PRAISE FOR

ESTEVAN VEGA AND THE ARSON SAGA

"Estevan Vega's dark fantasy bristles with malignant energy and throbs with ideas, bringing to mind the early work of Clive Barker crossed with the magical realism of Jorge Luis Borges. Sensual, sexy, and surgically precise, this is *Harry Potter* for the thinking person. Highly recommended!"

—Jay Bonansinga, New York Times bestselling co-author of *The Walking Dead: Fall of the Governor*

"*Ashes* left me speechless. The whole thing was like an Edgar Allen Poe poem...Where it's lovely and creepy all at once. Not only was *Arson* incredible, but *Ashes* is even better."

—Abigaile, Blogger, *Reading Teen*

"Vega writes well beyond his years...With his third literary attempt, Vega has hit his stride—one that can only pick up speed."

—*The Record-Journal*

"*Arson* is not to be missed. It is densely layered, tense, packed with surprising compassion, and written with great courage... Groundbreaking!"

— *Salt Lake City Examiner*

"In a fortunate writer's career, there is one book that inevitably launches its author to a new level of success and visibility, and *Arson* may very well prove to be just such a book for Estevan Vega."

—*Hartford Examiner*

"Estevan Vega's *Arson* proves he is an author to be reckoned with."

—*The Christian Manifesto*

"[*Arson*] could be compared to other young adult books such as *Jumper* or even a young coming of age super-hero genre story. And even at times flecks of the *Twilight* series."

—*Title Trakk*

"Estevan Vega is a fabulous storyteller. I have a feeling he's going to be a major force in fiction."

—Robert Liparulo, bestselling author of *Deadlock* and *The Dreamhouse Kings*

"*Arson* is every bit its namesake: a sinister story that slowly licks at the edges of your subconscious until it fully engulfs you in a firestorm of fascinating characters, twisting plot lines, and an explosive ending. A great read and Estevan Vega is a talent to watch for sure!"

—Jon F. Merz, bestselling author of *The Kensei*

"I really enjoyed *Arson*, but I absolutely loved *Ashes*. I recommend this to anyone looking for something different. Not something with rainbows and unicorns...Something dark and addicting."

—Jessica, Blogger, *Step into Fiction*

"I love when a book keeps you thinking long after you have finished reading it. It has been interesting watching this series morph from what I thought was a paranormal romance into more of a psychological thriller. It is in a genre all its own. Estevan Vega is truly a gifted writer."

—Gabby, Blogger, *What's Beyond Forks*

"Basically, *Arson* and *Ashes* are two of my favorite books. That is all."

—Asheley, Blogger, *Into the Hall of Books*

PUBLISHED WORKS BY ESTEVAN VEGA

TO
THEA

BE FEARFUL of The Thoughts of MEN
BE WARY of The TRAPS of The END!

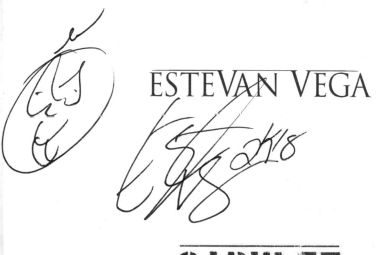

ASHES

BOOK TWO IN THE ARSON SAGA

ESTEVAN VEGA

CAPULET
ENTERTAINMENT

This novel is a work of fiction. Names, descriptions, entities,
and incidents included in the story are products of the author's
imagination. Any resemblance to actual persons, events, and
entities is entirely coincidental.

Capulet Entertainment 2015

First Paperback Edition 2011
First eBook Edition 2011

Cover design by Damonza.com
Edited by Audra Marvin
Layout design by Nikki @ DragonMoth Media

Published in the United States of America

For n.b., the girl without a mask

ASHES

BOOK TWO IN THE ARSON SAGA

CHAPTER ONE

HER SCREAMS TORMENTED THE HALLS. IN MERE MOMENTS, Salvation Hospital awakened.

"Oh God!" The stinging pressure intensified from inside of the young girl. "Oh, it hurts so much." The pit of her stomach bubbled up and bubbled back down. The gurney rattled underneath. A shirt, filthy and tattered, clung like life to her stuttering body. It didn't take long for the hot blood to mix with the sweat.

She jerked. "It's burning." There was fear in her tears. A hollow horror glared from her face. Both eyes rolled inside loose sockets, spinning like wandering spheres.

Outside, the wind tossed dead tree limbs. The branches scratched the windows, letting go of the leaves that once clung to its frail shape. The cloudless December sky watched, dragging the cold dark into itself as winter let slip the ashes of snow.

The halls of Salvation carried no sympathy for the harsh world outside, no love for a young girl unfit for the fire inside her. The emergency room doors swallowed the chaos for a moment, but its torment could not be contained. The panic. The screams. The stop and go of unsure wheels and squeaking metal.

Something unknown had come through.

"We need to get this girl into surgery now!" one of the EMTs shouted. His voice quickly vanished down the corridor. The white walls crept around them at every angle. "Miss, just try and relax."

"Daddy," her voice quivered. "Daddy…" Her lips couldn't say the rest. Her eyes could. Whispers slipped out. The silence underneath was troubling to those surrounding. She stared into her father's face, perhaps even his soul.

He weakly stared back, at first a solid stone. Then he turned away, a hollow cave.

Her heart dragged. The hard material gripping her back began to pull tighter. The fast jerks forced her head to spin, the face of her lover, Isaac, blending white with the surrounding world.

"It'll…" her father tried. "It will…be over soon, sweetheart."

"Oh, Henry," her mother gasped. "Darling, do something, won't you? She's our only daughter. She's my baby."

Henry didn't move.

She beat his chest. "For the love of heaven, do something. Pray for her, darling. Pray for her. That child is coming. Oh, sweet mercy!" She stroked Henry's jacket lapels, desperately trying to grasp to a hope that wasn't there.

He held her in a symphony of silence. His daughter sensed something not right, something horrible coming.

"Almighty God, grant her peace," her mother begged with quaking lips and tear-soaked glasses.

The next few seconds came like a flood. The emergency crew pulled her away from her parents, away from the past, away from everything she once knew. Isaac swore he'd never let her hand go. "You're gonna be just fine, baby, you'll see." He looked down upon the bloody mess. "Our son's gonna be so beautiful." His voice cracked. He wiped away a tear, glanced at one of the panic-stricken faces surrounding him, and breathed deeply.

She twisted. Her stomach blistered, and another crimson stream bled into the sweat on her shirt. A plume of smoke sailed slowly into the air.

"What do you want to name him, baby?"

Her teeth slammed tight like two gates coming together. Her eyes abandoned Isaac momentarily then drifted back fast. "Oh, Isaac…ahhh!" Her nails drove into his palm and drew blood.

"It's gonna be just fine, I promise. It's almost over. It's almost over." They rushed around another corner, the hallway growing darker and darker with each turn.

"Stephen. I always…liked…that name." She winced. "I think it means crown. Our son will be a prince."

"You never put those name books down," Isaac said. "Yeah, yeah, of course, baby. I like that name. It's perfect."

The dim lights flickered above. The smell of her shirt singeing reached his nostrils. It was disturbing to breathe in.

Silence consumed the entire hall for several long moments, stretched back and lingering. People's expressions spoke of worry and uncertainty. Their mouths lingered wide with shouts but no voices. Screams with nowhere to rest. It was enough to pull a human being out of a coma.

"Bring her in now, before we lose the child too!" she heard someone call. Trepidation filled her throat.

Isaac shuddered in bewilderment. "What?"

"Stay calm, okay? They're gonna do everything they can to help your wife," the EMT assured. He seemed about Isaac's age.

"Fiancée," Isaac whispered.

"Dr. Raymond," a nurse ordered to the receptionist, "we….to operate…quickly! Losing blood. ER…3." Not a full sentence or even full thoughts, just indecipherable syllables bonded to panic.

Would she die? Would her child die? "Isaac, I'm afraid." The sweat filtered out from her palms as she grabbed him. It all felt so different from when she had reached for his hand with closed eyes while trying to make it through one sitting of *Friday the 13th* in her parents' basement. Strange that such a thought would come to her now. It struck her how defenseless and hopeless he looked, despite his words.

"Oh no!" she screamed.

A thicker heat swelled through her stomach. *How far back are Mom and Dad? Can't they be with me too?* Perhaps they were too afraid to watch. *Daddy promised it wouldn't hurt, not like this.* Not like hell was being born into the world, a monster. It kicked and tore from inside. Her skin, now stretched, was beginning to peel black.

"I don't look very pretty," she cried. "I'm not beautiful at all, Isaac."

"No, Frances, you are…the…most beautiful girl in all the world." He tried to sound convincing, but she could tell when he was lying. He'd lied before, but tonight it was different.

"Isaac, do you lo—" Frances's voice sounded cut. She twisted her wrist then flung her head backward, almost snapping her neck. The gurney spiraled into the drywall, disturbing the naked and lifelessness it possessed. The EMT jammed his finger and cursed.

"I can feel him, Isaac," she whined, chewing the top layer of flesh off of her lip. It bled and formed a thin black line where chapped skin used to be. "Make it stop. Oh, please, son, you're hurting Mommy."

Her face was a block of wet brick, crumbling red and white, turning paler by the second. The freckles around her nose and mouth bleached away completely, like vapor. Strands of tugged hair stuck to a stained pillowcase as she kicked and screamed atop a paper-thin cushion. Her hands warmed.

A deep sound shattered eardrums in three blasts. The smoke alarms sang a haunting chorus. Seconds later, water began showering down upon them in furious drops, soaking them instantly and creating a sea of confusion. The drops of cold mixed with the blood on her face. Frances couldn't even feel her heart beating anymore.

"Sedate her!" a nurse ordered. "Sedate her quickly! We can't control this."

One of the assistants standing nearby rushed into a vacant room as the gurney screeched to an immediate halt. She clamored about inside, the clank of a metal bowl dropping, scraped plastic, and a curtain being torn. She emerged soon after with a three-inch needle that she shoved into Frances's feverish neck.

Her eyes went calm all of a sudden, but her body convulsed nonetheless.

"Holy—" the EMT gasped. As he looked down at her, he could see a face moving about underneath the dented flesh of her belly. It didn't look much like a belly at all; more like something sinister and unnatural trying to escape. "Keep her moving."

"Daddy!" she yelled, but no one came.

So afraid. The crowded faces. The loneliness.

"Baby, just be calm. You're doing great." Isaac stared deep into his fiancée, the skin around her eyes like crusted charcoal. Her gaze drowned in pools of fire.

"You'll love him, won't you, Isaac? Even if he's different." She peered into him then looked down at her belly, as it bubbled once more. Hurt violently consumed every ligament and bone. Another scream. "Stephen," she whispered, vision starting to blur. Her tight grip held tighter. Through the haze she saw Isaac howl in pain, the short spikes of hair on the bridge of his wrist singeing off.

The medics rolled her past doors that flapped back and forth, back and forth, until stopping suddenly, eerily.

The sedative was swimming in her bloodstream, she could feel it. But it couldn't calm her, not for a second. These stabbing birth pains remained, increasing. The muscles seemed replaced by something trying to escape.

Someone yelled, "The child is coming now, and if we're not quick, this girl is gonna suffer cardiac arrest."

"Where is Dr. Raymond!" one of the nurses yelled.

The veins moving through Frances's ghostly belly resembled black, misshapen fingers. In seconds, she was hooked up to machines and strange devices, hoses and wires confusing her brain and bringing back awful memories, and the face of a young boy.

Another half dozen alarms rang throughout the ER. A thick shower of rain descended over them.

The room got warmer.

Some of the people froze.

She wanted to be told it was going to be all right, for real. She wanted her father to be holding her other hand. Frances wanted to be saved. "I want my son. Just give me my—!" She quaked.

An older man stepped into the room.

"Doctor, thank God you've arrived," the EMT said, right before the doctor told him to get lost.

"Everyone, step back," Dr. Raymond commanded, sliding on a pair of latex gloves. A nurse fitted him and masked him quickly before he started reaching for tools. He glanced at the monitors, noticing the needle on the screen spike and then drop. Spike and drop. "Stay as calm as we can, everybody. This isn't elementary school. Let's handle this situation quickly. We don't have much time!"

The fear and uncertainty in his voice unsettled Isaac's stomach.

"Step back, son."

The nurses removed the rest of Frances's clothes and stood back, mystified.

"What is it?" Dr. Raymond asked, unsure why they would pull away during such an immediate procedure.

He drew nearer to her, her body now glowing black and red, even hints of white. In all his years, nothing could have prepared him for this. Raymond peered down, his peppered hair falling forward in front of entranced eyes.

It was moving inside her.

A set of fingers clawed unnaturally at the edge of the womb. He saw sections and ligaments shifting and sliding within the girl's belly, as she squirmed and shrieked, her voice climbing and descending the walls. The room seemed to shake. She ripped at Isaac's cheek. Seconds later, her fingertips began to melt, dripping into tiny pink pools on the tile.

"What is this?" Raymond said, his voice layered with a pounding fear that he could hear beating through his brain, fear that caused his hands to shake and his veins to wish they'd explode.

"Doctor, I've never seen anything like it before," one of the nurses said, horrified.

Raymond gazed silently as the girl shook the operating bed. The blood was now mixing with the flesh burning off of her spine, bits of her ribcage and skeleton beginning to show whenever she moved.

Water drained from the above metal mouths, soaking the curtains, faces, and tools. The echoes of voices swelled in unity. Frances watched the lines on her palms flash red before deforming into something misshapen and ugly. She swallowed hard, almost taking down her tongue along with the spit.

Isaac blinked, rushing to her bedside, the salty tears distorting his vision. "Be strong, baby," he tried.

Meanwhile, lights flickered overhead, shadows dancing with the darkness, then the light, then the darkness again. Shapes continued to disturb her soaking womb. She bit down, teeth chipping and splintering deep in her throat.

Dr. Raymond loomed, as a group of nurses fled the room, nothing but the hiccup of the doors flapping back and forth to keep them company now.

"What's happening to her?" Isaac asked, begging the doctor for hope with each word.

"I...d...uh..." A glob of blood bubbled up out of her belly-button. Raymond leapt back.

"Swear to me you'll love him. It isn't his fault. I never meant..." Her voice suddenly separated into a million fragments, slicing the air. The veins in her neck boiled, her throat mixing purple and red. Some of the items around her began to melt from the heat breathing out her body. The three who remained stared down at the operating bed at an unclothed, pulsating victim.

Her tears resembled hot coals. Smoke rose from her center, all of the glass in the room melting or shattering. Steam thickened the air. The doctor was motionless. One of the nurses fainted, sliding onto a table of sharp instruments.

A trail of spit had formed between Frances's crimson smile, as she stretched her jaw one last time to call out a name: "Stephen."

Then she collapsed, her head dropping back, eyes spiraling into emptiness. In a blink, the flesh on her belly peeled, a growing fire eating and folding the skin away from whatever was moving underneath, blistering the ripped flesh. All they heard was a slight murmur, one that came off the lips of a baby who couldn't have weighed any more than five pounds. Its skin appeared grainy, bits of ash and liquid mess wrapping the frail skeleton within what remained of the mother's womb. Slowly, it moved and bent its fingers, as Isaac saw its hands briefly surrounded by tiny, gloved flames. It didn't cry or long for breath. It simply lay still, silenced perhaps by the wind scratching at the window from the outside world.

Isaac flared his nostrils and fought to catch his breath, slowly moving closer to her body. There was nothing holding her head up, nothing to honor her. Smoke engulfed the dark room. The tops of her fingers had melted off at the nails, hands charred. He imagined the emotions Kay and Henry were enduring outside those swinging doors and down the hall. Imagined what it was going to be like telling them how she… No, he couldn't even bear the thought of her being gone, let alone conveying the terrible news to them. They never had been too welcoming of him, sure, but he did love them, at least enough for her.

But now she was gone? Now she was spread open and soaking in this mess of life, pieces of her fingertips missing. What happened?

Isaac thought his insides were going to explode. He glanced down at her, noticing that the thing still connected to her body did not even stir. "Stephen," Isaac mumbled. "Stephen Gable. My…s—" He couldn't say it.

Isaac forced his eyelids shut. He reached for it, but something stopped him midway. Its hands no longer glowed, but Isaac didn't wish to hold it. He remained disturbed by it.

"What…just happened?" Dr. Raymond whispered hoarsely, lip quivering.

Isaac stared at him, barely able to make out the holes in the old doctor's face. The alarms blared, but the sprinklers above their frightened, awestruck heads spun out of water, puddles of red and pink and clear fluid dampening their feet.

Isaac looked one last time at the doctor but not at the quiet, stained menace that had replaced the woman he loved. Perhaps this had been a mistake. Falling in love, getting her pregnant, being in this room at this moment. All of it. That's what he would have to tell himself in order to live without regret, if such a thing were possible.

"*It* burned through her." Dr. Raymond coughed, the dark realization culminating all at once.

Isaac breathed deeply and wiped his hands against his shirt. Then he moved back, every wary step pulling him closer to the exit, closer to escape from Salvation Hospital, and whatever had burned through.

He couldn't stay. Isaac couldn't be a father to this thing.

There was a beating in his chest just then. Perhaps it was his heart, or maybe it was something else entirely, a gut kind of thing. It didn't really matter. All that mattered was that he was leaving this place. He needed to. He wouldn't tell a soul where he was going. *It* was safer with Henry and Kay anyway. They'd know what to do.

CHAPTER TWO

17 years later

ARSON LISTENED TO THEIR WHISPERS. HE STRUGGLED TO MAKE out what was said, but it was all muffled; blending shapes and words looming over him.

Is this the hospital? his mind lulled. The feeling of suffocation set in deep in his lungs. Claustrophobia and fear and confusion. A nasty flavor lingered on his tongue, something he couldn't shake. The air didn't taste right, didn't smell right. How long had it been?

He tried to move, but he couldn't; tried to scream, but his vocal cords burned cold. "Who-h-where-the-kill-Emer-y." They were just small, simple words and half syllables bleeding out. He could feel his muscles fighting to do something, but a dark lullaby was fluently touring his veins. It didn't want him to.

"Wakey-wakey," one of the shapes said, hot breath crawling down Arson's neck. *How many of them are there?* Quiet voices came out like lost echoes, appearing and disappearing, but not enough to cancel the noise of machines and beeping panels. Wires twisted around every corner of the table, connected to metal creatures. They were wrapping him in their hybrid cocoon. They chirped and constantly blinked green.

Arson exhaled, the foggy shapes beginning to form vital parts for his mental image of them, like they were searching for true form. A gasp turned into several more ill words, too few for even him to know what he was trying to say.

Swallow, breathe, repeat. The process was numbing.

"You're dreaming, aren't you?" Arson recognized the slimy voice this time; it slithered out and cradled around his spine, which was now stuck to a cold bed.

"He's def-definitely dreaming," another blur said. From the volume, Arson guessed he was in some far-off area or in an office he wasn't able to perceive.

Arson blinked again, noticing the brief flickers of light tracing the outlines of every phantom within this space.

"Whatever it is, it's not friendly," the far-off blur said.

"The dose seems to be wearin' off, Krane. Somebody's starting to come to."

A brief period of silence spread over the room.

"How many failed experiments, Doc? How many godforsaken times are we gonna do this? Maybe your theory's whacked."

"Years of research and st-st-study are correct. The theory is sound."

"Stubborn jackass. Maybe you lucked out with the other one, but this is…I just don't see any point in searching for something that ain't there."

"You witnessed it with your o-own-own eyes."

"Not sure what I seen anymore. Maybe this fire thing's not like we thought."

"All brilliant men face consequence when they are on the cusp of something great. We're going to do this until we get what we need."

"And what's that?"

"More data. M-more-more…answers to how their minds work, so we can duplicate it perfectly."

"Leave it to a geek to get all excited over his toys."

Another gap of silence.

Arson struggled to speak, but the syllables wouldn't come out.

"I've got orders, Lamont." Krane started murmuring to himself. "Just do what you're told."

"Yeah, yeah, everybody's lips are chapped from kissin' somebody's butt."

Lamont. That was the guy's name. It was coming back, but only in part. *Remember, just remember.*

"Little punk's got some fight in him, don't he? Maybe we should get one of the loonies down here. Start ourselves a little circus." Lamont swallowed a full, groggy laugh, his hot breath circling Arson's nostrils. The smell pouring out from the row of crowded, unhinged teeth was familiar. Disgusting. "What dark secrets are crawling inside that messed-up mind?"

Several other phantoms surrounded the table, all staring down at him. Looming, lidless eyes. Arson didn't like it. Through the confusion, he perceived their coats, some white, some black, or shades of all colors. Some constricted by ties and long skirts. But what his mind focused on the most was the ugliness above him. Lamont looked like a horned devil.

Suddenly, their tones became clearer. "I think it's time," the one identified as Krane said. He looked at Arson through oversized, thick lenses. A stitch of tape held one piece of the frame to another, but the cheap plastic wanted to break.

The skinny apparition had changed positions. Far away. Then close. *It's hard to keep track. Hard to capture everything.* Now the blur hovered over Arson's bare chest as he began to add red lines with a permanent marker. The lines traveled in multiple directions from his naked upper torso down to his boxers.

"Get away from him, Lamont," Krane ordered. He leaned down and continued pressing the marker's tip against the soft flesh. A dark color bled short, sporadic lines across Arson's forehead. "Hold still," the voice assured. "It will only hurt a little." The figure turned to his assistants. "He's waking quickly. We need-need another dose." Krane finished tracing the lines and covered the tip of the marker, pushing up his glasses so they'd sit more firmly on the long bridge of his nose. One of his assistants stuck Arson in the neck. It stung. "Prepare to initiate Morpheus."

"Help me, plea—" Arson struggled.

Two other blurs wheeled a large device toward the table: the thing they called Morpheus. The machine's wide, metallic grip stretched to Arson's feet, while the remainder of it rested above his head. It was shaped like half of a coin, or a comb without teeth, hollowed out at the top and complete with wiry fingers that jutted out on each end.

Krane turned a switch and tiny spikes instantly protruded from a center wire and stabbed into the sides of Arson's temples, twisting until the machine got a verifiable scan. The hovering mechanical beast buzzed and sliced into his mind like a whirlwind, emitting a blinding light that kept Arson's eyes glued shut.

"It's like staring straight into the sun, ain't it?" Lamont snickered, fingering his tobacco dip with his pinkie and sliding the brown chunk into his gums. He savored the taste.

"Can you keep-k-keep it down?" Krane asked. It was clear the skinny doctor wasn't comfortable with spectators circling his work.

"Yeah, yeah."

Krane focused on controlling the movements of Morpheus. It was a meticulous machine.

"What...doing...me?" Arson gasped. Light penetrated his closed lids enough to create many wildly colorful splashes that corrupted his true vision.

"I don't think Mikey likes it." A sick cackle disturbed the air. "Looks like you're putting baby in a corner."

Krane was perfectly mute.

"Sure he's not gonna remember any of this?" Lamont asked, stepping forward. "'Cause I'd be pretty ripped if you were walking around inside my head."

Krane waited. "Lamont, shut your trap, b-be-before I give Hoven an excuse to remove you permanently. Besides, no one's brave enough for that journey."

Lamont mocked him silently, the dip in his teeth squishing back and forth. He folded his lips, producing a trail of mixed saliva that ran down the cleft in his chin. The sticky brown spit dripped onto Arson's cheek.

"Would someone get this brute away from my work? He's disrupting the trial."

Lamont felt a hand tugging at his jacket. "Take it easy. I'll leave you geeks with your rusty gadgets. Don't, uh, hurt yourself, yeah?" Then, looking at the orderly who had him by the forearm, he wiped his chin and spat. "Get your claws off. I know my way out of this nuthouse."

Krane muttered something under his breath, keeping his attention on the slab and the subject struggling to move. He walked over to the monitors, punched in some keys, and flipped his eyes toward the oversized screen to his left. The machine breathed, several metal fingers drawing nearer to the boy's skull. Their thin needles restricted the amount of blood.

Morpheus continued to scan Arson's brain matter horizontally then vertically. The blinding light forced him to keep his eyes closed. But he wasn't strong enough to fire up, not even a little.

Arson drooled involuntarily. He pressed his fingers together, hoping that by snapping them he might initiate some sort of spark. Where on earth was he, anyway? What did these men want?

The machine vibrated endlessly around him, a pounding, wretched sound, like a tortured baby screaming for his mother.

He grunted, weak. A coldness covered his limbs. It was useless. There was no fire left, nothing inside him but pictures of things he couldn't remember.

What had they done to him?

"Emery," he barely whispered.

CHAPTER THREE

SHE FELT NAKED. EMERY SHOOK HER HEAD VIOLENTLY, trying to stumble out of the fog. She was awake, just not fully aware. Her eyes started to drift. Her stomach and chest felt sore. She lifted up her shirt, confused by the slight scars that had never been there before, next to her ribs.

There were no clocks in this room to watch her. Little to mark the passage of time but peculiar stares now and then, a small meal, and plenty of fear to share with the shadows. The spells of fear or shakes, as she called them, were beginning to consume her more and more.

Peaceless. Sleepless. Forgotten.

Her mind was a jumbled puzzle. She couldn't remember which events came first and which second. Dreams and reality and everything in between. Some things she remembered clearly. Like moving into a new house near a boy who seemed different, cute. *Arson.* She couldn't forget him. Never. She remembered going bowling and having a strangely amusing night. Then volunteering at some hospital and meeting an old man. But in her memory, the old man didn't have a name.

It was so frustrating. Who knew thinking could get so complicated? With shut eyes, she forced herself to remember as much detail as she could. She had to in order to keep from scratching at the drywall.

It was summer. Somewhere in Connecticut, right? The 'rents were on the rocks because Mom didn't know how to keep her hands to herself; and Dad, well, he had loved the bottle a little too much.

Emery dragged her wrinkled hands down her face. Where was she? Where had she been? How many nights had she been in this tiny, deformed room? *More like a cell, come to think of it.* Were the screams she heard when she slept real or imaginary? She swore they came from somewhere above her, but she wasn't certain. Of anything. Was the air getting thinner? Would she eventually disintegrate because of some chemical virus being pumped into the ventilation units?

Don't flip out, Emery. Get a friggin' grip. Her eyes drifted to the corner wall, almost too dark to make out, but the glaring scratches cleared it all up.

No way out.

Had she drowned? Been knocked out for days, weeks? Had she been tortured? Suddenly, all the cheap slasher flicks she'd stumbled on over the years filled her brain with gut-wrenching scenarios. It felt like something ugly was crawling across her skin too. Arson was the only boy, the only person who had made her feel beautiful, for real; but he wasn't here. No one was.

Her face started to itch. She missed her mask. Emery closed her eyes and opened them. Blinked once, twice. Arson. The beach. A flood of angry memories stormed her. Mandy. Her sick friends. The worst and best night of her life. "We're going to fix your face!"

Screaming. Alcohol. Safety. Hatred. Violence.

Then the quiet.

Which part of it was real? *Arson.* He was real. He saved her. When she was freaking out. When the mask was burning. Yes, that's when he went…nuclear. She could still feel the fire licking the flesh on her leg as it tickled and then scarred some of her skin. She was ten years old, then seventeen, then ten again. "No!" she cried. *Where is he? What happened to my parents? What is this place?*

She couldn't shake the sensation like she'd been in this room before. As sick as it was, it didn't feel strange. But why? She seemed to sleep and wake up like clockwork but with no memories in between. It didn't make sense.

Emery cradled her arms on the floor. She shoved her head between her knees, fighting tears. The headache was increasing. She didn't want to think anymore.

Unless it was about Arson. His skinny arms, his curly hair. Those chapped lips and dirty fingernails. The sweet taste of his breath mixing with hers. Why could she remember some things and not others? What lay inside these walls? Behind them? Above them? What lingered in this thinner air? What was wrong with her?

Other than your messed-up face?

Other than being completely alone?

Why am I here?

She spent a moment biting her lip, and then she ripped at a fingernail until its edge tore off. The pain was a horrible friend. She wanted to hurt, as long as it was by her own doing.

"Can anybody hear me!" she yelled. Sometimes she imagined a person breaking down the walls and taking her out of this torment. She daydreamed that she had conversations about love, God, and death with the unknown world above her. But not now. Now, it seemed like nothing but emptiness. Her voice climbed up and down the walls and then died.

Emery couldn't keep the tears back anymore. She tried to concentrate. "Think, Emery, think." She was standing there alone on the beach. Slowly, the night's sick crowd appeared. Mandy and her friends tried to breathe, but air and hope were stripped, along with their...

Skin. And faces.

Arson remained. Dead on the sandy floor, but then he came back to life.

How?

The room still found ways to be dark. Ways to terrify her. She looked up, and the violent memory tucked itself back into the creases of her mind. She had hoped that just once, she'd find a window above her, or some sunlight. But there was only a door with no key. Not even a handle.

She felt hungry one moment, and the next she didn't. There were sessions she went to, but couldn't remember anything about them or discover a point to it all. Just some guy who wrote things down while eyeballing her like some sort of...

"Freak!" Leaning her back against the wall, Emery wiped her nose with a sleeve. Why couldn't she remember what had happened next? Suddenly she feared to admit what her thoughts forced upon her.

Arson was gone.

CHAPTER FOUR

IT FELT STRANGE TO MISS HIM. THE WAY HE ONCE STOLE glances of her. The pattern his mouth succumbed to whenever he used to mention her name. How his lips desired to press softly into hers. These were the stirrings of romance Aimee hadn't experienced in months. Dr. Carlos Pena, her boss, had forgotten her.

Before, all it would take was a knock on his office door to get a document signed and approved, or a smile and a whisper in his ear after lunch to have him buckling at the knees.

Now it seemed like running a marathon was easier than catching up with him. He was always in a rush to go nowhere, to be nowhere, without her.

"You've become a significant hiccup in my life. I have my routines. Right now, you're a distraction. I'm sorry." A hiccup. Not a *lover*. Not a *friend*. Not even someone he wanted to bring home. Just a *distraction*. That's what Aimee had become. To him.

All she could do was nod and fake understanding.

"Some of the others in this department are getting quite uncomfortable, Aimee," he said with his hands folded, focus drifting.

Aimee tried to think of anything but how she felt about him. Her infatuation was now mixed with revulsion. Still she hoped to find safety in the comfort of what she once held to be true, the love he so easily refused to give.

"How have you been feeling lately?"

"I thought you were reprimanding me. Did you bring me in here for a lecture or because you're concerned?"

"Perhaps it's both," he solemnly replied.

"Safe answers. You always were good at that."

"Aimee, given our history together, a meeting like this isn't what I would have preferred."

"What would you prefer, Carlos? Avoiding me like the plague? Ignoring my emails? My phone calls? You've been acting like I don't even exist these past few weeks."

Carlos raised his hands a bit. "Let's not get melodramatic. I realize now that I can't live in the past. What we had is no longer possible. Everything is different now."

"You mean, since Emery?"

"She's gone, Aimee."

An earthquake could've torn the room in two, shattered everything around them, and it wouldn't have mattered. She couldn't move.

"How could you be so heartless?"

"I'm sorry, that was harsh of me."

"Don't pretend to know me, Carlos."

"I used to. I don't claim to know this new woman anymore."

She clenched her teeth, trying to ignore the mist blanketing her eyes. The last thing she wanted was to feel weak in the same office that once empowered her.

"I loved you," she said.

"Did you? At any rate, it's easier this way. Trust me."

"Easier for you, but not for me." Her sleeve cleaned her nose.

She tried to hide the tears. "It was always easier for you. You love to ignore the blame, don't you?"

Carlos raised his voice. "*You* left me all those years ago! Or have you forgotten? And like clockwork, it was *you* who came crawling back months ago. This is your mess, not mine. Don't wait around hoping somebody else will clean it up."

Was she imagining this? Were they really fighting? He was everything she wanted. He had a better life, could provide better than a failed minister. And his lips would never pour out so much poison. This wasn't Carlos screaming at her; it was Joel. It had to be. Joel was the bastard who wanted to control her. Joel was the iron fist who no longer needed her, not Carlos.

"Kiss me," Aimee said. "Forget about your ego for one minute. Don't think. I don't want you to reason whatever this is—whatever we are—out. Just kiss me."

"What? You're acting juvenile."

"Do it. You'll forget about the garbage that has come between us. None of it will matter. We can run. You can take me away from all of this." There was so much noise and madness in her head that she hadn't even thought about what she was saying or if it even made any sense. Escape, love.

"Can you hear yourself, Aimee? You're acting purely on illogical emotions. Think about what you are saying."

"I don't care about logic. I want to feel right again."

"You don't *sound* right."

"Why? Are you that much over me? What are you afraid of?"

"I am not afraid. But you're…not well. I'm hearing whispers of you taking out your frustration and anger on patients." Carlos shuffled the papers on his desk as he searched for proof of her unbridled dramatics. "Last Thursday you threatened to shove meds down Jeffrey Wilton's throat if he refused to do what you said. And a month ago, Norma overheard you cursing at an orderly for no reason." Carlos leaned in. "Screaming, at the top of your lungs. The poor girl came into my office in tears."

Aimee's mouth twisted. "Did you console her, Carlos? Did you give her the *encouragement* she needed?"

"Don't flirt with innuendo!"

"Is that a request or an order, boss?"

"Enough! I'm sick of this! I'm sick of watching you deteriorate day after day. It's lunacy, really. Look at what you've become. You're not who I thought you were. You're not what I want anymore." Carlos pulled his chair back and walked around the office. "Your hair's a mess. Your makeup is undone, nails unclipped. And the attitude that you carry around is—well, it's infectious. Do you want this job? Nothing about you says you even care about anything."

"I care about *you*. I need you, Carlos."

"But I can't save you. Your daughter was, as you claim, abducted. But I'm a surgeon. I can't fix what happened this summer any more than you can. You have to get a grip on reality. What if she is not found? What if she never comes back to you? Have you prepared for that? Are you ready for that?"

"She has to."

Carlos circled around her and stopped right in front of her. He knelt down and held her hands. "It's killing me to see you like this, in so much pain. I have friends who can help you with these issues."

"*Issues?* I'm not crazy. My daughter was taken from me!"

"By whom? Do you even have anything to back up this conspiracy theory? Because that's all it is, a theory."

"They were both taken, Carlos, from this hospital. Why am I the only one who seems to remember that my daughter and her friend disappeared into thin air? It doesn't make any sense."

"What doesn't make any sense is that you're still rejecting reason. You're stuck in a fairytale. The police supposedly had a single lead that turned out to be nothing. She is gone, Aimee! Accept it. Try to move on. Let her go so you can get on with your life!"

"I can't."

His frustration bubbled out. "This problem is affecting your work."

"Right back to business. How appropriate. But for the record, it isn't." Aimee recoiled. "It won't anymore."

"It better not. This is the second and last time I am going to discuss this with you. Three strikes…"

"I get it, Carlos."

"Oh, that reminds me. I think it'd be best for everyone if you went back to calling me Dr. Pena."

Aimee wanted to smack him and kiss him at the same time. How could he be so unkind and still warrant her affection? How could he toy with her heart and then abandon it?

"Did you ever love me?" she asked.

"Once upon a time," he said gently, shaking her reality. "But we can't live in fairytales forever."

A trail of Joel's breath was stuck on the glass of the cooler. He reached in slowly this time to grab a bottle. Budweiser was his usual drink of choice, but today he felt like a Guinness man. The hard, sorta-burnt aftertaste of the beverage would feel right at home in his throat.

His lungs pushed out another piece of air; at this point, he regretted even calling it breath. Shifting his eyes to the tougher stuff was all he could think of. He felt crowded, though, with the thoughts and vindicated stares of folks around town. He'd seen a few of them before and even knew some by name. A reluctant smile and wave from time to time usually did the trick of silently telling them to mind their own business, but it didn't much work now. He wondered if they were thinking cruel thoughts about him or if their hearts were still soft with sentiments concerning his missing daughter. Joel just wanted to find what he was looking for and bring it back to his home, safe and sound.

He scratched at the hair starting to prick up on his chin and cheekbones, forming above his lips, with the sweat. He hadn't shaved in more than a week. His jaw felt like sandpaper. The hair on his head was grungy and sagged down over his eyelids.

Claustrophobia. The opening and closing of other worlds, these addiction cages man so eloquently called *coolers*. The chains he drank to make pain fly away.

But the claustrophobia—that came from the uninvited stares. Was it pity in their hearts or heartbreak in their eyes now? His opinion wavered by the minute. A second came and went, and he looked up to see them glaring back, no one saying anything. They wanted to say something, but every mouth was stitched together, soundless empathy that couldn't save him.

Joel cursed as a bottle of vodka he didn't realize was cracked suddenly slipped from his grip and shattered on the floor. Almost like a bullet. It hushed the place for a second, nothing but the bright lights above him and the startled breaths of others. He tiptoed around the mess for a moment before setting the bottle of Guinness down and hitting his knees. Blood from his fingertip mixed with the alcohol, so similar to the way the suds mixed inside with his veins, robbing from him the dark rhythms of sadness.

Joel's eyes danced from the splattered mess to the other culprits he wanted to consume. Captain Morgan and Dos Equis snickered. Cuervo mocked in the corner of the store while bottles of Skyy asked him to come closer. Some changed shape; others jeered. Was he drunk or mad?

It took a minute for the manager to come by. Her name was Myrtle. She knew Joel's name, empathized more with his loss than most anybody.

The first thing she noticed when she knelt down beside him with a towel was the cross dangling from his neck. "You look lost, priest," she said, concerned.

He snarled, ripping the towel from her hand and trying to clean the mess but spreading it instead. "I can fix it. I swear I can." And then, under his breath, "I'll bring her back."

"Mr. Phoenix, you don't look right. You're in here more often than I am. Feel like I should offer you a mattress in the back or something." She chuckled to herself. Joel figured she was trying to add some levity to the situation. "This place isn't going to heal you."

Joel looked at the heavy-set black woman with tattooed arms and a rolled-up pack of smokes tucked into her sleeve. She was one to talk. He got up off the floor, forgetting about his left leg being dampened by the vodka. The stink of it didn't much matter; it matched his breath, and the whole hum of the store. He felt okay in the stench, in the safety of these medicines.

Joel exchanged awkward glances with Myrtle and snatched his liquor from the floor. Then he reached on the shelf and grabbed some vodka and rum. A moment's hesitation called him to the magazine rack, a slight whisper luring him closer. He selected the latest issue of *Maxim*. A gorgeous, half-nude model lay gently hunched over her knees with a seducing stare—one that didn't judge him, one that wouldn't care where he'd been or why he wasn't strong enough to take back what he'd lost. A body tender and full of the lovely lust he had forgotten.

For a second, it was Aimee on the cover, tempting him, calling to him, but a blink set everything back to what reality had made him familiar with, and as he piled this new drug atop the other bottled saviors, he stopped to grab a case of cheap wine before heading to the register. "Just in case I get to feeling *romantic,*" Joel heckled, hoping Myrtle could hear him.

Minutes later he paid and returned to the grey world outside the store. Facing him was a cluster of small shops on the quiet highway he assumed was as vacant as he was.

Joel dropped the items in the passenger seat but not before grabbing the magazine and a bottle first. He snapped open the bottle, and started thumbing through the issue, waiting for it all to take effect on his body, his mind. The girls modeled in front of him for his entertainment and the taste coaxing a tired throat weren't fixing him. But he so wanted them to.

Another sip. Another loose page turned. Another sting at the back of his throat. Another bombshell calling to him. A tear suddenly hit the page. Joel hadn't even noticed he was misty-eyed. The skinny drop of water slid down a girl's soft frame and fell off the edge. He tossed the magazine to the floor, where he'd forgotten the pictures of Emery lay; the ones he had copied and plastered around the entire state. No, he hadn't forgotten at all. There were only a few left, but the entire spread was glaring back at him now.

The picture was the best he'd caught of her. It's because she didn't know he had taken it. A game of chess always kept her attention far better than he ever could. Right when she made her move and looked up to see his reaction, her eyes flashed with the light of the camera. It caught those eyes so poetically that Joel thought he was hearing song lyrics whenever he looked at the picture.

It was one of the few times when Emery had come out of her mask. He wasn't sure what made her come out that night, what made her feel safe again for no more than an hour, but he was thankful. She truly was beautiful, in spite of her scars. Those eyes, innocent and just longing to be loved, found him now as they had then. Their warmth took root inside his fallow chest.

If Joel didn't cover up the image, he'd drive this car into the store. *Myrtle would love that,* his mind hummed.

It was a terrible time for a joke or sick antics. But then again, he wasn't laughing.

CHAPTER FIVE

EMERY FINALLY CAME TO. A MIGRAINE TRAMPLED THROUGH her head. All she could do was hope that her body would keep awake long enough for her to catch a glimpse of the unusual shadow from the other side. Quite a few came and went, but one in particular—she could tell which shadow, based on how long it stayed in one spot and how its feet danced behind the door as it listened to her breathe—was curious, and she wanted to know it. If it had a name. She wanted to know why it was here, haunting her. She spent hour after hour wishing it were Arson finally coming to rescue her. He'd take her back home. Anywhere but here.

The taste of rust filled her mouth. The putrid soak of damp concrete stifled the air in her nostrils. It was the taste of no control.

She spent the next uncounted moments raking bent fingers through the greasy knots in her hair then leaned back against the wall and tried to hide from the darkness. "No," she said, shaking her eyes open again. "Stay awake." *Where is the food?* she wondered, hungry as ever. She fought to catch a clearer glimpse of the shadow lurking outside. Was it the one she'd been hoping for? She wanted it to come back and keep her company.

Emery held her head between her knees as blood began to rush. The sudden flood to her brain forced her mind to want to go black and stay lost somewhere. Head up, head down. She didn't even have shoelaces. Someone had dressed her, fitted these rags on her. What had she done to be treated like such a criminal? "I'm a person. A human being!" she yelled at the walls. They didn't seem to care. "Let me out!" She bashed once, twice, several more times against the concrete surface. The ridge of her hand leaked red.

Something suddenly moved across her feet. In the dark, she couldn't tell what it was. But a splinter of light invaded from the bottom slit in the door just then, long enough for the light to reveal that the creature had sharp nails for teeth and a slimy, hairy sack for a stomach. A thin, pink tail dragged behind it. She screamed, before kicking the rat across the room, praying it didn't find her again. She heard the creature squeal when it smacked against the ground. *Maybe it broke its little neck.*

Suddenly, there was new movement outside the door. She swore she heard breathing. Then footsteps. Then a deeper breathing. Closer and farther away; then closer again. Who was it? What did they want?

"Hey, if you can hear me, I need to get outta here. Hello? Can you help me, please?" She crawled toward the door, somewhat apprehensive about the furry villain that might still be lurking close by. "Please, help me."

The begging became sobs that were never heard. Or worse, were ignored. If there were a living, breathing human being outside, how could they keep her here, locked away from the world?

She listened carefully as the footsteps once more escaped her. No food this time; maybe dinner was later, or breakfast. It was easy to misplace hours in a room with no clock.

"Come back," she begged the cold sounds outside her door. "Come back to me." Her slippery mouth brushed up next to the wall. She tasted dirt, wanting to throw up.

Too late. She wondered if, because she hadn't eaten anything, particles of *her* were coming up out of the dead space inside. Parts of *her* erupting and splattering disgusting mess on the ground.

Emery scraped the wall with her nails like a lunatic. She hoped to find a hole, a stitch of brighter light, something real to hold onto. Then she pounded her forehead against the wintry surface. Once was enough to knock her out cold.

CHAPTER SIX

THE BACKGROUND HUM OF THE TELEVISION SOUNDED LIKE
a swarm of hornets. Joel hadn't changed the channel in a few hours.
He let the station play and play as he tried to filter out thoughts.
He wondered where the people who took his daughter were from.
Questioned what they'd want with a scarred teenage girl anyhow.
The notions he gathered were sick and perverse, horrible things no
father would ever dream his daughter might be forced to endure.

He remembered seeing a black sedan parked outside the ER
and a van full of roses being peddled by a clean-shaven yuppie
in his twenties. The whole thing didn't feel right. Did they have
anything to do with it, or was he just reaching?

He recalled being in the lobby of the hospital where Emery
had been ripped from his life. The stink of the air was enough
to suffocate him. Not clean, not filthy, just something gross and
weak in between. He was aggressively tapping his fingers on the
Formica countertop, waiting for someone—anyone—to tell him
where his daughter had gone. And that strange boy she kept company with. While he was waiting for the police to arrive, Carlos
Pena's eyes met with his, but only for an instant. The look on that

scumbag's face was something Joel could not describe with words or even feelings. It just kind of hung there, apathetic, removed. Joel wanted to tear each particle of skin from the man's bones slowly, rip the flesh from his weak carcass and send his body to the pit of hell for luring his wife away at the apex of his weakness. But he didn't. Instead he stood back and let the doctor walk away down the hallway.

His mind had been so busy that day, still reeling from the night before, when he'd taken off, inebriated and hopeless; tried to run out on his family, the only thing he wanted now more than ever. If only he'd known. If only he could go back to spend that last night with Emery.

No form of rationalization could help. He was there in that hospital in the flesh, but his mind wasn't. His mind was cloudy, angry and frustrated and confused.

A still unfinished sermon now lay amidst the clutter of scattered thoughts scribbled onto paper. Beside that were his ambitious lists of conspiracy theories and phone numbers to agencies that had yielded no leads. He remembered the search parties, the agents and officers assigned to their case before they were eventually pulled away from it all to attend to more promising endeavors. The world had given up.

He was convinced even God had given up.

No matter what he did, who he called, or how hard he searched, he had gotten no closer to finding Emery. The idea that she'd become another lost face on the profile wall of missing children at Wal-Mart terrified him. Could he really exist in a world she was not in?

As a last attempt at hope, Joel reached into his pocket to find the card with the name Redd Casey on it. Redd was an odd first name, he thought now, as he did when the schmuck of a lawyer handed it to him saying, "We've done all we can do for you, Mr. Phoenix." How easily someone could give up on him, force him to look for a new private investigator. How easily they could all wash their hands of it and pretend his Emery wasn't still out there. Joel wanted to call this one. He really did. But there was a clamor in his chest that wouldn't subside. He was Emery's father. He had to find her. But could he, on his own, bring her back? He put the card away. Didn't fit right in his hands now.

Feeling his skin, Joel realized it seemed more like leather, worn and creased. New wrinkles. He never knew anyone could age so quickly in mere months.

Joel got up to stretch his legs. Then he lingered in the hallway, on his way toward the kitchen. He scanned the guest bedroom, thankful that his stomach was growling; it allowed him to abandon the other infuriating ideas for a short while.

The guest bedroom was empty. It was where he slept, at night anyway. He'd given Aimee the master, thought she'd be more comfortable. That, and he didn't like being in there anymore. But most of the time Aimee complained that the bedroom's emptiness bothered her, made her fear the dark even more. That was familiar to him too, only he never voiced it.

When would Aimee come home? It was late. He missed her footsteps. Her nagging. He wanted to talk to her, even if it meant a fight might come because of it. He dug his nails into his hands. He wanted to be close to her, hold her again, that woman he called whore and wife. The smell of her skin seemed like a fading memory now, one he sought to relive over and over. But he never could quite get it right.

It was a mystery how close two people could be but how far they really were.

In no time, his mind drifted. He imagined Aimee and Carlos making love. Loud, almost violent passion. The kind that makes your feet go numb and your lower back tingle. He blinked twice, to make sure the picture went away.

Love. Odd how a four-letter word seemed so long, so stretched and out of reach. The truth was, he longed for that kind of passion, that forsaken romance. He looked down at his left hand, pulled off the ring, and was prepared to throw it out the window. But when he looked back at his hand, the ring finger now bleached white, he began to wonder if the stain was enough.

The front door slammed all of a sudden, shocking him awake to the reality in which he found himself stuck. Aimee shuffled in with a bag of fast food. He realized he had never made it to the kitchen.

She tossed him the bag, some fries spilling onto the floor.

Joel reached in. "Fries are cold."

"Coulda let you starve. Took me a little longer to get back tonight. Had a long day, something you really wouldn't know anything about." She took off her jacket. "What's the matter, Joel? A 'thank you' too much?"

He shrugged. "How was your day?"

"I told you. Long."

Joel's eyes dropped to Aimee's hands. He hadn't looked at them in a while. She'd taken off her ring. When, he didn't know. But it was gone. He put his back on, hoping it would be noticed.

Aimee walked by him, asking how his day was, more out of obligation than concern.

"Tiring," came his weak reply.

"It must put a real strain on the body walking to and from the kitchen," she jeered, no doubt anticipating a reaction. "You're drinking again too, aren't you? I can see why you're tired. You stink. Too much time alone in this miserable place. When would you find time to bathe?"

"How's Carlos doing? Did you give him my best?" Joel asked, biting into his burger.

"I'm not doing this tonight."

"C'mon, baby, don't you wanna fight? It's written right on your face."

"Instead of acting like some moronic beggar, why aren't you out looking for her? Why haven't you brought her back to me?"

"Ding-ding-ding. We have a winner, folks. All of life's mysteries and consequences are Joel Phoenix's fault. Thanks for removing all doubt."

"There's still a mystery I can't seem to crack, Joel. Just one." Her eyes narrowed. "Why I ever married you."

He was quiet.

"You should be out there looking for her, not in here, hiding."

"I have looked! We've looked. We've contacted half the state, for heaven's sake. I've called family and what little friends we still have. I've spent hours on the internet and on the phone, waiting for someone at those *elite* agencies to tell me they haven't found jack squat! Why am I not out looking for her? How do *you* sleep at night?"

Aimee hurried around the kitchen. She was searching for something. She yanked open cabinets and drawers, shoved items aside, broke a coffee maker in the process. Then she moved to the far end of the kitchen to the hutch they rarely used. There she found the wine. She poured herself a tall glass.

"He doesn't want you anymore, does he?" Joel asked, taking another bite. "Makes sense now. Your fantasy is over." He knew he struck a nerve when she didn't reply but rather stared coldly at him, the way a cobra studies its prey.

"Bet it feels good to lose it all. Lose control and get tanked," she eventually said. "I want to feel good, get stupid. Like you. That's what you want, right? You want me to feel like you."

"Let loose, baby," Joel snarled, but all he wanted was to pull the wine away from her lips. Tell her she didn't need it. But he was frozen in the situation his bitter words had created.

Aimee chugged the full glass and filled it once more. "Feels nice."

"Stop it," he asked finally, regretting egging her on. "The show's over. You don't need to impress anyone."

"The control maniac rears his ugly head again. Punish me, Joel! Why don't you tie me up in the closet? Tape my mouth shut when I have an opinion. I'm just a helpless woman with no will of her own. Isn't that right?"

"I never said that." He swallowed the rest of the burger and tossed the bag in the trash. "Be rational."

Aimee bellowed. "You are asking *me* to be rational? Priceless words of wisdom coming from a full-time drunk. Who are you to tell me anything? You've been irrational for months. It's your fault we're in this mess. Your fault we even moved out here in the first place to this freaking cow town!"

"Yeah, and having you as a wife is a real trip."

"I'm not your wife; I'm only a whore, remember?"

Joel chewed his lip, silent.

She was lit like a fire, blazing with anger and discontent. He watched her chug the glass until it was nearly empty. "I'm like this because of you. I'm tired of you! You can't even bring her back. You can't fix it, Joel. There's no miracle. There's no right word. It's your fault she's gone!"

"Is it my fault you went out and—" Joel stopped himself short.

"What, Joel?" she said, moving closer, aching for a response. "What are you dying to say?"

"I wasn't the one who had the affair, Aimee. Take a good hard look in the mirror. I have my sins, but you drove her away just as much as I did."

"For your information, I didn't sleep with Carlos, you deluded creep."

"But you wanted to."

Aimee took another long sip and got close to his face. "Yeah," she said, eyes taut. "I *really* did. Maybe I still do."

Joel grabbed her neck and pulled her to his mouth. He kissed her with passion, with rage, with desperation. For that brief skip in time, she was his wife again, the woman he loved and who loved him back.

But Aimee ripped away from him, chest pushing out and caving in with every breath. She smacked him hard on the face, and then hit him once more. The second time her nails broke skin. "Don't touch me like that ever again."

Once he caught his breath, he said, "We keep looking for the evil inside each other, Aimee. But the evil's out there. Someone took Emery away from us. I don't know why. I don't know how. But I swear to you I am trying. Don't you think I want her back as much as you do? I never stopped wanting it. I'll bring her back. I'll find her."

"Empty words from an empty man."

"Not this time, baby. Not this time."

Aimee finished her glass and put it in the sink. Then she turned toward him before exiling herself to her bedroom. "It's been over three months, Joel. I can't keep living like this. I won't."

His eyes felt paralyzed, his hands and feet cold. Joel reached for Redd's card again. He had little faith in what one person could do when all others had failed. But his hope hung on a chance, a thread that was soon to slip from his grip completely, he was almost certain.

He had no choice. He had to call before he went insane. Time was running out.

CHAPTER SEVEN

DR. EMANUEL KRANE MOVED NERVOUSLY IN HIS CHAIR UNTIL comfortable then studied the office. There were several things about it he knew for sure. He knew it was approximately eighteen feet by sixteen feet. He was also certain that the ceiling fan circling above him—the one manipulating the specks of dust in the air—had been replaced somewhat recently. But there was something different about the way it hummed overhead. So mechanical and precise. Inhuman. He missed the noise of the other machine.

Krane could have sworn that the windows were once covered by colorless shades, lackluster attempts to match previously bland walls. Part of him kind of liked their pale blur, though. The color on the walls was so new he imagined he might still be able to smell the paint. It had some sort of eggshell finish by the look of it—the lines and blemishes hiding beneath the newness, almost undetectable.

What Krane noticed most about each surface, however, were the cracks. In certain spots, he could still make out the slight imperfections. The places of life in the walls that someone had overlooked. The places where a patient most likely broke some poor nurse's jaw with a good punch, sending her flying backwards enough to chip it some. He then pictured a guy resembling Jack Nicholson ripping a bolted chair out from the floorboards and using it to shatter the pristinely clean glass in front of him, yelling "Here's Johnny!" before succumbing to immediate sedation. That was one of the ways things and patients were handled at Salvation. Quickly. And if possible, without incident.

In an era where countless psychiatric facilities were being abandoned and shut down, Salvation continued to expand. At times, the war for the human psyche had to be fought with extreme measures, here above all places. For in here, there existed an environment where apathetic loved ones could responsibly dispose of their *more fragile chain links*. At least, that was the euphemism Saul Hoven, Salvation's director of operations, had chosen. This was a place for the deemed criminally insane, a haven for the ones that wandered.

And he was right too. This place *was* a unique haven, a place constructed unlike any other. Sure, the surface world, this upper half that Krane stared at from the hovering office fixed inside one of the many corners of the building, was quite the usual asylum. Ex-convicts. Schizophrenics. The occasional serial killer. Menaces. But the other world—the world that existed beneath this one— was full of experimentation. It was a world for the prodigies; the beginning of something powerful.

It was easy to get lost down there. To get swept up in research and study and *them*. Was it possible to truly and wholly identify with them? Was it possible to really understand them?

Krane spent the next several minutes thumbing the leather-stitched sides in his chair, never coming to a conclusion, always circling back to the genesis of these wilting ideas. A full answer might come, but there was no telling when or in what form. He shut his eyes, had to force them closed. Keeping them open for such long durations was certainly taking its toll. Could he for a moment focus on something other than the imperfections? The problems? The weak links in his own chain? This wasn't some ridiculous homework assignment.

No, his mind reiterated. *It's the future.*

A sigh fled from his throat. Just relax. Being in this room felt like being in the disciplinarian's office. He instantly retreated to the fifth grade, when he grabbed Suzie's chest when she wasn't looking. He claimed it was a dare from one of his buddies, but everyone knew he didn't have any. There was a part of him—one not unlike the part of him that enjoyed locating mistakes and imperfections—that liked having that kind of control over something that wasn't his.

With weary eyes and sweat clinging to the armpit of his cheap shirt, Krane waited. The disciplinarian at this hour was Saul Hoven, a military man, aged more by his experience with violence than the number of years he'd endured in the world. He carried himself like a bloodthirsty general, and the people at Salvation mockingly gave him the title of God. It must have been born into him, a desire to have other people quiver in his presence. Maybe it was his way of silently letting everyone know that they weren't worthy to breathe the same kind of air he breathed.

"Care for a drink?" Hoven asked upon entering the room. "It's been a hectic morning. Not to mention I just got off the phone with the secretary of defense. Guy's a real class act."

Krane was mute.

"How do you do it?" Hoven added. "You're down there in The Sanctuary close to twenty hours a day now. You just don't know how to rest."

"Did I miss something? I mean, a man with your back-back-ground must certainly understand dedication."

"In my history of working with mad men, Doctor, there seems to be a fine line between dedication and obsession." Hoven had that twisted gleam in his eye, one Krane never could quite calculate. It could mean anything. Then he broke into a slight chuckle, really prolonged and breathy, with a groan at the end.

"I'm busting your stones, Manny. You're exactly the kind of blood Salvation needs. Our own personal Victor Frankenstein."

The doctor moved in his chair, slightly calmed. "I'll take that as a compliment."

"Take it any way you like."

"Well, I am rather conn-c-c-connected to my work. I l-love-love discovering new flaws in the code, something to be perfected yet."

"I imagine it also frustrates you, though. The cracks, the flaws. But we'll get to that." Hoven sipped the drink slowly then stirred the liquor before putting it up to his lips again. "But a brain like yours needs rest. One can only speculate what all that mess can do to such an *intellectual.*"

Saul Hoven stared down below at a sea of patients. "I want you to come over here for a moment."

Krane got up and walked toward the window. Hoven put an arm around his shoulder, but he didn't like it.

"Take a look. Tell me what you see."

Krane stared down at a dirty first floor. Nurses and patients were walking; some exchanged words, others simply moved for the sake of movement. One patient with tangled, wiry hair kept fidgeting with his toenail. Another skulked back and forth, engaged in a heated conversation with his sworn nemesis, who was, in fact—as one of Krane's coworkers tried to convince him—nothing more than the patient's shadow.

As his eyes moved a little farther down the long stretch of hallway, they found a woman hitting her head up against the wall outside the public restroom, for the moment unwatched by anyone but Krane. She then reached into her pants, and her hand emerged full of feces. She began rubbing it on the wall then smelling it. The motion repeated. A guard took notice and came toward her, but when he did, she turned violent, clawing at his neck with her filthy hands until a group of orderlies rushed to his aid.

Krane took it all in with a mixture of disdain and understanding. The mind was a tricky creature, Morpheus was teaching him.

"I thought you'd react the same as I had. As I do, come to think of it. But why is all of this so screwed up? We deal with madness day in and day out. You'd think we'd become desensitized by it all the same. But there's still something in us that looks at a girl frolicking in her own excrement and labels it nuts."

"They're misplaced, that's all. Insanity is a trick the mind plays on us. If w-we-we let it play too long, we g-get-get lost."

"Yeah, we do, don't we? Makes me think, you know. They're all like little children. Uncontrolled, little children."

Krane felt the expectation that he should agree, but he didn't fully.

"Manny, I'm aware your little underworld is a slightly different animal. Up here, it's pure chaos." Hoven sipped his drink. "And outside this facility isn't any different." He pointed in the direction of the nearest highway a few miles up the road.

Krane remained attentive. That's what men like Hoven wanted— to be listened to, heard.

"You see, I've been meaning to talk to you, on a personal level, for quite some time now. You've been here for several years, yet we don't get all that much face time, do we?"

The doctor shook his head.

Hoven rubbed his chin. "Let me be blunt. What exactly is it you think you're doing down there in The Sanctuary?"

Krane kept quiet.

"You're probably thinking you're trying to discover new miracles. The scientific explanation for why there are unnatural phenomena in our seemingly natural world. How is it possible that some boy can summon flames from inside his body? This is the question you want answered, isn't it?"

"Yes."

"But not me. We have The Source, Manny. We've already cracked that egg and made ourselves an omelet. So where is it all going? Where will it end?"

"I-I-I do-do-don't know."

"Wrong answer. You know more than anyone. There's always more. Always."

Krane circled around back to his seat. Hoven's eyes lingered on the window, or better, the weak links below.

Silence. After a long wait, "We're on the brink of a regime change, Manny. Can you feel it? The movement is happening. All around us. I can practically taste it. We've been close for years, and now the madness will all collide. Change is coming, make no mistake."

Krane hated when Hoven spoke of the future. The old man took a sick pleasure in it.

"We have the power controlled, for now, and we're studying it further. Providence. Destiny. In the palm of my hand. Feels invigorating. After all, what's the use in having a god if he never shows up and gives you what you want?"

Krane barely chuckled.

"Well, Doctor, our one goal is to replicate what we've begun. To create. These creatures hold the key to a future mankind has needed since the Almighty, in his *infinite wisdom*, thought it prudent to baptize the human race with a little rain."

Krane rubbed his thumbnail inside the chipping grooves of one of his teeth.

"We are so close to stepping beyond the boundaries your mentor left behind. But this is only the beginning. Just think twice before becoming like that old man. No attachments. No excuses…"

"No return."

The left side of Hoven's face slid up into a half grin. "Right. A man after my own heart."

Krane's stomach sank at such hollow words.

"As I was saying, Manny, we are getting closer to eradicating the imperfections. These abilities we bring to light aren't to be squandered. We are perfecting the gene in them, yes we are. Slow but sure. We're not ready yet, though. We're close, but we are still like them out there, little children—the weak links. We must be ready when it comes time. And when we are—" he sipped the last of the liquor "—all of this will be a blink."

Krane had noticed Saul Hoven's sunken shoulders before, but now they seemed to slouch even more. In his old age, he was becoming like a vulture with a short spine. His hair was cropped around the ears, and crept wearily toward the top of his scalp to form a neatly brushed flat-top. Lines started at each side of his nose and snaked down to the corners of his mouth, forcefully. Hoven's eyes had a sick glow to them too, a look of possession, like a king gloating over a kingdom of plagued rejects. Incurable, belligerent—a living dead. Krane knew it was brilliant after all to have constructed The Sanctuary beneath this unshakable façade.

Krane scratched at his neck, and afterward, rubbed the bottoms of his long fingernails on his pants. "I s-sometimes wonder, sir, if there is an end," he said.

"Just do what you do, Manny. Do what your mentor taught you, pathetic waste that he was."

"He w-wasn't a waste," Krane barely whispered.

Hoven didn't even acknowledge the comment. "You know, Manny, I never believed I'd see the day when human men became gods. But that day is coming quicker than we know. The Good Book is right, I gather. The world isn't what it used to be. Not anymore. The skies and the grounds are old and tired of us. We've slipped. We've strayed. We're zombies, like them. We're looking to start over. We're looking for a second chance."

"From us?"

"From us," Hoven said definitively.

Krane's eyes grew heavy, the silence of the moment calming him briefly. Hoven could conjure purpose all he wanted, but months had been spent and there was little to call successful. The dreams weren't delivering the sort of promise he knew his mentor had envisioned. They were too sporadic, too jumbled. They didn't explain enough. What was he missing? What could he do differently?

"How are the boy's sessions with Carraway going?" Krane finally asked.

"As good as they can."

"Which means not v-vcr-vcry well. Tell you the truth, I didn't think enrolling Carraway into our selected was a g-goo-good-good idea. But there *was* a part of me that hoped... Sir, what if the arson's body doesn't m-manifest the ability again?"

At this point, the female subject didn't matter. The Phoenix, as he called her, was an anomaly all her own. But the arson mattered. Because if he could really create fire, and if they could control it the way they had so far controlled The Source, then Hoven really was right. The day would come when men could become gods.

"Cure your unbelief, Doctor. We'll get that fire back. My over-seers wouldn't have it any other way. But perhaps you shouldn't focus your attention on the when as opposed to the how. Like, how will you handle 219's powers when they do return?"

Silence split the room.

"Minor details, right, Manny? Minor details. Don't panic. We just need the right thing to call those flames out again. Get me whatever data you have. I want to see what he's been dreaming. We have spent a lot of money on Project Morpheus. I need confirmation that the machine is still operating as it should."

"Yes, sir," Krane agreed. He stood up, gripped with fatigue. It had been a long morning.

CHAPTER EIGHT

KRANE HATED THE SOUND OF SAUL HOVEN'S VOICE WHENEVER he called him by the nickname *Manny*. Like they were friends. It was obvious why he did it. The same reason the low-lives in high school did it: to get under his skin, create a vile home, and live there.

Along with the frustration, new doubts stumbled in. What right did he have to experiment on and cut open these children? These subjects? Creatures Hoven liked assigning numbers to in order to subtly identify them. There was less of a responsibility when a life boiled down to a series of random digits. It was clear that there was no room for conscience in that mental sepulcher of his.

Get a grip, Emanuel. You're on the brink of a regime change.

He figured the more he let Hoven's agenda into his brain, the easier it would be when he was cutting holes into theirs or stitching up the boy's chest. But was it only Hoven's agenda or had it become his own just the same?

Krane dragged his feet into the nearest restroom, ignoring the odd looks from patients and nurses. He knew he didn't belong on their turf. Whenever they spotted him, there were snide looks and occasional grunts. No one up here fully knew what took place inside The Sanctuary, but there was enough knowledge for them to realize it wasn't exactly *friendly*. Most left their curiosity at the front gate. But he'd been lost below so long that the upper level felt strange.

He headed for one of the urinals. After draining himself, he moseyed toward the sink, gazing into the gaudy mirror bolted to the wall. A ripe whitehead waited to spread on his left cheek.

"Great," he moaned, drawing nearer to the glass. "Just another thing to help me look terr-terrible. You can't even insult yourself right, st-s-s-stupid skeleton."

The stuttering had come when he was six. Dad didn't beat him raw. Mom actually baked cookies. *He* was the sore imperfection. He couldn't form the words right, the sounds. So many syllables felt so awkward on his lips.

Krane motioned both thumbs to the surface of the whitehead and pushed together until the pus squirted against the glass. The fresh spot was disgusting, but he'd bled out the imperfection. Now it was glaring at him, a wicked and judgmental stain.

He needed to recharge, to rest, if such a thing were possible. The human body could only expel so much energy before going completely dead and needing more.

"Brilliance is no good to anybody if it's wasted," his mentor had once said. During those long nights Krane had spent studying for tests, Henry Parker was there for him, going through the motions with him. He'd gone to school for medicine but learned so much more about surgery, about the blood, the mind. How to really ask questions and experiment. It was out of respect for a brilliant man that he offered his talents—the promise he made to himself to finish what Parker had begun, even though his mentor had forsaken it all those years ago.

Nearly seven and a half years had been spent perfecting what was left behind. The legacy of genius reduced to machines and medicines and formulas and lab rooms. Rooms that seemed like dirty secrets now.

Krane recalled his first invitation. The Sanctuary was a basement in some alley. Some time passed, and it became part of something greater. Salvation Asylum assumed the location of the once hospital, after a gas leak on the lower level completely left its former existence in ruin, providing them with a new arena to play. The asylum was reconstructed under new ownership—government ownership. The outside world would believe it to have been funded by private businessmen, and they'd be half right. But these businessmen were among the most powerful leaders in the world. Hoven irreverently referred to them as the Magnificent Seven. No one knew their true names or even what they looked like, only that they kept the media out of the asylum staff's hair and checks in their bank accounts.

Back in the days of the alley, Parker had been trying to bring dead things back to life. Then his obsession shifted to injecting potential regenerative qualities into certain species of plants and living creatures. It started with flowers of any kind; then pets, living or dead; reptiles, warm-blooded, cold-blooded. If it moved, walked, or crawled, it could be tested. But he argued never to test humans until they were sure the experiments could work successfully.

You're not sure, Krane's thoughts intruded. His conscience had become a frequent interloper.

The chief concept behind Henry Parker's work was his notion that the sum of the human person resided in the mind. All actions, reason, will, and soul. He reasoned that humans did what they did because their minds birthed certain ideas and told them to. Much of life resided in the blood, Krane knew, but the purpose and control of that life rested in the mind. A reciprocal miracle.

Project Morpheus was born less than five years later. "If I'm right, this machine will act as a filter for the human psyche," Parker said. "It will not only articulately study brainwaves, but in time, I believe we will be able to take pictures of the real landscape in one's mind. We will essentially harvest one's dreams and thoughts and memories." The possibilities were endless. One day, he believed that they'd be able to record such sessions in real time and dissect them piece by piece. "If what I'm telling you is true, Morpheus might confirm that the potential for something far more special than mankind has ever dreamed of resides within our psyche. A link to the supernatural."

This mechanical god of dreams was constructed before Parker discovered what they would call The Source, also known as Subject 217. Krane was just out of med school, still wet behind the ears. He had his doubts. "Sir, that's not possible," he argued then. But it wasn't until The Source that the trials began to show signs of producing significantly positive results. He knew that now. Still, a long time had passed since the more progressive cerebral scans.

"My research, my life, has led me here. I am telling you, we are finally getting our hands dirty for real. Think of the questions we might answer; think of the power we might create."

That was it—create. It sounded like a simple, pretty idea back then.

Krane blinked, coming back to himself. He was so tired, so faithless. *What if we're wrong? What if we're wrong about all of it?* Maybe the vast human race, with all its intricacies and its fragility, couldn't handle this new shift in genetic structure. What if it weren't possible at all?

But we've already done it, his mind reminded him. *We can do it again.*

He found his reflection once more, blurred by the recent smudge of blood and mucus mixing on the glass. Krane washed his face, startled by the skeleton of a man staring back. A middle-aged soul with no real power and no true form.

He was far from insane. He wanted to finish what he'd started, to play his part in the game Parker forfeited long ago. But Krane knew he had to ensure that the right people had this power when the world became. Maybe that was his mentor's intent all along: to uncover that lost human particle, the anomaly he named *the God gene*, and to dictate who could have it and who couldn't. To control it for what was to come. But the old dreamer didn't stick around long enough to see how the story would end.

A chill snaked down the doctor's spine. It really was a game with a curious conclusion after all. Like chess. But Krane was sick of playing as a pawn.

CHAPTER NINE

"HOW ARE YOU FEELING TODAY, STEPHEN?" THE SHIFTING blur asked.

It was a struggle for Arson to keep his head up. So heavy. So very heavy.

"It's all right, Stephen." The blur spoke softly. "The sedative is still navigating through your system."

"Sedative?"

"Yes. Don't worry, it's…it's not harmful. It keeps you somewhat contained, as we've discussed before. Harmless, really." The figure's head appeared to have another one attached to it, one that disappeared and reappeared like smoke. It had a dizzying effect.

"Who are you?"

"Good grief, don't you recall, Stephen? I thought we were past this. I am Dr. Nick Carraway, your psychologist." The grey vapor held out his hand but was met with a long stare.

With a snap of his fingers, he urged Arson to follow his index finger as it moved. "Come back to earth." The man wore a stoic expression. The movement of his lips seemed too coerced, and there were some wrinkles scattered about loose skin and jutted cheekbones. Sharp ears stuck out through salt-and-pepper hair. Gentle, younger, and seemingly freer eyes gazed into Arson's warring windows.

"You're…" Arson managed before slouching in his chair, "not like the others."

"What others?" A long pause. "Oh, you mean, the other orderlies? Well, I can't say I agree with you there. After all, the skeletons that skulk about these halls are mere clones of other clones. That's what most of the patients here say, anyway."

"Patients?"

"Yes. You're in a psychiatric facility. But you're safe here."

"Where is 'here'?"

"Salvation Asylum. This is a haven from the fears of the outside world." The doctor kept looking at Arson like he was supposed to recognize him or something, supposed to remember this big room, but he didn't.

"You…you're strange," Arson gasped. "This place is different." Arson took a moment to scan the area. His pulse quickened, and his pupils dilated. The room had no windows. That part was familiar. There was nothing on the walls, but he felt like it was meant to calm him. Still, it wasn't working. Where were the lively flowers or the bright photographs of a carefree family that often decorated a typical doctor's office?

"Where is everybody?"

"There aren't many here like you, Stephen."

"Am I in some kind of trouble?"

"Please, enough with the games. This is the same room we've conversed in for the last several months."

Arson's ears became alert. He drew his wandering eyes up from the crisp floors and felt his chest cave in. Months? Had it really been that long since he'd scooped ice cream at Toby's or tucked Grandma into bed?

"Hmm," Carraway said, massaging his jaw. He set his notepad down and pressed his hands together. "Is all of this still foreign to you? Can't you remember?"

Arson shook his head, still drowsy, eyes weak and heavy.

"It's not abnormal. Don't be afraid. This is part of the process. It can sometimes be the case. Many of my patients can't fully comprehend space and time because they are sometimes outside of it, if only in their minds. Black-outs and temporary memory lapses are...can be some of the side effects of post-traumatic stress disorder."

"What are you talking about? What happened?"

The doctor appeared bothered by the thought of having to exhume the dark details of the past yet again. But Arson's eyes begged to know more.

Carraway eventually replied, "Stephen, your grandmother..."

"Is she okay?" Arson let the blanket keeping him warm slip off his shoulder. He sat up straight at the mention of *Grandma*. His head was spinning as he watched beads of sweat slip from each lid. Warm and cold and confused. "What?" he struggled to say, feeling the twist of reality return.

"She's dead."

Arson's mind splintered just then. "No, she's not. I just saw her not too long ago. She's safe, at home."

"Home? Are you sure?" Carraway questioned. "This isn't the first time I've told you. You can remember that, can't you?"

A million voices were screaming inside his head. Arson fought them all, hoping he might decipher something true within the chaos.

The doctor continued, "It must feel like a blink to you. Time can be like that sometimes. But you haven't spoken to Kay Parker in months, I'm afraid. Your grandmother...well, as much as it aches me to say this...is gone."

"No. Don't lie to me. You're sick," Arson said, finally starting to recognize the air in his lungs and that chill clawing up the back of his neck. His senses returned, but his mind was still a maze.

"I know it's painful to grasp. I understand your anger, your fear. You have endured immeasurable trauma and stress. But you're all right now, and believe it or not, I think you're getting better. There will be healing soon." The doctor reached out to touch him.

"Leave me alone," Arson said, shoving his heel into the table. The guard in the corner rushed to the doctor's side.

"I'm all right." Then, addressing Arson, he said, "Please don't be frightened by me, Stephen. I'm not here to cause you any harm. All I want is to help. But you're in control of all of this. You must not let yourself become a slave to these irrational behaviors. Let me help you."

He appeared sincere, but Arson wasn't able to fully trust his senses. Any of them. Not yet. How did he know they weren't messing with him? That this wasn't some kind of conspiracy? The fact that he couldn't smell right or even taste anything in his mouth, apart from something bitter, was strange enough. Every sound was a piercing drum-beat pounding against his skull. His chest and stomach ached. It felt like a hole had been made right at the center of him. "Was I cut?"

"The wounds you carry are self-inflicted."

A wave of perplexity flooded Arson's mind. Hearing the doubt in the doctor's voice troubled him. He wanted to scream. "Is this a nightmare? A bad dream or something?" he asked.

"No. It's quite real." Carraway let reality do some work before continuing. "My efforts are to secure your safety. To bring you back home. I can free your mind from the burdens and the strife you carry. You don't want them. You don't need them." Carraway's voice was a whisper. "We've gotten quite close during your time here. Can't you remember?"

Remember? No, I can't, he thought. *I can't remember anything after I exploded and tore the flesh from their bones. I can't remember anything except her face.*

"I'll try," Arson said.

"Good. I know you better than you might even know yourself. You can trust me, Stephen."

The more he called him by that name, the more it seemed to sting. He wasn't Stephen.

A slight flinch disrupted Carraway's posture. He slid his glasses on and thumbed through the print-out affixed to the notepad on his lap.

"Why do you want to help me?"

The doctor set his pen down for a moment. "Because I'm your friend."

"I'll bet," Arson said, slouching. "This is just your job."

"I want to set you free. This place is for those who need…a little more attention. For those who can't find the way back themselves." He folded his lips and awaited compliance.

Arson settled in his chair, studied the doctor up and down.

"It'll all come back to you soon. Nothing stays lost forever, not even memories."

"Memories," Arson said. "Tell me what happened. Tell me!"

Carraway's nose twitched. "Let's not bother with specifics right now. The mind remembers in part. We must give it time. Your grandmother's death will come back to you when you're ready to fully accept it."

"I'm thirsty," Arson said, smacking his tongue. He wanted to know why he was here. He didn't believe this man, in spite of how innocent and welcoming he appeared.

"Let's get you some water." The doctor snapped his fingers, and with that, the guard accompanying them left the room. But he didn't walk through a door. The wall just moved forward at the pressing of the guard's hand. This room had no doors. Sighs rushed out of them both.

"Stephen, what is the last thing you remember before entering this institution?"

"I'm not crazy, Doctor," Arson spat, crossing his arms.

"I never said you were. Now, please, try to focus all of your energy on your last memory. Concentrate."

Just then, the wall opened again with a snake's hiss, and the guard entered with a glass of water. He set it down on the table and returned to his position.

Arson reluctantly shut his eyes, thinking back. He couldn't tell this man that the last thing he remembered was burning the faces off jocks and sluts. He wasn't a murderer. Instead, he thought deeper, reached for memories he hadn't experienced in some time. "There's a dock by a lake. I'm drowning. Waves, small waves rock my head back and forth under the current. No, I'm not drowning at all. I can't breathe, but…but I'm safe. Grandma's yelling at me in my bedroom. Doesn't like me going in, not at all. She loves me, just doesn't know how to show it."

"Very good. This is an older memory, no doubt. Still, it's a start. What else?"

Arson's mind violently sprang to life. "Now I see a room, like this one. But I can't make out much of anything. It's so dark and cold outside. Winter."

"Go on," the doctor said, scribbling notes.

"A young girl? She's in pain. I just want to help her. Can I save her? I want to save her!"

"Try."

"I can't. All I can do is watch. I hate it. Oh no, she's in so much pain. Something's happening. She's burning." An aching sensation spread at the back of Arson's eyes, and then warm tears dripped down the sides of his face. "I can't even touch her."

"Who else is there? Can you see anyone's face?"

"No," Arson said, eyes shut. "Everyone's a blur." Goosebumps bubbled on his arm. "Nurses are freaking out real bad. This girl is pregnant. There's a man next to her. I can tell he's afraid. Doesn't want to be there. So much blood. Is she burning alive…from the inside? She can't take it." Arson felt his nose start to bleed. "I'm alone and I can't get out."

Dr. Carraway snapped his fingers a few times, but Arson remained in that dark trance.

"Help her! No! Somebody, please help her!"

"Stephen, you must come back," he said, shaking him. "Wake up! Stephen!"

Arson shook violently and screamed. "What? Did you hypnotize me or something?" He touched the soft flesh above his lips. "I didn't mean to bleed."

"No, there was no hypnotism. Are you all right?"

"I'm not sure. I feel like I don't know anything anymore."

A grin toyed with the doctor's lips. "How did it feel?"

"How was it supposed to feel?"

"Here, have a drink."

Arson reached for the glass, liking the way the cold felt in his grip, how the liquid satisfied the burning in his throat.

"Stephen, it seems that this world you were describing is very real to you. And perhaps it is. I cannot yet determine that. If it is, then what you experienced were your memories trying to come alive again in the present. Maybe you have forgotten them, but they are still there, waiting."

Arson stared blankly.

"These images exist inside of you. They're a part of you. But you must be able to discern the dream from the real. There is nothing you can do to alter these past events. It is rather curious," Carraway said, stroking his chin. "One sticks out the most. I think it's healthy that you have now experienced it, maybe for the first time. That's how this process works. You know, it's one thing if I simply spit rules of the mind at you, but as you can see, everything's different when you relive it."

Arson sat quietly.

The doctor eyed him as he drank. "Perhaps these are just your memories and that's it. I'd love it if it were that cut and dry."

"No. That last one, Dr. Carraway. *That* memory…isn't mine."

The doctor stared at him strangely. "I assure you, once we dig a little deeper, some of these mysteries will begin to make sense." He sighed. "I appreciate your willingness to cooperate. You're very brave."

It was like the man didn't hear a thing. "You're not listening to me. I don't feel brave at all."

"But you are. Perhaps I need to remind you of it more often." Dr. Carraway smiled, his teeth glistening like ceramic.

"Forget it. If these memories are real, what do they mean? Why can't I remember other things, like what I'm doing in here?"

"Give it time. We've been at this for months, as I've told you, but today is a breakthrough."

"Great. Cue the infomercial."

"Take it easy," Carraway said. "It *will* come together. Your mind is in startling disarray, searching for all of its lost pieces. On this journey, I can help, but I can't make it for you."

Arson's mind was swimming. Drowning. Maybe that would've been better. He fidgeted in his chair, his skin begging to crawl off. "This isn't right. None of it fits. I don't belong here. I'm a good kid, right?" Arson crunched his eyebrows together. "I don't steal. Don't do drugs. I'm not *crazy*!"

"Calm down. I don't think you'll gain anything from my divulging everything to you. I've already given too much, I fear. You're brave, Stephen, but that doesn't mean you're invincible."

Arson rubbed his forehead. His breathing became normal, but he was blinking fast, swallowing often. Still thirsty. He took another sip of water.

"You're in here for doing a very bad thing, *Stephen*," the doctor said. "But what happened isn't your fault, *Stephen*. You are here to get well, *Stephen*, mentally, physically, and…emotionally."

"Stop calling me that."

"But Stephen is your name."

"And what, what are you talking about?" Arson said. "Mentally well, what? I still don't see what's wrong with me. You keep speaking in riddles. You stupid doctors are all the same. No answers. Just questions. Forget you!"

"It will return. For now, let's continue with what we left off with last time. Perhaps you recall that I am helping you with not only your mental state but also your completion of high school requirements," Carraway continued. "We'll work on all your basic studies. There's no reason why you can't gain an education during this process."

What was all this? Rehabilitation and mental guidance? High school requirements? It was too much to soak in all at once. Arson wanted to fight it so badly, but for the moment, he decided to keep quiet, to go along with whatever sick joke this happened to be.

The doctor walked to the back of the room, where only a chalkboard hung, and began writing out a quadratic equation. "This is quite basic. I want you to come up here and solve this."

The last thing Arson wanted to do was solve an equation. His entire mind was an equation. "That seems complicated. Don't think I was good at math. I would've remembered."

"Very funny. But that's nonsense. You might surprise yourself." Dr. Carraway held the piece of chalk out, waiting for Arson to meet him.

Reluctantly, Arson got up and started by scribbling fractions and equal signs, hoping for some spark of genius to hit. But it wasn't happening.

"Get all of the variables on one side first. Then check to see if it is in proper form. Once it is, factor out the greatest common factor and deal with the remaining numbers." The doctor dragged his fingers across the slate board, one hand still in his pants pocket. "Once you solve for x, plug in the answer and check your work. This is junior-year stuff, Stephen. As I am aware, you passed algebra II with flying colors."

It sounded so simple coming out of somebody else's mouth. But there didn't seem to be any answers at all, only questions and equations with no values. Primes and confusion. No absolutes. Another twenty minutes were spent toying with diagrams and complicated theorems that Dr. Carraway assured him had been covered in previous sessions.

"Have you completed the written assignment for today's session, Stephen?" the doctor asked once they switched to English.

"Written assignment?"

"Yes, it was a writing prompt. I asked you to write about your dreams. What you recall specifically. Your grandmother, for instance, or your high school prom."

Arson shrugged. "I didn't go to prom."

"So you remember? Good. That's *very* good."

Wait, how did he remember that? He thought back to that night, tried to remember what he did instead, but it was all hazy. Was he working? Hanging out with friends?

No, I don't have any...except her.

"You look slightly nonplussed. That means confused, in case you didn't know. Should be one of the vocabulary words I had you look into. But I'm guessing you didn't complete that assignment, either." Dr. Carraway sighed, making notes. "Stephen, how do you expect to heal if you aren't doing your part? There's no reason your education should stop simply because you're in here getting better."

"Wait, stop this crap. Since when are you a teacher anyway, Doc? Just who are you!"

"Calm down, Stephen. I told you, I am your psychologist. I am also quite qualified to guide you through your basic studies. In addition to counseling you, I am your teacher, for the time being."

"And how long is that going to be?"

"Well, I suppose that's up to you. The overseers of this institution pay a lot of money to invest in the minds of those who need it. Play ball and they might let you go early. Your eighteenth birthday is approaching."

"Wait. What month is it?"

"December. It'll be Christmas in a few weeks."

"How is that possible?"

"It begins here, Stephen." The doctor nudged his index finger up against his forehead. "Once you realize this, the rest is cake."

A short pause walked between them.

"Speaking of cake, why don't we call it an afternoon? *But* I want those assignments, along with the reading, completed by the next time we meet. So keep busy." The doctor signaled his guard to bring in a slice of cake. "I snuck one in for you. It was mine, but we'll keep this our little secret."

Arson's face changed slightly. He nodded, slicing the fork through the moist triangle. "Your grandmother used to make carrot cake, didn't she?"

Arson remembered the taste of something similar. His brain flashed pictures of one of his birthdays, when he was much younger. The bitter face Grandpa made when Grandma forced him to eat it, even though he didn't want to. There weren't kids around to celebrate, no party to speak of. He must've been four or something, but the image was so hazy, he couldn't be sure. The taste of this cake helped recreate the static images briefly.

"I think so," Arson finally answered.

"Well, I wouldn't dare compare your grandmother's baking to this." A grin climbed up the side of Carraway's mouth, as he stood up. "But try to enjoy it. I'm not much of a cake person."

Neither was Grandpa, Arson thought. He shoved another bite down his throat and took a sip of water. "Please tell me what happened to my grandmother, Dr. Carraway. I need to know," he said sternly, eyes peeled and narrowed with anticipation. "How did she die?"

"I don't think that's something you're ready to hear yet."

"Please! Tell me."

Dr. Carraway looked at the guard, an air of uncertainty mixed with deliberate pause. He placed his hands on his waist, locking eyes with Arson. "It was a fire. She was asleep, the police believe, when the house went up in smoke. I'll spare you the details, but I'm afraid your grandmother didn't make it out alive. In fact, there was nothing left of your home."

Arson put his fork down. He suddenly felt very sick. A thick cloud hovered over his mind. He stared at the guard then back at the doctor. None of this was right. What kind of man would lie like that? Make up some kind of twisted story? Was he toying with Arson's emotions for the thrill of it? He couldn't take this charade any longer. Enraged, Arson got up and grabbed Dr. Carraway by the throat. "Get me outta here!" he shouted. "I wanna see for myself."

"Stephen, you're choking me. I'm here to help you. Remember?" the doctor said calmly, face blistering red. "Let go of me!"

"No more lies! None of this makes any sense," Arson said, his hands swelling hot around the doctor's neck.

"It will," the doctor struggled. "Your mind continues to remain unwilling...to accept...truth."

"Liar!" Arson screamed, before everything suddenly went black.

Arson's body thudded hard against the floor, unconscious.

"Thank you," the doctor said, looking at the guard who had knocked his patient out. Gasping for air, he reached up to touch his throat. It stung. The skin was burned.

"No way," the guard pointed out with big eyes. "Look at your neck. That little runt burned you."

Carraway rubbed his throat one last time. "I think this afternoon's session went slightly better than expected." He grinned, torn between concern and unbelief. These sessions had no end in sight. He wondered how long the boy's mind could take it all, if he could take it all.

Carraway reached down on the floor to grab his pen and notepad, staring one last time at the boy on the floor. "It seems the arson is back after all."

CHAPTER TEN

THE SHADOW APPEARED AND THEN DISAPPEARED AGAIN.
For a split second, it gave Emery the feeling that someone was there, watching over her, but it left so quickly that the only thing she could surmise was that the shadow didn't come to save her. Desperate for some hope, she put her face to the wall and yelled; the loneliness began to clothe her bones.

"Come back. Please, just talk to me. Tell me your name. Who are you? Why am I here?"

But never was there an answer. Emery lay there on the cold floor, kneeling and scratching in the dark. There was a stitch of light hoping to be noticed beneath the door, where the shadow toyed with her. She lay still and quiet awhile, counted all the lines in this room—this winter coffin—the ones she could see, at least.

Her vision fought to adjust to the black. Every now and then the lights flickered, like smoke from a candle, but the dark was messing with her logical mind. Sometimes she imagined shapes and colors crawling up the walls, things that weren't there. They had claws and fangs and yellow stares, but upon the next blink, the haunting apparitions disintegrated back into nothingness.

She screamed, bashing her trembling fist into a divot in the wall. "You psychos! Where am I! Let me go. I'm not the freak. You are. You have to let me go!"

They didn't have to do anything. They were already doing it. Whatever plan, whatever scheme this was, she was stuck here. Screaming and yelling orders didn't change her situation. It was all useless. She wasn't getting out. No one was coming to save her. No hero in a cape. No weird alien boy coming to light this cell on fire. *That's just not normal*, she reminded herself. *That's not how things happen in boring, real life.*

She was beginning to doubt if she had ever even really seen what she believed took place that night on the beach. She felt like old Ebenezer, trying to find fault with his senses. No Jacob Marley, no spirits, just doubt and loneliness to warm her and fear to reminisce with the cold.

"Arson. I need you." Emery rubbed her face. It was still ruined. This place created a need to somehow create a mask once more, to hide from the dark, from the weaknesses that still craved a way out of her.

Just then, the shadow slipped by a second time, its colorless, formless shape crawling underneath the door frame.

"Hello?" she called, leaning on her ribs and nudging her eye against the bottom slit. "Hello, please just answer. I need to know somebody's there." She started tearing up. "Please."

"Keep your voice down," the shadow said finally. "I can't stay long. I'm not supposed to be here."

"What?" Emery said. "Who are you!"

The shadow pressed a hand up against the door. "You have to whisper."

Arson pulled his lips apart, letting his mouth hang open. He wanted to scream, but this place put too much fear in him. No words found escape. Only the empty breath now exiled.

He was in a hallway. Stuck. Part of him recognized where he was. It was cloudy, though, like fog had somehow slipped into the old building he remembered as middle school. He tried moving faster, to get out, but the doors were locked.

Hello? he wanted to scream. *What am I doing in here?*

No answer came to settle his thoughts, just the open silence and the faces jetting past him. Smoke. Smoke and pictures of memories, drones he used to know. He recognized some, others trapped far too deeply in the past. He'd forgotten the year or the day, didn't even know what time it was, because for the life of him he couldn't find a clock. Not one that ticked anyway.

His heart was a gavel. *Boom! Crash! Boom!* He could feel it in his ears. And then a piercing sensation started to stir the fluid at the center of his skull, as if something were drilling there. *Vizzz,* it hissed. *Snip. Buzz. Crash! Boom! Vizzz!*

Arson thought about stepping into one of the classrooms, sitting in on a discussion of *The Outsiders* or maybe stopping in to see an old social studies teacher. But something blocked him at all the doorways. Other students were allowed in but not him. An invisible force kept him out. The echoed laughs of children chilled and haunted Arson at the core. The children could see him now. All of them—the boys and girls he wasn't sure even knew his name. But they remembered him, even if he didn't remember them.

"I am the outsider," he mouthed.

Arson blinked, hoping that might shut them out, but their eyes found him, studied him. Kids with long hair like his, but with grins stitched into their vile mouths, smiles he wasn't sure how to create. They pointed, stared, pointed. "Look at the freak!" they taunted. "Look what he did. Monster! Killer!" The teacher couldn't hear them. Maybe he didn't want to. Why did they hate him so much?

Arson looked down to scrutinize himself. To his confusion, he was covered in ashes. His hands were crusted over and black, drops of blood staining the bent tips of his fingers. His skin glowed red and then turned pale. Raising his hands to his face, Arson lightly touched the disintegrating flesh. Bits of his skin floated to the floor, charred. He watched the ashes disappear all around him as he stopped up his ears, begging for the madness to end.

I want to be free, he begged silently. *Get me out!*

Arson fled down the hallway, the piercing eyes of an old teacher and countless vile children creeping toward him as he drifted by. He swore he even saw Danny, lost among the voices, the faces, the condemnation. Another layer of skin tore off from his arm and floated to the floor. He could see bone.

He needed a way out of here, and fast. Past lockers and administrators' offices he stormed, eyes peeled and wide with anxiety. Posters of the evening's basketball game surrounded him. He was there, wasn't he? It was all so unclear. Was this real? Was he? Had he been in the bleachers when one of the shooting guards sank that three-pointer? Was he there to watch Mandy, with her skirt hiked up, float in the air with a rowdy cheer the whole gym clapped to?

Yes, you were. This is real. You're remembering. You must be. But Arson couldn't be sure of anything—not this place, not his conscience; or was that Dr. Carraway's invading now?

Why did only some memories return?

The rumor was that Mandy lost her virginity on the night of the big game. He'd wished so many times that it had been him. Before he met Emery and everything changed. *She gave me a new purpose.*

A strange stillness consumed the hallway. Everything went numb. A cold quiet dropped from the ceiling, spilling into him and all around him. Empty cold. Lifeless cold. Soundless footsteps and words that remained deep inside of him. Locker doors swinging back and forth to no clamor. Papers floating in the dead air.

Arson stumbled down the hall. Where was the exit? His body was getting sore, tired. He raced through a set of double doors. The only doors that would welcome him. Arson was sure this led to the cafeteria, which led to the parking lot where kids used to make bets on how long he could last without sweating like a Popsicle.

He flew down the stairs, not even feeling his feet anymore but knowing they were there to carry him, at least for now. The cafeteria hall was empty too. Except for a janitor who was mopping the floor at the end of the room. Arson couldn't see him clearly, but the man was working with a slow and calm disposition, like he was eerily anticipating Arson's next move as he soaked the mop's filthy dreads into water before splashing them across the checkered tiles. "They're waiting for you in there," the janitor spoke in a deep voice.

Creepy.

"Who is?" Arson asked. As his feet edged closer he tore awake with a terrified scream.

Furious curses exploded within the dim room. He was on a cold table again, removed from that prison with the checkered floor. He couldn't swallow. Breathing was a chore, and his lungs were fatigued and lazy. Arson swore he heard the crash of a machine, broken pieces scattering on the floor to compound the panic. His lips mouthed a silent, spiteful prayer that whatever it was would burn. That this whole place would be swallowed by flames and smoke. Frightened blurs stammered over his shaking body. "Lemme go," he begged, coming to. "Not...real... Get me... out..." His words eventually trailed off.

A sharp sting crept inside. Whatever sedative these sick people were pumping into him was growing more potent with each gasp. The dosage was strong and relentless, and he was weak to its charm. The needles spearing into his brain were quelled for now at the shores of a dizzy consciousness. Waves of pink flesh and blinding white light. He'd come back to the real world.

The heat reversed. He felt chills; then weakness; then nothing.

Emery focused all of herself on the words the shadow was saying. She felt a sinking in her gut, a skip in her chest. But the voice was young and soft.

"Emery?" He was hushed but anxious.

"What? Yeah. I mean, how the—how do you know my name?

"Doesn't matter," the shadow replied, its black shape sliding in and out of sight. The voice came from a person possibly her age. The boy's presence was like Arson's. For some strange reason, she felt peace with him on the other side.

"Oh—okay. Do you...work in this place?"

"There isn't time. Emery, I'm not what you think I am."

"Where am I? What are they doing to me? Why am I here?"

"You're in a place called Salvation. It's an asylum. At least, the top floors are. But down here, nobody knows you even exist. This is the invisible level, part of The Sanctuary."

"The Sanctuary?"

He seemed to measure each breath, almost as if it were his last. "You're a special girl. That's why they want you."

"No, I'm not. I don't have a clue what you're talking about. What are they after? When my dad finds out, he'll—" Emery broke down, wondering where her father was, if he were even alive. Would he ever find her? The shadow pressed his hand upon the cold surface again. "Place your hand against the door."

She unfolded her fist and placed her palm against the cracks and metallic splinters. "All right," she breathed out slowly. "I want to get outta here. Can you help me?"

"I don't know," he said. "The eyes of God are everywhere. But I had to meet you. I *had* to be sure."

"Of what?"

"That you were real. They've been talking. They're planning something, Emery. I can't let you be involved in what is to come. We have to leave. Soon. It will increase, get worse. I can't let that happen."

"Who are you?" she asked, panic creeping up her throat. "Are you going to hurt me?"

"No. I—" he cursed under his breath. "Someone's coming. I have to move fast before the cameras rotate again. I will find you."

Emery prayed that his voice would stay, even if he didn't. She imagined it was Arson, imagined that voice could save her completely. In seconds, the sound of his bare feet running down the corridor seemed to cause vibrations in her hand.

"What is your name?"

But she was too late; the shadow couldn't hear her.

CHAPTER ELEVEN

THE DOORKNOB TWISTED WITH A WHINE. KRANE DRAGGED his feet into the apartment. Defeat was a prisoner inside his wrinkled, sleep-starved eyes. Cracking his back, he let out a long sigh, and with it, pent-up frustration. The amount of damage incurred back in his underground city was a weight he wasn't prepared to carry. Not when he was so close to weeding out the imperfections.

The last few hours hadn't gone as he'd hoped or planned. But plans often changed. After all, besides testing a girl who didn't appear to show any signs of manifesting genuine power, he had the privilege of working with a subject whose body and mind were in constant flux, unstable and uncertain. Like the future. Like the dreams he and Morpheus fought hard to steal.

Was he stupid to think there was even a point to it all? The troubling idea toyed with him too often, and each time, he remembered his mother's words, words he believed were buried with the past. "Do something miraculous with your life, Emanuel. Help people. Change the world." Well, the world would be changed because of his work.

Hope I made you proud, Ma.

Krane rubbed the tension from his body by massaging his temples. It felt as though a stampede were crashing through his skull. He set his briefcase down on one of his ripped sofas and stumbled into the kitchen.

Cluttered countertops and unwashed dishes welcomed him. No wife to kiss, no child to scorn for homework she didn't have done. Just home, sweet home. Little ever changed in this apartment. The off-center picture frames hadn't been moved in nearly four years and were now weighed down by dust. Newspaper clippings and magazine articles were pasted and stuck to the wall at the center of the kitchen so he could easily scan the contents and judge the progress made. Words and pictures ran along the dull-colored Sheetrock, pieced together by sloppy glue and thumbtacks. His research. His life. Their lives.

The filth had never really bothered him, not in all these years. In fact, he wouldn't know what to do with himself if these rooms were clean. Odd how much of a hypocrite he could be, so quick to notice another's imperfection, perhaps quicker to notice his own, but unwilling to change.

A bottle of ibuprofen spilled out into his palm the moment he opened the cabinet door. He must've forgotten to cap it the last time a migraine fought to split his brain. He spent the next four and a half minutes reorganizing the shelf full of prescriptions before giving up completely when he realized it would never be as he wanted things.

He walked over to the sink, flipped up the faucet handle, and cradled a handful of water, drawing it to his mouth. It tasted like copper. He swallowed the pills and reached into the freezer to pull out a frozen dinner—Salisbury steak and mashed potatoes. With a sigh, he tore the package. After popping open the microwave, he tossed the frozen entrée onto the wheel and nuked it.

The microwave finally beeped moments later, not enough time to allow him to escape his thoughts, the ones still stuck in the obscurity of the lab. After forcing himself back to the reality he was in, Krane grabbed the platter without using a glove. He quickly jerked back with a curse. The pain made him think of the arson, probably afraid now yet unable to burn, even if the sick desire lingered to do so.

He imagined controlling that kind of power. Such power was beautiful.

Krane licked the burn already beginning to blister the tips of his fingers then found a fork amidst the dirty items in the sink and used it to eat. The clock on the microwave glowed yellow. He didn't bother to register what time it was. He was too busy thinking on what he'd say when Hoven came to prod for an explanation for the loss of visual data.

He just needed the arson to keep dreaming. Whatever mysteries roamed inside the fire-breathing teenager turned him hostile, made him react. Reacting, as long as it could be controlled, was a good thing. Losing expensive equipment wasn't.

Krane shuffled over to a sofa that was falling apart in the corner of his small, unimaginative living room. Balls of years-old cat hair, magazines, and papers with statistics littered the carpet. With the remote, he turned on the television, an outdated unit with a big back end. He proceeded to surf the static channels, eventually settling on a Travel Channel special. Some re-run of a magician's journey to prove he possessed true magic. His name was easily forgettable once he performed the first trick, but it was at this point that Krane became intrigued. He leaned up in his chair, pushing around the bad flavor of the Salisbury steak and soupy potatoes in his mouth, and focused on the screen as the magician began to levitate. Or so he was expected to believe. But he knew a scam when he saw one. The crowd, unlike him, was in awe; some were terrified. Even the camera man leapt back momentarily, perhaps not expecting such a stunt. "It's just television," Krane mocked. But was that all it was? A cheap stunt created for a gullible audience?

The next scene shifted to the magician in the middle of a downtown city square. Probably Chicago. Again, a crowd had gathered to hear him speak his slow, soft words, almost hypnotic. He began guessing their thoughts, and the people were amazed, like the crowd before. Next, he gave a homeless man a gold coin then allowed him to scratch a lottery ticket, said to be worth a fortune. As predicted, the beggar won several thousand dollars with the ticket and the coin.

Krane grunted. These were such trivial things. Hocus-pocus nonsense. As a man of science, he couldn't be perplexed, just frustrated at how easily people believed in such dull magic. It was nothing more than a trick, a distraction or the proper lighting. "Bring someone back to life. Heal an infant. F-feed a th-th-thousand men."

If a man could really do these things, without trickery, that man would become someone to be feared. Perhaps even one to be set on high, if he possessed the proper genes to rule. Why, then, was this vagabond hungry for an audience? He wasn't a god. He wasn't something to be feared. Why was he walking street corners and doing signs and wonders that undoubtedly could be manipulated or reenacted for an unintelligent target market?

"Nothing but ch-cheap-cheap tricks," Krane concluded, shutting off the television.

CHAPTER TWELVE

REDD'S OFFICE LOOKED FRAIL AND WORN DOWN FROM THE outside. Joel noticed a sign that hung on the front of the chipped vinyl siding, but he couldn't make out what it said. There wasn't much light. It was the kind of building you had to know was there in order to find it, and he surmised that was precisely the intention of the owners. Being built on possibly one of the worst corners Hartford had to offer didn't really help. On his way in, he'd witnessed two drug deals go down, just yards away. He got sized-up once, hard, by a dealer with dreads down to his waist. It was warning enough to mind his own business and find where he needed to go. No problems.

He waited outside for a moment once he arrived. A long moment. Maybe it was fear keeping him unbalanced on the outside. Maybe it was lack of faith in what this Redd guy, whose hidden office resembled something out of *The Exorcist*, could do to reunite him with his daughter. A cold wind sliced at his jaw, chilled his neck. He watched his breath unfold around him. His gaze drifted forth and back to littered streets and cracked sidewalks with gang symbols painted on them. It reminded him of his home in Camden.

New Jersey had left its mark on him for sure, but he'd tried to leave that part of him in the past, where it belonged. If he'd stayed in that filth long enough, God only knew what he might have been capable of.

The front sign's letters flickered one last time before the sign went completely dead. No more hum, no more distraction. It was just there, a sight of lost light, hung in the dark for all the world and this lonely street corner to miss.

Soon after, he found himself taking in the warm air of the office. The exterior was gravely misleading, and the quite-normal interior calmed him down some. A small desk waited at the center of the room. A receptionist with a headset sat behind it. Her fingers no doubt punched away at an email while she simultaneously finished up a phone call with someone. It was admirable how efficiently some secretaries did their work, becoming more like liaisons or emissaries than mere desk workers punching a clock.

The woman had tenacious curls flowing from the top of her head down to her chin, and it fit her just right. Her makeup was neither overdone nor underdone, complementing the blouse she wore. But what dragged him from despair was her welcome. It had such a life to it that Joel nearly surrendered all his apprehensions right then and there.

"You look like you're carrying the world on your back, Mr. Phoenix," she said.

Joel sat down slowly. "How'd you know my name?"

"You're our six o'clock. I pinpointed your demeanor, anyway." She studied him briefly. "Thought you might look something like this. Hope you don't mind my saying so."

"No, it's all right, I suppose," he returned.

"Redd'll be off the phone in a minute. If we take this case, I'm sure we'll put your mind at ease. We haven't let a client down yet, and we certainly don't intend to. We're a small operation, but we take care of our clients' needs like they're our needs. Can I get you a cup of cocoa to warm up?"

"Uh," Joel hesitated. "Sure. That'd be nice."

He couldn't help feeling like he was a patient, about to get seen by Dr. Redd. He pictured the "turn your head and cough" routine several times before getting weirded out by it.

"Here you go," the kind girl said, returning with a steaming cup of cocoa. "Man, winter's definitely here. Now be careful, it might burn you if you drink it too fast. Sort of like a reverse brain freeze, I call it." She had such a bright personality that Joel's emotions wrestled some with it but only slightly. The truth was that he wanted to be at ease, swooned by the quiet of the place.

"Thank you so much," Joel said, taking his first sip. "It's pretty good."

"And it's homemade," she chuckled. "From the bag. I love those little marshmallows too. They rock."

This young girl's persona made him wonder what Emery might have been like if she had not gotten burned. *She* was computer savvy, people savvy. *She* had had such life, such ambition as a little girl, and then one accident—one night—changed everything. If he blinked enough times, maybe this girl would become his daughter.

She went back to feverishly typing away at the next group of emails or whatever she was working on.

"Can I use your bathroom?" Joel asked after some waiting.

"Sorry about the wait. As you can see, it's not Rockefeller Center here. We try to keep a low profile, but sometimes we get swamped with calls from clients and business folks. I'm sure you can imagine how complex certain cases can get. But all you asked for was the restroom, and here I am talking your ear off. The answer is yes, you can use it, small as it may be. Walk precisely six and a half steps to my left and the bathroom is the first, the only, door right there."

Joel said thank you with a smile; inwardly he returned to the frontlines of a battle, where his thoughts continued warring. A hundred doubting scenarios came all at once. The second-guessing was killing him. Maybe it was merely the pressure from Aimee to get out there and "do something again." He only hoped this wasn't a mistake.

Joel checked his pockets. He had a roll of a thousand dollars. Close to all of his savings. The last few months had been tight. Shortly after relieving himself, Joel paused in front of the mirror. "Maybe this can change things," he admitted.

Joel sighed as he let the water run over his hands. After drying, he reached into his back pocket to find the picture of Emery and one of the flyers he'd posted in nearly every city in Connecticut.

As he stepped out, a voice called to him. "Joel Phoenix?"

"Yes?" he answered.

"I'm Redd Casey."

Joel froze slightly.

"Right. This is the awkward, *'I'm-actually-a-chick'* moment. I get it a lot. I'm ready for you now."

Joel wasn't sure which he was more shocked by, the fact that Redd was a woman or the fact that someone as firm and strongly attractive as she would refer to herself as a *chick*, especially considering her line of work. But he disregarded it and entered.

"Please sit down," she invited. "Let's talk about why you came to see me."

Joel adjusted his jacket before sitting then folded his hands. "As I'm sure your secretary, uh…"

"Jana," Redd firmly added.

"As I'm sure your secretary, Jana, informed you, I am searching for my daughter. She was taken over three months ago." Joel tried not to sound so weak and desperate, but it was the only tone his voice managed to create.

"Right. I'm terribly sorry for your loss, Mr. Phoenix. It's not easy, not by a long shot, to lose someone you love."

"You speak as if you've lost someone."

"Haven't we all?"

"Recently?"

Redd hesitated. "A long time ago. But let's stick with your situation. Emery. Tell me about her."

"What's there to say? She's wonderful. Spontaneous. Funny. Sarcastic. A bit rebellious." He swallowed and pushed his lips together as these one-word tags came like bullets out of his mouth. "Fragile. Beautiful."

"She definitely sounds like a seventeen-year-old," Redd said, rotating slightly in her chair.

"I loved her."

"Use the present tense, Mr. Phoenix."

"I beg your pardon?"

"When you refer to her, always use the present tense. Don't allow yourself to think for a second that you've lost her for good. Odds are already against us. The last thing we need right now is doubt. If we're gonna find her, you need to be with me in here." She pointed to her head and then flipped open a notebook. "Should you decide to work with me, this little notebook is like our bible. Are you a religious man?" Redd asked, nodding to the cross hanging from his neck.

"Used to be. But I suppose, to some degree, we all believe in something, don't we?"

"Not here to judge," she said with a shrug, making a note or two before her eyes returned to his. "I'll be collecting notes about your daughter from you, anywhere I go, and from anyone I meet. And then I'll use that data to track her down, if I can. Of course, you'll be in the loop every step of the way."

Joel simply nodded. He wanted to work with her personally, but this would do.

"Do you have a picture of Emery?"

"Yes," Joel said, almost flustered. He handed her the crinkled photograph.

"There was an accident?" Redd asked.

"When she was a little girl, her face was burned and scarred," Joel said slowly. He didn't like to talk about Emery's condition or what had happened to her; most people didn't really care, but Redd seemed different. When she asked something, it practically demanded an answer, and Joel wanted to supply one. "It's been a struggle for me and my family ever since."

"I can imagine. Your wife…are the two of you still together?"

Joel looked down at his hand, toyed with the ring on his finger. "Separated. It's complicated."

"She didn't feel up to the meeting?"

Joel forced another sigh out.

"Complicated, right. Sorry. I try not to dive too much into the personal, but I find it's better if I get to know my clients a little. We've all got problems, complications, but my uncle always said that it's how we deal with the crap this world chucks at us that shows our true colors."

"Sounds like a smart guy."

"When he was drunk, maybe. He tended to spit out little proverbs like that whenever he hit the bottle. Strangest thing. Some men turn into bitter animals after a drink and others into prophets." She chuckled but only slightly. "Anyway, I'm not at all trying to make light of your situation. It hurts, may even kill, inside. I am so sorry for everything."

"None of this is your fault."

"If only that could make everything right again for you. To be honest, I want to find your daughter, Mr. Phoenix."

"Thank you. And, please, call me Joel."

Redd blinked slowly after his comment. "Now, before I go and label this an abduction, you're absolutely certain your daughter didn't run away? Checked with family? I mean, there's nothing you or your wife did to trigger a reaction or cause her to high-tail it out of this beautiful state, right?"

"She's not the kind of girl who runs away like that," he said abruptly. "She wouldn't."

"Point taken. I just don't want assumptions to rule this case, that's all. I want to be thorough and diligent."

Joel was distracted by her long red hair, noticing how it was the only vibrant thing in the room, how he wanted to stare at it forever. Her almond-shaped, green eyes fit well inside a soft but determined face. She had direction and fuel behind them. Her full lips formed every word, and in no time Joel was wondering how long he'd be captivated.

"Is everything all right?" she asked. "You seem distracted."

"Yeah, everything's fine," he said, brushing it off. He hoped she didn't think he was a creep.

"I'm assuming you've exhausted other avenues before coming to me?"

"Yes."

"Ah, the justice system isn't what it used to be. Sooner or later, there'll be anarchy, I'm convinced. You can't really trust anyone these days. It's sad but true."

"It's a huge risk to put your faith in someone, only to have it ripped away," Joel said. "For more than three months, I've heard all the excuses and polite rejections, and swallowed all the bull. Enough to make me choke."

"Gotta love all the bureaucratic charm. But you're here now, and we're gonna bring your daughter home. I want to be honest with you, though. It's not easy. Right now, she's nothing more than a thousand pixels on a flyer, a name on a list. I'm gonna make her famous. You'll see. It's not all doom and gloom. There's a big, wide world out there. And I network pretty good with others in the field."

Joel nodded.

"But I want you to understand that I can't just punch some digits into a computer or make a few calls and have her miraculously appear. She was taken, okay. You've done phase one walking through my front door. Now it's time for phase two: keeping the pace. It's a marathon, not a sprint. It has been more than a hiccup in time that she's been gone, so I don't want to mislead you into thinking I've got superpowers, 'cause I don't."

"It's difficult. I get that. You don't have to stress it any more than you've already done. I've been living without her for the last three godforsaken months, and I'm losing my marriage, my sanity. I'm quite familiar with what's difficult."

"All right, then, we've officially begun," Redd said, making several more notes. "Now, it's getting late, and this city isn't exactly friendly once the lights go out."

"Don't worry about me. You're talking to a Jersey boy. Grew up in Camden. Like I said, I'm familiar with difficult."

"Well, difficult and dangerous aren't a good combination. I'll be in touch in a day or two, after I send out some preliminary stuff to people I know. In the meantime, stay calm. I'll do everything I can."

Joel motioned like he was getting up, but leaned back again in the chair. "There is a boy. His name is Arson Gable. He was the last one who saw my daughter."

"Arson? Is that the kid's birth name?" she asked.

Joel shrugged. "I don't know. I only met him a few times. He seemed…different."

Redd leaned in. "Different how?"

"Not sure. It's a vibe I got. Different than your average teenager."

Redd took down the name and the address Joel gave her.

"He was my neighbor," he said.

"Was?"

"Well, that's just it. He vanished the same day Emery did. And his grandmother was the only other one who lived with him. Haven't seen or heard from either of them since my Emery was taken."

"Okay. And you're thinking this boy and his grandmother might be involved somehow?"

"My gut says that old bat had bigger things to worry about than a seventeen-year-old girl with a scarred face. But I've been wrong before."

"This is good. I'll look into this Arson kid's record. If he's been convicted or arrested, we'll know about it. And if something concrete comes up, we'll act accordingly."

"I should have pressed charges or something when it happened. I was so lost."

"Don't beat yourself up. It happens. Things fall through the cracks. You're human." Her soft stare peered into his. "Did this boy have any friends, close-contact kinda people?"

"Like I said, I didn't know him. Met him a few times, and they weren't exactly moments I was dying to relive."

"Sorry. It's obvious I'm badgering you. It's not intentional. I'll back off for now until I get something, if I get something."

Just then, the phone rang, startling them both. Redd checked the caller ID and pressed the lowest button on the dial pad, sending the call to voicemail.

"You don't have to ignore them on my account."

"No," she said. "They'll call back."

Joel stood up and extended his right hand toward her. "Thank you, so much, for meeting with me. And again, I'm terribly sorry about the initial meeting—awkward-frozen-stare thing. I just assumed—"

"Not a problem. Most everybody assumes that because my name's Redd I must look like Clint Eastwood or something. Truth is it was a nickname given to me by my uncle. Name stuck."

"I'm thankful for people like you in the world. It was a pleasure meeting with you, Redd."

She nodded and shook his hand.

"Now, do I give you the deposit, or does Jana handle it?"

Her cell phone vibrated, and she reached into her pocket, checked the ID, and said, "I'm sorry, they're persistent. I suppose I should take this now. Get the feeling it's urgent. Jana can handle the deposit and the paperwork to get your case moving forward. It isn't much. I'll be in touch soon, Mr. Phoenix."

"Joel," he tried to say as she closed the door and answered the call.

CHAPTER THIRTEEN

THE SPIDER HAD THREE PAIRS OF BLACK, GLASSY EYES. SPINY needle legs reached out from a brown gut and hinged upward before bending back down. The creature's slowly executed moves put Arson on edge. Before going completely still, the spider crept along his wrist and stayed there for a moment.

A fog drifted over Arson's mind. He sucked in a deep breath and tried to focus. Turning toward the spider, he found a mysterious sympathy lurking in his bones, sympathy for this creature. A sigh thrust out as the back of his hand became a platform. The spider's spear-like legs stabbed into ill skin. There was a slight pause, and then it located a crevice in the wall in which to hide itself from wandering predators, though Arson knew nothing else had gotten through. Nothing but the fear of not knowing what was to come or the nightmare of being completely forgotten.

His jaw crunched tightly. Aching ligaments and muscle and bone. And the fragile want of company.

He couldn't get his thoughts straight. Couldn't tell which were memories. Worse, he didn't know which memories were his own.

Did they belong to his mother? His father? How was something like that even possible?

He shook. *It's just the drugs. You can't have memories unless you've actually lived them.*

Or could he?

Everything was a mess. His brain felt like jelly, sandwiched between his ears, which seemed to echo every faint noise traveling between the walls and under the door. The door with no handle. What was wrong with him? He'd thought all his life that he was a mistake. But if that were so, why was he here? What did these *blurs*, apparently doctors, want with him, anyway? As far as he knew, his curse was gone.

But had he simply traded one curse for another?

He pondered Dr. Carraway's words. How he said with such confidence and finality that Grandma was dead. Arson didn't believe it, but what if it were true? What if Grandma really were dead? Arson's guilt was a sickness infecting him. His knuckles flared white, quickly shaping a fist. He listened for the crack, the air fighting to get out, the way *he* wanted out. Never in a million years did he think it would be possible to feel more alone than those nights spent locked away in his bedroom.

But this was worse. This was way worse.

Lifting his shirt up, Arson led his eyes to the marks that crawled across his chest and down his abdomen. The dark made it difficult to focus clearly, but he concentrated his vision until the faint scars showed. They still looked new. He then pressed his fingers against his left wrist, noticing three numbers tattooed at the edge of his palm. 219. What did it mean? When had he been marked with this, and why didn't he feel it or notice it before?

Because your head's a mess, that's why. Because you screwed up and went nuclear. You didn't save Emery. You took her away.

"No!"

What did these monsters do to him? And why couldn't he remember?

He felt the sides of his temples, rubbed the bruises and slid his fingers along the crusted blood staining his hair. His spit tasted like metal; the smells of this four-wall tomb were enough to make him hurl. But little would come up even if he did.

He picked at the dirt filling in the space beneath his ruined fingernails and then scratched at the spots of acne he could feel swelling on the left side of his cheek. What new weapons were they using to slice into him? Was it his mind they wanted? His power? His blood? Where was Emery? He needed her. He had to know where she was, if she was safe.

Was she even alive?

Dream and reality turned to static, blurred and confusing. Fiction. Fact. Lies. Truth.

A kid could go crazy thinking about getting out. Maybe he was closer than he thought to that edge. He'd seen all kinds of twisted movies. The kind where the hero quickly becomes this sadist who goes on to commit unimaginable sins. It didn't take much for a sane person to lose it. It didn't take much at all. Arson just wondered how long he could keep his balance before he also spiraled off the cliff.

Hours were spent screaming curses at the walls, at himself. There was no making sense of it, of any of it. All it did was cripple the noises in his throat. Arson folded into himself, trying to heat up but turning cold instead. His body had been so off lately. Sweat drained from unwashed pores. The stink of his armpits hovered around his face. The ratty t-shirt clinging to the bones and loose skin on his body was faded and ripped, dirt staining the collar and flipside.

"Sooner or later, we all pay for our sins," Arson murmured, the spider suddenly unveiling itself from the crevice once more.

He spied on the creature, the same admiration for its beautiful design, but without hatred. He squinted to better glimpse its short, bent fangs. It was a recluse. *Like Grandma*, he thought. He'd seen several of them in the woods behind the cabin, even killed some. But never had he been this close, eyeing one so wicked and hauntingly beautiful. Arson's face, now damp with sweat and filth, smacked against the floor. He was so weak, hungry, lonely.

The spider moved closer. "Are you my enemy? Or have you come to save me?" Arson stuck out his hand to touch the recluse's mud-colored body. He kept it there. Could it see him or hear his voice, sense what little warmth drifted from his skin?

Suddenly, Arson felt a sting, a quick stab. Glancing down at his pale arm, the flicker of light reaching in from underneath the door and reflecting off the dark-white walls, he was curious how long it would be before his skin changed color. Maybe the bite would kill him. Maybe.

The poison slipped deeper.

He didn't scream. He watched as the spider retreated to its vile home, leaving Arson to his. His eyes were misled bullets, waiting to be shot out. Muscles flexed lethargically. Every inch of him became weaker, but he still had strength to think, to fear for Grandma's life and Emery's.

Before his next blink, Arson lost himself inside that middle school cafeteria again, standing atop the checkered floor. The janitor mopping carelessly. The haunting, open room. But he didn't want to walk through. Afraid of what lay on the other side. He was tired of this dream.

CHAPTER FOURTEEN

JOEL WELCOMED A HOT SIP OF HIS STRAIGHT-BLACK COFFEE and finished reading the latest issue of the *Record-Journal*. He couldn't help but think his daughter's name should be somewhere in between the black lines and white paper. But she wasn't. No picture, no story, nothing. Her vanishing wasn't a big enough piece to run more than once.

His mind felt like putty as he tried to pull himself out of a near hangover. The last article he'd read before shutting the paper kept gnawing at him. It involved the unveiling of a new government facility, some unspecified place in Massachusetts that today went public. More locations like this one were already in plans for construction, the final and most prestigious edifice heading for residence somewhere in New York.

The article expressed the government's first and chief priority of protecting the way of life for every fabric of humanity, stating that these locations would open a window to study the human condition more thoroughly, to locate man's greatest strengths and greatest weaknesses.

"It is a fight to create and discover new potential in the human genes," the writer pointed out, "and make way for a future without the limitations mankind has endured since the beginning of time. Volunteers for these new projects will be compensated and their identities kept confidential." As Joel read, he found himself inwardly surprised by how easily people could be swayed. But it was becoming even clearer now. No one read between the lines, and the reporter issuing the story left it vague. She didn't dare question who funded it or the process by which these people would be studied or tested. And she certainly didn't raise a half-educated eyebrow as to the ultimate motive.

How many locations like these would be built, and who would run them?

Was it ethical to study human beings like this in hopes for a better world?

Massachusetts. What was it that kept drawing his thoughts there? It was like he couldn't escape it. The people assigned to look for Emery months back had searched the surrounding states, in addition to combing the country via other networked locations, but for some reason, they stopped searching Massachusetts after just two days. Could there have been more to look for after all?

Joel's thoughts switched again like a loose lever. He was drawn back to the summer. Earlier in the year, right after the oil spill in the Gulf, the president had revealed America's three-year plan to protect against future tribulation.

A new agency emerged from the ashes of crisis. D.A.T.A.: Defense Against Terrorism Abroad. The very name sounded strange and suspicious, but the president pledged that it would be a more potent and effective agency than anything the world had ever seen. It was a better, more cost-effective solution for National Security, and this new program extended the jurisdiction of the president specifically. International borders that were previously unaided by American efforts now had his protection and intelligence.

China became the first to make the headlines, and the president issued a thrilled response to the States' new partnership with this foreign power. He called it a new and inspiring alliance between two great empires of the world. "Freedom always comes at a cost," the president remarked, "but it's a cost we're willing to invest for the security and the safety of our children and our world. Change is never easy, but it is change that has kept the American heart beating, and it is change that will keep it beating for generations to come."

Joel played the television broadcasts back in his head a dozen times while he read the new article about this location just hours from this hick diner; he couldn't help but try to piece the two together.

When the Gulf crisis hit the press, it was chaos. But shortly after, D.A.T.A. was unveiled, and for weeks, it distracted millions from the panic, which always held Joel to his suspicions. He recalled how, at the time, he was bottled up with his own familial suspicions, too much to give credence to his thoughts of injustice or sorrows afflicting others. But he knew that whenever a great tragedy or attack happened, it was for a reason; it had a purpose.

His coffee was now almost cool. As he finished the last few sips, his mind continued to wander. It seemed strange that so much could happen in so little time. In less than two years, the world had begun to change, spiraling almost out of control. But was it merely two years, or had this process been in the making for years prior, decades even?

Someone was in control. With poise and clarity the pieces were moving, toward what end, Joel didn't have the slightest clue. But he knew he needed to stay sober, now more than ever. If there were some new, violent plot coming, he was nowhere near prepared. Emery had been taken, and since then he'd been gone. Might as well have vanished with her.

He still had questions desperate for answers. Where exactly was this location? Who was running it? And could he be held accountable for the sins he'd commit when he learned who had taken his daughter?

Joel was finally beginning to pay attention, for real. He was sober now, and he'd stay that way if there was a heaven in the sky. Joel was waking up to everything, to the reality that this world was no longer the place he and Aimee had grown up in.

It was changing before their eyes.

Joel's tongue was still alive with the flavor of the coffee. He grabbed the newspaper he'd been reading and paid the tab for his breakfast. He was glad he'd gotten off the couch and come out today. A candle, however faint, now flickered to life inside of him. Boston was only a few hours away. Joel knew where he had to start looking for Emery.

CHAPTER FIFTEEN

ARSON COULDN'T REMEMBER HOW HE'D GOTTEN INTO THIS room or what the pile of assignments in his lap was doing there, but his spine tingled still, and his hands were stiff and in need of blood flow. Finally, he forced his jaw open to get a word out.

"How'd I get here?"

Dr. Carraway answered, "The guard found you in your cell, unconscious. We're lucky we found you before the venom spread any further into your system. You know, a bite from a recluse isn't something people in your condition generally wake up from."

"My condition?"

"Your current weak state, Stephen. You haven't exactly been eating. Though I can't imagine why. Aren't you hungry?"

"What? Yes. I mean, I don't know."

"Slow down. Let your thoughts rest a moment. You were bitten by a brown recluse, and we found you unconscious. Do you understand what I'm telling you?"

Arson nodded, but he desperately wanted to wake up from all of this. Wake up from this dream and go home.

"It's a good thing we did. I fear what might have happened

if we hadn't reached you in time. Don't worry; sometimes those little vermin sneak into our facility. But we'll flush them out. We have the best people on it. If it crawls, it's getting sprayed to the underworld."

"Dr. Carraway?"

"Yes?"

Arson breathed slowly, the chills sinking into his blood. "Why is it so cold in here?"

"I'd hardly call seventy degrees cold. Now, my professional opinion would be to hold off on our session for today." A slippery smile parted the doctor's lips. "After the morning you've had, I—"

"I think I'll be okay," Arson said, locking his arms tightly. He didn't like it when the guard eyeballed him like that. Big, macho dude standing with that pissed-off look on his face. The guy had one of those handlebar mustaches that no doubt made a snarling threat easy to pull off. He was also equipped with a puffed-out chest and monstrous arms capable of carving out some bimbo's name in the side of a brick.

"But is your buddy gonna stare at me the whole time?" Arson asked. "Don't think I'll be doing any tricks today." He tried to push out a sarcastic laugh, coughing instead. It felt like there was an ice block stuck at the center of his throat.

Carraway put down his pen and took a seat. He gave the guard one of those looks Arson was familiar with. The ones he'd seen in movies. Something detectives might employ when working with a drug lord who didn't want to talk. Reluctantly, the guard left them alone.

"Is that better?" he asked.

"Sure." Arson sighed, rubbing his arms. The friction wasn't helping much. "What are they doing to me here?"

"I've already told you why you're here."

"No, you haven't. Not really."

The doctor crossed his legs and chewed on the tip of the pen. Furrowing his brow, he looked Arson up and down. "We've already discussed this. Your mind isn't—"

"Isn't what? Ready? Ready for what? I just woke up from being bitten by a brown recluse. I've been locked away in some stupid cell for who knows how long. I want to go home."

The doctor's face flashed white. "If you're unhappy with the conditions of your r—"

"I close my eyes and I'm trapped in these dreams. Dreams that aren't mine! What does that mean? I wake up and I'm either hooked up to machines or in these stupid sessions with you."

"Stephen, it's perfectly normal to feel this way."

"Don't feed me that crap. Nothing about this is normal." Arson looked down at his lap. The papers with handwriting that wasn't his stared up at him. A book he only vaguely remembered seeing before sat in his lap. "What's this book? Why do I have it?"

"That's *The Great Gatsby*, by F. Scott Fitzgerald. Fantastic choice, by the way. I have a copy myself." A book with a tattered cover slowly appeared out of the doctor's pocket sleeve. A few loose pages fell out, but he picked them up quickly. "It's your favorite book, isn't it?"

"Where'd you get that?" Arson recognized the book in Dr. Carraway's hand.

"This one was passed down to me by my father. He was a closet Fitzgerald fan."

Arson jammed the heel of his hand into his forehead, cleaning off the nervous beads of sweat like a wiper blade. "I want to remember. What is all this? I mean, is this some messed-up reality show?"

"This isn't a game, I promise."

"Then what is it? Maybe you can't hear me right. I…*didn't*… write this!" Arson started tearing the pages and throwing them onto the floor. "In fact, I never did any of this. I didn't do these assignments. I'm not supposed to be here. I don't even know if you are who you say you are. You know what I think? I think this is all just a bunch of bull—"

"Stephen, there's no need to be melodramatic. My name is Dr. Carraway. Nick Carraway."

Arson locked his gaze to the television monitor and the cameras peering at him from all angles of the room. He felt himself stir with rage, imagined what it would be like to see them explode to pieces of electronic trash on the floor. He bit down hard, chipping some teeth, he was sure. The veins in his neck pulsed, the cold slowly reversing. Nothing happened, though. Was he crazy for thinking he could do anything? The fire was gone, wasn't it? Maybe it was all part of the dreams.

Dr. Carraway hesitated momentarily. "I'm going to be honest with you. But you might not like the answers you get."

"I don't care. I need to know. What's…happening to me? Why am I here? What is this place, really?"

The doctor removed his frames, setting the notepad on the floor. He scooted his seat closer to Arson and slouched forward. Face to face now. "A few months ago, there was a fire, as I told you before. Your grandmother didn't make it."

"Yeah, sure. You've sold me this garbage already."

"Just listen to me. The firemen got her out, but her lungs collapsed. They filled with smoke. Her body…just couldn't be revived." Arson listened, still unsatisfied with this version of the truth, still wondering when the camera crew was going to pop out of the hidden doors and yell something stupid.

"You were standing outside the cabin, watching as the firemen arrived at the scene. Is any of this sounding familiar?"

Arson shook his head.

"It isn't easy for me to tell you this, but…the police identified *you* as the culprit." Dr. Carraway's long forefinger jutted out as he issued blame. It might as well have been a nine-inch dagger. He slowly continued, "Kay Parker had no enemies to speak of. In fact, reporters claimed she rarely even left the cabin. I'm sure you could testify to that. Broken bottles—Molotovs— littered the crime scene."

Dr. Carraway opened a manila envelope and pulled out three glossy images of a burning cabin. Arson knew the place. It was his cabin. *His* home, consumed by fire. "Your clothes reeked of smoke and alcohol. The police found a pack of matches in your back pocket." The doctor's final words slowly spilled out. "You were convicted of arson."

A memory flashed at the back of Arson's mind. He saw Mandy and the scumbags from the bonfire party. It was a summer night. He and Emery were at Mandy's house on the other side of the lake. He was nowhere near the cabin. In fact, he could remember being in a hospital bed but never going home. That was it. Why couldn't everything blend more clearly? So many parts were missing.

"This is crazy. You can't be serious. I am not a criminal. I wouldn't burn my own house. I would never hurt Grandma."

"I believe you. But it's pretty condemning evidence. And... sometimes, Stephen, we hurt the ones closest to us without rhyme or reason."

"No, no. That's not how it happened, all right? I was at a bonfire party with some friends, and things sort of spiraled out of control. I made a mistake, but there's no way I did this."

"Really? Because I've gone through the report several times, met with the officers assigned to the crime scene. I've gone over a number of scenarios. If I am lying, why hasn't your grandmother come to see you? Where is she when you need her the most?"

Arson clenched his fists. "I...I don't know."

Carraway leaned back in his chair. "I don't write fiction. Here, check for yourself; it's all there." He handed Arson the folder with an array of contents inside. Arson refused to look at the evidence.

"I will say one thing, though. Something the police report never said." The doctor surveyed him, and he didn't like it one bit. Arson suddenly felt like telling him to go to hell, if they weren't both already there. But he couldn't say anything because some part of him believed it.

Dr. Carrway leaned even closer. Arson could smell his breath, how it stunk of onions, mustard, and chicken. He listened to the doctor speak again. "I personally think the cops made this whole thing look like something it wasn't. I don't think you used matches or alcohol at all. That's kid stuff for you, isn't it? In fact, you aren't exactly like other teenagers, are you, Stephen?"

Arson blinked, sucking in a deep breath.

With a soft sigh, Dr. Carraway slowly brought his hand to the tie he was wearing and removed it. Then he allowed his neck some room to breathe. A scar in the shape of a hand glowed faintly against the flesh on his throat.

Arson gasped.

"During our last session you threatened me. Against my better judgment, I told you the truth. But the truth wasn't something you wanted to hear. When you began to strangle me, you left this scar behind. Tell me, Stephen, what teenager can grab a man's throat and leave a second-degree burn?"

Arson wondered if eternity had come and gone. He swore that his ability to create fire was no longer there. Never thought it could return, but it had apparently, without him even being aware of it. What was wrong with him? His body?

"I swear, I didn't know I was doing it."

"So you *have* done this before?"

Arson nodded. He looked up at Dr. Carraway, feeling like a lost puppy wanting to be found again. "I don't know how I can do it. Did it."

"Did it?"

"I thought it was gone. I mean, I was…in that hospital bed."
Arson's eyes spun, a jolt of realization coming quick. "And that
agent, he drugged me or somethin'. I couldn't light up or do anything to stop him. The fire abandoned me."

Dr. Carraway narrowed his gaze, growing defiantly impatient
and slightly nervous.

"They took her."

"Stephen, enough of this! No one has taken Emery anywhere!"

Arson's head jerked. "What did you say?"

"I said no one took your friend. I can't keep indulging in these
adolescent fantasies."

"I never said her name."

Dr. Carraway choked up suddenly. His eyes became distracted.
"Don't be absurd. Of course you did. Emery, your girlfriend, right?
Emery Phoenix, that's what you call her."

Arson twitched his eyebrows, his forehead sliding back. "What
I call her?"

"Precisely right. You have imagined her. I've told you several
times that these mirages will be of little help to you. Your psyche
is still very fragile. We need to get inside your mind. We need to
figure out how it works."

"Who's 'we'?"

"You and me, Stephen. For the past several months, we have
been trying to fix you. Your memories, your corrupted idea of
the way things happened in your life. It makes perfect sense for
you to want to escape. Your thoughts feel like dark prisons. It's no
wonder you sought to create a companion for yourself. Loneliness
can be cruel."

Arson's eyes were angry, his lids like pale sleeves. He couldn't
take staring at Dr. Carraway any longer.

"Try to comprehend it all. It's a struggle to let these memories
go. It's almost as if there are two parts of your mind fighting for

control. But one side isn't real. It is only fantasy. A dream. Your imagination to want. These *fabrications* are misguiding you. This bonfire party you keep referring to never happened. We've interviewed numerous students from the local high school, none of whom even knew your name."

"It can't all be lies," Arson said, shaking. "It can't. It's not!"

"You needed to be reborn, to be something other than what you've been your entire life. Complacency can make us think and do strange things. The story of the phoenix—the goddess of the stars who dies and is reborn once again from her ashes— is precisely what you needed to believe in. It's obvious you would choose her as a lover. You said the image gave you hope that one day you could be something important. A hero."

Arson closed his eyes, picturing himself staring at comic books from the scatter across his bedroom floor. The *heroes* he idolized. The *monsters* he identified with. He was someplace in between, lost. But he'd burned every one of them, hadn't he? He'd burned the comic books, and he'd burned the twisted schemers at the bonfire party.

He'd burn everything if he could, if it meant protecting her.

It was not fiction. It couldn't be.

"Stephen, it's not all that difficult to comprehend, really," Carraway said, interrupting his thoughts. "You needed to be loved."

"Grandma loved me," he bit back.

"Did she? Not like this, she didn't. She couldn't, right? She didn't know how to love you the way you wanted, the way you needed to be loved."

"Shut up!"

"You're going to be all right. Just be honest with yourself. Allow yourself to believe it. This may not be what you want to hear, but it's the truth."

Arson lost himself in a stir of frantic thoughts. The doctor had said Emery's name. How did he know her name? Were they responsible for taking her, for taking them both? Where was she? Indecipherable, faint whispers slipped off a dry tongue as he tried to piece the puzzle together.

"It's never easy, but I can see the horizon. We're almost there. We will find answers, I promise. I hope that after today, we can finally put this silly Emery Phoenix business to rest. You don't need her anymore. You need people you can trust. You need people who are real and not some figment of your imagination. *I* can help you. Let me help you."

Carraway reached into his briefcase. His hand soon emerged with a bottle of water. He unscrewed the cap and began to drink. Arson focused on the bobbing of his throat, the sound the water made as it left the bottle and slipped inside those paper-thin lips.

"Now, are you finally ready to accept the truth, Stephen?"

Arson was back at Mandy's beach, the ground uncertain beneath him. He looked down, seeing himself covered in black, burnt ashes, his breaths shortened and heightened by panic and fear of losing everything he cared most for. It wasn't a dream. It wasn't some conspiracy. Arson knew he wasn't the criminal this stupid doctor made him out to be.

This was crazy. All of it. This place…he had to get out. These walls, this doctor. It wasn't right. It felt like a nightmare. The same as the middle school cafeteria. Everything in sight meshed together.

Can't focus.

Can't think.

This is real, Arson told his mind. *I am real. Emery is real. This doctor…*

Is.

A.

Liar!

The doctor took another long sip. "Stephen? Are you ready?"

Arson glared at Carraway, the calm changing to frustration. Frustration becoming rage. An animal being attacked and cornered. A child being beaten for an unknown crime. A boy too unloved to be what he wanted most. Until…

All of a sudden, Arson could see the air bubbles trapped inside the water bottle multiply. The doctor didn't even notice at first. The more Arson focused on his thoughts, the more the bottle bubbled and pulsated. Within seconds, Carraway spit out the water with a curse, pulling the bottle away from his mouth.

"It burned my lips!"

It didn't stop, though. Arson was far too focused to let it end here. Emery. Mandy. Grandma. That horrible room. A young woman screaming.

Blood.

So much blood.

Arson's eyes began to burn. His pupils turned from hazel to crimson, sparks dancing inside his eyes like bloody diamonds.

Emery!

The bottle turned red, then black, and suddenly split from the center, the plastic instantly melting then bursting, liquid spilling everywhere. The violent stream of water burned a hole in Carraway's lap and singed his tie. Charred plastic, exuding smoke, lay ruined and twisted on the tile floor. The doctor's eyes at once came to fearful life.

"Stephen, what have you done?"

Arson's words escaped like dark poetry. "My name…is Arson."

And then everything went black.

CHAPTER SIXTEEN

"**WHERE ARE YOU!**" **AIMEE SHOUTED INTO THE CELL PHONE.**

"Massachusetts," Joel said calmly. "I left a few hours ago."

"Why? What are you doing there? And why didn't you tell me?"

"Don't blow this out of proportion. Can you just calm down so I can talk?"

"This is calm, Joel. This is *very* calm." How dare he just pick up and leave like that? What right did he have to abandon her to this lonely house with just a note left behind to say he'd be back when he made it right? It wasn't fair.

"The license plates, Aimee. Do you remember when Emery was taken?"

"What are you talking about? Of course I remember. I was there, same as you."

A long breath stifled the phone speaker on her end. "We gave it to the police, and after some minimal research, they were led to Massachusetts, right?"

"Yes," she responded reluctantly. "But the case went cold, or have you forgotten?"

"It went cold because they stopped looking."

"What is this, Joel? Are you trying to prove your masculinity by taking off on this witch hunt?"

"It's not a witch hunt. I'm close, all right? I feel it. I know something's not right. C'mon, Aimee, the news the last couple of months, the *accidents*, the crises. It's all screaming that something's not right."

"I'm not a politician, Joel. What does any of that have to do with finding our daughter?"

"Aren't you listening? I'm feeling something, in my gut, my soul, that's leading me here. I'm piecing it together the best way I know how."

"Your gut? Your soul? I'm not hearing this. This is crazy. You know, you're good at trying to piece together lost causes." She hadn't meant for that thought to come out. And now that it was out in the open, she wished she could take it back.

"I spoke to the private investigator, Aimee."

A long pause.

"Did you hear me? I called the investigator."

"I heard you. What did he say? Is he another leech, or can this one actually help us?"

"Well, for starters, he's a she. And yes, I *think* she can help us. I think she really wants to."

"Well, isn't that nice." Aimee's tone turned vindictive. "Was she attractive?"

"How is that at all relevant?"

"Just answer the question, Joel."

"No, I'm not goin' there. The whole reason I brought her up is so you can't hold it against me. I'm trying to keep you informed. Good communication, right, baby?"

"Hold what against you? The fact that you scheduled an appointment with a private investigator and didn't feel the need to tell me?" Aimee knew she was overreacting, but if she didn't explode now, when Joel could hear it, he'd never know how much horrible tension was building up inside her. Besides, he should feel the repercussions of keeping her out of the loop. Emery was not his daughter alone. Emery belonged to her too, or didn't he get that?

"You had work. You're always working now."

"We all have our reasons, Joel. The banks don't care what our family situation is right now. The mortgage payment's still due."

"Admit it, Aimee, you hate being in that house. You hate being with me."

Aimee didn't want to answer. She feared what the truth might bring.

"It's useless fighting. Doesn't even matter. I met with Redd and talked about opening up a case to find Emery. And she agreed to work with us. I think she's committed."

"Good. Somebody should be."

"I'm doing the best I can," Joel's voice cracked through the phone. He sounded distant, like he was talking on speaker or heading into a tunnel.

"Your best? You took off and left me here, Joel."

"You have to work, don't you?"

She grunted. "Easy scapegoat."

"Look, don't play the saint. I left because I had to. I will find her. I believe I can find her. And whatever help I need, Redd'll be there."

"I'm sure she will. Did you inform her about your covert mission?"

"As of now, we've only spoken twice. Like you, she thinks I don't have much to support my theory. But unlike you, she allows a little room for my better judgment. Some things take faith, Aimee. A lot of faith. And I'm not sure what to believe anymore, but at the very root of me there's still a man looking for purpose, desperate for his little girl. And until I stop breathing, I'm gonna look for her, starting where everyone else gave up. I'm awake now. I'm finally awake."

Aimee laughed a bitter kind of laugh, and she dragged it out to let him know how ridiculous the remark was, especially coming from him. Had he left because of Emery, or was it to escape her completely?

"Aimee, I don't know who we can trust anymore. Here's Redd's number, if you wanna talk to her." Joel dictated the number but stopped short because Aimee told him she already had it programmed into her cell.

"Joel, if you're out there, hours away, alone, then what's she doing?"

"She sent out Emery's picture nationwide. She has connections we didn't have before. While she's doing what she can on her end, I'll be here, until something else comes up."

"And what about money?"

"I took some from our savings. My account's nearly drained."

Aimee cracked her neck, frustrated, yet not without concern. "You mean, *my* savings? All right," she finally caved. "Just remember, this isn't some Wednesday night crime drama. The answers aren't gonna magically fall out of the sky. There are no writers making sure you come out the victor."

Joel's sigh filled the speaker. "Just tell me you believe in me, please."

"I believe *you* believe in it," she returned, cold.

"Try to remember who we were, Aimee. We weren't always like this."

"But this is who we are now." She waited for something, anything, to come from his end, but maybe she'd hurt him too deeply. "And you left me behind. You could've died, for all I knew."

"Careful, Aimee, you're sounding concerned."

"Stop it, jerk," she said in a hushed voice, like she wished it were a secret. Was he right? Was she concerned about him or just angry that he'd left her, alone with her thoughts? "I'm not concerned, all right? I want to believe you, Joel. I swear. But it seems like you're acting on a whim, and we need more than that."

Then the sound of his voice nearly shook her. "*You* need more than that!"

"But you don't know where you are, or where to go. How are you gonna search there with no official lead?"

"I grew up in a city, remember? Cities change their names, but their souls are the same. If she's here, I'll find her." Aimee struggled to accept Joel's determination. She hadn't seen him this focused since he had it set in his mind that he was going to start a church so many years ago. He seemed different.

"I made a few thousand copies of Emery's picture. Already put up half a dozen on every block. Got chased out of a restaurant too." Joel seemed amused, and she wondered if he was smiling. "Wish you could've seen their faces. Bunch of cold people."

"You left Camden for a reason."

"I left Camden for you. Your father didn't trust us there, remember?"

"He didn't trust anyone anywhere. But I think deep down he admired your passion. You stood up to the man."

"Well, I wanted something then. Now is no different. Listen, what we have, it's not normal. It's not life. Something has to break. It has to."

"Yeah," Aimee whispered in a barely audible sound. She didn't want to tell him that she was holding back tears. "I have to go."

"Yeah, me too," Joel said.

"Be careful," she added before hanging up.

The phone lay cradled in the palm of her hand. Aimee couldn't speak for a moment. She felt literally frozen. Her ear was still warm with the sound of Joel's voice, and for the first time in months, she didn't feel it was out of place. She felt possessed by the sound of each word, embraced by his tone. What it was she felt at the core she didn't know for certain.

A static sound, now nothing more than an echo inside, shook her like a wave. But if just for a moment, she could wish for that wave to belong to anyone, it would be Joel. She knew it. Love? It wasn't love. It couldn't be, not anymore. Not in a long time. But *something*. Something strange. Something foreign to her. Safety.

Aimee walked into the garage, a cold room she hadn't ventured to in months. As she searched for a bin labeled *Family Stuff*, she felt a longing in her chest. To be held, told she was loved. Carlos didn't love her anymore, and maybe he never had. Joel probably hated her so much. One day, her coworkers believed, acceptance would come, and she'd be able to move on. But tonight, the concern lingered.

At long last, she found the big tub of family items. What lay inside were photo albums, Emery's first *A*, and some old recordings. These memories were the only things that could keep hope alive in her.

Lately, this was where Aimee came to escape. Joel was usually asleep by the time she managed to choose a family episode. She thought about asking him to watch them with her once or twice, but she believed he'd tell her no, and she reasoned it was better to view them in peace.

After selecting a disc from the collection, Aimee shut the lid and exited the garage. She poured a glass of wine and walked into the living room, putting in the disc and waiting for it to load. In seconds, her daughter's face lit the television. The glare of the dimming afternoon light reflected off the screen. Emery was only five. The wind carried her daughter's hair everywhere it wanted to, tossing it like flecks of sand. Her eyes sparkled inside the lens of the camera that watched her every move, every smile.

And then she'd laugh at something Joel had said, a joke any normal adult would think was amateur at best. But Emery loved her father's humor, always had. The laughter poured out of the speakers and brought a smile to Aimee's lost face. She touched her skin as Emery touched hers onscreen. It was beautiful then, unscarred, soft, and innocent. Most of her baby teeth still hanging on behind those tiny lips Aimee loved to kiss so often.

"Why are you watching me with that camera, Mommy?" her little girl asked.

"Because I want to remember you," came her reply.

"But you love me. Will you forget me?"

"No. Of course I won't forget you. But the beach is beautiful today, and so are you. I don't want to ever forget all of this magic."

"Did you hear that, Daddy?" the little girl said. "Mommy thinks I'm hot. Hey, isn't that what Daddy called you yesterday right after he tucked me in? I heard you guys smoochin' in da hallway." She laughed as the story poured out of her. "You thinks I was sleepin', but I'm slick."

"You *thought*, Emery. Thought is the past tense of think. And apparently I'm gonna have to kiss Mommy more in private." A young, shirtless man stepped into view. Aimee embraced the sound of the young couple kissing. Did she even recognize them anymore? A part of them, maybe, but not completely.

"I knowed what I was sayin'."

"Yeah, tell Daddy to mind his beeswax," Aimee heard her younger self say. It was so strange hearing the way she used to sound. Odd how a voice can change, like a body, or the spirit within it.

"Daddy," little Emery said. "Mind your beeswax. And you have to obey, because I'm hot."

"Okay, sweetheart. But your mother wants to crack open that new book, so why don't we go catch a wave." Her husband grabbed little Emery and put her over his shoulder. She screamed playfully, laughing as he took her toward the water. The waves rose and fell along the shore, their foam and fury colliding. The sand was alive with a thousand feet, families, and the tents they brought with them to enjoy a beautiful summer day.

"We were a family once," she said, wiping away her tears. So many things were lost.

She watched the final few seconds of the recording as the camera panned upward, catching a glimpse of a kite lost in the wind with nothing but the sky to fall into. The sound of Emery's innocent laughter was the last thing Aimee could hear before the screen turned to static.

CHAPTER SEVENTEEN

SAUL HOVEN STORMED DOWN HALLWAY FOURTEEN. A LOOK of murder was in his eyes. He was out for blood. Two doctors and a secretary silently followed him on his right and his left as he issued a dozen and a half curses. He might have even invented a few new ones.

Hallway fourteen resembled an outdated penitentiary wing. It hosted receptionists and armed security personnel at both ends, making it impossible for anyone to get in or out without the proper clearance. Once allowed in, however, there was a lot of screaming. Sometimes crying.

The rooms built into the hallways had doors with no handles, all of them removed when the facility underwent serious recon-struction years earlier. Going from a hospital to an asylum altered certain luxuries, deliberately. Hoven always made sure to refer to this place as a clinic for physical or mental rehabilitation, basically an asylum with a fancy tag. Didn't matter which euphemism suited him best, though, because in the end, crazies were crazies, the sick were the sick. This place, with all its world-class screw ups—the paranoids and schizophrenics and the ones who saw creepy-crawlers at night—was home. Eat, sleep, crap, and eat it all up again in here. A dorm building wrapped inside a frat house within a university of chaos.

"Oh, look, the Almighty is here for a visit," a receptionist murmured as he passed. He didn't pay her any mind. She'd be replaced by the end of the day tomorrow.

Being the director of a goliath of a facility had its advantages. If working for the government some thirty-two years had taught him anything, it was how to be a leader during times of war. And this place was a warzone all its own. Getting things done, no questions asked, came at a price. So if being mocked was the currency, he'd pay it gladly. With one word, he could financially cripple any pathetic pencil pusher. With a single phone call, he could secure a meeting with the prime minister of Spain and then secretly go to bed with his daughter, and there was little anyone could do about it. It was a kind of power ordinary people didn't or couldn't fathom—a fantasy for most men. A gift for his cooperation and assistance as leader of this facility.

This thirst was an all-consuming ambition for more control. He lusted after it, lived it, breathed it, worshiped it. In his mind, real power avoided the weak and favored the strong. It was a masterpiece idea. A five-letter word trapped inside greed, both fueling a wish for more, with the knowledge that more would never be enough. It had never been about numbers, dollar signs, or flashy romance. It was about being a god.

The reward for leading this location to grander heights—leading mankind—would undoubtedly come soon. But not yet. For now, he was quite content with being the eyes, ears, hands, and feet of Salvation. But it was really draining when the world came crashing down on top of his shoulders.

"Will somebody please tell me what happened in that room?"

His secretary shuffled some papers, her eyes shock-lit. "Sir, we're not entirely sure, but it looks like—"

"I keep you around to take notes, Nina, not to offer your opinions," he bit back, motioning to one of the professionals beside him.

"He finally did what we've been hoping he'd do for months, sir. He got hot."

"Did you expect that to sound like an attractive punch line? Elaborate! Details, facts. Let's go."

"Well, Stephen Gable turned a bottle of water into charred plastic, without ever touching it. Carraway said that the boy simply looked at it, and it exploded."

Saul Hoven stopped midstride and leaned in. "Are you retarded?"

The doctor twitched his nose then bit his lip, clueless.

"Next time you want to blurt out the subject's name, don't! I work hard to keep our work *our* work. I don't need any of these loonies jumping to hasty conclusions. And beyond that, I don't need to give some self-righteous quack with a grudge any reason to put his nose where it doesn't belong. Am I absolutely clear?"

Nod.

"When it comes to *them*, no names."

The doctor mindlessly followed Hoven down the long stretch. When they stopped at a set of enormous white doors, Hoven leaned down and lifted up the top of his right eyelid. A light beamed out from the side wall and scanned his retina.

"Access granted. You are free to enter," the overhead speaker chimed.

Through the doors and across the next room, they waited for the elevator. Once it arrived, a loud *ding* welcomed them in. Hoven pulled out a key and inserted it into a small chamber at the side of the elevator. The chamber popped open and displayed another

button. On it was engraved THE SANCTUARY. He pushed it in
with his thumb, and the elevator began its descent.

"I knew it. I never should have agreed to those sessions!
Everybody's so concerned about the property. To hell with this
nonsense of making them feel like they're normal teenagers. The
psych evaluations haven't amounted to jack squat, anyway." He
counted his breaths. "I'm losing my cool. And that twit Carraway
is making quite the mess of things."

"Sir, isn't this what we wanted?" his secretary asked.

Hoven turned harshly to her, and she backed down.

"With all due respect, she makes a valid point. We've been
trying to get 219 to engage his *ability* since we brought him here.
We expected there to be consequences, and so far, they're minimal.
Shouldn't we be more optimistic about this?"

Hoven started to nod; his eyes were burning embers. "Are
you all really that thick? Everyone's got a point. But the fact of the
matter is that our goal was simply to get 219 lit. We've accomplished
that, but the subject was never supposed to fall into a coma!"

A hush fell over them.

Hoven was already calculating the potential damage, loss, all
while formulating another move. On the surface, these frenzied
emotions poured out like rage, but underneath he was really
disappointed he had missed seeing the arson come out to play.

The elevator doors chimed open. Out they stepped. The basement level was far colder than the usual temperatures above most
of the time. Being several stories below the ground didn't help. A
damp smell thickened the air.

"Nina, find me Dr. Carraway, and find him fast!"

Nina quickly separated from the three of them to search.
Hoven led the other two doctors farther down the hall. The
concrete floor made The Sanctuary feel like a Costco, but the
walls were covered by thick sheets of steel, bolted down. In each

corner, a nano-camera sat tucked into the wall, with larger ones at the centers. They slowly rotated, scanning the room with red eyes.

Hoven took a sharp right turn, passing one of the neuro-specialists and some orderlies on their way back to one of the top levels. He didn't bother ever getting acquainted with most of them. Didn't need to. He knew Carraway, Krane, and a few others. Everybody else was furniture. The amount of money coming in from the unnamed investors was enough to keep the majority quiet. The threats on their families if they ever decided to play Judas controlled the rest.

They walked by a door that had the numbers 218 painted across it in thick-as-blood black paint.

"Sir, why are we keeping the girl?"

"Because she was there when our fiery friend decided to blow up. We have reasons to believe that she too possesses an ability."

"What?"

"We're calling it regenerative transference. Our best guess for now is that *she* brought him back to life, after the fire took over."

"What logical reason do we have to think this?" one of the doctors asked.

"None of this makes traditional, logical sense. But she was there. She saw him lose control. She touched him when he was dead…and then he wasn't anymore. If nothing else, we'll continue scanning her memories and slicing through that small frame of hers. Maybe she'll give us what we need."

"And if we don't…I mean, have we discovered anything yet, sir?"

Hoven's lips stretched back. "Subject 218 is playing her part. As of now, her mind isn't as cluttered with the code as we'd hoped. But perhaps there's a flaw to Morpheus after all."

Out from one of the doors at the far end of the space, Carraway came rushing, Nina trailing close behind.

Hoven clapped. "The fool of the hour. I say there is no darkness but ignorance."

"Sir, what took place in that room was…unexpected." Carraway made sure his shirt was completely buttoned and his tie hung tight around his throat.

"Oh, really? At what point did you surrender control, you idiot? You know what, don't even answer that question. Just tell me what you said to put the subject into a coma? Hmm? What did innocent little Nick Carraway say? I want to know. It better be good. Because something triggered this episode. And now we have a potential weapon who's fallen into a coma."

Carraway's gaze betrayed him. His mouth hung in awe as he weighed his words carefully. "I think I slipped, sir."

"Oh, well, alert the press, genius here thinks he *slipped*. If this were as cut and dry as you breaking your backside on a patch of ice, perhaps your terminology would hold some water, but since we're dealing with an unstable subject inside a facility that costs billions of dollars to run, I don't want to hear that you slipped. I want to know exactly what happened!"

Carraway sucked in a deep breath and then blew it out slowly. "I mentioned the girl's name. The kid saw right through it."

"You pathetic, stupid little…. If he wakes up, and you pray he does, he'll be dying to ask a lot of really ugly questions."

"What if we erase some of his memories," the other doctor suggested.

"That wouldn't be a good idea. His mind is fragile, sir," Carraway said strongly.

"Yes, it is. And now it's worse because of your little screw up."

"Saul, I can fix this. It was a mistake, but I can get him under control again."

"Forgive me if I don't give you my vote of confidence. And it's *sir* in here, boy!"

They followed Saul Hoven deeper into The Sanctuary, where they performed the experiments. Spikes of green light shot out from the floors like almost-invisible lasers. Rusted staircases climbed up toward the ceiling, and their platforms hosted massive monitors, some of which were still short-circuited or working with waves of static streaming across from the arson's violent episode several days earlier.

As vast as the room appeared to be, it still managed to become cluttered with asylum personnel. Suits and hot breath. They hustled around a table, upon which lay a young girl with a ruined face. Wires trailed from one place to another, with seemingly no beginning and no end, entangled. A panicked Dr. Krane hustled from his seat on the platform to the operating table, where Morpheus was lowering above the girl's forehead.

Saul Hoven approached the cold table, the others keeping their distance. "Hello, my dear," he said in a voice so thick it bled out. "Are you frightened?"

The girl's head spun, eyes rolling behind droopy lids. Her mouth hung limply, her ruined cheeks following suit. She managed to nod while a slow tear spilled down the side of her face.

"Sir, it might be best to take a step back as Morpheus c-com-commences!" Krane shouted from one of the platforms.

"You're going to give us what we need, princess," he whispered, stroking her arm and then her bruised, naked chest.

"Why…why are you—"

"Doing this? Because I have a vision. Now, relax."

Many watched as the Morpheus dome positioned itself above the girl's face. It exploded with light. Her head slammed back against the table. The pain from the tiny needles stabbing into her temples was obviously overwhelming her body.

"Krane, get over here. We have…a situation."

"Wh-what-what else is new?"

"Now's not the time. 219 has regained his ability."

"Incredible! This is what we've been waiting for." Krane set the few working monitors to full stream and paraded down the stairwell to meet with Hoven. "But you're not happy with this, are you?"

"What gave that away?" Hoven asked, frustrated. "He's slipped into a coma."

"Sir, with all due respect, we've been trying to get him to bur-b-burn since his arrival."

"Your doubts were beginning to take root, weren't they?"

Krane nodded.

"Well, your doubts are currently irrelevant. What are we going to do about this?"

"If you're asking for my professional opinion, nothing. We'll continue the treatments."

"You want to sedate him and put him under that machine while he's in a coma?"

"Why not? The eff-e-f-f-effect should be the same. Perhaps Morpheus will work more efficiently now that his ps-s-s-psyche is probably looking for a way out. This is a gift. We may now have a clearer passage into his mind. From what we've gathered, in there, the boy exists only as the a-ar-ar-arson. We might have more control."

"Well, I'll be. You do have a dark side. But tread softly, Manny. Keep him under our control."

Krane eyed Carraway and the others standing in the circle.

"Check his vitals regularly."

"I'll do my best."

"Do better. I want that power harnessed, Krane. This is not a boy, remember that. He's an instrument to be used. He's the property of the U.S. government, and soon, the world. He will help usher us toward bigger and greater things."

"That's what we promised Adam, isn't it?"

"Stop," Carraway hissed.

Hoven breathed his hot breath over a cowering Krane. "217 hasn't been much use to us lately, or have you forgotten about that?"

Krane recoiled, cheeks flushed. "You're right. Mere self-doubt, I gather. It's-it's nothing, really. I'll keep working."

"Doubt if you must, Manny, as long as you don't raise the white flag on me like that coward Parker did. I've already got one stupid flake," Hoven said, that last comment aimed at Carraway.

"You brought the fire out, didn't you?" Krane asked with a grin. "Maybe it was a good idea we l-let-let him play after all."

Saul Hoven scraped the top layer of his lip. "Maybe. Let's hope you're right about this. I want his dreams. I want his code. Get the flames to manifest again, without incident if possible. Back to work! And don't get sloppy or it'll be you on this table." He leaned over to watch as Morpheus continued drilling into the girl's temples. "Sweet dreams, princess," he whispered over Emery's body as she writhed in pain.

"I wonder if the pain ever stops," Carraway added.

"One day," Hoven answered, knowing that for him, for some, the pain would end. Gently, he stroked the girl's hair back, her eyeballs frenzied behind loose sockets. "But not today."

CHAPTER EIGHTEEN

JOEL SHUT HIS CELL PHONE AND ENDED THE CALL. HE LIKED the way Redd's voice sounded from the other end—sexy, uninhibited, certain. She had a presence that he could feel, even when he wasn't in it. It was a nice reprieve from the grueling arguments he'd been enduring with Aimee.

"Maybe I should come up there and meet you," she'd said. "Some friends of mine went to Suffolk, so I know my way around the streets pretty good."

"No," Joel had returned with slight hesitation. The truth was that he wanted her there, could've used the company and support, however little she could offer as premature as the case was. But not yet. This was something he had to do by himself, for now. Joel knew the retainer he'd put down would only last him a week or two, so he had to move fast.

She eventually caved when he politely refused to divulge his location, and said she'd "resort to the usual tricks, then."

Joel caught himself smiling as she said it, knowing the comment wasn't without a hint of sarcasm. But even in sarcasm, she was attractive.

Careful, he thought, staring at his ring finger. *Don't swim out too far.*

It was hard to swim out too far when, for the last two and a half decades, he hadn't even left the dock. Sure, his eyes caught a pretty woman now and then, smiled coyly at a set of bright baby blues from time to time, but other than that, feelings remained mere feelings. Whatever this was, he didn't know how to handle it. It was like returning to a pivotal moment in his teenage years and getting to feel that new crush all over again. The feeling was a warm, almost hypnotizing sensation. He liked it. He could easily get used to it if he weren't cautious.

Joel returned to posting flyers of his daughter up on the city block. His eyes wandered back to where he was parked every five seconds, wondering how long he could let his hazard lights flash before a nosy cop dropped by to pay him a visit. The cool wind whispered through his dark hair and brushed against his just-shaved cheek as the staple gun bit into the paper and pinned the picture to the telephone pole.

After posting a few more images of his daughter, he got back in his car and headed south down Boylston. Once he'd blanketed that entire area—from church to grocery mart to liquor store—he was caught at a red light.

Close by was a basketball court and beside that, a skate park. He'd frequented places like this as a teenager, but he'd not revisited one since. Nevertheless, he revisited with each trick he witnessed from afar. That was him once, hopping poles to pull a pop-shove-it, something the Tony Hawk video games trademarked for the twenty-first century. The long, unwashed hair and the ripped jeans were only part of the ensemble; the attitude was the icing on the cake. It was almost like being brought back to an era once forgotten.

No matter how long he would've liked to stay captive there, though, his mind was ripped from memory after a series of horns forced him to notice the traffic light above flashing green. Signaling an apology, Joel switched lanes and pulled into a curbside spot.

Some of the kids were skating; others sat lounging inside their cozy hoodies, relaxing in the smell of their cigarette smoke. He noticed a few were placing bets on who'd smack their face the hardest or break a bone while trying to perform a nasty move. A black kid with cornrows handled the bets. Joel choked back a laugh, remembering placing a number of bets himself, more often than not stupid attempts to prove skill and masculinity. Looking back, it was just plain lunacy. "Street cred" didn't hold a lot of weight anyhow when a fight broke out.

Two kids slid down a pole just then, one falling off and smashing the right side of his face against the pavement but not before crushing his groin on the metal rod. A spew of curses flowed, and all the boys hugged their manhood in empathy.

The bookie motioned for the kid to pay up once his balls stopped swelling. Then he raised an eyebrow, laughing at the ridiculous positions the hurt skater tried to stay in to avoid pain. Nothing seemed to work.

Joel stepped out of his car to get up close. To his left, a skilled group of athletes were earning their pride with a basketball game, a fence dividing the two separate worlds. He watched both arenas with his fingers lost inside the metal holes, wondering who'd fall next or fumble a ball and thus forfeit a game.

This venue was a city in and of itself, a place for weary teenagers to go to release the crap they felt inside—the struggle of making it through high school in a messed-up place. This was their ESPN, their temple, and this little bookie, with skin like coal and wearing nothing but a wife beater and a faded, tattered jean jacket to match his over-sized gym shorts, was their priest. He held their redemption, and they offered their tithes if only to be a part of something greater than themselves—to earn a way to be accepted, if such a thing were even possible.

"Looks like we got some paparazzi, fellas. Try not to choke in front of Casper." The boy was amused by his own comment. He turned and winked at Joel. The few kids Joel actually made eye contact with blew smoke rings in his direction. He couldn't make out their faces, but he assumed they could make out his.

"What's the matter, ladies? Too much pressure? Fifteen and a pack of smokes says Ricky breaks his butt during the next trick."

"Fifteen says I land it, slug," Ricky said, grabbing his board and smacking the bookie's hand with fifteen bucks. Then he headed to the top of the court's half-pipe.

"Yeah, he's cocky, he's crazy, he's Ricky!" the bookie said in a high-pitched voice, like he was some auctioneer or a boxing announcer. Then, he followed it up with, "But he's still gonna fall and break his butt. Be sure to send a note to his future ex-wife and kids, people." Another sarcastic laugh split his mouth, and he hugged his side. Then, counting his money, he challenged another skater. This time it was a newbie for twenty-five bucks. The challenge was accepted.

"Like moths to the flame," he chimed. "Ricky's gonna break his butt, and this clown's gonna break his hymen. Ha-ha-ha. Show me whatcha got, baby." Then the bookie turned to the basketball court, catching the last slam dunk and the biggest guy on the court bragging about it. "Guess that covers the bet you made me last week, Chico," the boy said. "Must feel good to be all paid up. Say hi to your moms for me."

"Screw you, Kyro!"

"Tell her I'll be by later. I'll sneak in, and we'll try not to wake you up." Kyro put the wad of cash in his pocket, sent a text, and focused on the next group of kids ready to make fools of themselves. Joel was in awe of how effortlessly this kid ran the grounds, almost without reproach. Here, it was like he was an untouchable priest with a motor mouth.

"You want in, Casper?" Kyro asked, flashing Joel some of his cash.

Joel shook his head no. He was envious of so much vitality, so much wild ambition, not unlike what had drawn him to this city. He blocked a wind of dust from coming into his line of sight and pulled a few flyers out from his back pocket.

"Have you seen this girl?" Joel asked Kyro, who was more focused on watching his friends, or victims, smash their faces.

"No, I ain't seen nobody. You a dark blue?"

"Dark blue?"

"You a cop or something? Why you comin' around our hood asking if we seen somebody? I ain't no snitch."

Joel walked around the fencing and approached the kid on his own turf. Instantly, a group of teenagers surrounded Joel. "Take it easy, guys. I don't want any trouble."

"Then you best get on outta here."

"You've got a big mouth for someone so small," Joel said, ignoring the big hand on his chest urging him to be cautious about his next words.

Before either of them could blink, one of the kids—Ricky, if Joel remembered correctly—flipped off his board and bruised his backside on the concrete step. The other skater landed the trick no problem, but no one was attentive enough to cheer.

"Pay up, man," Kyro ordered, almost out of breath.

Ricky flipped him a few bills. Kyro turned to Joel for the first time and eyed him. "Give me the picture," he said.

Joel handed him the photograph. The boy glanced at those around him then dropped his eyes back to the page. "This some kind of joke?" he asked.

Joel shook his head no.

"This chick looks messed up. What happened to her face?"

"Doesn't matter," Joel said. "Have you seen her or not?"

"We haven't seen nobody like this. You're on the wrong side of tracks, Casper."

"Yeah, guess so. Well, keep an eye out, will ya?"

"Who am I supposed to tell, anyway? The po-lice? Shoot, is there even a reward? Rich white boy like you's gotta have some coin."

Kyro's subjects all agreed with nods and grunts.

Joel feigned a halfhearted smirk. "You don't seem to be doing bad yourself."

The boy reached into his pocket. "How about you do a trick for us, pops? Maybe we'll tell you where the girl is."

Joel's face flushed red.

"Now he's listening, fellas. Look at his face go all blank like that. You heard right, Cass. Get your used carcass up there and show us whatcha got. Maybe our memories'll come back. Get you what you want." Kyro leaned in close. "Maybe."

Joel grabbed the kid by the shirt and tugged hard. "If you know where my daughter is, you better tell me."

"Or what, pops?" one of the kids behind said, nudging the tip of his knife into Joel's back. "Careful, amigo. You ain't back home."

Joel wiped the spit from his lip and let Kyro go. "You have no idea."

"You want something, and I want something. Show me whatcha got," the bookie said, grinning. "Tell you what, I'll throw in a little something extra for ya, so you can buy your broke self a new pair of shoes or a necktie or somethin.'" Kyro flaunted a hundred-dollar bill.

"I don't need your money, kid."

"You will if you wanna get outta here. You crossed the fence, gotta pay your toll. Ricky, give this old dude your board."

Ricky groaned.

"Shut up and give him the board, before I break it off in your tailbone!"

"Fine," Ricky said, still wincing from the pain of his fall. He handed the skateboard over.

"We got you a ride, Casper. Now go fly. 'Less you wanna give my boy behind you an excuse to go home and polish his blade."

Joel grunted, took the board, and climbed the steps. A crowd of cheers followed every move as the dark sky loomed. The cold snaked into his nose and mouth, sliding through his blood the more he let it in.

What was he doing here? Was he trying to prove something? Just what did he have to prove, anyway, to these project kids? He was a grown man, not some sixteen-year-old punk with acne. But still, it felt invigorating returning to his youth. Like taking a dare and having the guts to follow through with it. Only question was whether he could land a trick without breaking any bones.

He swallowed a cool, deep breath and brushed his hair back. Stretching a bit, he slanted back farther so he'd have more room to skate some before leaping onto the pole. Blinked twice, twitched his nose, lost sight of why he was here or that he was completely moronic for stepping into the fence line on somebody else's turf to begin with. He knew better.

If Aimee were here, she'd no doubt be condemning the very notion of trying to prove himself to a bunch of kids. Taunts haunted the air from below, while *tsk-tsk* and kissing sounds filled his eardrums; they were trying to distract him, psych him out. But it wouldn't work. Not this time.

With one deep breath, Joel Phoenix was a sophomore in high school, dressed in a v-neck t-shirt and jeans with holes in them. His long hair dangled in front of his eyes no matter how many times he brushed strand after strand back. In no time, he was skating and leaping in the air, catching the cold, unchanged steel beneath the board.

Balance was hard enough, let alone thinking about which move to land. He had about four and a half seconds to decide. Some of the crew below shot their fists in the air, others spat slander, and some just sat in the fog of their cigarettes.

Joel blinked and felt his knees drop, felt the almost weightlessness of his body atop the thin board. A few sparks shot out from the wheels along the grind. Propelling upward he managed a varial heelflip before crashing down onto the concrete.

Only problem was, the board went flying into Ricky's face, and Joel ended up on his back. But he couldn't stop laughing.

"Just stay down, Ricky," Kyro said before applauding Joel's move. "Not bad for a senior citizen."

"Hey, I'm not as old as I look," Joel said, catching his breath.

Kyro helped him up off the ground and handed him a hundred-dollar bill.

"Thought you said I couldn't keep it. The toll, remember?" He was still trying to put air in his lungs.

"You're right," Kyro said, taking back the hundred and handing Joel a twenty. "I should keep you around. Can't skate worth a crap, but you got a good memory."

"Speaking of memory…"

"Look, I ain't seen her around here. That's legit."

Joel got up close. "You little liar. You hustled me?"

Kyro's lips split into a grin. "I said maybe, or are you deaf? Look, I think we were all *amused* by you. So now you can leave. Unless you're a cop and you got a warrant to search this place, get lost!"

Joel held hatred in his eyes. The boy had truly hustled him to get what he wanted: a desperate man to prove himself in front of a crew of teenagers. For amusement, for a show. And they got it.

Joel's body was still reeling from the fall. Pain swam inside his bones. He coughed and started walking from the scene, the photograph of Emery blowing away in the wind.

After Joel had started his car and driven off, one of the kids went up to Kyro with a wallet. "Casper dropped it when he took the fall."

"You take any?"

"Nah, man. He only had, like, forty-six bucks in there. Didn't touch nothin', I swear."

"But you counted it, though." Kyro said more with his expressions than with his words. He opened up the wallet and searched it. Credit cards, past receipts, and a bunch of other stuff he had no use for. Last, he checked the license. "Joel Phoenix," he said. "East Hampton, Connecticut?"

"Connecticut?" Ricky said, finally through whining about the incessant throbbing in his head. "Wasn't your gramps buried there?"

"Don't talk about him, Ricky."

"Just saying…"

"Yeah, well don't. Unless you want me to rearrange your face."

Kyro was frozen. *Who are you, pops?* he wondered, closing the wallet. "I'll catch you guys later." In minutes he was another shadow in the city, chasing a man he had never met before tonight and the ghost of a grandfather he once loved. "Got me a body to follow."

CHAPTER NINETEEN

A HALF-LIT SIGN, CHIPPING PAINT, AND BUMPER STICKERS
swallowed the glass-door entrance of the gas station. Flickering
lights hung above the pumps, and a peculiar homeless man lay
by the dumpster at the side of the building with a cigarette. Other
than that, there wasn't a soul around for miles.

Joel wasn't sure how he wound up here, wherever here was.
The last sign he had seen was for Cambridge. Maybe he'd taken
a wrong turn. It was too dark to tell for sure, though the bridge—
which should've been in plain sight from here—was nowhere.

He stepped out of the car and headed inside to pay for gas and
round up some driving junk food. He could tell the store clerk,
young as he was, and implanted with several piercings, knew he
wasn't a local. And the way those eyes followed him as he went
around selecting candies really got under his skin. If there was anything to warrant mistrust, it was this store, that clerk, this whole city.

"Just roll with the punches," he said in a hushed voice.

"Can I help you with anything?" the clerk said in a rough tone.

"I'm all right, thanks," Joel returned, rolling his eyes. As he
studied the small, cramped space, with walls of products the

wrong person might need at the right time, he thought about how easy it'd be to just snag one of the candy bars, a bottle of soda, and split. Right as the thought came, though, he noticed two cameras watching the store. Someone could always see.

Joel grabbed a Twix and some sour snacks and glided toward the cooler. He wanted so badly to reach for a beer, something strong to numb the swarm of insects buzzing around in his head or to take his mind off looking for Emery, just for a second. His leg started to shiver, and the tension climbed his bones. He ached for strong drink, wished it would wash through his veins. Soon his hands turned clammy as he drove each nail into the fleshy surface of his palm.

With a deep breath, he opened the cooler and pulled out a root beer. The IBC bottle looked like beer, even felt like a bottle of Bud in his hands. The chilled glass felt right within his sweaty grip.

Joel brought his items to the counter, the cameras catching it all. The idea of being watched still bugged him, but he was almost out.

"So where you headed?" the clerk asked in a thick accent. All of a sudden, the guy was Irish.

"What?" Joel replied.

"You must be going somewhere."

"Yeah, everybody's going somewhere."

"That's not exactly what I meant, friend. I mean, you don't look like you're from around here. And I know these parts very well-like. Seen just about every face there is to see this side of Boston." The guy licked his lips strangely. "Plus your plates kinda gave you away."

Joel looked back at his car parked beside one of the four pumps the station had to offer. "I'm looking for someone," Joel said in a somber way.

"Who might that be, friend?"

"I'm not your friend. Ring me up, please, and save the FBI routine. I didn't take anything from your store."

"Never accused you. Besides, nice guy like you looks like he's been roughed up enough for the both of us. It'd be a royal inconvenience for me to reach behind this counter to get me bat and use it to split open your skull over a pack of sweets." The clerk spit the threat out in such a calm, unsuspecting way that it threw Joel off balance. It was difficult to respond to a guy who laughed while he mentioned opening up your skull with a baseball bat. "My mum always said I was born for Fenway."

Joel shrugged, the discomfort creeping into every facet of his being. He just wanted to pay for the items, fill up his tank, and disappear.

"So who'd you piss off, friend? Was it a guy or a skirt?" The accent was beginning to drive needles into Joel's brain.

"A couple of punk kids. Wasn't a fight. I skated for a little while and fell off.… Why am I explaining this to you?"

"Just making light conversation. No need to get hostile on me. Nothing wrong with getting to know your patrons. But if you don't want to chat, so be it." After the clerk rang up the items, he took a long sip of his beer. "That'll be eight-fifty."

"Are you allowed to drink while you're working?"

"My uncle owns the place, friend," the clerk said, putting down the beer and leaning in close. Joel inhaled the stink of his breath, imagined the same flavor soaking into his own gums. "You know my uncle?"

Joel shook his head no.

The clerk lunged out, intimidating and angry, and Joel suddenly felt his skin jump back. "Then leave it alone. Now pay up and be on your way, yeah?"

Joel reached into his pocket, pulled out some lint and a dollar with some spare change. It wouldn't cover the amount.

A halfhearted smirk sent him digging for his wallet, but it wasn't there.

"What's the holdup, friend?"

A long silence. A lot of staring.

"Can't let you walk off with my nice uncle's merchandise, can I? What kind of nephew would I be?" He took another sip, and Joel let his mind linger there, eyeing his throat as the drink slipped down into the man's chest. It was then that he realized how dry his mouth was. "Pay up or hit the road. If you're lucky, maybe you'll find your daughter."

Joel's ears pricked up. "What did you just say to me?"

"I said if you're lucky, maybe you'll make it a little farther. You know, you got that crazy look in your eye, like murder. I reckon you got some unfinished business."

Joel settled back into his skin, rubbed his forehead. "Get a grip, Joel. You're fine, you're fine. Just tired and frustrated, that's all." A deep breath dropped into his lungs as he continued to check his coat for cash. Empty. His hands moved to his jean pockets. Empty.

"Nothing left, huh? You lose your wallet in the fight too? Hope you at least gave the skirt a run for her money." The clerk bellowed a sick laugh. It infuriated Joel how little respect he was getting from this pierced-up low-life. *Shut up*, he kept wanting to say. *Shut up!*

"You want any gas or not, friend?" The clerk's voice dripped with sarcasm.

Joel just stood there, wanting to throw a punch, but knowing a bat would cut open his head if he tried. He swallowed, waiting for his wallet to miraculously appear. But it didn't. Obviously, he wasn't crazy, but he felt like he was losing it. How could he have been so stupid going to those kids? What was he thinking? He wasn't some teenager anymore.

Joel blinked, drowning in the mistake of losing something so valuable. His wallet had everything. "They must've stolen it," he surmised.

"What's that you're saying?"

"Those little punks…they must've taken my wallet."

From behind him came a voice. "I hate liars. I really do."

Joel turned around and saw Kyro standing there, covered in sweat and heaving. "You? Were you following me?"

Kyro wiped a bead of sweat from his neck and flung it to the floor.

"You took my wallet. Give it back to me, you little thief!"

"I didn't take your wallet! It fell out your butt when *you* fell off the board, loser."

"Them's fightin' words, boy," came the clerk's voice. He seemed interested as to where this téte-a-téte would lead.

"Tell you what, Casper, say another lie and I'm gonna make you wish you never met me."

"Is that a fact, Kyro?" the clerk said, leaning on the counter. To Joel, he said, "Is this the slugger that ripped you off?"

"You know him?" Joel said, surprised.

"Told ya, I know just about every creature in these parts."

"You stay outta this!" Kyro said, shaping his finger like a gun. It was almost tough.

"You're still a motor-mouth, kid. But your friends aren't here to back you up this time," Joel said, walking closer.

Kyro pulled out a blade. "Think twice, Casper."

"My name's Joel, you little thief."

"I know what your name is, stupid. Checked your wallet. Don't worry, I didn't take nothin'."

"You best be putting down the blade, boy. No need for this to get nasty." The clerk grabbed his bat and placed it gently on the countertop. It rolled back and forth along the crooked surface.

"Your last name's Phoenix, right? And you're from Connecticut?"

"And?" Joel said, standing still.

"You knew Abraham?"

"Who?"

"Don't lie to me! Don't play games. Did you know Abraham Finch? "

Joel searched his memory. "It sounds vaguely familiar. What does that have to do with me?"

"Abraham Finch died in Connecticut. The suits left him in some hospice unit to die." Kyro's tongue slid over chapped lips. Short tears spilled down his cheek. "He died a few months ago. My aunt said the last thing he talked about was some little girl. Said her name was Phoenix. Emery Phoenix."

Joel's heart leapt into his throat. Surprise and wonder filled his stare. For a second, he forgot how to breathe.

"Abe was my grandfather. Now I'm gonna ask you one more time, and don't you play me. Did you know him?"

"Not personally, no."

Kyro cursed aloud.

"But my daughter knew him. My wife, she works at that hospital. This past summer, Emery volunteered for a few weeks. I wasn't father of the year then. I'm still not. But I remember that name, Finch. She told me about this strange, funny guy she met. I wish…" Joel's thoughts searched for direction. "I wish I listened more."

"Emery, that's your girl?" Kyro asked. "Man, oh man." Kyro pulled out a crumpled photograph from his shorts. "This is her? This is Emery?"

Joel nodded weakly.

"Those sick bastards!" Kyro began. "Abe would skin me alive if I let anything happen to her."

"What are you talking about, boy?" the clerk said. "Man's gotta pay me first, 'fore you gents go searching for the holy grail."

"Pay this chump," Kyro said, putting away the knife and throwing Joel the wallet. The boy grabbed a Slim Jim before heading out to the car. "Put this on the tab. Then we gotta fly, you hear? I'm ridin' with you." The boy spoke with an urgency Joel could not ignore.

A minute ago, he was swinging a blade, and now he spoke like they were old friends. Joel smirked; it was hard to believe any of it was actually happening.

"And I need twenty-five on pump three," Joel said.

"Now we're talkin', *friend*," the clerk returned with a dirty smile.

CHAPTER TWENTY

"I DIDN'T KNOW SHE WAS YOUR DAUGHTER," KYRO ADMITTED, finally breaking the silence in the car. "I'm sorry, man."

The right words just didn't seem like they wanted to come, so Joel was content with saying nothing. He was focused on the road, now foggy in front of him.

"So what are you doing? What brought you out here?"

Joel turned toward the boy then looked back at the road. "A hunch, I guess. Something in my spirit led me."

"Yeah, right. Tell me for real."

"For real?" Joel said, almost mockingly. It was unclear what this kid's angle was. He wondered if it was stupid bringing him along, but he had to take a chance if it meant finding his daughter. Maybe it was time to risk honesty with this kid. At length, he said, "She was taken."

"Taken? Man, you sounded like that dude from *X-Files* just then. You practice sayin' that?"

"No. Why don't you stop joking about it!"

"Sorry, pops. You look like you ain't heard nobody joke with you in a hard minute."

"Will you stop talking like that?"

"Like what?"

"Like a thug."

"It's where I'm from, man. Respect that."

Joel felt his eyes roll.

"Do you even know where you're going?" Kyro asked.

"Haven't got a clue. I've been searching blindly, asking people if they've seen her. I feel like an idiot. Putting up flyers. I'm exhausted. I don't know what to do anymore."

The boy choked up a laugh. "So you turned to Kyro. My man knows what's good."

"I didn't turn to you. You had my wallet and we had a mutual friend." Joel noticed a set of eyes glaring at him. "I meant you and my daughter."

The boy, who looked like little more than skin and bones, kept glued to the photograph, as if waiting for Emery to speak. The way the outside light—what little there was—flickered on the image made it seem like Emery's eyes were alive.

"Man, oh man, you can't forget eyes like that," Kyro whispered.

"Yeah, you're right. My Emery was a beautiful girl."

"That's for sure. Look, like I said, I didn't know she was your girl when you came up to the skate park. I wouldn't have hustled ya if I knew, swear it." He tapped his chest and put it to the roof of the car, as if he were communicating with God or something. "So what happened to her face?"

"Who are you, kid?"

"I'm the guy who's helping you out. Now what's the deal?"

Joel forced himself to explain. "When she was a little girl, her mother and I left her alone with her cousins. We hadn't had a date in forever. There was a bonfire accident, and certain parts of her face got burned, okay?"

"Shoot," Kyro said. "That's heavy. My aunt, she was tellin' me how my gramps knew this girl and she thought he was half-baked 'cause he kept spittin' about how this Phoenix chick wore a mask all the time. Freaky stuff."

"*This Phoenix chick?* She isn't freaky. She's my daughter! Emery was a very special girl."

"I'll bet," the boy said, hushed so Joel couldn't hear. "She's kinda hot. Little makeup will fix her right up."

Joel glared disapprovingly. "She wore the mask to hide from the world. And sick degenerates."

"I resent that. I got a four-point-oh GPA, sucka!"

"She's not some object. She's my flesh and blood. The world never understood how special she was. *I* never understood. I was selfish." Joel rolled his jaw back and forth, looking like he wanted to cry.

"Let it out, Cass, I won't tell. We're just two dudes on a road trip. It's straight."

"No, it isn't *straight*, Kyro. And this isn't a road trip. I let you come with me because you said you'd help me find Emery. So far all you've been doing is running your mouth, so much so I can't even think."

"Ouch, man. I get more respect from my crew."

Joel gritted his teeth. "Fine. I'm sorry. Look, my mind's a mess right now. I don't have a lot of patience, and I don't have a lot of money. So can you help me or not?"

Kyro glanced down at the photograph again, taking in Emery's face, her innocent eyes. He bit down hard, feeling his teeth jam up against each other. "It's all comin' back now. Look, Casper, you gotta promise not to flip out, okay? Be cool. And remember, I got a knife."

"If you're smart, kid, the last thing you do is go around bragging about a weapon you wouldn't have time to reach for anyway."

"Point taken," Kyro said, cowering back slightly. "I'm not as tough as I look. I act tough so fools think I'm tough. I travel with a crew…"

"So nobody messes with you. I get it."

"Aight. So remember, stay cool." After a short pause, he said. "I think I might possibly, sorta-kinda know where she is."

Joel slammed on the brakes as soon as he heard it. Kyro's face smashed into the dash, and a curse flew out.

"Easy, man!" He grabbed his head, but there was barely a bruise.

They were stopped in the middle of the road, no one coming on either side. Fog enveloped the car.

"You wanna run that by me again?" Joel turned red.

"Why do you think I'm with you, man? I'm on your side, remember? I want to bring her back, same as you."

"Tell me everything you know right now!"

After a series of heavy breathing and twitchy blinks, he said, "There's this place called Salvation Asylum. It ain't exactly on the up and up. Ain't for normal people, if you know what I'm saying. It's for the ones that got issues. The ones that aren't all there."

"A mental hospital? What does this have to do with Emery?"

"Yeah, Salvation is a mental joint. It used to be this big-deal hospital, the normal kind. Years ago it burned down, though. And, boom, this place took over. Shoot, I think the devil runs it or something."

"Get to the point, kid."

"I heard a bunch o' little birdies talkin'. They say it gets weirder. They say there's this place underneath where they take some of 'em…and do things."

Joel's face read defeat. "Enough. This isn't a stupid horror flick, Kyro. Do you know anything or not?"

"You don't believe me? Crap, I thought we was bondin' just now."

"You're about to be walking back to that skate park in a second, unless you tell me the truth."

"What aren't you g'ttin'? I am spillin' the truth, man. This place is real."

"How do you know?"

Kyro took a deep breath. "Because I got out."

Joel sat back in the chair and put the car in park. "Wait, you were a patient?"

"*Were*, exactly. Past tense, pops. And I got out. Shoot, now you're gonna think I'm some psychopath. I'm tellin' the truth, nothing but, swear it. Salvation's real."

"But you're barely sixteen? Why would they put you in a mental hospital?"

"Man, I'm nineteen. Felons ain't exactly looked upon like saints, case you hadn't noticed. I look young and all, but you do the crime, you do the time." Kyro chewed his lip and finally removed his hand from his forehead. "Look, let me give it to you straight. I loved Abraham. He was like my father. Hell, he was better than a father. He adopted me when I was wicked young. Nobody else gave two pennies about a little street thug. He did. I had no family. My aunt was high most of the time. I mean, that chick finally got her act together, but it was too late. Fast forward a few years. Abe gets sick. I went cuckoo."

"Why?"

"'Cause Abe started dying! What don't you get! He was sick for years before it got to the point where they tossed him away like some used-up trash. The white suits put him in that hospice unit to die. That's where Emery met him." He started to tear. "That man was Hercules. He didn't need nothin' from nobody. Especially no yuppies in suits. Bunch of heartless murderers."

Joel could finally see this kid for what he was: frail, always watching his back. Sarcasm masking a lack of confidence, smirks hiding fear. Joel was so focused on his daughter that he had been blind to the tragedy of Kyro losing someone he loved.

"I lost it. I got wicked violent." The boy lifted up his sleeve to show Joel the cuts he'd inflicted on himself, wounds he'd have to carry for the rest of his life. "I wanted it to go away, man. The pain. Started stealing pills from people. My crew's families, they're all screwed up. So it wasn't too hard to drown in something other than pain for a while. Man, when Abe got sick, I split. Just ran and ran from it. What a coward. What a stupid coward."

"It's human to want to run, Kyro. Try to escape it if we can."

"Yeah, but ya can't. The truth's always there. Nobody can run forever." The boy was sobbing now. He wiped his nose and eyes, hiding his face in the dark of the car. "My aunt couldn't deal with me no more, and after I got busted with the prescription crap, I started doin' whatever I could to lose myself. Dealin' and thuggin' and takin' a swing at a cop once or twice, it caught up. Judge wasn't so nice. It was either the joint or the funhouse. Guess they thought that place would fix me or something."

"I'm sorry, kid. Really, I am."

"Yeah, whatever. It's nothing." Kyro tried to laugh, but he couldn't, not fully.

Joel sensed a splinter inside, and maybe it was growing. Still, he had to know more about where Emery was, and he hoped, deep down, that this hustler wasn't up to any new tricks.

"I wasn't in there for long, but if you got half a brain left, it doesn't take long to figure out it ain't legit down below. That joint's got many levels, man. That's how I found out about Emery. Every now and then, they roll in with new meat. Somebody that ain't crazy. No one knows what happens to them, only that we see 'em come in, but we never see 'em roll out."

Joel gripped the wheel tightly.

"They tell us we're imagining it all. And you know what? We believed that garbage. No questions asked, just keep quiet so you can get out. But being on the streets taught your boy how to keep his lips shut and his eyes and ears open. I listened to everything."

"Everything?"

"Yeah. Sometimes you hear the nurses talking about something they ain't supposed to be knowing about. That's when you act real cool, like you're Rain Man or something."

Joel's chest was prepared to cave in. "What'd they say about Emery? Is she all right?"

"Look, I don't know. I started asking questions. You can see the fear on their faces, fear that told 'em I was close to finding out something I shouldn't know. Man, thought they were gonna ice me. Suddenly I got dismissed way earlier than I was supposed to. If I stayed in there any longer, I woulda gone bat—"

"Tell me what happened to her!" Joel said, cutting him off.

"I don't know nothin' for sure. This was months ago. I only overheard a few details. But I put all that stuff outta my head. And then you showed up, brought it all back. All I know is I seen these eyes before. I wasn't supposed to, but I did."

"So maybe Emery's still in there."

"Big maybe, Casper. That's if those creeps didn't do anything to her. Crap, I shouldn't have spilled my guts. Not sure what good any of this is gonna do anyhow. I just had to tell you. Abe woulda wanted me to."

"Don't say that. She's there. She's gotta be. She's alive, and I'm going to bring her home."

"Okay, Superman. Be real, unless you got a death wish."

"You have to take me there."

"Are you crazy? They all know my face in there. And I ain't exactly made nice with Jesus just yet. This cat's not stepping within a hundred yards of that prison." Kyro started to squirm. "That place isn't right."

"You know where to go, where to look. I need you."

"Maybe *you* should check in," Kyro said, interlocking his arms. "You're crazy enough for the both of us."

"Maybe you're right. That might not be a bad idea."

"Wait, I wasn't serious. You really are insane."

"Take me there, please."

"They're backed by the feds or somebody high up. You show up at night, they're gonna pump you full o' lead. Use your head, stupid."

"Then we'll go tomorrow."

"Look, Casper, you keep talking crazy and I'm bailin'. I mean it. I'll take off down this long, creepy, really, really dark and foggy road, and I'll split. Kyro out."

Inflection wandered into Joel's throat. "You actually sounded serious for a second."

Kyro sighed and, trembling, stepped out of the car and darted into oncoming traffic. High beams flashed, and a horn startled them both.

"Get back in the car, Kyro, before you get yourself killed. I need your help on this. I need to find my daughter."

"You need to find your mind, 'cause you lost it. That place you want to go to is hell itself, for sure. We don't even know if she's alive."

"I have to believe you're wrong."

After waiting a long moment, Joel started to drive, hoping the boy would stop him. He was right. "You're sick, man. Real sick, you know that?"

"Yeah," Joel shrugged. "C'mon, I'll pay you to help me."

"Thought you said you was almost broke."

"Almost. After you, I will be. Get in."

"Four hundred, large."

"Fine."

Kyro swore under his breath. "Could I have hustled you for more?"

"I don't know. We live in the real world. No reverse button. Now get in the car."

"Plus you spot me for food and lodging."

Joel tapped his fingers on the wheel. "Once a hustler... Done. Get in, for crying out loud, before that driver comes back to finish you off."

Kyro moved around the car and stepped inside. "This is suicide. Man, this is suicide," he kept saying.

Once the car door slammed shut, Joel hit the gas and headed south. "We'll wait until morning, but I don't want any tricks. You bring me right to the devil's doorstep."

"It ain't gonna be pretty. Do you even got a plan?"

"Still workin' on it."

"Yeah, definitely suicide. You done lost your mind."

The fog started to dissipate. Joel flipped open his cell phone.

"Who are you callin'?" Kyro asked.

"Put your seatbelt on, and please, keep your mouth shut."

CHAPTER TWENTY-ONE

REDD'S FORK SLICED THROUGH THE SILKY BLACK SKIN OF a chocolate mousse cake. As she lifted the frosted piece to her lips, she begged for peace.

"Want another cup of java?" the waitress asked.

Redd nodded. Her phone was vibrating when the waitress, one of the gaudy-makeup-and-a-nose-ring types, drew closer to pour fresh coffee into her mug. Redd checked the phone but didn't pick it up.

She knew she was wavering a bit, too much probably at a time like this. It was paramount to stay with the course, to stay dedicated. She couldn't slip and let her emotions get involved in all of this mess, and it was clear that was exactly what was beginning to happen.

She had shouldered the risk of accepting this case, and she knew what the end result would be. She knew it would come eventually, no matter how many times she sent the reality to the back of her mind, hoping it wouldn't find its way back.

"Just do your job," she mouthed, almost silent.

"You look like something deep is on your mind." The waitress nosed right in.

Redd's lips broke, and she flashed a smile. "It's this case I'm working on." Why did she say that? She was more than familiar with what always came next, and she hated aimless dialogues. "But it's just a case."

"Oh, really? You a cop or something?"

"Or something."

"I always wanted to be a detective. Finding bad guys and putting the right people behind bars just seemed like something right up my alley."

"You crave war?" Redd said, almost like her words were in search of a target. "Because this job, my line of work—it's a war. There is no clear conscience, no sense of perfect justice, no certainty of winning the fight. I gave up on my thirst a long time ago. It just never seems to let go."

The waitress was taken aback. She probably hadn't expected that kind of answer from what she surmised was no more than innocent chitchat.

"So what held *you* back?" Redd asked, hastily deflecting the attention from herself.

"More like who," the waitress returned, putting down the coffee pot.

Way to go, Redd. You caught the big fish.

"My ex. We were in love. Until I smartened up. I can't exactly blame him, though. The loser gave me something pretty special." The waitress pulled out a wallet-sized photograph of a small boy with a face that seemed to reach right out of the picture. His soft features brought back kind memories from her childhood. "His name's Timothy. Tiny Tim, I call him. He hates that, though. And that's why I love it."

"He'll come around," Redd said, staring at the picture. "He's beautiful."

"Gee, thanks. Say, are you okay, miss?" the waitress asked. "You look lost in there, almost like you've seen a ghost."

"Yeah, sure. I'm fine. Your son, he just rem… Take good care of him."

"My name is Paulina," the waitress said, returning the photograph to her front pocket. "Hope you don't think I'm weird. I carry his face around with me everywhere I go. It's like he's a part of me, you know?"

"Can't argue with that, now, can I? You love him. I understand. He's pretty lucky to have someone like you looking out for him."

"You think?"

Redd nodded again then took a sip of her coffee.

"Well, like I said, that jerk gave me something pretty special."

"I don't mean to impose, but what happened?" *Careful, Redd. Don't let your emotions take you over. Don't second-guess it.*

"Tim's daddy was all about Tim's daddy. When he wanted something, the creep just took it, plain and simple. Took me. Took my heart. Then he started taking other things. First it started out small—my mom's necklace, my father's watch. But once the darkness has you, it doesn't like to letcha go so easy."

The hairs on Redd's neck stood up.

"He liked taking things, thought it was his right. Ended up breaking into people's houses while they were asleep and knocking off cheap stores. Guess he liked the thrill of it. One day, a detective—like you—came into the picture. Took him away. Guess he'd gotten careless living two lives, you know. He murdered two young boys, said it was an accident. But they all say that, don't they?"

Redd connected to what she was hearing. It bothered her. She could see that Paulina still missed him, a little crushed that life had dealt her such an unfair hand.

"Maybe he's gone for the better," Redd tried. Those words were easy coming out, but once they escaped, they just hovered there with the silence, waiting for her to realize it wasn't that easy to let someone go. She knew that whether a person was good or evil, they became a part of you.

"I suppose you're right," Paulina muttered. "Suppose it's for the best. Tim's good and fine without him."

"And you?"

"I'll be okay, I guess. I loved him too much. Wish things coulda been different. I wish he wasn't taken away. But when you do something that hurts other people, there's really no other option. People like you are out there to help us. People like you, you're just doing your job, can't be blamed for that."

"No, certainly not," she slowly answered.

It didn't take long for Redd to leave the counter and get lost in the night. She felt the cold wrap itself around her effortlessly. "Can't be blamed," she repeated, but it didn't sink in. It wasn't right, and it didn't take a brain surgeon to see that.

But it'd been so long; she'd gone so deep. She hated the shell she had become, a tomb of what had once held her soul.

Escape it all before you get too deep. Before it goes any further.

Paulina's story engulfed her mind. *Block it.* She had to block it. It was too hard to think about him. It was too hard to remember, especially amidst all of this. She had to make the terrible memories die.

Her phone vibrated again. Different number.

Redd picked up.

There was a need for her now; she could sense it in Joel's voice. The way he called her, practically begging her to come out to Massachusetts to meet with him. He sounded so desperate, but not in the way Aimee was used to hearing him sound, not the form his tones were taking lately.

This time, his desperation was well warranted and revived. The more she thought of it, the more she felt it was similar to the desperate, lovely technique he had employed when they were dating. Aimee once relished the opportunity to be with him, to be cradled in a manner obviously foreign to her own father. With Joel, it was always simple. Yet strangely, over time, it became complicated. Now it was like they were two rogue planets spinning out of control.

Joel refused to elaborate on anything over the phone. It was too important to get lost on some digital signal, he'd said. All she knew was that he finally had uncovered some useful, concrete news about their daughter, and that was enough to carry her out of the lake house and onto the road to meet him. Like a relentless moth to the flame, though, her mind wanted more specifics. And she'd get them soon.

Aimee checked the clock, which was right beside the monitor displaying her total bill for the trip. Taxis. She hated them. Always had. Her young driver was ever quiet during the first half of the ride, and it bugged her. What Aimee disliked most about traveling with strangers, particularly taxis, was that she had such little control over the path she'd be taking. The driver chose the routes and, if it got quiet enough, left her with too much room to think. Thinking led to feeling, which led to regrets, which became real and living things that eventually ate her up inside. Too much time to think always seemed to rip open the floodgates of the past, and she was already drowning.

But were all of these superstitions real or just her ailing mind searching for a lifeline? As she pondered the road her life had been on since summer, Aimee was overtaken by an unfathomable turbulence telling her that maybe she'd taken the wrong way. But these backseat notions, did they have any validity? Dear God, maybe all of it—Carlos, the fights, threatening Joel with papers— maybe all of it was her fear trying to find a mask to hide behind. In hindsight, maybe her daughter had the right idea.

She held her phone tightly in grip, wondering if she could talk to him again, like lovers do. Talk to him as if their worlds were still in true orbit. Talk to him like she'd already apologized and time had forgiven them both. For a brief spell, she thought if only he'd said the right thing or if she'd loved him harder these last few years, they wouldn't be two rogue planets. They'd be set right. They'd be strong, on purpose.

Aimee brought her knees into her chest and sat cradled against the window. She didn't care that the driver exchanged several stares with her. She was a little girl, waiting for Daddy to come home. Waiting and waiting to tell him how sorry she was that he'd gotten angry with her for doing the wrong thing.

But her youth eventually ran dry of the words. The sorry, it stopped coming. Replaced with malice and bitterness. They were the fuel that kept her war with her husband burning. She shouldn't say sorry, not to Joel. Her father taught her that much. No matter how deeply she meant it, wanted it, needed it, she couldn't say it.

It was past midnight and the fog was getting thick. Uncertainty was like a looming darkness all around her. Transparency, like a shallow light she could not escape. How she wanted things to be different. Watching film after film of their life's work together made Aimee rethink it all. Why did she do it? Why did she toy with this game and risk the future ruin of her family?

Oh, it can't all be my fault, she reasoned. *Wherever I have failed, Joel did too.* She had her father to thank for these arrows in her ready quiver. Still, the justifications she spent on herself didn't make it right, didn't reach the root of her pain.

Aimee was now transfixed by the luminescent shine of the clock, how its numbers took new shape every sixty seconds. It wasn't as if she'd never seen a clock before, but this time she was wishing to see the numbers in reverse.

CHAPTER TWENTY-TWO

THE DOOR PUSHED OPEN WITH A HISS, AND FAINT LIGHT CUT into the black. Emery was curled up on her back, tossing prayers into the darkness. Ones she believed would never be answered.

"Arson?" she gasped.

The figure moved closer. "Emery, you awake?"

She leaned up, wiped her eyes. Had it finally happened? Had Arson finally come to save her? She reached out to touch his skin. Cold breath shot out from his mouth. She got even closer. She hugged him. It felt like Arson. It had to be him.

"Yes. I'm awake now. Now that you're here."

But as the boy pulled away, she realized her mind was mistaken. She was wrong. This savior, this frail shell of a person, however much it resembled the boy she loved, wasn't Arson.

"Good," he whispered quickly. "We need to move. Now."

She recognized the voice. It was the voice that belonged to the secret shadow. The one she'd missed. She had been wondering where he had gone.

"What are you doing?"

"I'm getting you out. Right now. We're both getting out."

"How?"

"Keep your mouth shut and your eyes open at all times. Do exactly as I say if you want to get out of here alive. You've stayed in this hell long enough." He hugged her tightly then let her go.

Emery got a clear glimpse of his face just then. A young stare carved out of pale-white skin, a hard and bruised surface. Black circles lined the bottoms of each eye. Cheek-bones protruded out a bit, and his lips seemed thin enough to miss if she weren't looking closely. Short spikes of facial hair flashed out in certain spots of his lower chin, and it seemed a razor had gotten to his scalp before a comb. The boy was bald.

"Stay close to me as we move." The boy stuck out his hand and looked at her with young eyes, the kind she figured were made of heartbreak and loss, the dark color of uncertainty.

She waited. "Where are we going? Who *are* you?"

He grunted. "My name is Adam. Now, do you want to stay here or come with me?"

She doubted a moment. She didn't have a clue who he was, where he came from, or where he wanted to take her. How had he found her, anyway? What in the world did he want with her?

Emery slowly nodded, still shaky. She'd made up her mind. "Go with you."

"Okay Grab my hand. I'll protect you from them."

Emery reached out, and he snatched her palm, tugging her closer to himself. His pulse beat inside his grip. He clutched her hand tighter as he peered around the lit corner, searching for faces and warm bodies.

When she stuck her head out of the doorway, she saw two massive guards lying face down on the tile. One guy's leg was twisted and his neck was purple. No movement. The other one was pressed up against the wall in a strange position. Both were unconscious. Disassembled gun pieces lay on the floor beside them. But she noticed Adam had a gun nudging up against her. One of theirs, she imagined.

"What's that for?" she asked.

"Don't worry about that. I might need it. For now."

"Don't worry," she mumbled. "*Right.*"

The cameras twitched back and forth, so Adam kept his hand pressed up against her chest. "Wait. Be very careful," he said quietly. "Wait for them to rotate again."

She was still, quite uncomfortable with his hand groping her like some excitable jock. But she didn't say anything. So far, he wanted to help her, and that she was cool with. Emery swung the loose strands of hair away from her eyes and waited until the cameras looked away.

"Run. Now!"

Adam held a black stick in one hand and dragged her along with his other. As she raced with Adam down the hallway, she couldn't help but wonder how such a seemingly unmuscular kid was able to take down two guards nearly double his size—guards who had guns and death sticks.

"Where are we, Adam?"

"I told you before," he snapped. "They call this place The Sanctuary. It's where God and his false prophets gather."

False prophets. The Sanctuary. This all sounded crazy.

"Gather for what?"

"Haven't they studied you? Taken you in for sessions?"

Emery searched her memories. It was all still hazy. Part of her felt drugged; the rest of her was scared.

"They're getting better," Adam said, unable to wait for her answer. A curse tore out of his mouth. "You probably don't remember anything." He lifted up her shirt and stared at her skin.

She fought him. "Hands off!"

"Keep your voice down."

"Well, don't grope me like that."

"I was hardly groping."

The cuts were gone.

"It worked faster on you here," he noticed, "but not your face."

"What are you talking about?"

He hesitated for a moment, looking at her mutilated skin. From where she was standing, it seemed like he wasn't all that terrified of it. The look in his eyes was almost like compassion or sympathy. "Why couldn't my blood heal your face?" he wondered.

"Wait, what? Your blood?"

"Later," he returned, not bothering with an explanation. "We can't stay still."

Emery trailed closely behind him. He stunk. But maybe that was her own stink rushing to her nose to be reviled. She was sweating enough.

Adam had dirt and blood encrusted underneath his nails. The back of his head had scars that she could see but couldn't focus on. The world around them was getting darker. It was quiet. Way too quiet.

"How did you do that?"

"What?" he shot back.

"Take out those guys back there. What are you, part cyborg?"

"Not even close. I'm just a little different. You'll get it eventually."

"Oh, really?" she said snidely.

"I have to get you free from this place, before—Shh! Don't move."

They waited. And waited. Until an opportunity to continue presented itself.

Then, after a moment of running, it was back to the walls. They came to a stop at the end of one of the hallways. White walls with black lines running together. She was sure this place was a maze. One of those rooms inside of another room, none of which really had an exit. This all felt like a nightmare, one that this puny, bald hero was attempting to save her from. Nevertheless, if looks could kill, he'd collect a trophy. Adam held that big black stick like he knew how to use it. She imagined him bashing somebody's brains in like some juvenile maniac with a bad attitude.

Emery held her breath when she heard footsteps, warring with the panic begging to let out a scream. A shadow reached forth from an open door somewhere around their left corner. Adam's back hugged the wall. He counted silently.

One, his mouth moved.

Two…

The footsteps drew closer. He gripped her hand tighter, and Emery eyed him while he ground his molars. She didn't like whatever was coming. Whatever sick plan he was conjuring couldn't have a happy ending.

"You're hurting me," she whispered. "Easy on the death grip."

He didn't seem to hear her. But in point-five seconds, he suddenly let her go and swung his right wrist up so fast she wondered if it was all taking place in slow motion. The sound of a man's nose cartilage crunching inside an ugly mug crashed against her eardrums. Emery covered her mouth in awe.

The man used his leg to swoop underneath Adam's feet and trip him. But Adam unleashed an ungodly assault on the man's entire body while on the floor. Blood splashed inside the tile grooves.

She couldn't tell if the man was a guard or some doctor or scientist, and it didn't really matter. She feared for his life.

Adam dropped his fist into the man's throat and then dug the back of that death stick into the ribs. She swore she heard more cracking sounds. A spike of panic climbed up her spine.

"Stop! You're going to kill him. He can't hurt us."

"Not anymore," Adam replied, wiping loose spit from his mouth. "I trusted you. I thought you were my friends."

She stepped over the man, now gasping for air. "You'll never make it out," he said, struggling to breathe through missing teeth. "It isn't s-s-s-safe for you outside these w-walls-walls."

Adam eyed him from where he stood, circling the body like some kind of lion. "I need something from you."

Emery listened to the smacking sound of Adam's bare feet against the tile. She was shivering. But it didn't bother him.

"A-Adam, you don't have to do this." The frail whimpers resumed. "Don't run."

The man's head tilted back. Emery could see the look on his face. She was full of fear for him, for the life that hung between sanity and violence, the will of this strange boy who could kill if he needed to. She knew she should feel something—anger, hatred—and she did. But maybe this was going too far.

"Don't worry. I won't cut you open like you did to us. But by the time they find you, I'll be long gone. Look at me."

Adam pulled out a device from his pocket. It was the size of a mini voice recorder. She'd never seen something like this before. A lip protruded from the top of it, one that had a scanner. The only thing she could compare it to was a supermarket bar code scanner. But she didn't have the slightest idea what to call the device.

The man tried hard to redirect his eyes.

"Now, now, let's not be feisty. There is another way."

Emery watched the man's lip quiver. Adam proceeded to bash the stuttering fool's face in with the black stick now spotted with blood. He dropped the weapon and forced open the man's right eye until he heard a beeping sound. The scan was complete.

"Whoa," Emery said. She couldn't feel her hands, and her feet ached. "What do you need his eye scan for?"

The cameras had circled around. No time for an answer.

"Adam!" she screamed.

"They're watching now. Let's dance."

Just then the lights flashed. Flickers of red and yellow ran along the walls and the glass. Light beamed and vanished, beamed and vanished. A loud alarm blasted down the hall. Adam turned to her. Then they started running, into the maze.

"You're insane, you know that?" Emery chimed, forgetting she practically clung to him. The cry of the alarm was the sound of chaos, a deep boom, like something wicked was trailing closely behind and gaining. "Do you know how to get out?"

"I've memorized a way." Adam took wide steps onward past a set of double doors. In order to avoid coming footsteps, he dragged her into the bathroom. There was a closet in there where they hid for a few minutes, until they heard their pursuers being pulled away by distance.

"It's so cozy," she murmured. "By the way, you can stop staring at me."

"I'm not."

"Whatever." She realized he hadn't been staring. But it seemed easier to think of him as some kid who *thought* she was a freak than coming to the realization that she might actually be one.

The closet was crowded. Claustrophobic. His cold breath seemed to come out wet but dried on her skin. His heart beat against his ribs, and she could feel it tickle her chest.

"I think it's okay now," Adam concluded, stepping out of the dark. His eyes pierced the still air. "C'mon."

With panic racing through her, Emery traced his footsteps, holding tightly to Adam's waist, where the stick he held dug into her side a bit. But she dealt with it. No way she was letting go.

They entered what seemed like the end of the maze. A snake-like hall lay before them, white rooms set inside the walls. A nickel-plated elevator stood like a centurion at the end of it all. They drew carefully closer, Adam focused on taking the lead, despite the obvious apprehension Emery could see staining his eyes. It was like with each step, his eyes grew older, a deep, mysterious blue, outlined by his pale, leathery flesh and crimson cheeks.

What if they took another step and some line was tripped? A line that would send tiny spikes into their bodies? Or a net that shot up from the floor to steal them back to their secret dungeon?

Immediately her mind birthed images of her, cold. She couldn't move, could barely talk. Voices like a distorted, gut-spinning swarm. Mirages looming over her face. A thick haze drifting above it all.

Adam lured her forward, her hesitation more and more apparent with every step. An eerie drip bled down her back. The alarm's relentless shriek shattered her ears. The lights messed with her head too.

Bright. Dark.

Bright. Dark.

Haze.

Bright. And dark again.

He pulled out that scanning device from before and exhaled. Emery assumed it would be used to grant them access to something. Something that, at this point, seemed to put more fear in her than hope. Would it open the elevator standing in sunken, tarnished spite at the end of this corridor?

Suddenly a noise rose above the sound of the alarm, or perhaps pierced through it. With a chime, everything went still. Like a violent sea, the elevator doors slowly parted. She fought the fear growing inside her. Emery's eyes exploded as five people, some with weapons, stepped out.

The silence seemed to strip her naked. Adam shoved her in the chest suddenly, flinging her body to the other side fast enough for her to slam against metal and Sheetrock and catch a tranquilizer fly past.

Her head spun.

Adam, clinging to the wall, took a glance at the group gaining on them then stole another look at Emery. With a scream, he sent the large black stick whirling through the air, aiming to break the nose of the frightening bald man who was coming toward them. She recognized him. The agent that gave her chills. The last day she ever saw Arson.

Adam grabbed Emery's hand then reached for his gun and fired off a few shots before racing back the way they'd come. Dodging several darts and bullets seemed like it came easy for this mysterious, blue-eyed rescuer. But he didn't dare tempt fate by looking back; he just followed his instincts. And his instincts seemed to say to take a sharp left.

"They're shooting at us!" Emery yelled.

"Thanks. Hadn't noticed."

"Are they trying to kill us?"

"I think this is them being friendly."

Emery didn't like the sound of that at all. "How are we gonna get outta here?"

"Just trust me," Adam urged, barely having to catch a breath. "I know another way. There are tunnels we can use. They'll lead us out through the sewage line."

"Forget it! I am not crawling through crap."

"Then you can stay here with them. I'm sure you'll love Christmas dinner."

Emery watched as he quickly slid into a divot in one of the walls. A small passageway, really, but he managed to squeeze through. A fear-filled glance shot behind her as she listened for the stampede of angry men desperate to bring her back to her cold prison. Her heart leapt into her throat, but she followed, sucking in some breath. They traveled deeper into the wall, her chest and ribs struggling not to cave in completely.

"Adam, they're coming," she panicked. "They're coming!"

He snatched her wrist and tugged her toward him, pulling her in through the wall and then making a slight shift in direction.

A maze within a maze, she thought. "How do you know these things?"

"Time."

The bald man chasing them stopped midstride and stared into the wall. "Gotcha," they heard him say as brown saliva slid down his jaw. His nose was split open and running red.

When he reached into his coat for a pistol, Emery shuddered. "Gun! Gun! Gungungun!" Just then, she felt Adam drag her backward a little farther. Seconds earlier, he had been pressed up against a vent of some kind. But he must've kicked it in.

Their pursuer's face was a cloud of rage. His eyes were black coals.

In seconds, Emery swore she heard the sound of a trigger being pulled, followed by a dart splitting air molecules and dust above her. Then she felt a deep sinking in her gut. They were falling. Into the dark.

Into the unknown.

CHAPTER TWENTY-THREE

EMERY KEPT HER MOUTH CLOSED TO KEEP THE MAJORITY of rusty grime and soot from dripping in.

"Don't let go yet," Adam warned, his grip starting to come loose. "And try not to look down."

"I can't see anything. How high are we?"

She could hear the struggle to keep holding on in his voice, the way his tone stuck to the inner lining of his throat, almost like it felt more comfortable being stuck than escaping. "Emery, I'm gonna need you to let go soon, when I tell you."

"You just said—" A sliver of brown slime oozed down her lip. "I'm gonna puke."

"Please stay focused," he groaned. "When I tell you, let go."

"It's so dark in here."

"It wasn't my first choice," he admitted. "Look, Emery, just trust me. You'll be safe."

They heard the sound of banging metal and heavy breathing. The enemy was getting closer. How much longer before they were both dragged back to those cells, left alone, separated?

"Now!" she heard Adam say. The split-second between when the word left his mouth and when she actually let go of him seemed like hours.

She kept falling. Wasn't sure if it was forever, but the black surrounding her made it feel like it. She felt weightless. She felt open. She was back on that cold steel table, bright lights flashing at her, through her. The strangers crept closer. Hot breath. Needles. That painful cry between her ears.

And suddenly she hit water, or something else. She nearly sank in. The putrid smell of waste invaded her nostrils. She wanted to vomit. No—she was vomiting. There wasn't much to puke up, but still she swore one of her organs was looking for a way out.

A few seconds later, there was another splash.

"Adam! Oh, where are we?"

"I told you, the sewer route," he said, spitting. She couldn't quite see him yet, but she followed his movements. "This is the only way out. There's a smaller tunnel up ahead. We're going to have to crawl."

Thinking about what Adam just said seemed to make things worse. The eerie darkness, the stink of this underworld, how her hair was tangled in filth. She hated feeling the sticky, gross threads clinging to her neck. "Get me outta here, fast!"

"Take my arm."

"Where are you?" she asked, trying to follow his voice.

After a few awkward seconds of wading through the dirt and waste, Emery reached out, and he grabbed her hand, slipping from her grip with the first few attempts. "Try to hold on. Grab my shirt. I know it's weird."

"Weird doesn't even come close."

"You're stronger than you think, Emery." His voice sounded slimy. It felt unclean and unknown.

Yet hopeful.

"Once you get past the smell, it's almost okay," Adam said.

"If by *almost* you mean—"

"Shhh," he whispered. "Hear that?"

Emery shook her head.

"Swore I heard something." They kept moving. Adam said they were almost at the part where they'd have to crawl. She couldn't really make out anything with her eyes, so she touched things with her hands. Metal. Slime. More metal. Her hands surveyed the circumference of the tunnel he expected her to crawl through, the waste sliding between their fingers.

"Don't touch your face. You won't be right for days."

"Gee," Emery sarcastically began, "and that was the first thing I wanted to do. I can't see anything. I hate this." She took another whiff and wanted to vomit again.

"Emery, there's no turning back now." She felt his hand touch her, her legs screaming to be out of this pool of filth. "Was this the best idea you could come up with for a first date, Shawshank?"

"What? I'm just—"

"Trying to get me outta here alive, I know. Look, just go in first. If the hookman decides to jump out, I want to make sure he has something to gnaw on while I make a crawl for it." She laughed, thinking of how ridiculous her statement must have sounded.

"I'm getting you out of here," Adam said, stepping into the cramped tunnel. "I'll protect you. I won't let anyone hurt you again."

"That's what Arson said," she mumbled under her breath.

"Stay close behind me," he told her. "We're almost out."

"On a scale of one to insane, how sure are you?"

"Pretty."

"Don't sound so convincing. You know, I never thought I'd be wading through crap with some skinhead I barely know.

Not that you're an actual skin—whatever. Funny how things turn out."

"Funny," Adam said, crawling forward. "Wasn't exactly my choice for the perfect word. Messed up, maybe. Sick. Not funny."

Emery followed behind him silently, at least for a few seconds. "So how many times have you done this, Shawshank?"

"Stop calling me that!"

"I thought we had to whisper." She knew she was being diffi-cult. She also knew he was looking back at her with one of those reprimanding faces her mother loved to employ, even though she could barely see him. "Something just moved past my leg. It's a freakin' rat. I hate rats."

"Just be quiet and c
-**rawl faster. He'll move on."

"Easy for you to say. Do you know how disgusting rats are?"

"Emery, do I have to remind you that you're literally crawling through human feces?"

"No!" she bit back. "Don't touch me, you little vermin."

"Was that directed at me or the rat?"

Emery was somewhat amused, but she wasn't going to show it.

"So, Not-Shawshank, a.k.a. Adam," Emery began, "what is this, escape number seven?"

"What?"

"How many times have you tried to break out?"

He didn't answer.

"How long have you been here? Where is *here* anyway?"

"You like to talk, don't you?" was all he said.

Silence carried them another two minutes before Emery heard something above her.

"Is that…a truck? Adam, that's, like, one of those eighteen wheelers or something. Oh, I've never been so happy to see a grungy truck driver before."

"Yeah, don't get too excited yet. We still got a little bit to go. Move faster, will you, there's no telling how close they are behind. If they follow the right pipeline, they might be waiting for us."

"You're not actually saying—"

"Keep moving, that's what I'm saying. No looking back. No second chances. We linger too long, and they'll take us again. They'll take you, Emery. So just keep close. I think I see some light up ahead."

"Good. Hey, is that the highway above us?"

Adam groaned. She could tell he was getting annoyed. "No. But it's one of those side roads, one that carries you to the interstate."

"I'm loving your confidence."

Again, Adam kept quiet. She was getting used to talking to herself. The smell of the tunnel, black garbage coating every piece of hair and skin and clothing, permeated through her.

He jerked her forward. "C'mon. If I'm right, these tunnels should bring us just far enough to make it past any cameras, and hopefully no one will see us."

Emery swore this kid was off his rocker. Did he have any idea how ludicrous this all sounded? *Hopefully* and *if* and whatever. It was like this kid memorized everything but the words to make her feel safe with him. She wished it was Arson getting her out. She wished he was her hero. She wished…

"See," Adam said, tugging her forward out of the lip of the tunnel and into puddles of mud. She panicked a little when she noticed a camera, but Adam told her it was one of the broken ones they just kept hanging to keep trespassers out. The fact that he knew so much about this place made her feel weird.

It was pouring violent rain. Adam spent the next moment letting it all soak into him, his body absorbing the sharp, wet bullets. Like he hadn't seen rain in years, or ever.

She studied him purely in that moment, focusing on the image of him—arms stretched out like someone about to break into song, the mud and filth slipping off his face with the water. This skinhead stranger dragged her out of the jaws of lions and into the rain. She should've been happier. But she wasn't. She couldn't be. Not yet.

It seemed like more than seconds, but that's all they were. That was the time it took them to get from being knee deep in strange, random mess to cutting through a forest, where Adam told her a road would welcome them. She wasn't sure how time had stopped for them, as if it knew what they needed and how far they had to go. She just followed him, blind hope filling the open spaces in her brain. Whatever lay on the outskirts of their former prison had to be better than a cold floor and no mattress.

And the rats. She shivered at the thought.

Emery tried not to look behind her. Adam told her it wasn't good to look back, but she was never good at following laws to the letter. She was unsure if it was fear or hope or stupidity that called her eyes back to that giant prison, which at this very moment, looked like a jewel of brightened darkness in the distance. And it didn't matter. Her gaze lingered there for a long moment before she reminded her legs to stay in motion.

Adam tugged her forward. Something else wanted her back. "A little further. Just stay focused, Emery, and don't be afraid."

He kept saying that. *Don't be afraid.* Telling her not to be afraid was like telling her not to breathe. She'd lived with this new, heightened fear for so long she couldn't shake it. It stayed with her. Lived inside her skin. Emery kept her head down then forced her eyes up so she could focus on Adam, only inches from her, his hand cold just like hers. Shaking just like hers.

"It's late. There shouldn't be a lot of people out. We might be able to hitch a ride."

"Is that legal?"

Adam eyeballed her for a long moment.

"Right, we're two lab experiments that just escaped from a facility no one even really knows exists. Hitchhiking it is." She fought to catch her breath, but her heart was pounding like a hammer. "Gotta keep reminding myself this isn't a dream."

"It's your new nightmare," Adam said, grabbing her hand tighter and ushering her deeper into the woods.

She wanted to wake up now. She needed to. Emery flicked some excess dirt from underneath one of her fingernails. Still grossed her out. It felt like some living thing existed under her nails, squirming around to aggravate her, mess with her head.

She hated that it was working. Emery drew slightly closer to Adam's shoulder, ignoring whatever slimy, mysterious pool she had just stepped in.

When Emery next turned her head, she noticed nothing was looking back at her. Not some horrible dungeon. Only nameless darkness. How far had they gone? How long had they been running? She hadn't kept track. The trail they were on was so black she fell half a dozen times, nearly sprained her ankle. But Adam promised her he'd get her someplace safe. *When*, he couldn't say for sure.

Her spit felt like glue at the back of her throat, sticking but not providing her any kind of satisfaction, and it couldn't quench her thirst. A plume of her own breath escaped like a lost fog from her mouth, and it bothered her to be reminded of how it smelled. How both their bodies reeked. She was glad the mud covered most of her face, though. It felt cool, hidden.

Arson was the only one who gave her peace without her mask on. And he wasn't here. But she so wished he were. "Just don't think about it," she accidentally said out loud.

"Don't think about what?" Adam replied.

"Nothing," she quickly answered, lagging behind him. She wanted to trust this kid, hoped she could, but what if this lame, un-thought-out escape plan...

No, stop it. He's trying to save you. Trying to get you free.

Her thoughts were getting louder.

I really miss him.

Another five minutes went by before Emery could hear anything other than the sound of crunching leaves and squishy mud. But she began listening more intently. The slide of tires against wet pavement. The honking of horns. Adam said he could hear the sound of windshield wipers, but that was too freaky for her to wrap her head around.

A bolt of lightning split the sky, and soon after, the boom of thunder groaned somewhere far off. Where she wished they could be. Where she prayed they might make it to, if they were lucky.

"Emery, can you hear it? We're so close. The road is close."

"Okay. I trust you." The only reason she trusted him was that she didn't have a choice— and because she'd heard for herself the noise of traffic, however sporadic or remote. They really were close. But would there be anyone willing to give two kids a ride who looked like the two of them did?

She hoped. Adam kept leading. *Soon,* she fought to convince her mind. *A few more steps. A few more breaths. A few more...*

Light flashed in front of her, nearly blinding. A horn cut the dead night air, startling them both. In their haste, they had darted out too far. But the truck driver was clearly spooked. His rig turned hard and slid as the brakes shrieked to a halt atop the slick white lines of the road.

Emery and Adam stood there, unsure, uneasy.

The truck driver cursed several times, rolling down the window to make sure his voice was heard, and then stuck his head out into the rain to get a better look at them. "What the—"

Emery watched Adam's chest expand. Only now did he start breathing heavily. *She* never stopped.

"You kids come outta that there woods? You look like you're running from Satan himself."

Tears of rain dripped from their faces, and they both nodded.

"Well, where the h—" The trucker abruptly began laughing, like a cynic who'd just stumbled upon a reason to believe in something. "I must've had a few too many drinks at Marty's. Good God, you both got some filthy color on you, for sure. Enough mud on you to scare an old fart like me half to the grave. Where'd you come from exactly?"

"Look. We need to get lost *now*," Adam replied forcefully. "Can you help us?"

"Depends, short stack. Where are you and that pretty little zombie friend of yours headed?"

Emery folded her arms and watched Adam turn red.

"Easy there," the trucker snidely said with that same peculiar laugh. He scooted his hat back a little on his forehead, revealing he didn't have much hair. Some rain trickled into his truck. "I'm just futzin' with you, though you scared me good. Nearly robbed me of my skin, God forbid. You two weren't thinking right, dartin' out in front of my rig. I could've given you a one way ticket to meet your Maker."

"Can you help us or not?" Adam said, growing impatient. The rain was starting to cleanse him physically, but mentally, Emery knew there was still something uncleansed underneath. No time for small talk.

"Now, I asked you where you're headed, and if you can't give me a straight answer—"

"New York." Adam hesitated. "Bethpage, New York."

The trucker grinned wildly. "I'd say this is rather fortuitous, then. I'm coming from Boston, got a shipment to Farmingdale and some family in West Babylon. Looks like tonight's your lucky night." The slick shine of his yellow teeth made Emery's skin crawl, but she wasn't sure if there really was something weird about him or if she was acting paranoid.

She looked at Adam, and with one glance she knew it was okay to step toward the truck. Emery hadn't bothered to look at the vehicle, but when they got up closer, she noticed it was blank, but the side body looked painted over.

There was a part of her that wanted this stranger to be a guardian angel, but a strange sensation came to life inside her. Another step closer, another step away from that terrible place. Wherever Bethpage was, maybe it was better. She hoped to God Adam would protect her, if he *could* protect her.

Adam followed Emery into the cab.

"Come on. Step right up. I don't got all blasted night. I'm one nut hair away from missing a deadline."

"What are you carrying?" Adam questioned.

"Whoa-whoa, wait a tick." The driver reached behind him and got a towel, placing it on the seat. His facial expression told them they were now free to sit down. "Good Lord, you two smell like a sewer."

Silence.

"Just close the door behind you, kid."

Emery sank into the seat, sandwiched between two strangers. An uneasy chill clawed at the back of her neck.

"Name's Bruce."

"I'm Adam."

Bruce glanced her way, waiting for her introduction.

"Emery," she finally said.

"Now that we're all acquainted and official, you two would be wise to fasten your buckles. I got a thing about deadlines and a penchant for driving hard."

Emery wasn't sure if she was more surprised that this driver was willing to pick up two strange kids who reeked of crap or that his vocabulary appeared so refined. For a trucker. She immediately made up a mental story of him dropping out of Princeton to deliver produce, but it didn't distract from how bizarre tonight had been or how uncomfortable this driver made her feel.

Emery breathed deeply, closed her eyes, and leaned against Adam as Bruce pulled back onto the road with a grunt.

CHAPTER TWENTY-FOUR

"WHAT ARE YOU DOING HERE?" THE SMALL BOY ASKED. "HOW did you get here?" Shadows confused his face. He lingered far away, lost in the center of the cold hallway of the school. Arson knew this place. How recently he had found himself trapped here.

At first Arson didn't speak. But the frightening shudders once entombed within him wanted new life.

"I said, what are you doing here!" the boy asked again.

"I'm not sure," Arson finally replied, stepping closer.

"Don't. I don't want you to see me."

"Why?"

"I just don't."

"Who are you?"

"No. We're not playing that game." The boy remained hidden. "You know this place, don't you?"

Arson nodded. He stared at the walls. Every heartbeat was a jagged and chaotic mess. His surroundings eventually finished shaking and fell into focus. The blurs and lines and colors collided in the dark-light. Posters and jerseys crowded the halls. Jewel cases were lined with athletic awards and photographs of people he used to hate. There was no doubt, no question that this chamber was every bit as lost and confusing as he remembered.

In these hallways, kids were worshiped, like they had powers. Arson wished now that he could light his fingertip and make it all disappear. Prove to the world that he too was special, had powers. But he didn't. For a while now, his powers had abandoned him.

His brain was so screwed up. Why couldn't he simply control what he remembered? Did he want this, or was it part of a plan? Asking wasn't the issue. It was the lack of answers that infuriated him.

Cold. Gloomy. Dark. Just like the middle school he'd somehow wandered through in his past dreams. This place was high school. He was sure now. A few things were different from the middle school halls, but it was mostly the same, a similar kind of ruined world.

"Why are we all alone? Where is everyone?"

"Everyone?" the boy replied, like he was surprised Arson would even ask. "I don't know. Why don't you tell me? Were you expecting a party?"

Arson was about ready to lose it.

"You wanna hurt me, don't you?" the boy said. "Well, go ahead. I'm never getting out of here. You'd be doing me a favor."

"Why?"

"Because I hate it here. They never let me out."

"Who?"

"The memories. The past. I'm stuck. Like you."

The boy stood up with muffled sobs, but his face remained distorted inside the black. Arson wanted to see him—feel him—know he was real because he couldn't shake the thought that none of it was.

Just then, the boy took off down the hall. Arson tried to follow his shadow, but he couldn't. Simply blinking was too long of a distraction. The only thing that remained was the darkness.

Hoven was a vulture surrounding them. Carraway, Krane, and Lamont sat like prey in chairs around Arson's comatose body. Their eyes circled.

"How did this happen?" Hoven asked calmly. Krane knew the man was boiling underneath.

"Adam is strong, s-s-sir. You knew what he was cap-cap-c-capable of. And he's very angry."

"I thought we suppressed it."

"Some of it, maybe, but obviously not fully. Not to mention, he feel-feels that we have betrayed him," Krane said, his hand still shaking as sweat beaded off a wrinkled forehead. "I knew it was only a matter of time."

"Well, let's send him a sympathy card, then," Hoven mocked, polluting the air with his vile words. "This wasn't supposed to happen. In the last three days, the two most powerful subjects this facility has ever encountered—it's like they're being taken from me!"

"One of them is still here." That was Lamont, feeling the need to add his two cents.

"Oh, you mean this one here? He's in a coma, in case you haven't noticed."

"Yeah. But look at the screens. Morpheus is still pickin' up a signal. His body may be fried, but that twisted mind of his is still in Wonderland."

Hoven turned briefly to stare at the hanging monitors then rubbed his temples. "Dreams or no dreams, we're losing control." Hoven's mouth folded. He loomed. "How 'bout you, Nick? Care to contribute anything to this enlightening dialogue?"

"I wasn't there when 217 escaped, sir. I can't speculate."

"You can't speculate," Hoven uttered, his voice like an imprisoned and angry chorus, at any moment ready to explode into a violent crescendo. "And where were you when this *escape* was taking place, hmm?"

Carraway kept quiet.

"Right. When it's time for answers, everybody's deaf and dumb. It astounds me how people so bright can be so weak and stupid."

The Sanctuary, with all its open space, felt claustrophobic and terrifying as the vulture skulked around the meat. "Frankly, I don't care what you were doing, Nick, or why, only that you facilitated this escape."

"Sir, I—"

"Shut your hole! I'm not finished."

Carraway sank back in his seat.

"If you were not there to stop this from happening, then you facilitated." His lips formed the words perfectly, each sound and syllable harshly echoed. "We have a mess on our hands, gen-tlemen. It's nasty, and I don't like it. Can any of you comprehend the gravity of the situation?"

"I'm quite s-sure we can…sir," Krane replied.

"This isn't a science project, Manny, this is business. This is a war. I've already got enough blood on my hands, men. All we need is for one pious reporter to go rogue and get in the middle of all we have worked so hard to secure. We're not ready to go public with our *extracurricular activities* just yet. In time, but not now. Our superiors would have our heads on a plate if something like this gets out. A screw-up like this is all it takes, that's it, and this Sanctuary gets torn down, with all of us inside. Get the picture?"

"I thought we controlled the press," Carraway fought back.

"We do. But something can always slide through the cracks. We don't control the others. The ones who built this place. The ones who pay our salaries, our healthcare, our families, in order that they remain uninvolved. That's all we need, for the president to get involved."

Hoven hovered over them. Reflecting green lights spiraled over and through him, providing a frightening atmosphere for him to breathe out. Every footstep, every gasp, was supplemented with a terrible emerald glow.

"Sir, Adam can't survive out there. So much has changed since we took him. He needs us. He'll return with us. He'll re-r-r-re-realize he's all a-alo-alone out there."

"How can you be so sure, Manny?"

"He'll be lost, sir. Adam needs to belong. He needs purpose. We g-gave him meaning. We-w-w-we showed him what he was capable of."

"He took 218."

"The Phoenix child is of little consequence to us now," Krane said, trying to inhale through a broken, bleeding nose.

"He's looking for her, in that mind of his," Hoven said, nodding toward the comatose body. "I'd call that consequence, Doctor."

"Y-yes, you are correct. But where there is Adam, there is the girl. We w-w-w-will bring him back, and the girl as well." His rib made a cracking sound he didn't like. He winced, but the pain stuck.

"The game keeps changing."

"Adaptation. It's beginning, sir. We need to ch-ch-c-change. Like they do."

"You're right. Perhaps my frail shell works a little too slowly. My becoming hasn't taken full effect as I believed it would."

"In time." It was a hiccup in good judgment, Krane believed, that allowed Hoven this fraction of vulnerability. "They're changing quickly. I've begun to notice it with this boy the most. The arson's blood, it keeps adapting. His brainwaves, they're changing too. A constant flux of movement. If my calculations are correct, I don't foresee he'll be in a coma much longer."

"All speculation for now, Doctor," Hoven replied.

"Yes, and therein lies the rub. The energy never st-s-stays in one place for long, which makes it increasingly more challenging to locate and absorb his mental codes." Krane leaned up slightly, his teeth clenched at the thought of readjusting his ribs or the bandages. "His DNA structure, the whole of it, is unstable. Con-constantly becoming more unique. It is growing, the way Adam's once did."

Arson's body suddenly jerked, and they didn't move for a second. One weary second crawled into the next.

Hoven's face formed a cryptic grin. "So, Manny, it would appear that the situation gets better."

"The Source has gone for now, but we have collected more than enough samples to advance the tr-tri-trials at our other locations."

Hoven eyed Lamont first, then located Krane. "Manny, I'm keeping you here because you are familiar with all of this better than most. But don't think for a second that we'll make it out of this unscathed. One more mistake like this, and this facility will be considered compromised. I can't have that. I will not have them take this away from me!"

Krane nodded weakly.

With hunched shoulders, Hoven loomed over the steel bed where Arson lay—a thin body connected to hardware and scattered machines. Wires and needles and Morpheus working together to feed nearby monitors with wandering images. A dark school hallway. Static. Open doors and empty rooms. To someone who'd never seen any of this, it would look chaotic, but there was a sick order—the order of the mind—that gave reason and purpose to everything unfolding on the monitors.

"It's fascinating, isn't it?" Hoven's voice slithered out. "Morpheus and him." He stood over the body. "Their connection. Even in a coma, you mystify me, 219. Don't worry, we'll get her back home where she belongs. You'll all be mine."

"There is something else, sir," Krane said.

"What?"

"While I am confident that the arson's mind will wake up in time, the coma *is* affecting his cerebral pathways. The landscape has evolved. I want you to be aware of it. There are so many trap doors in his mi-m-mind. The potential to complicate our ef-f-f-efforts is great. These dreams may become more and more…violent. I think a part of him believes they're real. It is my understanding that if the arson cannot separate what is re-r-r-real from imaginary…"

"…he'll be stuck in Wonderland," Lamont chimed.

Hoven took a peek at the images as Krane played back some from the night before. The monitors glistened with pain and blood. Horror. A boy who set an animal on fire to sit there and watch it burn. Then a mother bleeding from the stomach as a burnt knuckle reached through her flesh from the inside.

And then something neither of them had expected. "This was the strangest of th-them all." Krane skipped ahead to another image. A needle being injected into a young boy's arm. Across from him on a table was a girl Krane recognized, a face he hadn't seen in close to twenty years.

"Is that…?"

"Adam," Krane said. "And Frances…the arson's mother."

"There must be a mistake," Carraway interrupted. "What exactly are we watching here?"

"His memories."

"But these aren't *his* memories. He wasn't even alive. The boy mentioned something in our session about this, but I wasn't sure… wait, how can this be?"

"The arson is quite extraordinary," Krane replied. "The w-won-wonder does not end with Adam."

"Are you sayin' that this kid is havin' dreams of things he ain't never lived before?" Lamont asked.

"Look at all that we've seen Adam do. Is it so strange to us?"

"How long have you known, Manny?" Hoven asked, more like a demand than a question.

"A few weeks. Since the beginning of his trials. But I wasn't sure what these memories were. I'm still l-l-learn-learning some things too."

A sudden jolt later and the images flickered to a hospital room full of smoke and splashes of blood. And then, without warning, the jitters and the monitors became empty school hallways.

"The mind, in our dreamscapes, can some-sometimes blur scenarios together."

"It still doesn't make any sense. You're certain these are his dreams, only the memories aren't?" Hoven sternly asked.

"Dead certain. Morpheus discovered these final two late last night with a clear scan. But look here." Krane pushed a button on the remote and the screen switched again. "He's back in that school hallway."

"What is he doing in there?"

"I don't know. For one r-reas-reason or another, he's drawn to that place, and places like it. I think there's some-something he must…face there."

"The past," Carraway offered, sinking back into his seat.

"Don't be scared." Hoven paused, his tongue sliding back and forth across the wasteland of dry lips. "Your son doesn't know who you *really* are, Isaac. Not yet, anyway. His mind's a mess. Let's just hope he doesn't put all the pieces together."

"Right," came Isaac's solemn reply.

"You are a secret," the old vulture whispered over Arson's body. "But we're finding you out. And this is only the beginning. When you find your exit, we'll be waiting." He ran his fingers slowly down the center of Arson's chest as he ignored the groan of Morpheus efficiently working to decipher a coded mind.

"When will you have enough?" Isaac asked. "When will we be done with all of this? Sooner or later—if he's capable of what Krane is talking about—he'll learn who I am."

"Are you worried? Take heart. His body, his blood, his mind… it will, like his predecessor, Adam, play its part. When we start over, our new world order won't remember the small sacrifices we made to ensure our future. All that will matter is that we played our part. They're pawns, Isaac, just pawns, remember?"

"Yes, sir," he answered.

"You knew the risks. You hired Lamont to catch for us this little lamb. But do not be troubled. After all, you're a patriot. A fool at times, but nonetheless, you will be taken care of."

Isaac nodded.

Hoven was ice. Turning to Lamont and to Krane, he said, "Bring the others back. Use force if necessary. Just, for the love of St. Peter, don't kill them. They belong to me."

They understood.

"Make no mistake, gentlemen, this is a war."

Lamont toyed with the gun at his side. With a hoarse whisper he said, "We'll bring 'em back, sir."

Hoven circled around Isaac. "Keep the faith. It's too late to turn back now. Much too late."

CHAPTER TWENTY-FIVE

A CURSE EXPLODED FROM EMANUEL KRANE'S THROAT. HE stared down at the tiny red puddles collecting in the bathroom sink. With a grunt, he dabbed his face with water, letting the cold slip inside his tired skin.

"Give it some time. The sting goes away after a bit," Lamont said, his voice scratchy from screaming orders at security for the last fifteen minutes.

"Time is always against us."

Lamont shrugged, enjoying Krane's agony. "That puny punk's got some kick to him, don't he?" Lamont eyed his reflection. A dark-purple line crept down past his half-shut eyelid. He chuckled, forcing the cartilage in his nose back in place. "The girls will appreciate the battle scar."

"Stay focused."

"Look, I sold it in there, all right. I played along nice, like we agreed. If you ask me, Hoven's gonna find a new place in hell to stick you once he finds out what's really going on."

Krane turned to Lamont. "He won't."

"Whatever you say, Doc. Your neck is on the line this time, not mine. But it's pretty stupid to let one of them escape like that."

"Finding Adam was never the issue," Krane said, hating every second of the pain. "I want-wanted him to escape. To ensure m-me that everything's working as it should. Adam is special. Without him, we'd be lost. It's because of him that we are here."

Lamont froze for a moment, chilling Krane with beady eyes. "And you let him get away."

"Quite right. I *let* him get away. He's being track-tracked as we speak. Saul Hoven merely doubts our ability to return him. Finding him, that's no challenge. Br-bring-bringing him back may be. His powers will return soon, so we must be vigilant and act quickly."

"I guess I just underestimated the little mutant freak."

"Adam is no freak," Krane replied, his jaw crunching. "Adam is special."

"Yada-yada. You think all of them are special. Scarface hasn't exactly given us much of anything. Great body, though. So young, so fresh. Man, high school was a trip." Lamont's eyes glowed with lust.

"You're a sick, blind fool. You've seen the powers of one with your own eyes."

"Well, I'm not really sure what I've seen no more. Bein' cooped up in this nuthouse these last few months makes me question if I'm still me. Shoot, I'm becoming more and more like you whack-jobs. This hole messes with my head."

Krane's wrist trembled. A bone splintered inside his hand and he struggled to hold back tears of anguish.

"Easy, Doc. It's just one little job, right?" Lamont snickered, applying a band-aid to the scar on his face, ignoring the dry blood.

"Saul Hoven is a menace, you know that, d-d-don't you?"

Careful, Emanuel. Tread softly. Hoven is the lord of this arena. Don't allow your doubts and your sentiments to ruin your position in all of this.

"He has his moments, I s'pose," Lamont agreed.

Krane's jaw shifted. With a slanted gaze, he eyed Lamont from the vanity mirror. "That menace doesn't have any notion of real power. A vulture is only as strong or as int-intelligent as his weakest, underestimated prey."

"So which one are you, Doc, the vulture or the prey?"

A cold silence split the air, and Lamont stepped back, rigid.

"Adam is The Source. He is precious to me. And we're going to bring him back."

Lamont grinned.

"Adam be-belongs with me." Krane tended to his wounds. "Hoven doesn't understand it the way I do. But a dog of war l-like-like you should be able to understand keeping things close to the chest."

"Yeah, well, seems like everyone's trying to run their own circus show, and I'm stuck riding backseat in all this chaos." Lamont got close enough for Krane to pick up the stench of tobacco escaping from his cesspool of a mouth.

"What is the mission worth to you?"

"Keep your coin. I'll do this one for free," Lamont said. "Already gave Hoven my word."

Krane's lids were grey splinters.

Leaning over the sink, Lamont spit a string of brown slime down the drain.

"Such a filthy habit."

"Vices, mmm, we all got 'em." Lamont rubbed his fresh bruise. "You plan on letting Carra…I mean, Issac in on your little operation?"

"This doesn't concern the arson. Besides, that freshman thinks he's ready to play in my realm, but he's not equipped to handle what's coming."

Lamont paused a moment. "You know, Hoven thought Isaac

was getting too close. Startin' to wonder if it's you we should be worried about."

Spit.

"You're not my keeper, Jeb."

"Easy, Krane. I'm not judgin'. You know as well as I do that this messed-up world wasn't built for peace. It's chaos, and I thrive on it." Lamont winced slightly at the purple bruise and furrowed a brow. "Adam ain't gonna go quietly, especially now that he's got Scarface with him."

Krane nodded, understanding that there would be blood, there would be violence, and there would be loss. But such things in times of war were inevitable.

Seconds passed, and Lamont let himself out, abandoning Krane to the dim lights of the bathroom for the moment. The sinister reflection got lost inside the glass. He wished Henry Parker were here. But he wasn't. It was up to him to claim his rightful place. This was how the story would end, not in peace, but in violence—a war with new weapons and a new order of beings.

Emanuel Krane, worn and sick with fatigue, dragged his body closer to the door at length. Soon he'd disappear inside some hallway. The purpose and potential of a turbulent future were now clearer than ever before. He was closer. They all were. There was no return. There was no undoing.

It was coming.

All that remained would be tears and bloodshed.

"Cry havoc and let slip the dogs of war," Krane murmured.

"Hello?" he screamed. "Hello!" It got louder each time. But nobody ever came.

Arson wasn't sure how long he'd been calling out or how long he'd been walking down this narrow school hallway, but it was getting old. This was too real.

Time slipped by, or maybe wasn't there at all.

Arson swallowed. His spit was a cold slide down his throat. Goosebumps raced up his forearm. His body became a living, breathing block of ice. He panted. He blinked.

Alone.

Hello?

Alone.

The t-shirt was tight against his chest, almost like it didn't fit. Hair sank weakly in front of his eyes, the grease from each loose and curly strand sliding inside determined facial creases. He coughed, and it felt like a chisel hacking away his insides.

A flash of light blurred at the end of the hall. Lockers. Images reached and called out to him from within the twisted metal cages, and suddenly it wasn't quiet anymore. The sounds erupted like distorted, tortured laughter. He recalled the bad homework piled on top of hatred and never fitting in. This place was a world of rejection. Would he ever escape it?

After shifting left, he stopped, frozen. Panic held him there with impunity. He stared into a stained, grungy locker. In there was a little girl with hair covering most of her face, head tilted low. She was breathing heavily. Arson waited for her to speak, the silence baiting him. Pity lingered inside. Then remorse. The hardest to endure was the fear.

Regret stung like acid in his lungs. The girl wore ripped jeans, dripping with dirt and black water. Messy, ruined hair covered the lost eyes that glowed like ashen lamps. Her black shirt and the fading flame bleached into its center seemed to shoot out from her small frame. Was it coming for him, trying to kill him?

"What do you want!" he screamed. "Who are you?"

The locker cage swung back and forth, its unsure creak enough to turn his bones into splinters. He took a step back, but the girl's tarnished face tilted and changed. He could barely identify those dark lamps; they wanted his soul. She was still and eerily pensive, her tiny hands drawn to tiny sides, where bent fingers carefully made him their target. Though her lips didn't stutter, he felt like she was saying something to him. It was a sentence of blame and judgment.

Spiders crept around her feet, their spiny legs moving all around her as they spun tormenting red webs over her. Once he stopped the shivers and could focus, Arson caught a glimpse of her scarred hands, burned to the bone, the nail crusted with blood. Slowly, the girl's neck dragged her head from side to side, and the angry hum of lament and understanding came at Arson like a flood.

It was dark. It was light. It was cold. It was his fault. For everything.

He blinked and shuddered. "Sooner or later…"

What did you do, Arson? He heard her mind speak while lips stood still. *What…did* you *do to me?* And then her thoughts became daggers. *What did you do to us?* In that moment, he wondered if this girl's identity had become someone else. "Emery?"

The girl's head silently shook no, but as she did her face became a mask. The image faded in and out, reversed then came back. It happened over and over, and he turned away but was drawn back again. The mask came closer.

In his hand was a lit firecracker. When it exploded, his grip turned hot and birthed a flame. He stared back at this frightening image. The way the mask seemed to choke the girl's face and throat, like stretched fingers bending around broken skin. Her hair and flesh were singed, but those eyes never wandered from his.

"Emery, I can save you. I love you. I'm sorry!"

Once more, her head dragged from side to side.

The white mask. It was an empty, lifeless thing.

A scream shot out from within the locker. All of a sudden, the tarnished white mask melted off. The girl's shirt tore from her body. All of her clothes burned, exposing the marks on her skin.

Arson was heartbroken and afraid. It wasn't the fear of being harmed, but the fear of *doing* harm. The murderer that lay dormant inside him. The pain he knew could consume as a result of his lack of restraint and good judgment.

"Beauty to ashes." Arson could see his breath as the metal cage slammed shut.

CHAPTER TWENTY-SIX

EMERY'S HAND REACHED FOR ADAM. THEY'D BEEN DRIVING for a few hours. The strange quiet mixed with bad classic rock forced her to squirm. She wanted out of these clothes. She wanted out of this cramped space. She wanted a hot shower, wanted someone to hold her, for real, and tell her it'd be all right, that she'd make it out of this thing.

Bruce reached for the gearshift and stroked the inside of Emery's thigh. She wasn't sure if it was accidental or on purpose. She cringed nonetheless, closing her knees as awkward thoughts raced within her. How long until they reached Bethpage? What did Adam expect to find there? She still didn't have a clue why she trusted him, only that he'd gotten her out. But the uncertainty ahead was still bothering her.

"Are you all right?" Adam asked.

She stared back in aggravated silence.

"Don't worry. I'll take care of you."

That was close, but it still wasn't enough.

"No need for you kids to whisper," Bruce said, showing off his toothy grin. "We're all friends here."

There was something off about him.

Adam swallowed hard, clearly trying to keep his cool. "So how long have you been driving big rigs?"

"Ahh, heck, ask me a real question, kid," Bruce replied. Once the quiet had its play, he continued, "About eighteen and a half years, I guess, give or take some months. It's a weak job, but the pay ain't too bad for the work, and there's a few other added perks." His wink insinuated something indiscreet.

"One-night stands…charming," Emery sighed under her breath.

"Plus meeting roadies like you gives me a reason not to drive this big rig into a sycamore at seventy-five just outta pure boredom." His eyes panned the cab space. "Rather interesting, though, don't ya think?"

"What?"

"My coming along right as you and the hostile one—" Bruce sent another playful wink her way, "—are storming outta the gates of hell. You'd think you were abducted or somethin'."

Emery squeezed Adam's hand. Her pores thickened with sweat, and the lingering seconds were several lifetimes. Her cheeks and neck itched.

"Relax," Adam whispered. "He doesn't know anything. You're safe."

"Easy for you to say. He isn't groping your thigh like a horny sophomore."

"Just…relax," Adam said.

"Now, *friends*," Bruce started with a groan, "you're making me feel all left out."

"Oh, it's nothing," Adam replied, sticking his head out to get a good look at the stranger. "She was just telling me one of her friends lived off that last exit back there. It's been years since they've seen each other."

A nod. "Oh, want me to drop you off there?"

"No, no," Emery said firmly. "It's all right. My buddy here just doesn't know when to keep his mouth shut."

"You sound ticked off."

"She's fine," Adam said.

My hero, Emery thought mockingly.

"No worries. Just trying to be friendly."

A little too friendly, she thought.

"So, got any kids?" Adam said. He was bad at small talk.

"Two. A daughter that won't talk to me and a son that hates my guts. Oh, and an ex-wife that'd relish any opportunity to eat my heart out with a spoon. Yeah, I got me some family."

Their faces shifted from nervous to disturbed.

"Rough."

"Yup, well, they caught me well and good…in bed with their aunt. Mommy and the kids didn't respond too fondly to the family reunion, let's just leave it right there."

"Got any regrets?" Adam asked.

"Do I got regrets?" Bruce slurred. "Some, but that isn't one of them. Shoot, I was gone to them before the rendezvous with ol' Aunty. Good riddance. Geez, you two stink like a crapshoot. Should we stop and get you cleaned up? I'm no Betty homemaker, but you two are filthy as a mother." His nostrils flared as he distracted his mind from the smell with more idle chatter. "You know something, kid. Every Tom, Dick, and Harry's got their thing. Infidelity was mine. Doesn't make that tramp any better than me. I mean, let me tell ya, she had her issues, same as the rest."

Emery sank into herself. Her mind wandered to thoughts of her parents. How her mom had done *to her* what this peculiar trucker had done to his family. It wasn't right. It was sick. Her stomach flipped, and she felt the crunch in her nose as the grungy stranger carried on.

"I loved their mother, and I loved them good, cross my heart."
He took a moment. "But I guess I just loved myself more." That
toothy, stained grin of his came out of hiding a second time.

Emery snarled.

"Suppose they'd be about your age. Haven't called 'em in a
while, you know. Last I heard, my daughter was afraid she'd been
knocked up by some reckless card player and Zach was busted
for possession of marijuana. A lot of marijuana."

Emery wasn't sure if this guy wanted sympathy or an award for
Best Deadbeat Dad. It was alarming how dysfunctional parents,
families, everybody could be. There was no normal anymore.
There just wasn't any room for normal. Dysfunctional was the
new normal. Heartache was the normal. Separation. Lies. The
more she sat and listened, the more she wanted him to shut up.
She found herself wishing they'd never jumped out in front of
this truck, never asked for a ride.

"You know, no matter whatcha do, history's destined to repeat
itself." He popped open a can of beer. Suds spilled onto his crotch
and dripped down the bucket seat, but he ignored it. The conversation, it seemed, had gotten the best of him.

Adam and Emery shared a concerned stare.

Bruce's eyes moved over Emery. She was starting to panic.
No way this was safe, or even legal, for that matter. She wanted
to get out. She blinked. With his free hand, Bruce brushed her
hair away from her face. Adam flinched but did nothing.

It felt like spiders were dancing along her sickly face.

"Kayley, my baby, she even looks kinda like you, come to
think of it. Real pretty face, you know, without all the sexy scars."

I want my mask. I want my freakin' mask. I want Arson.

Emery chewed her bottom lip. Anger tugged at her eyes and
pulsed in her forehead. "I want my mask," she finally said.

"Ha-ha, what?" Bruce cackled.

"I said I want my mask, you sick slob."

"Emery, take it easy. We're getting closer."

"Not close enough. This pig is making me nauseous."

"Now, now, pretty bitty, what's got you all worked up?" There was something sick in his smile, something twisted in the way Bruce spoke. Stiff hairs covering the lower half of his face started to move when his hot breath blew out. His flashing eyes were violent, black needles.

"Nothing, I'm just fine," Emery said with gritted teeth, nudging up against Adam.

"C'mon, freakshow, I won't bite…I'll only nibble."

"Bruce, lay off the beer. And leave her alone. You're making her uncomfortable," Adam ordered.

Bruce burped. "Maybe you should shut your trap when I'm talking to the little lady." His palm pushed a strand of filthy hair behind her ear.

The seconds between his words and his touch were horrifying. No one had touched her since Arson. And she didn't want anyone to. She despised the thought. Why didn't Adam just take care of it?

"Don't touch me, you creep. I'm not one of your messed-up kids you can feel up and use. Now leave me alone."

Bruce got ugly and took his focus off the road. Beer suds coated his toothy, blonde smile. Before the next blink, he swung at Emery, his knuckles slicing her cheek open as if his hand were a blade.

She screamed.

Bruce took another swing, his can of beer slipping from his grip and spilling onto the floor mats. The stench of beer filled the cab. With a curse, he tore at her with his fingernails. The dirty claws were like rusty nails.

A shower of panic washed over them with the screech of slick tires sliding across the interstate. They doubled over, Adam's temple crashing against the dash. His stare jumped from the road ahead to Bruce's tormented composure and back to the road again. The truck was a wild beast on wet, black silk. Other eighteen-wheelers steered clear of the scene, speeding off into the mist.

"Let us out. Let us out now!" Adam ordered.

How much longer? Emery wondered. *God, how much longer?* She felt filthier. She felt rage, filled with panic and a longing for someplace safe. A place removed from the nightmare of these last… *how long had it been?* She wanted to escape, from that facility, from this trucker. From all of it. *Get me out,* she thought, about ready to cry. *Just get me out.*

Adam suddenly jerked Emery's body forward, accidentally shoving her chest into the gear shift, and with a quick thrust he jammed the heel of his hand into Bruce's beet-red mug. The trucker's jaw broke and seemed to hang limply in the air, part of the bone jutting out of baggy, stubbly skin.

Nearly shredding to pieces from the pain, Bruce cut the wheel to the right hard. The road divots shot vibrations up their seats as the truck slid toward the breakdown lane.

"Got a pair of brass balls on you, don't ya, kid?"

Adam didn't flinch. Instead, he struck the driver a second time and Bruce's head quickly turned the driver's side window into a spider web of cracked glass. As he beat the hound, Adam kept yelling "Prove it? Prove it! Prove it!" It was as if his mind had gone to a different place. A place of hurt and confusion and unbridled rage. Curses spilled like blood.

Emery glanced up from her huddled position and saw Adam's eyes flash. He was like an animal finally free from its cage. "Arson." She didn't mean for it to come out, even if it was breathed to life in the form of such a faint whisper.

"I'm not a monster… You hurt her! Never again. I'll kill you… It's okay, just don't tell mom and dad. It's okay. I wanna be strong… like you."

Another blow. Another grunt. Harsh cracking sounds Emery didn't like but was starting to get used to. She'd seen this warrior, but in this moment he had enlisted in a new war with an unclear enemy. Where was Adam exactly? What was causing him to act this way? And why did he sound so weird? She was thankful for his defense, but somehow she couldn't escape the possible notion that he was fighting for someone else.

"Don't you ever touch her again!"

Emery sat still and witnessed Adam grabbing Bruce by the throat. With one squeeze, his dirty fingernails bit into the trucker's hairy gullet, and drips of red suddenly burned black.

"Adam!" she screamed as the truck spun toward a ditch. He twisted the wheel in a frantic fight to gain control again, but the truck jackknifed and then crashed, its wheels a slippery mess and the three of them thrown over one another's bodies. The driver's window exploded, and glass showered over them, cutting up their arms. Then the truck ripped off the road and tore through a wall of soaked trees. Emery's head swam.

The color faded from Adam's skin. He fought for breaths. "Are…you…k, Lana? You o—…won't let them hurt you. I won't let him hurt you."

He faded completely.

She was still shaking. She couldn't stop. Bruce wasn't moving. Adam wasn't moving, but she knew *he* was still alive. How long before Adam woke up, and was she still safe with him?

She wanted to scream, but her lungs wouldn't give. The pain was a hornet's sting. Her body swelled and ached. The rain bled on her face, cold, as she whispered Arson's name again.

CHAPTER TWENTY-SEVEN

THE EARTH FELT LIKE IT WAS SHIFTING BENEATH HIS FEET.
Mud glossed the lower edges of his sneakers, which hadn't properly worn in the way he liked them to just yet. They were a birthday present from his baby sister. Lana never forgot. She'd gone off to ride the Ferris wheel, but he stayed behind. Adam didn't much care for heights. "I'll meet up with you after," he'd said.

A brisk wind tossed his hair. It was a perfect night for the carnival. He loved their bright lights and colors and sounds. He loved the loudness of the crowds. He enjoyed the uncertain weather and the grungy-looking carnies. This place made him feel normal.

Adam was sure his sleeves were hiked up so he wouldn't get too hot. One thing about Mom was that she always saw to it that he was warm. But she didn't really understand how his body worked. No one did but Lana.

Sometimes he was warm; other times he was cold. His body changed like the weather changed. No rhyme or reason; it just changed. It was challenging, near impossible, to make it stop or slow down. But he'd survived these last few years with it. Wasn't sure how long the changes would last, but in some ways he was grateful for them. It wasn't a normal, everyday occurrence that allowed a sixteen-year-old boy to taste real power.

And tonight, he'd show *them* what that meant.

Adam pulled his sweatshirt hood over his head and felt his two bony shoulder blades sink. The material fitted nicely around his small back. He swore his muscles were growing too, even though there wasn't any actual evidence to support his theory. Tiny hands, dwarfed by the extra cloth of the sweatshirt, absorbed most of the night's chill. His spine snaked as he walked, shaking off the persistent cool breeze as best he could. Beneath it all, he was wearing his favorite shirt, the shirt of the phoenix rising up out of the ashes. Its colors—black and orange and red and white—were much like the colors of this carnival, the one that rolled into Bethpage every October.

Adam looked to his right. He saw a father cradling his son, who was trying to devour an entire caramel apple on his own. There was such love there, a joy he liked to see but didn't really believe in. His eyes moved to the left, and there was a group of friends playing with a hacky sack, betting on who'd drop it first. Some bent the rules to slant the odds in their favor while others swore at the ones shouting do-over. Kids were funny.

Straight ahead there were cattle races and sports car auctions. He could hear men hollering out in anticipation. Then he listened for their wives, the sounds of disapproval and even worry pouring out of their voices.

Where is it? *Where are* they?

Adam hoped that wherever Lana was, she wouldn't see or hear. Upon their arrival, Lana asked that he make a promise to her, a promise that he wouldn't do anything *supernatural*; that he wouldn't react to the taunts or the rants of the boys and the girls who, just one week earlier, had given her belly bruises she refused to show Mom and Dad.

"I promise," he'd said, easy enough. She believed him too. He could see her faith in her eyes, those heartwarming, pretty eyes that found some sort of redemption in every human being. She hadn't become calloused or distorted, like him—not yet. There wasn't an ounce of hatred inside her. Adam didn't understand how a girl who'd been treated so harshly could find enough compassion to offer it freely to those who didn't deserve it.

Children of ruin, that's what he called them. That's what Mom called them too. Dad was too busy to deal with it, the spears of ridicule, the taunts Adam had told him about time and time again. Too busy. Too concerned with better things. His children weren't a priority. "You'll be okay, son," he was assured. "And your sister will be okay." But what was okay?

Adam scanned the crowds, the food cabins, the game stations, and each and every sly vendor eager to make a buck off naïve adolescents. He studied their eyes, their hands, their mouths. He moved from person to person, looking for his sister's tormentors. He knew they were here. He'd find them.

The smell of cooked sandwiches and cold sodas filled his senses. He'd polished off a hot dog minutes earlier. Didn't have a whole lot of money and Lana wanted to go on rides, so that didn't leave much to spare.

About twenty feet away there was a group of high school kids. He finally found the ones he was looking for. The one he assumed was their fearless leader had just torn open a pack of smokes. Adam saw the flicker of light that consumed the tip. The boy inhaled a breath of smoke as his face violently sized Adam up, the creepy way it always did. Seconds later, the entire group turned to look at him.

"Hey, check it out," he keenly heard the smoker say. His name was Derek or Devin or something like that. "Look who came out. Hey, freakwad, what do you think you're looking at?"

He hated when they called him *freakwad*. Adam just stood there, his eyes focused on the cigarette, the smoke, this douche bag's greasy hair.

He blinked, and the kid started choking. The more he tried to breathe, the scarcer oxygen became. The wind circled the group, but still he couldn't breathe because Adam had constricted the kid's throat from a distance.

Adam blinked again, and the kid was allowed to breathe. He watched the smoke slip out through the holes in that tormented body. Like a retreating viper. After his enemy got up from his knees, he saw the smirk on Adam's mouth and gave him the finger. No words. The cigarette had burned the smug leader's hand, but he didn't have a clue what had just happened to him, and no one would be able to explain it.

"Let's lose the freakwad, huh?" one of them whispered.

"Yeah, I'd like to lose him for good. Look at him smiling as I'm choking. Little puke. I oughta rip him apart."

"Let's lose these tickets first, baby," the kid's girlfriend said, rubbing his chest. "Then you can have your fun. I wanna ride the Ring of Fire."

She noticed Adam out of the corner of her eye, it seemed. And she blew a dark-lipped kiss toward him. Not inviting but mocking. Her wrists were tattooed, and an ear full of piercings often left Adam slightly uneasy. The crowd walked around him and his enemies, but Adam stayed where he was. He was completely in his element, connected to the force within his body. It rushed and spread. He breathed in. Exhaled. Breathed in. Exhaled. The people scattered. The group moved.

Then he moved finally. He was hidden enough. The starless sky hung over them. A few city lamps glided upward nearly fifteen feet and provided the carnival space with a golden, artificial glow. The night fell colder. He could see his breath as it escaped tired lungs and reentered. His teeth clenched. His fists were almost bleeding. Something was awakened in him.

And he liked it. It was time to pay them back.

Out of nowhere, a gloved hand reached out and grabbed him. Pulled him close. "Are you two kinds of crazy, boy?"

Adam was rigid, uncertain how to respond. Who was this stranger?

"I've seen that kind of look in a boy's eyes before. I'd get on outta here if I was you. They'll peel the flesh right off your skinny bones if they get the chance."

"That's not going to happen, not to me." Adam shook free of the man's grip. He defiantly turned to find the group he was after. "They will pay."

"Puny thing like you. You're either crazy or stupid."

"I'm special. I'm different." Adam clenched his teeth together, and the man's wrist snapped. A curse flooded out of the carnie's throat.

With every step closer, Adam began to savor the excitement of what was to come. He didn't really know how to control all of it, whatever dark message was inscribed on his blood or in his head, but whenever he thought something strong enough or felt something powerful enough, it happened. It was like a voice haunting him from within, something he was called to.

The group's sick leader sat in the ride first, along with his girlfriend, who clung to his waist like some needy pet. They were making out before the ride director even closed down the lock to their seat. The remainder of their small clan sat behind them, loaded in nice and tight. They were eager to take a spin on the Ring of Fire.

The breeze tickled Adam's eyes as he looked up, hands in his pockets, sweatshirt pulled open. He briefly glanced down at the fierce bird etched into his t-shirt. So fearless and alive. He felt known by it and accepted. Then his eyes returned to the ride, how it glowed and sparkled in all its strangeness and attempted uniqueness. His jaw slackened, and just then, one of the screws to the ride twisted slightly out. With a twitch, another.

The ride director stepped back after assuring every rider was locked in. Unable to move. The leader of the group mouthed a string of curses at Adam. A few more bolts and screws came loose at that precise moment, flinging hotly out into the grass. Adam was controlling it. The careless crowd was an easy audience.

Deep breath.

Are you sure about this, Adam?

Yes.

You can't take it back.

I don't care. I have to fix it all. I have to change this world. One. Sick. Scum. At a time.

Without warning, the ride began. The next thing Adam knew, he had caused the metal shoes on the carts to spark. With his next breath, the lights sitting upon the plastic and the sheet metal boiled to a loud pop. A few teenagers waiting in line jumped at the noise of what sounded like a gunshot.

He was shaking. He was afraid. The memory of them punching Lana in the chest, in the belly, stormed his mind. How they hit her to cause him to react. How she screamed, praying he wouldn't. He remembered most how he just stood there watching it all take place. Like a god who didn't care. Able yet unwilling to unleash *it*.

But tonight was different.

The insides of his ears sounded like waves crashing. All of this took no more than ten seconds, but this hurricane came so violently and so strong, it was as if time had ceased to exist. Suddenly, he lost his nerve. Suddenly, he felt unstable.

Never turning back.

But I have to. What if I die?

Can't turn back.

His eyes burned to a hot black. The eyelashes seemed as though they would disintegrate and smelled like something burnt. People swarmed. Their voices climbed high into heaven. A stream of smoke slithered out from Adam's nostrils and open mouth.

This wasn't a game, or anything like it. It was revenge. It was...justice. Silently, the huge, hollow disc was consumed in flames. The fire crawled from chrome piece to jagged edge, the screws and bolts and metal washers melting and popping as the cart, which held the group of tormentors trapped inside, flipped upside down. Their screams of horror descended, and their eyes even met Adam's for a brief skip in time before the tail of the cart was dragged backward. It rapidly spiraled off the magnetic track. Splashes of blood decorated the lawn.

Terrified screams consumed the night. People from far away froze to watch the fire advance. In seconds, the flames had devoured most of the ride. Glass from the shattering light bulbs showered down over they who now longed to escape. Anyone too close to the Ring of Fire fainted from the heat. Dread danced through the swarm of bodies.

Flakes of ash slowly fell to his feet. The huge, hollow disc cracked at the apex and dropped with a violent noise and returned to the earth, disintegrated. Adam lost motive. Conscience abandoned. But of all the things in the world, sorrow never came once. The bodies of those who'd ridiculed his sister, who harmed him with their wicked actions and corrupt hearts, were buried underneath the metallic remains. They were gone.

The crashing waves ceased for a moment. He recognized a voice in the chaos. Unmistakable. So precious it was almost painful to hear.

"Adam!" the voice shouted. "Adam!" it shouted again. But he could not find her face. He knew whom it belonged to, but where was she?

"Adam!" It was Lana. Sweet, precious Lana. Where had she come from? How did she find him? What had she seen?

A black cloud rose above the lost ashes of the ride's disintegrated frame. The flames, upon her arrival, were sucked back into the cold October wind and removed from the carnival, from her. Adam scraped the soot that had dried on his cheeks like tears.

Lana's eyes found his. "You promised me," she said, crying. "You promised."

CHAPTER TWENTY-EIGHT

SUDDENLY, LANA WAS RIPPED AWAY FROM HIM. SOMETHING was pulling him out of the carnival, out of the past. Sirens. Thick drops of rain spilled onto his face.

"Adam! Wake up. Adam!"

"I promised...I...promised," he said weakly. He breathed in the night, the smell of Emery's skin. Her touch was smooth on his chest. His lips split, chapped. His throat was dry, and his eyes wouldn't stop spinning.

"Wake up! Adam!" It wasn't Lana. Emery's voice called him out from the dream, brought him back here, where he had to stay. He had to get up. There wasn't much time. The sirens came closer. Closer.

His face felt torn open, cut, bruised, but he didn't have a scratch on him. "I swear your face smacked against the windshield," Emery said, doubling over. "You had cuts. Where did they go?"

"They don't all stay. C'mon, Emery," he replied slowly. "I have to get you outta here." He stood up then fell back over.

"Easy, Adam. Your body's still in shock."

He groaned. "There's no time for it to be in shock. We can't linger here too long." He took her hand, and pulled himself up.

The sirens in the distance vibrated the air. Emery shook slightly, but there was a hairy knuckle digging into her belly-button. The hair from Bruce's hand tickled her in a way so vile she couldn't put words to it.

"Adam," she breathed out slowly. "Adam. What happened?"

"I made them stop."

"What?" she said, confused. "What are you talking about?"

"Huh?" he returned, the faces of Emery and Lana fading in and out. "Whoa. I hit him. I hit him, Emery. He's not waking up." Adam's voice sounded calm, but when he caught a glimpse of her in considerable pain, he seemed regretful. "No."

She quickly shot a glance over at Bruce's throat. Unnatural stains like tar and black blood created a gruesome scar.

Adam kept searching for a pulse, but his efforts were more for her than him. Bruce had already gone cold, and Adam didn't want to fix it. It was better this way. It was good to keep this villain silent. Better off dead. His forehead had an open gash crusted red, and one of his teeth was jammed into the steering wheel.

"He's gone. How long was I…?" Adam said.

"I don't know…three minutes, maybe," she quickly replied.

"It felt like so much longer. Emery, we need to disappear, and fast. Someone's gonna call the wrong people, and they're gonna want to take us back. I'm not going back."

Adam shoved Bruce's grizzly wrist off Emery's abdomen and reached inside the man's pant pockets. In a few moments, he emerged with a wallet and some cash.

Emery's convicting glance reminded him of Lana. He felt obligated to defend his theft. "We're fugitives. We need the cash, and this creep doesn't need it where he's going." His face was already soaked, the color of his skin scrubbed almost clean by the drips seeping in from the cracked windshield. Chips of rock scattered the hood of the Mack truck, one of the side lights gone completely and the other flickering like a summer lamp.

He shoved the money in his pocket, and went back to digging for anything else. He found a pack of smokes, a couple lottery tickets, a condom, and…

"A stiletto," Adam said. "Baby doesn't play well with others."

"A knife? What kind of trucker was this creep?"

Adam raised his brow and Emery didn't reply. She kicked Bruce once in the chest, propelling herself off the seat as soon as Adam had pried open the passenger door and slipped out. One last glance at the incisor sticking out of the steering wheel made her rethink how brutal his beating seemed moments earlier. But the pity for such a low-life pig was gone almost completely.

"Gross," she said under her breath as Adam dragged her by the armpits off the seat and into the mud. "I need a shower."

"Yeah." Adam shrugged.

"Ahh, my leg fell asleep." She winced, limping while the circulation and blood flow bloomed inside her calf muscle, her feet still aiming for balance.

"Well, they better wake up quick. It's a few miles left to Bethpage."

"Adam, why are we going there? What's in Bethpage?"

Adam was quiet. "The past. My home."

"Your home? What makes you think it's still intact? Not to mention, what if we get there and those maniacs are waiting for us?"

"What is this, Adam? I'm not in this for the thrills and the mystery and intrigue and all that crap, okay? I want to go back—"

"Where, Emery! Back home? Think again. Life as you once knew it is gone! They took you. You're a pariah, just like me."

"Yet you want to run back to your past?"

"We'll stay together," he said, ignoring her. "We're safer that way."

"Safe, sure we are."

"Stop it. Don't you see? They'll come find you. They'll always find you. Nowhere is safe."

"And Bethpage is?"

They started walking in silence.

"I have to try, Emery. I have to see it again, just once."

"You're not making any sense, Adam." The mud creeping up her ankles didn't sit well with her, but it was only a few hours ago that they were climbing through sewage.

"Save your breath and jog."

"Whatever, fearless leader."

"Emery. I'll protect you no matter what."

"Yeah, stellar job so far. Can you trust me too?"

He was frozen.

"Didn't think so. None of this is clearing right now. What you did in there, where we're going, that messed-up place we took off from. One big shipwreck, and I'm just drowning out in the middle of the sea. Alone."

"You're not alone, Emery."

"Says the boy with a million secrets."

"Sorry I let this happen to you," Adam tried.

She just nodded and began running with him. They quickly vanished into the night, the call of sirens and bright lights like violent raiders in pursuit.

"Bethpage," Adam panted. "We'll be there before dawn."

CHAPTER TWENTY-NINE

KYRO MOVED FROM THE MOTEL COUCH TO THE BED ABOUT four times before Joel told him to keep still. The boy held to the notion that he was just trying to get comfortable, but it was obvious he was anxious.

"I merely said you have to take me there," Joel said. "You're not going back there to rot."

"Yeah, but obviously something's not clickin' in that sophisticated brain o' yours. That place is evil."

"Kyro, I can't just leave her in there. I have to know. It's not a choice anymore. I *need* to know if my little girl's all right."

"Yeah, well, when you're first in line at the pearly gates, don't say nobody warned you."

"To be honest, I don't think I'm gonna make it there, kid."

"Please, whatchu done in your life that's so bad?"

Time skipped a beat. "I lost a church, lost my daughter. And my marriage is falling apart."

Kyro leaned up from the mattress. "So, what are you, like, a priest?"

"Sort of. I was. A minister. We're like priests, but we don't sing our sermons."

Kyro was amused. "I don't know if you're allowed to be makin' fun of your own kind, Preacher."

Joel fought back a tornado of grief in that brief second. He unzipped his bag and pulled out a Bible. Felt the leather in his hands. Stared at the gold-trimmed edges and marveled at the way some of the pages were falling out. "Can't believe this thing is still around," he said under his breath.

"Whaddaya mean? How old is that thing?"

"A lot older than you. One of my professors, someone who became a very dear friend of mine, gave it to me when I finished seminary. I was fresh outta school, didn't have a clue how to run God's business. I was still rusty on a bunch of the key verses too. Then I got this thing." He held the thick book tightly in his grip. "It changed my life."

"Yeah, so they say."

"That's not what I meant. I mean, it literally changed my life. This guy, this teacher of mine, he didn't seem like he believed in anybody or anything except the Good Book. One of those fire-and-brimstone dudes. *The whole world is goin' to hell* kinda guys."

"A real d-bag, huh?"

"Easy. But yes, I guess you could say that. When I graduated, here he is with this warm smile, ear to ear. I remember it all like it was yesterday. Man, it was hard to get my own family to believe in me. But this professor, he shakes my hand and looks at me like the fate of the world rests on my shoulders or something. A real deep look. And it's like there's this block of lead in my gut I can't take. I'm thinking the whole thing isn't real. How could he be proud of me? How could he show off a grin I'd never even seen before?

"He leans in real close and says to me, 'This thing changed my life; it'll change yours. It'll change the whole damn world.' It was the first time I'd heard him curse. When he handed me this beat-up book, it wasn't just a book anymore. He had it highlighted and underlined, stuff scratched into the margins. This was personal. It was special to him. He believed in what it meant, believed it had power to change people."

Kyro was hunched over, elbows on his knees, chin on his knuckles. "What do you believe?"

"I'm washed up, Kyro. I don't know what to believe anymore."

"Well, no wonder you lost that church, man. If I was God, I'da kicked you out too."

Joel held a look of shock and wonder. No one, other than Aimee, had hit him between the eyes like that. "God didn't kick me out. His *chosen ones* did."

"That's real pathetic, Cass. You're old. Whatcha gonna do now? Sulk? Cat like you don't got a whole lotta options. You gonna go snag a job at some convenience store? Yeah, that's doin' something for the world."

"A lot of those people have hope," Joel replied. "They're meant to be there."

"Yeah, but are you? If that's all you want to accomplish in your broke life, then keep feeling sorry for yourself. Keep being this weak loser. And that's what you'll stay."

"Who do you think you are, kid? I don't even know you."

"If you're smart, you'll listen to me this time. Shoot, I ain't a moron. I know when I see somebody that's got potential and they just blowin' it."

"Look in the mirror, Mr. four-point-oh GPA. Why aren't you at Yale doing something with your life?"

Kyro went blank. "Guess I never really thought about it. 'Til now."

Joel wrapped his knuckles around the black book's threadbare skin. His mind was on that platform, shaking hands with a senior professor. But so much was different now.

"You wanna know why you failed, man? 'Cause you wanted to."

Joel shot back a hard look of disdain. "You don't know what I've been through. Don't pretend to know what you're talking about."

"Looks like you've been livin' on everybody else's faith, man. You don't got any o' your own. I'm a street kid, but if it's one thing them streets learned me, it's that a punk that don't believe in somethin' ends up dying for nothin'. Why you got that cross on your neck, man? It ain't gonna save you. Don't mean a thing. None of this crap's gonna save you if you don't believe in it." A grin moved across his face. "Shoot, I'm feelin' a hallelujah or an amen…or somethin'. I'da schooled you in seminary."

Joel wanted to break down and laugh. He felt a spark in this young boy he hadn't seen in his congregation or even himself in so long. Unbiased, uncalculated honesty. The truth staring him in the face. Kyro, as dim as he seemed, had a light in him. A church and a street corner really were closer than they appeared.

"You're wrecked, Cass. You got pages comin' out your eyeballs, and you're fadin' and rusty. But you ain't dead yet. Drop all that trash you got in your head, man. Shoot, what's so bad that you can't let it go? That stuff'll catch ya quick, leave you for dead."

Joel's nose flared out. "I didn't just lose my daughter or my wife. I lost God. I'm nothing. I'm gone beyond repair."

"Abraham used to say that's devil talk. He wasn't all damnation neither; he was a half-full kinda brotha. Before the end, he talked about heaven and angels and stuff, but I didn't listen. Too busy…doing my own thing. Sometimes you're so close, but you miss it."

"It's not our job to save the world, Kyro. We can't make anyone believe."

"You're right, so let's just quit. There is no hope, no heaven, no hell. Just you and me on this wild suicide mission. Look, dude, unlike you, I was always a skeptic. I never really took any of that angel-fairy-God stuff past Sunday mass. But you, you had something. It's in there someplace. You know it is. I think you just needed somebody else to believe it was there." Kyro untied his shoelaces and flung his sneakers across the room. They hit the door as he leaned back on the mattress, hands behind his head. "Man, oh, man, cats like you are so desperate for attention." A gasp. "White people."

Joel flipped open the Bible.

Kyro reached beneath a pillow and pulled out an issue of *Maxim*.

"Where'd you get that?"

"Your backseat. What's a priest doing with skin mags anyhow?"

"I'm not a priest."

"Whatever, man. You got good taste, though." Kyro studied each individual page at length before turning to the next. "Mama got curves."

"Give me that. What are you doing?" Joel said, snatching the magazine.

"I could ask you the same question. A religious, *married* dude like you shouldn't have such, oooo, naughty stuff. I'm just glad the pages weren't stuck together."

"Easy, kid. And I don't want you going through my stuff again."

"Yes, massa, no sweat. So sorry, I am, massa." Kyro quipped, no doubt thinking himself witty. Less than a minute later, there was a knock on the door. "Hide this," Joel said, tossing Kyro the magazine.

"Thought I wasn't supposed to touch your stuff," the boy returned.

In a panic, Joel snatched it back from Kyro and stuck it in the laptop case, and half-zipped it. When he opened the door, a slender woman with brilliantly crimson hair and a long brown jacket stood there to greet him. Her cool breath invaded the room first.

"Hello, Redd," he said, lengthening the pause between their stares. Her comely face was precisely what he needed to see. "It's cold out there, huh?"

"Yeah, like you wouldn't believe. So are we gonna stand around and talk about it, or are you gonna let me in?"

Joel smacked his forehead and welcomed her inside.

"Who's the kid?"

"This kid got a name, lady. It's Kyro," the boy said rather forcefully.

"Didn't mean to offend."

"No sweat. Just keep it real."

Redd and Joel exchanged mixed glances. "That's the only dialect he knows," he whispered.

"I can hear you two," Kyro chimed.

"So, Joel, tell me what you know," she began.

"Well, maybe you should go first," Joel offered. "You're the… professional."

She licked her lips and dropped her suitcase on the bed opposite Kyro. He raised an eyebrow but didn't say anything. "My contacts here in the states haven't really found much of anything. I expected we might run into snags along the way, but the landscape is bleaker than I hoped. One thing you might want to prepare yourself for, Mr. Phoenix, is that your daughter may not be here."

"Here?"

"In the States. I've spoken to a lot of people, a ton of agencies, and some high-ups in government. Things like this happen. I think, given your scenario, your circumstance, we might have to spread out past our own borders."

"What, like, Vietnam?" Kyro exclaimed.

Both of the adults kept talking as if he'd not said a word. Joel sat down, his body heavy on the sinking mattress. The springs whined every time he moved.

"It's a harsh reality, to say the least, I know. But it's one that, at this point, we really need to accept," Redd said. "There's a reason the agencies you hired before me stopped. The rest of the world's a whole different animal. Those pansies probably never wanted to get their hands dirty. Jurisdiction and foreign policy and all, it gets real complicated, real fast."

"You've dealt with a situation like this before?" Joel asked.

"But why would somebody want to take his daughter out of the States, lady?" Kyro added before Redd could answer.

Redd dropped her hands to her hips, shifted her jaw slightly, and responded, "The farther she is away from home, the easier it is for her to stay lost. There are sick, sick men all around the world in disgusting trades. Sex sells to the highest bidder. It's filthy."

"And you think that's what happened to Emery, huh?" Kyro said, his voice stiff with unbelief. "What do you believe, Casper?"

Joel wanted quiet in the room. He had to think. Redd had decided to meet him here, in some dilapidated motel, to discuss a new lead he'd encountered because of Kyro, yet she was now thrusting an entirely new theory toward him, and he wasn't ready for it. He knew what Kyro had told him, and he hoped that was the truth.

"I think I know where Emery is." Joel said it with near defiance. He didn't care what doubts had permeated through him these last few minutes since Redd's arrival. Her reality was that his Emery might now be traveling as excess cargo in some filthy, foreign sex trade. But here and now, he was compelled to make a choice, to decide which theory made more sense. Kyro was looking at him with the most honest face he'd seen in this town, and Joel could not ignore the reality warring within him. The reality that he had to believe that what this boy was selling was the truth, albeit an unsure one.

"I think Casper means *we*," Kyro added.

"Casper. Cute," she said. "What basis are you two going on?"

"There's a facility called Salvation Asylum. Kyro said he was there as a patient. He knows it inside and out." Redd did not react. Joel didn't expect her to have heard about the facility; he never had. So he moved to the desk, where his laptop sat idle with an image of the enormous mental facility in plain view. He drew her attention toward the screen. "This is it."

Redd's eyes followed the cursor as it staggered across the screen. New images loaded and came to life before them. Pictures of doctor-patient sessions, a clean facility, and a pledge to keep safe and to protect "your closest family treasures."

"That last part's a bunch of horse crap," Kyro said. "Oh, they sell peace and warmth and happiness, but it ain't real. That place is evil, and it always stunk."

"*This* is where you think your daughter is, Joel?" Redd said, leaning in close. Her hand fell gently on his back, tickling his spine just by being there. Sympathy poured out of her. "I know you must want it to be true. I know you want to say you've finally cracked the case and found her, but this place…Emery isn't there."

"How do you know?" Joel replied.

"Because in my dealings, I have, once or twice, been there. Sometimes you get brought to strange places doing what I do. And they keep getting stranger with time. There was a firm that had some *unpleasant* experiences with them. Decided they wanted to file suit. My team was brought in, years ago, to investigate before pushing a procedure into full effect. Turns out it was just a cry wolf. Nothing. We searched that place high and low, interviewed just about every sane soul in the building. It is what it is. A mental institution, put there to help people. Emery wouldn't be there."

"Man, this broad's talking junk."

"Settle down, Kyro."

"This is whack, Cass. I was telling you the truth. Why would I make that stuff up? That place is real. Whatever you're lookin' at on that screen, *that's* the lie. Open your eyes."

"He seems pretty passionate about this," she said.

"I have no reason not to trust him."

"Really? And when did you two meet?"

Seconds of silence intimidated them. "Tonight."

Redd returned to a straight, stiff posture. "Where?"

"In Boston, some skate park off Boylston."

"The city? You picked up this juvenile delinquent—" Redd turned toward Kyro "—no offense—in the city at some *skate park*? Look at him, Joel. His socks don't even match; he's dressed like a homeless kid. Doesn't exactly scream, *Trust me.*"

"Cass, she don't know what she's talking about. I am who I am, lady. Take it or leave it."

Redd removed her smile as her eyes became two narrow slits. "I think I'll leave it. Stop wasting this poor man's time. I don't know what kind of game you're playing, kid, but it better stop. After everything he's been through, to toy with his life like this, it's demented."

"I ain't toying with nobody, *Redd*, whoever you are. You don't know the first thing about me, so screw you if you think you got me all figured out. I spent some time in that hellhole, okay? And it ain't what you think it is, and it definitely ain't what that computer says it is. I'm not crazy!"

"Talk about a living, breathing contradiction right there, eh, *Ky-ro*?" She said his name mockingly. "A boy who says he's been to a nuthouse claims he's not a nut. Who would've guessed?"

"Screw you! I did my time in there, and it messed me up. But I ain't lost it. I know the things I seen, things I heard. It's the truth. I don't give a rip if you don't believe me."

Kyro threw himself back on the mattress, tried to get comfortable. With his arms locked inside each other, he started breathing heavily. It was obvious he was hurt by Joel's mistrust and some detective's uncertified analysis of him.

Joel cracked his knuckles. "Is that necessary, kid?"

Kyro stewed in frustration. His breathing remained a thick, stifling addition to the already suffocating room.

"How old are we?" Redd asked him.

Kyro gave her the finger and rolled over.

"You're quite the snake charmer, aren't you?" Joel said to her.

"Yeah, well, I never got the award for delicate ice breaker, but I'm a straight shooter. You hired me for a reason, Joel. I think you should trust my judgment."

"Man, forget this. I'm outta here." Kyro found both his sneakers and put them on without tying the laces. "Good luck finding your girl, Casper," he added. The spite was enough to make Joel wish he'd at least defended the boy in front of Redd.

In seconds, Kyro was gone, but he left the door ajar, punching it as he walked out. Joel wished he'd called out his name or begged him to come back.

"I'm sorry if I crushed your soul a little bit, Joel. But I had to be square with you. Before I went off on my own with this agency, I worked for some big guns. We searched for needles in that haystack for several months, investigating, checking the books, the staff, room by room, whole nine yards. But we were lookin' for something that just wasn't there. I don't want us to waste any more time than we already have. If we keep running in the wrong directions, we allow more opportunities for Emery to slip right through our fingers. That's not what you want, is it?"

He shook his head. Confusion and apprehension blended within him. Joel wanted to hold Emery in his arms and feel her warm skin as they embraced again. Still, however strange, a part of him held onto Kyro's story. He wasn't sure which part, but it was there.

Redd's hand touched his cheek, and she knelt down to meet him at eye level. Her skin was soft on his. He could taste her sweet breath floating closer toward his lips. Several strands of red hair dropped in front of her glassy eyes. Joel could feel his heart racing.

Suddenly, he wasn't thinking about any of it. Not the case, not Aimee, not Kyro. He was only able to recognize the cracking in his ribs, the thick, pulse-pounding beat of a heart that jolted alive. One breath. Two breaths. He quickly lost count.

"I really should go," she said softly, almost a whisper.

"No, please stay."

Redd glanced at the two empty beds. "That wouldn't be very professional, now, would it, Joel?"

He released a long, shaky breath.

"I can't be your escape. You're a good man."

"You don't know me. Not really."

"I know enough. You are. And I don't wanna be just a mistake one night in your past."

Joel bit his lip. It was nearly impossible to avoid imagining what it would be like. He was ashamed to admit that he actually wanted it. There was a passion in him that, even now, at his most desperate, made his body long for the warmth a night of romance might bring. He knew he shouldn't have let his thoughts drift so far away, but the pounding in his chest refused to quit.

"It's late. We'll work out the next move in the morning. I was able to get the room next door. Goodnight, Joel." Redd leaned in and kissed his cheek.

As she stood up to leave, they both noticed a woman standing in the doorway. The door creaked farther open.

"Aimee?" Joel gasped.

CHAPTER-THIRTY

AFTER AIMEE CLOSED THE DOOR, EXILING REDD INTO THE outside parking lot, she held her breath for a while, wondering if she'd burst. Being in the cramped backseat of a taxi for several hours had been nauseating enough, but to arrive at the motel Joel asked her to come to—the one she rushed to—and find him receiving a kiss from a complete stranger—that was too much.

Her ears rang with the screams in her head. "What was that?" she asked.

"Nothing." Joel massaged his neck. A nervous tick he adopted whenever convenient. "Safe trip?"

"What do you care?" she snarled. "Is that *her* bag?"

A knock disturbed them. Aimee opened the door after waiting a bit, just to let the tension thicken.

"Hi, Mrs. Phoenix."

"Aimee's fine, Redd." Aimee put extra emphasis on the last few letters. She didn't like this investigator, and the distaste had nothing to do with her ability or inability to find their daughter, which at this point was flimsy speculation.

"There's no reason to feel threatened," Redd assured her. "Seems I just forgot my bag right on the bed there."

Aimee let that image settle in her mind. A dropped suitcase on one of the motel beds. Suddenly, the kiss she'd accidentally walked in on returned. It shouldn't have bothered her, any of it. The fact that this strange woman might have slept with him. She expected that, after some searching, she'd uncover a bra tucked under the mattress or a hair dryer plugged into one of the outlets in the awkwardly diminutive bathroom. Unwanted thoughts criss-crossed her brain: the two of them enveloped with one another, groaning, panting, kissing.

Redd walked right by Aimee, who was too lost in the awful fantasy boiling in her blood to even see the beautiful stranger grab her suitcase and exit.

"You can close the door now. Thanks for not making it weird," Joel sarcastically noted. "My goodness, you have impeccable timing."

"Is she the replacement?" Aimee asked, closing the paint-faded door.

"Don't start."

"Why? Did you already finish?"

"I asked you to come so we could talk face to face about all of it. About Emery. I don't want to fight anymore. I'm sick and tired of fighting. Besides, it's not like we're still together or anything. You made that very clear. Last time we had sex, I think NASA was planning its first trip to the moon."

"Very funny. So you had sex...with her?"

"Am I on trial? She's the investigator! We were discussing the case."

"Really?"

"Really. Not like it's any of your business."

Aimee hated this. She'd prepared for it, sure, but it was still somewhat surprising that it actually kept happening this way. She and her soon-to-be ex-husband were incapable of communicating without spiteful arguments. The road in front of her got wider, foggier. She wanted an exit soon.

"You're right. It isn't my business who you do or don't sleep with."

"For the love of…I did not sleep with her!" Joel yelled. "Get that through your head. Can we please derail this train?"

"Nice metaphor. Kinda fits, considering."

"You are unbelievable."

"You would know, Joel." Her eyes flashed, and her nose flared. Was there anything left other than empty quarrels and bitter words? She brushed by him rudely and went into the bathroom to rinse the fatigue from her face. Really she just needed to retreat before her transparency gave her away, if it hadn't already.

Aimee wasn't in there ten minutes before there was another knock on the door. She fixed her hair and cracked her neck. Then Aimee returned to the frontlines.

"Who is that?"

Joel didn't look all that inspired to acquiesce to any more of Aimee's probing questions.

A small black boy with obvious wardrobe issues stood in the center of the room. "Man, Casper, you get around," he said. "But I think we can work with this one."

"Excuse me? I don't know who you think you're talking to, but I am not some piece of meat for your twisted imagination."

"Is this your old lady?"

Joel blew out a deep breath and nodded.

"Not bad," the boy said, bumping his fist against Joel's. "She's kinda spicy."

"Who *are* you?"

"I'm Kyro. K-Y-R-O."

"Your name sounds like a pathetic comic book character."

Kyro took offense. "Look, we just met. Ease up, baby."

"*Baby?* My name's Aimee."

Kyro smiled devilishly. "Yes, it is. So you must be the culprit. You're the reason we're here—well, sorta."

"I don't follow."

Joel started to fill her in, but Kyro insisted *he* tell her how it all went down. "So my gramps was Abraham Finch. You knew him, I think. You worked at the hospital where they sent him to rot. Anyway, that's how he met *her*. Emery, your daughter." Kyro pulled the photograph out of one of his socks. Aimee recoiled. "Easy, baby, I showered yesterday. Look, this is how it is. Your girl and Abe, from what I heard, they was friends. She meant a lot to the old man. And the old man meant a lot to me."

"Okay?"

"Man, she's tight, but she ain't the sharpest tool in the shed, pops."

"Are you just gonna let him talk to me like this?" Aimee directed her frustration at the grieving mess of a man leaning, hunched over, on the motel bed.

Joel scratched his scalp. "Like what? That's how he talks… to everybody."

"All right, let me spell it out for ya. Your husband, Joel here—"

"Soon-to-be ex-husband," Aimee interjected.

"Whatever. He comes up to me and my crew, asks us if we seen her. After we mess with him a bit, and this knucklehead drops his wallet, I check him out. Start putting two and two together. I seen his license was from Connecticut, near the place Abe died. Last name Phoenix. Same last name as that chick that made old Abraham smile 'fore he checked out."

Kyro noticed Aimee still wasn't registering it all correctly, so he came out and said it. "I think I know where your daughter is."

"Yeah, but right now, it doesn't seem likely," Joel corrected.

"Why, 'cause some cute tail said so?"

"Redd's been there, Kyro."

"And I haven't?"

"She led an in-depth investigation on the facility and the staff. I think she knows a little more than you do. After I met you, I allowed my better judgment to get swayed."

"Nah, you got it backwards, dude. She ain't dealing straight with us."

"Oh, please. Let it go, Kyro. She's checked every inch of that place. Have you?"

Kyro choked up.

"Have you even seen this 'underworld' you speak of? Is there any proof at all that it exists? Solid proof?"

"Where's your faith, man? I came back here 'cause I thought if your brain had a second to cool off from all them hot flashes you been gettin' from Little Red Riding Hood, you'da come to your senses by now. But you're just dense. You believe whatever you want to believe. Forget this. Come morning, I'll find Emery on my own."

"Thought you said it was a suicide mission," Joel said.

"It is." Kyro's tone seemed to split. "But if you won't go look for your own daughter, I will. I ain't gonna be a little coward no more, man."

"I'm not a coward. But Redd is right. There's no solid proof. No evidence. Am I supposed to go in there and make a fool of myself?"

"You gettin' scared, Casper?"

"Look, maybe I was wrong about all of this. It was a stupid hunch."

"No, it wasn't. You was talking sense on the car ride in. I was a chicken. But this is real. Is *she*? Hell, do you even know her real name? Redd. Yeah, that sounds legit. What's she hidin' from us?"

"Stop it, Kyro. Just stop it."

"You gonna white-flag this one, ain't you?"

"Maybe I read into leads and believed what I wanted to. Maybe you're right about me." Joel's struggling smile eventually dissolved.

"Or maybe *you* were right," Aimee finally broke in. It was hard for her to admit it, but the compliment came out nonetheless. "I haven't seen you so passionate about anything in a long time. You drove out here to the middle of God-knows-where to look for her when everyone, including me, was against you."

"Here it comes," Kyro added. "If you guys start suckin' face, I'm throwin' that ish on YouTube."

"Give it a rest, kid," Joel sighed.

"Just sayin'. I ain't gonna sit here and feel like the awkward third wheel doing nothin'. Both of you got some serious lovey-dovey baggage to get straight before we go down that road, if you ask me."

"We didn't," Joel and Aimee said together.

"Look, Joel, I know you better than either of them. When you're this stubborn, it's for a reason. And I think this strange… thug…*person* is right." She ignored Kyro's rolled eyes. "Your gut brought you here, and it led you to him, who just so happened to be related to some hospice guy Emery volunteered for. Maybe there are bigger things happening here than any of us."

Joel still needed convincing.

"Your old lady's spittin' sense at you, Cass. My story's legit. Believe or don't, doesn't matter. Tomorrow, I'm finding a way to get in and get some answers. Or I'm gonna die tryin'."

"You seem like a fighter, Kyro," Aimee said. "Thank you for wanting to help my daughter."

"What can I say? Just a stupid comic book character that wants to change the world, baby."

"And a real smart mouth," Joel added. "Okay. Maybe there is something at work here bigger than all of us. I felt it before I even left, Aimee. But I couldn't tell you that then."

"Things are different now," she said. "I get that." Her eyes wanted him to stare into her. Still she couldn't believe how careless she'd been. She had reacted in the complete wrong way, getting angry at something she *thought* she saw. It wasn't fair to either of them.

"You back in, Casper? Let's go kamikaze on this motha."

"I swear, they're gonna invent a new language just for you," Joel sneered.

The kid chuckled. "Kyro-nese, baby. Respect that."

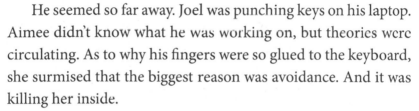

He seemed so far away. Joel was punching keys on his laptop. Aimee didn't know what he was working on, but theories were circulating. As to why his fingers were so glued to the keyboard, she surmised that the biggest reason was avoidance. And it was killing her inside.

Kyro had purchased a dozen candy bars from the parking lot vending machine, and he bought Joel and her cheese Danishes. The little spazz was hyper enough before devouring half the pile. Now he was sprawled out on the adjacent mattress like some wounded war veteran with six bullets in the gut. No doubt a sugar coma was working its way through his system. Candy wrappers and chocolate smears littered the comforter.

Aimee kept watching the ceiling fan spin overhead. Lying flat on her back, she counted every stain that tarnished the otherwise white ceiling. The smell of cigarette smoke in the room wouldn't leave her nose.

"Charming place," she said under her breath.

"It was all I could afford," Joel said.

She hadn't meant for him to hear, but she was glad he acknowledged her, glad she could share a few words with him, even if it wasn't on purpose.

"How can you concentrate with him snoring like that?"

Joel shrugged.

"What are you working on?"

At first it was as if he didn't have time to respond. His eyes were glued to the LCD screen.

"Joel?"

"Yeah?" he eventually said.

"I said, what are you working on?"

Reluctance held him tightly.

"Secret?"

"Just something I've been trying to write for a while. I don't know if I'll ever finish it, but it still wants to come out."

"You used to write all the time," Aimee said. "When we first got married, I couldn't pull you away from the typewriter. Competed with that thing for years."

He smiled. "And eventually won."

His eyes went back to the screen.

She had been hoping the conversation might evolve on its own, but perhaps it was too soon for wishes to come true.

Now Joel flipped pages quickly back and forth between his Word document and the Internet pages concerning the asylum Kyro had nearly convinced them held Emery.

"You've been looking at that screen all night. Aren't you tired?"

"Can't sleep."

"Did you tell your girlfriend that we're storming into Troy in the morning?"

"We'll speak in the morning. And for the last time, she's—"

"Not your girlfriend, I know."

"It bothers you, doesn't it?"

Aimee was good at hiding her emotions when she wanted to, though it was unclear how long she could keep up the façade. "A little."

"Nothing happened."

"You don't have to explain, right?" She coyly leaned up on her side and placed her left hand on her waist, hoping he'd catch a glimpse of the ring.

"Aimee, I…what are we?"

It was something her heart wasn't ready to respond to. The drive here from Connecticut had certainly been long enough to ponder the question, to cleanse the murky waters they'd both wandered into. But here she was, being asked a question that had lingered in the back of her mind for months. He asked her pointblank. And the safety was off.

"There's so much I used to know," Joel started. "And now nothing seems clear. I feel so much…unrest. Forget it."

"No, what is it?"

"There are two roads, Aimee. Who I am and who I hope to be when all this mess is over."

"Will it ever be over?"

"I hope so. Every choice, it matters. Everything we do or say, think, it has to matter. It collides and has a purpose."

Joel was speaking in circles, and she was waiting for him to make sense.

"I met Kyro only a few hours ago," he continued. "I've known him less than a day, yet I feel like there's a part of me in him. A part of that burned-out fire I used to have. My doubts made me second guess it all. The spirit is willing…"

"…but the flesh is weak," Aimee finished. Never before had those words held such potency.

"Something led me here, Aimee. Sure wasn't me. *Something* led me to him."

"You think heaven is still rooting for us?"

"There are moments when I believe and others when it feels like heaven is on the side lines waiting for me to fall."

"Maybe God is there. Maybe we just couldn't see him before. Maybe we didn't want to."

"We're not good, Aimee. I'm not good."

"No, we're not, but we're human."

"That doesn't make me feel better."

Aimee sat up and pushed a sigh out of her lungs. She never thought she'd be listening to one of his sermons again. But it was returning, however faint, that still voice she used to know. The one that lived inside Joel once upon a time, the one that got up in front of scores of people to give hope to the desperate.

"It's like a roller coaster. Up and down. Repeat. That snoring, smart-mouth kid, he believed in me. And I ignored it, Aimee. It's sick. I was ready to give up…again."

"But you didn't. We live in the moments between our choices, I think."

"He came back. I don't usually get a second chance. It's strange, you know, meeting him. In a lot of ways, he makes me think." Joel chewed his bottom lip and swallowed hard. "Maybe he's like the son we…"

Aimee brushed her hair back. "It's all right, Joel. It was a long time ago. We can talk about it."

"No, come to think of it, I'm not sure I want to."

"It happened for a reason, right?"

Joel's eyes cut right through her.

"The miscarriage was hard. I lost a piece of myself when it happened. Our baby. My son." Aimee choked up. "But we were able to focus completely on Emery, right?" She was searching for his confirmation, even though she knew it wouldn't come.

"Her accident changed all of us. But losing a son, there's no fixing that."

"It wasn't easy for me, Joel. It wasn't easy."

"You blamed me when you lost the baby."

"I was scared, okay? You weren't around. Gosh, you were gone so much. The stress, it was eating me inside. I fell down those steps, and you weren't there to catch me."

"I've regretted my decisions every day. Leaving you like that. But nobody had it easy, Aimee. We both lost a son. That was the hardest thing in my life to endure."

"Harder than this?" she asked softly. "These last few months have been misery."

"Whether you drown or burn, does it matter? You're still dead."

"Yeah." Aimee stared at his back. He wasn't typing anymore, but he never turned around to face her. Was it judgment for the guilt she'd put on him for so many years? Was it fear of looking her in the face? They had made a promise not to talk about it ever since it happened. But losing one child is complicated; losing both, unfathomable. Tonight seemed like as good a night as any to resurrect old demons.

Still, it was vexing talking to him so vulnerably. She kept noticing the ripples in his shirt, how his spine tugged gently against the fabric, or the manner in which part of his collar stuck up in the back. She studied his pale skin, the kind Emery had inherited from his side. His skin color changed enough for summer, though, most of the time.

How stupid were these thoughts, these useless bits of information? They wouldn't cleanse her of the trouble; they wouldn't give them a second chance. They were only thoughts. That was all they'd ever be.

Another tear slid to her lips. She could taste the salt and the renewed memories she'd fought hard for so long to suppress.

"Aimee, I should've been there," he said. "All those years, I should've been there."

"I drove you away. I was suffocating you, and you had your ministry. I just kept hearing my mom's nagging voice every time you left. It made me start rethinking what we had. That's not your fault."

Joel nodded slowly. "We can't change those things, Aimee, but the past doesn't have to follow us forever."

She was ready to change the subject; otherwise, there would be a river of tears collecting at her feet. Aimee unzipped her suitcase and pulled out a large photo album. "Do you remember when we met?"

"Of course," Joel confessed. "It was a U2 concert. Rained like crazy."

"My friend Gail set us up. Blind dates were never my thing."

"Me neither, as you quickly learned."

Aimee flipped the book open and selected a few photographs. Joel turned around and edged closer to the bed, to where she was.

"Here's one." She smiled, almost embarrassed. The picture she handed over was of herself in a white t-shirt. The rainstorm left her wishing she'd worn a bra that wasn't black. "I sure know how to kill those first impressions, huh?"

"We got soaked that day. I was just glad to get outta the house, even if I hated the band."

"They were not that bad," she fought to convince him.

"To an unrefined musical palate, perhaps."

Aimee shoved him gently. "I liked 'em. Just because you got dragged on a blind date, doesn't mean the band sucked."

"Yeah, maybe I was too much of a critic. I think you knew the words to every single song."

"Please, you loved my voice." Aimee said it more for her own embarrassed ego than thinking he might actually agree.

"I did. I loved to hear you sing. And when they came onstage for the encore, I thought you'd be lost in the magic all night."

Aimee was frozen, the way she was when they met for the first time. Hair messy, shirt soaked and muddy and showing off the only clean bra she had. She was tempted to sing an off-key note right here, but she didn't want to risk waking their new friend, who seemed to be lost in a strange dream and was talking in his sleep.

"Do you remember what happened next?" she asked him, looking down at the spread of pictures in the album. How young they were, in love from the first moment. Not caring about each other's pasts and uncertain about the tumultuous future. They were two naïve kids, ready to tempt love.

Joel placed the photograph of them down on the mattress, and with his hand, he lifted Aimee's chin. He stared into her eyes, and she, afraid to look away, stared back. Her makeup was running. She hadn't worn any for him in months, and tonight of all nights, tears had to come.

"I said you were beautiful." Joel spoke to her in a whisper. "And then I kissed you." Slowly, his lips got closer to hers, and she felt weak before him, her heart quivering and not knowing what to do. Did she want this? Was she ready to let him in again? Did Joel really think she was still beautiful?

Their lips touched. She could feel his fingertips inside her hair. With the other hand he held hers. Before she had time to think, Aimee pulled away. She could still taste him on her tongue, but there was no trace of alcohol, only the flavor from his lips more than twenty years ago. Familiar and inviting. She wanted more. As she leaned into his mouth a second time, Aimee returned to her youth; she was young and beautiful once more. She wasn't worn out and bitter.

"I'm sorry," she said, this time not caring if she bled tears. Where this new passion came from or how long it would last, she didn't know. But she welcomed it. It didn't matter if Redd had stolen a kiss from Joel tonight, because now Aimee had his complete focus.

It was their chance to put the clocks in reverse, to experience their first true kiss a second time. Aimee was reborn, remembering the way it felt to drown in a sea of rain, music, and unknown faces.

CHAPTER THIRTY-ONE

THE MAN COULDN'T SCREAM. THE RAZOR SHARP WIRE WAS around his fat neck before the door whispered shut.

A human body's first instinct is to fight for survival, to war with the evil seeking to end it. She knew the pattern of human stains well, and this body-flopping was usual. His vocal cords scratched, and his arms swung, phlegm sticking to her wrist as the violent dance carried her between seconds. His hot breath poured over her. Spit flew into her mouth. First she aimed to steal his balance, knocking out both kneecaps with the heel of her boot. And then he bowed before her.

She could see the veins in his eyes gaze up at her, asking for more time, vision ready to turn into a million colorful blotches against a wall of black. He was all shaky, elbows knocking back and forth, desperate for new air, like a baby from a womb. He managed to claw once at her face before his cheeks turned into pale-blue spheres with needle hairs reaching out.

The struggle was short lived, though, and this overweight terror proved little more than she'd expected. The obvious horror of approaching death forced every frail soul to its knees. More time, more breath, they always wanted. This chunk of human sorrow was no different.

And then, like clockwork, he stopped moving. Complete. Lifeless. Torn from this world. This part never used to bother her. The killing. Or, as she called it, recycling. But lately, she was developing a conscience, and she didn't like it.

The wire remained tight on her black-gloved palms until she peeled it from her grip. The metal cut into the fabric pretty good. Her victim had dented the closet door during their war, and now the hinge didn't swing right. A mirror had also broken, but that would be easy to replace. She had a few hours before sunrise. Despite her considerably small frame, she wasn't one to forfeit a fight.

After dragging him into the bathroom, she pulled a tight rope from her jacket sleeve. She tied it to the man's gullet and strung him up in the shower. He swung there until at last, there was no moving at all. No creak. No tug. The mess of an innocent man now hung by the thread she'd be hanging from if she weren't careful. Still, those haunting, bloodshot bullets shot right through the gate she once believed to be impervious to quiet suffering. Pain like this she swore she'd never have to endure again. And until tonight, she had kept that promise.

Why was this so difficult? The reasons and the rhymes seemed already obsolete to her. The curtain couldn't hide this guiltless man's shadow. And his phantom of a stare still searched for her even though her back was turned. The blood had to come off.

Instantly, she reached for the faucet and tried to scrub her skin. Her palms and wrists dried with black blood. Her own blood. The man had put up a decent fight. *Who is he?* she wondered for the first time. *What is his name? Does he have children?*

She imagined him as some overworked, discontented stockbroker who went to cheap motels to get lucky.

Maybe he was a frustrated, bitter uncle who had raped his niece.

What if he sold pot to middle school kids?

He had to be a threat. He had to be some kind of evil the world no longer had use for.

But she'd be protected. It was all part of the plan. She fulfilled what was necessary to ensure the future, to ensure her selection, her safety when the world had fully become. The details and the liner notes in between shouldn't have mattered.

But they were starting to.

The mystery of losing the one person you cared most about could make a person colder than death. What difference did it make how many she killed or how many she led astray? All of it fled toward the inevitable.

The faucet kept spilling out water as the cut on her chin dripped blood into the sink. There was only a small mark on the skin where the man's filthy nails had clawed, small enough most wouldn't notice. But underneath, that's what bothered her. It was her ruined humanity, her soul. She swallowed hard, taking sips of the water her mind perverted, convinced this was the blood of others and more to come.

There were no options, no more. She had to follow through with it, no matter how much it stung. It was quiet next door. Far too quiet. She wondered what conversations Joel and Aimee were exchanging, deeply aggravated by her carelessness. Why had she not planted a chip in their room? Was it on purpose? Was she really becoming that vulnerable?

"You're weak," she spoke to her reflection. "You're not like him."

But she *was* like him. She was strong. Strong enough to begin and strong enough to end. Wasn't she? She had to be. Tomorrow, if she didn't stop it, everything would change.

The vibrations of her cell phone on the wet counter sent chills up her spine. It was Saul Hoven. She wasn't ready to give a report. She wasn't prepared to confess that she was sick of the lies, sick of leading two broken people to the slaughter. She should've killed them when the arson was taken. Why had she prolonged the inevitable?

Because you didn't think they'd get this far? They weren't supposed to get this far.

Her cell vibrated again. And again. And again. It wouldn't cease, like a machine gun going off in her brain. Her blood curdled whenever the sound came. Her ribs embraced the impact of a frightened heart. And suddenly, a flood of tears slipped down crimson cheeks.

At last, she'd reached the point of no return. Joel, Aimee, and that thug boy knew too much. They were getting too close. Finally, she realized that this was the soul she had created, the horror she had painted with her own hands. She was cold and calloused. She was a soldier, a murderer.

Redd pulled out the 9 millimeter that was tucked into her lower back and put a silencer on the lip. She pointed it at the bathroom mirror, pictured it shattering. Then she nudged the weapon underneath her chin, closed her eyes, and pulled the trigger.

But nothing happened. Gasps later, she was blinking. A silent curse slipped out. There were no bullets in the chamber.

It wouldn't be that easy.

CHAPTER THIRTY-TWO

EMERY GROANED FROM EXHAUSTION. SHE'D BEEN WHEEZING for the last four miles, and the shin splints should've hurt more, but the shivers, they were new. "We need to stop."

"I think we're finally here," Adam answered, staring in awe at the untouched, lonely house at the end of the crumbling road.

It was a dead-end street, perfect for raising small kids or fitting in with the rest of suburbia.

"You *think* we're here? Adam, I have blisters and cuts on my feet. You better give me something more than *you think*."

Adam moved toward the house, erected like a horrifying statue, a piece of a former great empire. A garage sat closed on one side, a patio barely tucked into the corner of the other. Depending on the angle and vantage point, someone might miss it. Connecting fences surrounded the once lush, emerald landscape. A bleach-white door sank at the center of the house's anorexic chest. Shattered windows looked out of place but couldn't look at all. The straight path toward the pale entrance betrayed the house's sense of health—torn from ridge to split, defaced and longing for peace.

This house was ill; wounded and left alone. He remembered
the grass so thick in his dreams, and now the blades were damp
and slick remnants of the past. Similarly, the two houses he once
recalled nestled tightly in the earth beside this lonely home were
no longer there. Full houses were now empty crypts. Their ruin
was all that remained, save the dug-up driveway and exposed yard
with tape surrounding it and signs jammed into stiff soil.

Adam felt Emery's body slide next to his. Her chest brushed
against his shoulder blade. "This place brings to mind some
sick memories."

He turned to her in shock. "You've been here before?" he
said quickly.

"No," she said solemnly. "I was just thinking…of our house
back in Connecticut. It was a dump like this place. Dad tried to
spruce it up, but I was only there for a summer before—"

"—you were taken," he whispered.

Emery's expression changed. Every crease in her face looked
like pain, and underneath it was fear. Adam felt it too but didn't
show it. He stood rigid, eyeing the home from forty yards away
in utter silence and near trembling. Adam wanted to go closer,
but he couldn't move.

His eyes split from the scene, and he scanned the other
homes on the block. The few surrounding the empty spaces.
He turned to find wooden fences, cracked gravel, and broken
chunks of sidewalk with grass crawling through. Time-worn
lives left behind. Colorless flowers trapped inside forgotten,
rusting coffins.

The air was suffocating. He swallowed hard, shifting to another
house. Missing roof parts and chipping shingles were among the
more obvious crimes. A spigot shot water across a patchy lawn.
How long have the owners been gone? he wondered. *Days? Weeks?*
Come to think of it, he hadn't noticed any vehicle parked in any

driveway, no car on the entire block. Nothing but a bike with twisted handlebars and flat tires and a tiny windmill spinning an eerie tune as it creaked with the loose wind.

His eyes swallowed the surroundings. Like some horrifying episode of *The Twilight Zone*. The quiet, dead-end street was a grave full of trapped memories. Spring days, summer nights, cold winters by the fireplace with an open book penned by his favorite author. He blinked, a cloud of uncertainty rolling over him.

It was a grey morning like today.

Deep breath. The conscious wind thought about tossing the hairs on Adam's wrist as Emery's scarred chin and neck nudged against his back. A permanent fear lingered. He could feel it. He knew she could too. The scars on her skin rubbed him strangely. Adam didn't want to be touched, breathed on, talked to. Not now.

He sniffed and took his first step toward the home. Its color was a blend of white and grey, black shutters lining most of the shattered windows, except one in the top corner of this oddly familiar dwelling. He waited for the sound of a barking dog or a delivery man dropping off a package no one had ordered. But the silence nearly crippled him, this haunting home calling him closer.

His eyes itched. Adam scratched, and his focus became the home once more. Emery winced behind him whenever she moved her feet.

"Whoa," he said, dragging his fingernails across his lips. "This was my home."

Emery was centimeters behind him now, but he didn't want her to see him cry.

"Danny!" Arson screamed. "Danny! Danny!"

The cold in Arson's throat pushed hopelessly out of him. He

needed someone to talk to. Someone who could remind him that this prison wasn't his home. Not even close.

Where is my home? What is home?

Where is Grandma?

Emery?

What happened?

How did I get here?

Things moved when he wasn't looking. Things danced to life and crawled back to death with one blink. The lockers hung open, the windows now stained. Where was the puppet master?

Hate fueled him forward. He was back on that street, watching the flames consume a man's house, the poor soul trapped inside. It was him. He was burning, his skin melting off and forgetting him with the remains.

No.

As Arson raced down the hall, he noticed one of the classroom doors was open. Almost inviting him in. Grandma sat there, looming, cursing at him for spilling a bowl of cereal on the rug. But he was only seven. "Why are you so cruel to me, Arson?" she asked, that icy stare like a strangling fog. "It wasn't enough that you took my child from me?" She broke down and cried.

The sound of her tears collapsing on the tiles was too loud to bear. Arson thought his ears were bleeding, but it was only pain.

He watched the frigid scene peel back.

Grandpa walked in from a long smoke and held his wife. He smelled like the world, like sweet fire. He was the burning Arson remembered, wanted to keep. Grandpa hugged him and assured him it'd be okay.

Did he know then how much of a lie it was? "You're different, that's all. It's not your fault, Stephen. You're not like other kids," he whispered with that half smirk he wore so well. "Sometimes your grandma forgets."

"Why does she call me Arson?"

Grandpa couldn't reply. Instead, he buried the boy's tiny frame in his arms.

But then the classroom door slammed shut. Arson went to open it, turning the handle until his palms went raw. There was no going inside. It was locked, and he was trapped on the outside.

What kind of place was this?

Everything here felt so real. He was real. These memories were real.

The thought of losing Grandpa again infuriated him. His blood boiled. He missed Grandpa so much. But pictures of his grandmother suddenly fluttered in instead. Some pictures were happy, most were violent.

Run, the whispers of this place taunted. *You always run.*

"Leave me alone!"

Run away from all this. Get out.

A deep scream started in his chest and crawled harshly up his throat until it tore out of him. "Danny, where are you! Come back. I know it's you. I couldn't forget. Never. Please come back!" The shivers were beginning to bug him. They didn't go away, no matter how hard he tried to burn.

The fire lay in his bones somewhere, still dormant. But how had the fire come out before? Had he imagined it all? His hand had been on fire, right? He flicked his fingers; made fists then flicked them again. The flame was what he really needed.

"Pull yourself together, Arson. You fell in here. You have to wake up and get out." But the hopelessness inside him grew teeth. The acid in his gut drowned him from within. Anxiety. Fear.

You're all alone.

No.

Loneliness is fear. Fear is loneliness.

Shut up!

A shadow crept out in front of him suddenly. "What's the matter, baby?" a soft voice whispered. He turned behind him to find Mandy standing there with a mask melting in her hand. It didn't burn her perfectly manicured nails or those beautiful knuckles. She was wearing the red bikini from the night of the bonfire. It held her breasts firmly, the scarce bits of light tracing the lines that led to her center. Barefoot, she moved closer to him.

"Do you remember when we were kids, Arson?" she said with a twisted smile. "Do you remember when you burned that wolf?"

Arson was confused. What was she talking about?

"You brought me to the woods. Said you found a lost wolf burned by some kind of monster. Why did you lie, Arson?" When she said his name, the s seemed to slither out from her tongue. It lured him.

But he found the strength to draw back.

"You burned it alive, Arson. Didn't you? You were always different. I knew. You were always a freak."

"Stop it."

Suddenly, the halls became a forest and the lockers became trees. The two of them were surrounded. Arson was twelve. It was November air. The smell of the cold and the end of fall. Leaves cracked under his feet, replacing buckling tiles. He stood still. The wolf saw him as it devoured the carcass caught within its sharp bite. Bloody teeth. A hungry growl.

"All of God's creatures are beautiful. All of God's creatures are damned." He learned the phrase from Grandma. She spoke it to him often before bed. It was the polarity of life. She said it was good for creation to realize its beauty and its devastation. How things could begin beautiful and end in suffering.

Flakes of snow slowly showered underneath the charcoal sky. A half moon tucked itself inside heaven's grip. The dead wind stirred only a little. Arson could feel his hair like needles prick the back of his neck then curl at the tip. So cold it was almost impossible to breathe.

The violence was sudden. One minute the wolf was devouring a meal of bloody meat, and then it lay still. A sharp whimper disrupted the cold as the wolf burned alive, the fire quickly crawling into its damp fur. The creature's eyes were engulfed, a pair of colorless spheres. This wasn't power like the comics. This was horror. The beast clawed and howled into the dark only slightly. It didn't take long to die.

Grandma had taught him about sacrifices. How religious orders once mandated a sacrifice for the atonement of sin, to receive forgiveness from the heavens.

Arson did remember. Arson remembered it all perfectly. But it was buried here, in this realm somehow. The dark he wanted to escape. Arson had taken Mandy to the woods to show her the dead thing. His sacrifice for her affection. Some terrible beast committed the evil against this creature, he'd told her. He'd told himself. Not a scared boy. Not a firestarter like him.

Not a monster.

"You remember it, baby," she said seductively. "You were the monster. You remember it, don't you?"

Arson's pulse quickened. Panic spread across his body. He had to get away from her, but it was like she held him there. He couldn't move.

"Scared, freak?" she said, pausing upon every twisted syllable. "F-r-e-a-k." Her face was completely held together, nothing melted or scarred or ruined, as if the night of the bonfire had never occurred. This was the girl he used to fantasize about. How he adored her. How he even found pleasure in her.

"I was stupid," he whispered. "But I'm not a monster. I swear."

"You're so adorable, you know that?" she whispered, sliding her tongue up his neck. Her mouth slowly found his. She tasted like smoke. But some part of him liked her being here with him. At least he wasn't alone.

"You were so easy, Arson. I had fun playing with your little brain. Your stupid…little…brain. When I was a little girl, I thought you were a retard, but I learned quick. You were just different. You weren't like the rest of us. You burned that wolf and then you told me your little white lie. So clever." With one hand she moved to his shirt and rubbed underneath. "But I had fun, until you turned on me. You ruined us, Arson. You ruined *everything*. Don't you want me?"

Her nails scratched at his chest. Eyeliner dripped down her cheek. "Was I just like the wolf, Arson? Lost inside the woods, waiting to be burned?" He watched as some of her lashes peeled. She dragged her lips across his once more, breathing into him with soft moans. Moans that turned into curses. Her ashtray mouth poured dust into his throat. But in seconds, he was coughing it all up.

"You want me, Arson," she said, reaching for his belt. "You *need* me."

He dragged his heel back, his heart lost somewhere in the empty space of the in-between.

"What did you do with her?" Arson's eyes slipped down to the mask in Mandy's left hand. It was still melting, and Mandy couldn't feel a thing. The mask locked inside was torn and crippled with stained edges, the hollow gaze searching him out. "Where are you hiding her!" A scream ripped through him. Veins on the side of his temple pulsated, nostrils pulling with disgust. This dream world was feeling more and more real.

"We're gonna fix her face," Mandy said, suddenly lighting a cigarette. Her lips toyed with it. She let her tongue dance around the tip. He wished the cancer stick in her mouth would ignite, and he marveled when it actually happened. The spark was gone by the time the cigarette pinched between her ceramic smile began to melt her. In a blink, the flame crawled toward her stained lips, a flab of skin sliding back and forth as it withered.

"Look at me, freak!"

He kept his eyes shut, wishing her away. Begging whatever force governed this dark world to take her.

Then her voice got deep and nasty, and it sounded like a growl, distant from the inside. "We'll fix her, Arson. We'll fix her goooooood. And then you'll die here with me!"

Sweat bled down his neck. He felt it slither along each dent in his spine. Then suddenly, she vanished.

The cold spread through his chest. "Help!" he yelled, his voice stretching what seemed like a chamber of a thousand miles. He'd wandered these halls before, but never had he been this lost, so afraid of what lay around each corner, what new hell hid in this forever dark.

"Get a grip, Arson." Like whispering to himself would help any. This place was creepy. He wondered how something like this was even possible. How many other things or spirits were here with him? Did they exist here or did his mind create them? Was he merely the visitor?

Arson concentrated on his grip. He stared down at his hands. He knew he could, if he wanted to, birth a flame. Well, couldn't he? He'd done it hundreds of times before. He thought back to how he practiced watching things burn behind the cabin. When Grandma... wasn't herself. No matter if he ran or stood still. There were two holes chiseled out of him. Where Grandma and Emery belonged.

He loved them both more than breath itself.

Arson chugged a wad of spit down and blinked fast, sealing flesh to flesh. He imagined himself lighting like a whirlwind, imagined that it would all happen with one furious thought after another trampling through a mind consumed.

Still nothing. Now. But before, he had made Mandy burn, and before she showed up, his grip was on fire. It happened, though he couldn't control it. Not in the slightest. But the fact that it happened erratically and without warning didn't mean he had his powers back. It didn't mean he could go nuclear whenever he wanted.

"You can do this." Arson smacked his hands together once, twice. "Now, let's go!" Once his nerves settled, he stood straight and rigid, his mind quieted, his muscles limp. He embraced the cold and felt his eyeballs roll. Nothing bitter, nothing violent. Just the chilling, quiet whispers.

Arson swung his leg up into a radiator with a curse. "Who am I!" he screamed.

A voice suddenly startled him. "You think that's gonna help? Screaming at the top of your lungs like a lunatic?"

Arson turned back around, shaky, to find the voice. "You?"

"Yeah, me." The boy remained hidden. "Look at you. You're a mess. You got stupid. You can't control your stupid temper. And that means you definitely can't control your powers."

Arson's eyes flashed, his heart unsure whether to keep beating or to skip one. "So…what, you're an expert on anger management and magic?" Arson whispered, flicking his fingers in hopes to call out a spark.

"It isn't magic. It's science. That's it. Mankind has always possessed the ability to do what men for generations thought was impossible. But it is possible. Case in point, you."

Arson returned a confused look.

"Yeah, it's true. And you've always known, haven't you? C'mon, you hit this one big. You tapped into the mother ship, Sparkie. Now, will you quit being such a baby? Obviously, throwing a pity party isn't going to get your powers back. That's not how it works in here."

Arson smirked. "What would you know about it?"

"I know a lot more than you. You think you're so big and bad, do ya? Then why are you stuck here? How'd you get caught?"

"Look, just shut up, Danny!"

The boy held back a laugh. "Easy."

Arson grunted, combing stiff knuckles through his hair. He shocked even himself. Minutes ago, before Mandy showed up and threatened him, he *wanted* to see this boy, talk with him, but all he could think about right now was turning the fire back on.

"What are you doing here?" Arson asked with a shrug.

"What are *you* doing here?"

"So, we're playing that game again?"

"You seem to like playing games...with people's lives," the boy said, sounding more like a frustrated detective than a lost ten year old.

"What are you talking about?" Arson barked.

"Don't act dumb. Ever since you were a kid, you know, that mistake you made? That stuff makes you who you are. You wrecked that little girl's life. Killed your own mom. Your grandmother hates you."

The boy spoke with such explicit execution.

"But that...wasn't my fault."

"You think that fixes anything? You think that makes it all better? 'Oh, sorry, I ruined your life, but it's okay because I've been feeling bad ever since.' Wake up. It isn't that simple."

"You were there too," Arson seethed.

"There it is...your scapegoat. Blame *me* for everything. I mean, get real."

"You're the most real thing I've seen since..." Arson's mind tripped.

"You start to forget about time in here." After a short pause, the boy said, "So you saw the slut, huh?"

Arson's neck jerked.

"She's hot, but can you imagine if you went all the way with that psycho chick? Then you'd really have some bad feelings."

The shock spread across Arson's face. Was he hearing correctly? Did this ten-year-old boy just call Mandy a slut and then go on to talk about going all the way?

Ghost, Arson, he's just a ghost.

"I'm not a ghost. I'm more real than you know."

"You can hear what I'm thinking?"

The boy nodded.

Arson's gaze stretched down the derelict hallway. "You seem kinda smart for a kid who's ten."

"Have you seen this place? Got nothing but time in here. You get *smarter*. You probably will too, if you survive."

The boy started walking away again. Arson watched as the boy's brown hair flopped back and forth faster as he walked.

"Where are you going?"

The boy's quiet steps gave Arson another round of chills. "Look, don't leave me, okay?"

"You scared?"

Arson looked away then slowly said, "I need to get out of here."

"I'm not strong enough to help you," the boy confessed. "I don't know how to get out."

"Don't leave me again. You left me before. You never came back." Sobs held his voice. "Not now. No. Please, Danny! Please!"

Arson followed the boy through a set of double doors. A slow draft lulled the swinging portals forth and back. He imagined the sound of their creak unhinging every joint and bone in his back. He drank a slug of lukewarm spit. His skin crawled. Each knuckle was prepared to crumble in his grip.

The boy was gone again.

Arson turned around, unraveling the dust and the dark.

Everyone was gone. Everything was gone.

Everything but the cold and the walls.

But then, something called him into that room. The room that rested behind the double doors that swung to an otherworldly melody. The room with the checkered floor.

The room, Arson thought. *The room where I was born. The room where I killed my mother.*

He'd seen the moving pictures in that place, how they came to life and gave him memories he'd never acquired on his own. It was an impossible mystery. Arson didn't like it, didn't understand it. He just stared at the black and white tiles glistening as the slivers of silver moonlight reflected off the surface. Was that pain or terror or catastrophe removing the embers inside him?

I have to face it.

The cold moved closer. Slowly, the doors groaned with haunting finality. He felt a pinch in his spine as he walked through.

CHAPTER THIRTY-THREE

THERE WAS A PIECE OF WALLPAPER STICKING OUT OF ONE of the floorboards. Adam wanted to put it back, to fix that loose piece barely hanging on. He fidgeted with it, used spit in efforts to paste it back against the wall. Where it belonged.

Adam hadn't used many words in the few lost moments between when he'd walked through the front door and now. Emery's footsteps soothed him a bit, but they didn't fix much of anything. They sure didn't fix that chunk of lead in his gut.

Wary eyes approached every corner. He reached for the weapon he'd kept concealed most of the night. Held it tightly, like it was breath, or God—hope in something ordinary eyes couldn't see.

His elbow snapped into place. His back clung to the walls, uneasy. He snorted a deep breath through his nostrils, the dust and stagnant air shuffling in. With gritted teeth, Adam swore he felt the veins in his forearm blister, but when he checked, they were appropriately hidden beneath his skin. What was wrong with him? He kept telling himself to stop freaking out.

"Adam, are you all right?"

He swallowed. His mouth was begging for water. He heard Emery's voice, but it sounded like a muffled echo. This house was a cave. He kept imagining lions coming out to devour them.

"Theresnolionstheresnolionstheresnolions," he repeated with rapid blinking.

Emery kept her distance, and fear thickened within her with each step on the wooden floors.

Adam's finger licked the trigger. His slippery grip was temptation enough to pull it. All he needed was a reason.

His mind was doing laps. He couldn't believe it. He couldn't believe how little it had changed. This was home. It'd taken him years to return, but he had finally come back. Familiar, but now a part unknown. Did it remember him? Could a house remember souls? How strange it had been to glide through the front door minutes earlier. Breaking in was easy enough. He could feel more of his powers, his strength, returning.

"This is your home?" Emery asked softly, leaving a thin trail of blood behind every painful step she took. So did Adam.

His lungs inflated. He didn't answer her. This apprehension remained, and he didn't wish to speak. His neck jerked out around every corner and scanned the area. The ornate living room with dressed furniture. The calm, neat foyer where he used to come in muddy from a day of playing in the rain.

Mom used to get so angry.

He shifted left. The guest bedroom, where The Grey Man slept during his visits.

Adam's eye twitched. He blinked a bunch of fluttered blinks.

Emery didn't see him. She was clinging to his back, though. Her grip was so tight he wondered if she was penetrating skin.

It was like every corner had a shadow he wanted to be rid of, a villain he had to destroy. But nothing was certain. He couldn't even feel his footsteps any longer. There was a numbness spreading through. The blood and cuts may as well have had calluses. Yet it brought a peculiar sense of awe, how this house remained so untouched, like it was removed from the world altogether.

He'd already circled around the spot where the slice of wallpaper reluctantly refused to remain joined to its counterparts, as if being bonded to one of its patterned brothers were too painful. His ankle nudged the lonely piece as Adam cautiously skulked past the vacant kitchen and scaled the stairs. Step by step he traced his memories up this flight. Only he was happy, not like now. Not like…

"Where are your parents, Adam?" Emery asked.

Adam put his index finger to his lips and pushed out a soft breath. "Stay there. I'm going to check upstairs."

"Fine," she whispered in return.

Adam may as well have been an apparition for the next several minutes, wandering the upper level. But when he came back, there was an unforgiving, mysterious clarity in his eyes.

Adam methodically placed one leg in front of the other and descended the stairs toward Emery. Behind him there was so much black, space that light seemed to abandon. Before him he saw Emery, looked into her, wondering if he was actually looking *through* her, because it felt like he was. His vision blended clearer. The lead in his chest was melting.

"What's up there?" she asked desperately.

"My life. Emery. I *am* home." He swiftly scanned the house and returned to the lower floor near the entrance with disappointment in his eyes. "Emery, I…"

Suddenly, he was drawn to a picture frame set atop glass. It was littered with dust, but the people lost inside were known ones. The Grey Man's face called out to him from within the oddly plain frame. He had thick eyebrows and an inviting aura. His arm sat along a younger boy's sloped shoulder. The boy had long, dangling hair that suited him well, considering the soft features he possessed.

Curiosity forced Emery to ask, "Who are *they*?" With that, she drew closer to him. Her presence felt invasive.

Adam blinked. Images belligerently crowded his mind. He blinked again, and they vanished. Then blinding green light; then darkness. Foggy breath blurred his vision, followed by a white room and men barraging him with questions.

And the needles.

His arms still stung. His spine tingled.

Emery touched his shoulder, but without thinking, Adam swung his hand into her chest, and her body flipped back. She collided with some furniture and then smacked the wood floor hard with her elbows. "Adam, what's wrong with you!" she yelled, catching her breath.

"I'm sorry. Emery, I…" Adam slowly brought the butt of the gun to his right temple and squinted. He bit down hard. There was nothing he could say. He only hoped she might forgive him.

She gasped and winced in pain. "Man, you hit me like a truck. Knocked the wind right out of me." Her eyes grew wide. "So who made you freak out?"

"What?" Adam asked, helping her to her feet.

"Who's in that photograph?"

There was a moment that drifted by, almost as if to forget them and move on. But even moments couldn't forget something like this. Adam's gaze fell into hers, still in pain. "You're looking at one of them," he said slowly.

Emery's gaze turned from painful to perplexed. "Adam, this photograph was taken years ago."

"Yeah, I had hair back then."

"No, Adam, *years* ago. I mean, are you listening to yourself? That's crazy. You're only, like…"

"Eighteen?"

"Or something like that," she said firmly, even though it came out as sort of a question.

Their eyes locked. "Yeah."

Emery digested what he was telling her with just one word. "And who's the other guy?"

After a long sigh, Adam replied, "His name was Henry Parker."

Adam was running down the stairs. His young body, feeble legs and all, raced down each step until his socked feet brushed against the floor. Henry Parker—The Grey Man—was waiting.

Adam's eye caught Henry's aged profile from a distance. It appeared tampered with, somehow, by the faint light, which acted more like a border around the doctor's otherwise grey countenance. His cheek had a muscle that twitched often. Adam never really understood it, but he sort of got used to the strangeness of it. With a furrowed brow, those fifty-something, frost-covered eyes drifted through time and space and captured the young boy. His first thought was to wonder how old this man really was; his second was to wonder what this stranger wanted. Adam had thought long and hard, calculated what manipulative, seedy plots lay behind those wintry eyes, but he concluded that perhaps the frost might soon melt.

A slick and heavy rain tapped along the windows, and a grey world lingered somewhere outside their front door, a passageway that separated the different worlds. The cold and the warmth, two brothers that never found peace…until The Grey Man came.

Adam's mouth formed his name first. "Henry." But they made no other sound. Adam's unsure mother had been leaning up against the frame exiling her from the kitchen, where a ceremony of silence had gathered in anticipation of her son's arrival. The boy intently studied his mother, watching as her innermost thoughts began taking shape in the form of disconcerted glances and all-of-a-sudden shrugs.

The tapping of Henry's fingers on the kitchen table harmonized like a lullaby. Pinky first. Then ring finger. Then the middle one. And lastly, the index, somehow always the loudest among an almost speechless council.

With the method of no ordinary man, The Grey Man turned. "Henry Park—" Adam started.

"Yes, Adam. Yes, it is me." A warm smile formed the short words. "I have returned as I said I would, when the world could arrange for us to bring you to a new home." His speech sounded so final, so definite. It defined the air around them, held captive the next few moments. "You are not frightened by me, are you? Certainly not, my young friend."

Adam found himself repeating the word *friend*. He liked how it came out. The gentle manner with which his tongue slid from top to bottom, almost welcoming this visitor again, for what may have been the seventh time in two years. Friend. Not enemy. Friend. A hope. A chance to become.

A chance for the world to become.

Henry Parker's arm was draped over the back of the chair now, his fingers never quitting their tapping, the impeccable nature of it soothing and unadulterated. Adam noticed his fingernails, their precision. He took in the sight of Henry's top hat, the colors blended with the rain and the mystery of the world he found little hope in. The soft ridges of Henry's knuckles as they slowly wrapped round the knots of a creaking chair whispered chills down Adam's spine.

"You're here to bring me…with you?"

"That's why I've come, son."

"Don't call him that," Adam's mother broke in, but his father soon swallowed her remark with a forceful hush.

"Adam, your parents will understand. Time brings all things to light."

It was as if in that moment Adam could look into both of his parents' eyes at the same time. How he wished he could feel as they felt. How he wished they could feel as he did. His crystal stare shifted with a blink, and Henry Parker stood up slowly. "You can come to me now, Adam. I won't hurt you."

"It's okay," came the voice of his father. It sounded like reason, reason to trust. Reason, excuse, faith.

"We can be friends," Henry exhaled, offering his hand. "You'd like that, wouldn't you? We'll be friends for a long time, I imagine."

Adam hesitantly reached out to take the old man's hand. "You will become, Adam. There is something beautiful inside you, something strong. You are the first we have ever found, the only human creature that we know who is born with it. You possess this strength in your blood and in your mind. I call it the God gene." Adam always knew he was different, but before Henry, he never believed what he'd be capable of.

"I have searched far and wide for you, my boy," Henry continued. "I can assure you our meeting is no accident. The stars are in position. The heavens have spoken. I've been looking for something like you…for so long."

"Something?"

"Someone, my friend. Forgive me. Some*one*."

Adam showed his teeth as he smiled. Henry had already checked his body for irregular bruising, disrupted brain activity, a frail heart. But what was found was that the irregularities, if any were discovered, proved to be improvements in human DNA.

Adam understood his role, to become something even more than what he'd achieved on his own, what his body had learned to do. And Henry was his friend. To a young boy, such a purpose seemed divine.

"We are going to change this world, you and I. You, Adam, are the first of this new kind. But there will be more. Like you. Soon. Very soon. I have no more doubts. There will be many."

Henry was like a giant over him. Adam seemed so small. He could feel his brows shift, his lips chapping the more times he licked them. The man's coat danced with the coffin of dust surrounding them, a flicker of light catching Lana's bright hair just slightly.

"Don't worry," Henry said. "Your sister will be all right. We'll make sure she is taken care of. They will all be all right. We're doing this for them, you see, for all of us." A moment's pause, and then Henry's huge palm cupped Adam's shoulder. "It is time."

Adam was ready, but there was a faint part—so faint—that longed for his family to endure this journey with him. Science and men and God. But no home. He felt searched and hollow, yet still he could not bear the thought of being left behind when his purpose was great. He had to go. He had to become.

"You will be The Source for the others, Adam," Henry's words came out so clearly they seemed to cut. "The beginning and the end of all things."

This utterance contained the lyrics of the future, but such dark words still did not bring him full peace.

"I am ready now, Father," he said softly.

CHAPTER THIRTY-FOUR

THE UNFORGIVING CREASES IN ADAM'S JAW BEGAN TO TAKE new shape. A wounded, childish form. Before this, Emery had noticed how frail and deceptive his body appeared, but currently he was like a lost boy in search of answers, maybe revenge. Staring at him, she found herself strangely connected. She swore she wouldn't cry, though, no matter how sad or depressing his story got.

"Any of this freaking you out?" he asked, the overhead light making his eyes seem like clouded embers wanting to ignite.

She sighed, "No. It's actually not freaking me out, which is kinda freaking me out." Emery allowed the hesitation to play inside her. "It sucks, being taken from your family like that. But I'm a big girl. I can handle it." Her voice was a familiar kind of worried.

He sort of nodded, sort of shrugged. Dragged his elbows along the edge of the creaking kitchen table.

"Okay." He paused. It took several moments for him to gather the guts to say what came next. "I'm...a little older than I *look*."

"Yeah, I figured. But what does that mean?"

"Emery, like I said, I'm different. I have these things that I can do. Staying young is part of it. My body heals very quickly, so I can regenerate. It's part of the drag."

"Okay?" she said, processing.

"I was born…" he stopped briefly then continued "awhile ago."

"Years…ago?"

"Decades. About forty years ago, give or take a year. They had me in that place for so long, I almost forgot all of this. The real world. A person's *real* touch." Adam reached out and grabbed her hand. In that moment, she felt a mixture of safety and danger. "I forgot love."

Emery gritted her teeth. Sympathy pulled her toward him.

"I thought I'd never long for the normalcy of the world. Thought I'd never need them. It was them who needed me, right? I was going to be their savior. But I was wrong."

"It seems like the normals on the outside have everything figured out. But maybe they're the freaks. Maybe it's them we should watch out for." Emery grunted. She brushed her hair to the right side of her face and tried to forget about the goosebumps popping up on her skin whenever Adam stole a glance. Whatever strange feeling put them where they didn't belong, she wasn't afraid of it anymore.

Adam picked up the photograph once more. The one with him standing next to The Grey Man. He squeezed it. Emery wondered where he'd gone those few seconds that seemed like hours. The more his eyes scanned the image, the more lost he appeared to be, transported somehow to a place she couldn't go.

Emery looked down at the photograph then back at Adam, wishing he would return from that trip. The picture of him looked worn with age, crippled and fatigued. Two faces trapped inside the black and white world of the past. But after studying it a bit more, she realized Adam wasn't crazy. He couldn't be. He just couldn't be.

Okay, Emery...you've dealt with this kinda thing before. Remember when Arson went nuclear on the beach? Okay, this is like that. Right?

Right?

The silence didn't lure her any closer to comfort.

She had no response. The mysteries kept spinning and spinning. She wished it would stop. She glanced at Adam then back at the picture then back at him. "Weird," she barely uttered. He hadn't really aged a day since the picture was taken. Except for the fact that he looked like a skinhead now, nothing changed.

Then Adam shook. "No. I don't want it anymore. Get that away from me!" He cursed, swinging his fists at nothing. When they came back down, his fists broke the table in half.

Emery jerked with a scream. She hadn't even realized that she'd scooted out from beneath the table in time to dodge his violent episode, but she was thankful for instinct.

"What happened, Adam?" she said, sucking in breath after breath. Her heart cruised inside her.

"I begged him to stop. I begged all of them. But I gave them too much control. Those backward devils!"

"Adam, what happened?" she asked again.

His teeth started to chatter. "They wouldn't stop." His words shattered out his mouth. "Had to get out. I had to be free and choose for myself. I had...to...save you."

In the panic, she got up and rushed to his side. The sweat had pooled around his eyes, and a stream of red dripped down the ridge of his nose. Emery got up close to him. Then she touched his cheek. His skin was almost burning.

"I lost myself, Emery...for so long. Adam disappeared. I was The Source of their new campaign. I was 217." The words almost bled out of him. "They gave me a number." He lifted up his shirt and pulled the top of his loose sweats down slightly. There were three digits inked into the skin on his hip bone. "They gave you one also. 218." Adam pointed to her eye. At first, she seemed puzzled, but when he found a piece of glass and handed it to her so that she could get a look for herself, his words made a horrible kind of sense. Three eerie numbers had been tattooed behind her eyelid like a dirty secret.

She gasped, "What did they do to me?"

"They'd give everyone a number if they could. To erase who they really are. To turn them into whatever they want. But I was more than a number, I thought. I was powerful, right? I mean, didn't they know how strong I was? They did things to me I can't forgive. And I let them."

There was new anger swelling in her blood. She felt the rage in him and accepted it as her own.

"He was…my friend." Another curse poured out of him and climbed up the walls. "They take. They take and take and take! Henry just wanted my mind and my blood."

Adam paced from room to room, skulked the dark halls of his former home. His neck snaked around one of the doors. He peeked inside. She watched him stall at the entrance as he breathed in the stillness of the room. Bright colors coated the walls; a pink comforter dressed the empty, stiff mattress. It was like the room was waiting for his sister to come back.

Slowly, he spread out his hands across the bed. "Lana," he whispered. "Gone. Like everyone else." He seemed sickened. Adam reached for the handle and slammed the bedroom door shut.

Emery was dying to ask more questions. "So what can your blood do?"

He turned toward her. "Henry said it was the most powerful substance he'd ever studied. It could do things no medicine, no drug, nothing else in this world could." Adam scratched a dry scalp. "It healed you after those monsters cut you, right?"

She wasn't prepared for what came next.

"My blood can even create. It has healing capabilities, to replace and repair lost or damaged particles inside human beings. Sickness, disease. They said it could save lives…and create others. It *did* create another."

"What are you talking about? Like a clone?"

"Not exactly."

"Then what?"

"Henry had a daughter. He loved her and wanted to make her better. He wanted to heal her."

"From what?"

"Just listen, okay?" he said, his hands jittery and uncontrolled. "Frances dropped by the facility a few times. She was sick. Real sick. And Henry started intensifying my treatments. His focus wasn't the world anymore, it was her. He didn't care about wars or foreign nations. All he cared about was healing his daughter. He became obsessed." Adam cursed again. "I was just a stupid lab rat to him. But I was the good guy. I wanted to change her. Fix her. I thought that if she were like me, she'd never be sick again."

Adam stopped, his nostrils flaring. She wondered what dark things his mind was bringing to light. "Henry increased the drugs, even erased some of my memories a few times so that I wouldn't remember what he had to do to me. Didn't know it at the time. The doctors lied and said I was some lost psych patient, that I shouldn't be wandering the halls. I got out of The Sanctuary a couple times without them finding out…but it didn't matter. It got worse. They still hurt you. They still hurt us."

The world was soundless. It was the world men had made. The world God let them make.

"He didn't want me to remember any of it. He just wanted her to be healed, and the menace would do anything. I was the key. I should've known it wouldn't stop with me." Every movement ended. His eyes got lost again, like someone was calling him. From a peculiar place at the end of all hope.

"Stay with me, Adam. Stay with me."

The light was gone from both of them. Adam walked like a paranoid creature, shoulders hunched and brooding eyes pulling out from behind frigid lids.

"Why can't I remember more?" she said, squinting, as if that would help any.

"They don't want you to. They can play with your memories. Take some out, probably put some in. Until you don't know what's real. They cut you open, Emery. They tested you. You're like me. Born, not made."

She started rubbing her stomach, her neck.

"That world, that place is a prison, not just for your body, but for your mind too. You can lose it all in there."

She scratched gently at her face.

"Stay long enough and you would've ended up dead. Or worse."

"Adam…"

"No, Emery. It's not right. I let it go long enough. Too many years. God only knows what they've been able to do, to create since I've been their…*property*." His back hugged the wall, his head slamming against one of the glass picture frames in the hallway. He turned around and grabbed it. Slammed it down. It shattered even more, the glass spraying the hardwood floor.

"My family's probably dead. All of them, gone because of me. I was so foolish."

"But you're not alone, Adam," Emery said, reaching for his hand.

Eternity wouldn't be enough time for her to tire of staring into his conflicted eyes. They were crashing waves. With each blink, she witnessed the birth of new ripples, ageless seas dropping and pulling and sinking. She was almost crying, for him. His eyes were real, and they could know her. Did he feel her confusion, experience the aching in her face? Perhaps that wild, Atlantic foam held such tears of sorrow.

"You're so beautiful, Emery," he finally said. Adam lifted one of his hands to touch her cheek. He blinked once, then twice. His fingernail stroked one side of her cheek. His focus never departed.

She was frozen in front of him. Something inside her began to shift. Something was changing. It felt like pain at first and then became a soothing sensation pulling across her entire face. With only a teardrop's worth of energy, Adam's touch was healing her. She shut her eyes, her mouth, as his hand moved from her cheek to her forehead. The ruined chunks of flesh she had come to call her own for so many years became a clean and unpolluted surface. Flawless skin appeared with scattered freckles around her nose. The missing part of her hair began to grow back, almost like each strand was being pulled up from her scalp by some invisible thread. In moments, silky brown hair covered her left cheek.

Emery couldn't breathe. Shock and wonder bloomed within. The scars were no more. Like an infection, the healing spread. What once was a parasite on her ruined flesh became a transforming agent, soft and unspoiled. Skin perfected and made new.

Adam stepped back. She noticed a change in him as well. His palm was covered black, tarnished by the miracle. A stain left behind from the healing. Perhaps his body would absorb her ruin. He now looked displaced, his mouth wandering and thirsty. He was weak.

"Adam," Emery whispered. "What did you do?"

Slowly and weakly he replied, "Changed you. Made you better."

Emery rubbed her skin, her jaw, her forehead. With big, glowing eyes, she felt the patch of newly grown hair where once had only been dead flesh. It was smooth. Real. "You…healed me? You fixed it. After all these years, you made me beautiful."

Adam nodded with slow breathing. "Like the angels."

There were no true words, no form weak syllables could make to express her joy. Tears swelled. Her heart was a gunshot in her ear. She swallowed hard, wondering if her soul had drifted off for the minute.

Adam's measured blinks and unhurried movements forced her closer. Had this event truly weakened him? If so, how much? This power he spoke of, could it be contained or controlled?

She wondered if that power felt anything like what had happened to her on Mandy's beach when Arson came back to life. But that wasn't her focus now. For the first time, she looked at Adam deeply, intensely. Nothing supernatural. Nothing magical. Just beauty. Desperately alive, the mystery of this free, unrequited sensation filled her mouth, her soul, her heart. She blinked and wrapped her fingers around the back of his neck. Emery leaned her mouth into his and kissed him with every part of her being.

There was a unique taste on his tongue. Perhaps it was her imperfection filtering through. But she could not stop. His lips caught hers and pressed back into her with whatever strength his body still possessed. As if gravity were pulling them together, his teeth toyed with her bottom lip, kissing her more and more deeply.

Adam breathed into her and said, "Emery, we are the same."

CHAPTER THIRTY-FIVE

ISAAC GABLE LOOMED OVER ARSON'S TWITCHING BODY. The boy was quiet most of the time, the screens flashing to life now and again. There was something hypnotic about watching the lines of liquid food flow into Arson's body.

Isaac had never taken time to watch him before, to watch what Morpheus—what this facility—was doing to him. Up to this point, it didn't matter. Arson didn't know him, and Isaac did well to forget his previous attachment to the boy as father, and realized this was business. The business of survival.

"My own flesh and blood is a menace. A horror. I never would've believed it," he sighed over the boy. "Never in a million years."

It was clear what was coming. Isaac knew it. Everyone in this facility knew it. He'd sat in on enough video conferences with the heads of state in foreign nations and the president to know there was no stopping what rulers had put in motion. Puny men like him had no opinion. All they could do was be smart; all they could do was *become* one with the system, to become with them.

As he looked over the boy, felt his slippery flesh, Isaac was transported back to the hospital room, to the birth of this unnatural thing—boy, creature, clone. Whatever he was. What part of Arson was he? What part did they share? Anything?

Isaac now touched Frances Parker, the love of his youth. She in turn squeezed his grip, praying for him amidst the screams and horrors of the emergency room. The needles, the trauma, the fear-drenched cries that could not be contained.

How much pain had she suffered because of this? How much had she endured to bring this animal into the world? Perhaps he should have strangled the child when it escaped the womb, charred and fragile mess that it was.

"Henry, you lunatic!" Isaac seethed. "She was your own daughter. Your own flesh and blood." Tears cradled his eyes. He remembered Frances being led into a room not unlike the rooms where he assisted in "studying" Arson and the girl with the scars. A room not unlike a prison cell, surrounded by white walls and cameras. Needles pumping blood and brain fluid into her veins, changing the course of history with every injection.

"You knew. You knew it all along. How could you? I hope you rot in hell, Henry!" The scenarios that waited at the back of his mind were cruel things—what he'd do to Henry Parker if he were still on this earth. Memories were like loose triggers firing rounds of hatred and violence. He recalled Lamont's phone call. Remembered following Arson to and from work several times a week. How he watched the boy's life unfold, only to be ripped away from it all.

And there he was again. Isaac couldn't beat the memories. They were far too strong to subdue. The sun watched him break into the boy's hidden life, that worn-out cabin beside the lake, a hell of a home. Kay was not so surprised by Isaac's arrival. Maybe she knew he was coming all along. Despite the curses and the tormented blows she doled out, maybe she was waiting for him all these long years. To set her free.

In that moment when he returned to a past he had forsaken, he was no longer Isaac Gable. He'd become something else entirely. They all were becoming. They were changing by the hour, by the minute. Less and less they cared for others, for what this world could give. What love could give. The wealth would come, along with promised new life. When the world passed away, when the age of man was ended, a new race, a new beginning would come, and they would be gods and kings.

The scratch of Kay's voice was a dirty splinter in his head. "I let the devil in my house." Her words were soaked in venom. How gifted she was at being evil. He'd never fully allowed himself to realize it until the time came when he had to. After smashing her head into glass, beating her, and throwing her weak carcass down a flight of stairs, Isaac was only barely satisfied.

With a blade he opened her up. Rage and revenge were the only blood passing through him. "You stood by and did nothing. You let them do it to her. You're filth, like he was." There were no tears that day. In the violent quiet, there was nothing. Blood soaked his gloves, his neck, and his suit. He'd been really messy taking care of this one. He knew Hoven would never send him to handle this kind of business again. Redd was a much better handler of such vile deeds, but it didn't matter. Not really. Finishing Kay the proper way was all he'd wanted. He wasn't a hired hand; he wasn't a killer. He was a man who could kill; he was a man who did. A chapter in his past was now closed.

Isaac suddenly realized he wasn't alone in The Sanctuary. A few surgeons and nurses brushed by him. He knew they were watching him like the vultures they were becoming. Quite good at searching for meat to devour, even among their own. He noticed Arson beginning to shake. A few of the monitors picked up his nightmare. A new school hallway that led to a room the monitor was unable to broadcast. Nothing but static and grey dots.

The boy's mind was growing stronger, there was no longer any doubt. He began to wonder if there was even any point to starting over. If mankind was damned to fall from the start, what made any of them believe by creating a new breed—beginning with his son—that mere broken, fragile earthlings could survive?

But perhaps it was better to be on the side of the devil than to oppose him.

CHAPTER THIRTY-SIX

EMERY STEPPED OUT OF THE SHOWER AND WIPED THE FOGGY mirror. She was still shocked the water hadn't been shut off. How long had Adam's family been gone? Where did they go? Were they taken, like them?

And worse, were she and Adam really safe here?

She quickly found her reflection in the glass, a reflection she never thought she could call her own. She touched her face repeatedly, making sure nothing had changed since Adam had removed the infected skin.

She breathed in the hot air around her, feeling new and restored, until pulling down her lower eyelid. The numbers tattooed there were haunting, terrible reminders of her capture. Of what they wanted her to be. Nothing more than a number, like Adam.

The next several moments she spent lost in reflection, combing her new hair strands, getting used to them being there. It seemed right, the way she was always meant to be.

Adam was waiting outside the bathroom for her. He'd shower next. For some reason, it wasn't all that awkward to have him wait there for her, like a guardian soldier or something. He just wasn't ready to leave her side. An offer to wait inside the bathroom with her was too much, though, and Emery told him not to get overly paranoid.

Oddly, she was beginning to detect a transformation in herself. Strength she'd never used before, a sense of calm nestling up along her spine. Was she finally all right? The longer she remained away from home, away from her parents, away from Arson, the more she possessed a certain independence. Adam had similarities to Arson, sure, but he was worlds different too. When they kissed, something electric, immovable, and incomprehensible existed between each breath. Something strong. Dangerous. And beneath it all, there was joy mixed with shame. Emery knew she loved Arson; that wouldn't change, could never change, she was sure. But kissing Adam was powerful; it moved her, burned the chaos to dust. He unloosed a phoenix she swore could never again be contained.

But how could one kiss do so much to her? How could one boy—one man—(she still was a bit confused about that) nearly cripple her?

Emery's shoulders sank, her spine hunched somewhat over the vanity. Her feet were cold on the tile, but she was thankful to feel something. After all the running barefoot, she thought she'd never walk right again. But Adam's touch had healed that pain as well.

Somehow the healing was spreading. But how? How in the world was he able to heal her in the first place if his blood could only heal a part of her before? The parts where the sick doctors split her open. Maybe his power was greater when it was he who unleashed it instead of a copied, diluted form.

Her mind was running circles. She wanted to kiss him again, to feel whatever it was that made her like this. But right in front of her, somewhere lost in that new reflection of hers, the scarred girl she once knew longed for the boy who played with fire and lived in a cabin beside a lake, the boy who saved her life, in more ways than one.

But would she ever be that girl again?

Like seeing a picture for the first time, Adam marveled at Emery's beauty as her feet hit the cool floor outside the bathroom. A plume of steam and heat was caught between the two spaces, lost somewhere in the confusion of the last few hours. He followed the drops of water that trickled along her clavicle, and held onto every second her eyes spent with his.

"Why are you looking at me like that?" she said.

"Like what?" he returned with a gasp.

"Never mind."

The skin beside his eyes crunched together as the words left his mouth. Using the heel of his hands, he pushed himself up, or tried to.

"What's the matter?" she asked him, her towel nearly falling off as she rushed to his side.

"I'm weak. It isn't good for me to be weak. It's part of the transference. When I healed you, that sickness was imprinted on me. It became a part of me, at least for a time."

A revelatory flood enveloped her. "A part of you? So when you heal something or someone, you get weaker?"

"Yahtzee," he wheezed. The pain waltzed through his veins. He wasn't sure how long it would stick around to aggravate him. "Eventually it goes away. That's how it used to work, anyway."

"Used to?" Emery asked, helping him up. He wasn't happy to take her aid, but the lethargy wouldn't let him argue.

"Before tonight, I haven't used my powers. They wouldn't let me. They kept me hooked to machines and kept injecting me with some chemical crap. Spider venom, I think, but I'm not sure what it is. It never took away my powers; it only subdued them. When you've had the gift long enough, you start to know when it's there. You feel it moving inside you, even if you can't fully control it." Adam winced. A rock was breaking in his chest, crumbling to bits as he breathed. "I think my feet fell asleep," he said, struggling to get up. "I hate this."

"I'll turn on the shower for you. You can relax."

A laugh suddenly swallowed Adam's voice. "Relax. I wish."

Emery helped him into the bathroom and turned the handle to the shower. Adam removed his shirt and noticed her eyes descend upon him. "I think I'll be fine in here," he said with a smirk. "Check the drawers in my sister's room. I think she left her clothes in there. Wherever they went, they must've taken off in a hurry. They were probably running from those evil men."

"Adam, maybe they are still alive, then."

"Maybe. Or maybe they were killed."

She hated his debilitating tone of voice.

"I don't want to think about it right now. Look, the clothes might be a little outdated, but hopefully they'll be fine until we find a store far away from here."

"Right. I'll be fine…out…side," she said.

He nodded. As the door to the bathroom shut, steam once more enveloping the walls and the empty space, a new pain was released in his body. He stopped for a moment.

It went away.

Seconds later, the rest of his clothes came off, and he placed one tired foot into the tub, the other slowly behind. He felt so weak, so taken. Each breath trailed behind the last, its origins unknown. His nostrils sucked in the hot air and steam as warm clouds piled above him and transparent lines surrounded a chilled frame. He liked the smoke, the warmth. His family was gone, possibly dead. The only thing that felt right was hiding in the smoke of the past, the innocence he once possessed but now abandoned for something darker and more real.

He kept picturing *her* face, those blameless eyes, that glow she had that he never could name. It was fixed in him to remember her above all others. His sister, Lana. His tears blended with the hot water dripping over him. It could cleanse his body from the world's dirt, but the dirt underneath remained always.

Was he dark? Could this rising violence rule in him? How long before it was let out and never put back?

Hands clenched, Adam turned one of his abilities on again. It was faded at first, but slowly a ball of fire was held in his grip. In seconds, the fire became one with his hand, and his wrist and palm glowed with heat, fingertips lit like the sun.

Inhale. Exhale.

The fire couldn't stay, and a curse split the warm rain draining from the spout above his head. "It's beginning to come back. I know it is. I can feel it."

His mind drifted momentarily to the scumbag they'd left in that rig miles back. Bruce, the one he'd killed, the throat he'd singed with his fingertips. Adam swallowed. He knew he was weak and that, if given enough time, his powers would fully manifest once more. It was a mindset. It was a conscious thing, some spiritual-mental connection he'd learned to do when he was a kid. No one ever taught him. His powers could be endless, so long as he tapped into them. So long as he remembered that he controlled them and not the other way around. This weakness in his body, bubbling in his veins, wouldn't stay for long, couldn't. It would pass, and his strength would return fully. But time, he knew, was no more an ally than death itself.

Adam liked the hot needles of warm water splashing against his forehead. The needles turned into beads that rolled down his back and purified him. When he opened his eyes again, he watched the dirt from his body sink into the drain like a brown snake returning to its filth.

"We return," he mouthed, almost soundlessly. "We all return to what we are." The steam held him. His lungs longed for more breath as he pondered the mystery of the human race and what he knew it would become.

Just then, sharp pains came back. Adam hugged his side. Something like electricity surged through his ribcage. His bones vibrated, and he could feel the numbing tremors in his head. He winced, banging his fist against the wall.

And then again, it wasn't there.

Reeling back from the stinging attack, Adam held still. The water now felt like knives stabbing into his skin from all angles. His face, his arms, his legs. Visions of Krane and the false prophets. Their needles. Their spells. Their attempts to control him, to use him.

Suddenly, he was surrounded by their smoky façades. The empty steam now had faces and hands that reached out to capture him. He wondered if they were reaching into him to pull out the only thing he had left. He waved away their fading faces and finally lifted his head. He knew in that moment he wasn't ready.

Another electric jolt consumed his insides. All of his fears came alive again. He shuddered with the realization. "Oh no! They're coming."

CHAPTER THIRTY-SEVEN

BLACK SPIT SPLASHED INSIDE THE FOAM CUP LAMONT HELD while he drove. He was operating a compact, onyx Mercedes. It was Hoven's ride, but Lamont had snatched the keys before they left Salvation. One of the *perks* of being a dog of war, he sarcastically mentioned to Krane, who put up a mild fit about the situation, only to eventually sink into the passenger seat without further comment.

Lamont moved the tobacco dip around in his teeth, letting the juice and the flavor of the poison soak in. "We're close, boys," he radioed to the following brigade.

"I hate that god-awful habit, Jeb," Krane said. "How do you enjoy the taste?"

Lamont looked over slowly. "How's the nose, Doc?" A moment passed. "Keep quiet."

They were on the interstate toward Bethpage, New York, which lay just miles from where a new Eden was nearly constructed in Babylon. From the highway, a stretch of several different vehicles followed closely. A silver Tundra first; then a black Cadillac. Behind them were a rusty Firebird and several white vans. It was imperative to remain inconspicuous, and even while following, Lamont made certain that every now and then a car or two from the passing traffic found its way among them. Farther back, about half a mile, were two Suburbans—one red, one green—and a charcoal Nissan Z. The sports car was the lookout.

"Hey, Marcus." Lamont spoke into the radio after spitting again. "What's the sense of having a lookout if he's half a mile behind me?"

A brief pause, and then, "Don't get your panties in a twist, I'm coming. Got a soccer mom in front of me and a truck on my side. Working my way up. Wouldn't miss this rodeo if it killed me."

Lamont waited a moment to respond. "Move quicker. This isn't the time for you to get a piece. Quit checkin' her out. Stay focused."

A laugh stifled the radio. "What can I say? I'm only human, boss."

Lamont mused on that thought. "Yeah, well, no time to be human. Not today. Krane's little toy is gettin' excited. Means we got a signal. We're close. I need the lookout up ahead. So move your butt."

Krane sighed and scratched at a few spots on his forehead. Lamont looked over, slightly perplexed by what he saw: a group of black spots at the top of Krane's scalp, most of which were tucked beneath a major receding hairline. Below those, on the back of his neck, Lamont noticed a sliver in the flesh, almost an opening near the spine. It was purple and looked to be layered with puss. Krane was relentlessly scratching at that as well.

"Something bothering you, Manny?"

"D-d-don't call me that, you vapid mongrel. Hoven does it, and I hate it with every fabric of my being."

"Easy, tiger. I'm just having a little foreplay before the action starts," Lamont answered with a chuckle.

"Cute. But if you haven't noticed by looking at my fa-f-face, we're dealing with something very strong."

"That's why we brought the ammo and the extra bodies. We'll bring him back. Got enough venom in the trunk to make him squeal nice and good." A moment passed. "Say, you want to tell me what them marks are on your skin?"

Krane dropped down his visor. A mirror flipped back, showing him a cruel reflection. His splintered nose and swollen eye, a jaw that kept slinging back and forth when he talked. And the sores. "It's nothing. Just a minor infec-tion-tion, that's all."

"Don't look like any infection I ever saw."

"And I suppose you'd be the expert, hmm?" Krane rolled down his window a bit, the cold from the frosted winter dawn invading the car space. "It's nothing serious, just my body o-overreacting to some allergy medicine. It ju-just itch-itches and stings."

"Right." Lamont stared and felt the cold on his neck. "You mind closing the window?"

"The cold feels good." Krane stuck his neck out into the air. The sliver near his spine split a little more, opening. Just then, snow began to fall.

"You must be aching for frostbite. You know, you're acting mighty strange."

"Focus on the road, Jeb," the doctor returned, pulling his head back into the passenger side and rolling up his window.

The computer device in Krane's lap beeped. He stared down at a screen, smaller than a laptop display, with fixed points and a grid, colored yellow. As their vehicle drew nearer to the target, a green dial spiked.

"We're very close. Yes, we are," Krane said with a smile.

"How did you ever get one of them tracking chips in him anyway?"

"I don't have o-o-one in Adam. There are three. The ribcage, the back of his neck, and behind o-o-one-one of his eyes."

"Well, I'll be, Doc. You're just full of surprises, ain't you?"

"No intelligent father willfull-willfully submits his son unto the world without knowing how it will all play out. I couldn't release him without first taking a few precautions."

Lamont roared with amusement, a splat of black ooze shooting out and tearing down the doctor's cheek. "Don't suppose this *son* took too kindly to it."

"Adam didn't know, although by this point, I'd be surprised if he hasn't figured it out."

"Why?"

"Because once the devices are engaged, he can feel them. My God, he went right to B-B-Bethpage. Home. As I imagined he would."

Lamont folded his lips and scowled. "What's the endgame, Doc? What, we mass produce this crap. Then we sell it to companies, and pharmacies buy it up like it's the new Jesus Christ. The formula that'll take away the sins of the world. Change 'em into somethin' else."

Krane scoffed. "Don't be so m-m-myopic, Jeb. That is only a fraction of the endgame. In a sh-short-short while, with enough of the world becoming, as predicted, we should be ready to un-leash-leash Phase 1. All thanks to our Source. The agents in Adam's blood, they are…perfect. Acute and flaw-f-f-flawless. In addition, he employs more of his brain than all of the genius men who have walked this earth. He is unlike anything this world has ever seen."

"Blows my mind how you let this one go. You spend years looking for freaks like them and when you got 'em, you let 'em go."

"The girl wa-wasn't part of the strategy."

"But still, it's a bogus plan, don't ya think? Why not play it safe and keep what you got? Men like you can't keep it together. Always gotta push the limits."

Krane sighed. "We were abus-ab-abus-abusing him, and he couldn't take it any longer. I had to see that there was purpose left to our keeping him. Adam was tired. He ceased response to the experimentation, to the t-t-t-tests, all of it. His body was wearing. After years of these trials, his blood stopped producing in its purest form. His blood, his brain fluid, they are the keys to our future."

"You're putting a lot of faith in one stupid runt."

"Need I remind you that this *runt* is a grown man? Regardless what you think of him, he is The Source. The arson is merely a replica. Beautiful in his own way. But not pure. His bl-b-blood may be more complex, more of an anomaly, but Adam's is without spot or blemish. He is the true origin of their kind in modern times. Before Doc-Doc-Doctor Parker located him, there was no other." Krane picked at the infection on his neck.

"You gotta wonder, is this it? Was there more of them before? And if so, why didn't they survive?" Lamont spit again into the foam cup, and switched lanes.

Krane was mute.

"If you ask me, you're all a bunch of greedy little rats, trying to control the world like she's your personal whore."

"No, not all of us. Some of us are sim-s-sim-simply underestimated," Krane replied. And then, under his breath, he said, "But it won't be that way forever. When the change comes, it will be quick. It will be a quiet dawn like this one. When it happens, the ones who are left will begin again. We will be new and perfected."

A heavy silence crawled between them and their words. The doctor's stoic and moonlit eyes drifted off into the winter dawn. Another beep climbed into the air, and two thirsty grins split their mouths. They were very close. Lamont pulled off the exit and headed south.

CHAPTER THIRTY-EIGHT

"EMERY!" ADAM'S VOICE SHOOK THE HALL. "WE HAVE TO GO now!" He nearly broke the door handle to the bathroom off when he opened it, his slick body snaking back and forth toward her.

Emery was still in shock that he had darted out the door naked. "What happened?"

"I felt it. Something's not right. They're coming!" Adam spoke with interrupted breath, his eyes drifting like fog over her. She followed him to the bedroom, but innocently looked away until he threw on a pair of boxers and jeans. When she turned toward him again, she saw a red sliver near his ribs.

"I should've known. I walked right into it. This is where they wanted me. This was so stupid. I didn't think." He paced back and forth, his face, arms, and forehead dripping with sweat or water from the shower. It was all probably mixing together now. His chest didn't stop moving. "This was a trap. And I played into their little game."

Suddenly, Adam stopped speaking, nearly frozen in place. His jaw hung like a tortured Slinky, and his knuckles were bent unusually. Torment was written across his eyes.

"Adam, don't do this. Please, what's wrong?" A panic quickened Emery. She ran to his side.

"No. Ahh! It stings so much. There's something there. Something inside. Feels like it's moving." He grabbed his side, not wanting to let it go. "I think I know what it is."

"Spill it, buddy, 'cause I'm on the verge of having a serious panic attack here."

"I overheard them talking once, about a tracking device they started to use on animals. Some African thing that didn't make sense to me then. I think they put one in me." Again, he felt it, this time stronger. And this time, it wasn't only in his ribcage; he felt it in his neck and face, and it grew every time he moved.

"Adam!" Emery watched him fall to the floor. The veins on his face bubbled the way a child's does when he holds his breath. Would he turn blue, black? Spit slipped down through his teeth, and the carpet drank it up. A coldness bled in him, knew him by name, like it was calling to him. His lips peeled the more he toiled in pain.

"That son of a—"

The window to their right instantly shattered. And a small metal ball smacked hard against the floor. In seconds, the ball made an explosive hissing sound and a thick gas clouded the bedroom. The stench and fog was nearly blinding.

"They're here."

Emery's voice shook with fear. "They're gonna take us back." Each stuttered breath slipped out quivering lips.

Adam read the terror coming out of her, the fear these monsters below thirsted on. He couldn't let them have it.

"Let them try! Hold your breath, Emery, as long as you can. This gas can knock you out." Adam felt the pain, the stinging, vibrating, relentless misery coursing through him, and stood anyway. Clenched teeth. Stiff knuckles. His eyes were shifting colors. He lifted himself and stared down at the bodies surrounding the house. The vehicles sandwiched between one another. The earth their meaty tires destroyed. His focus was Krane, broken and bruised up.

"Come-c-come down, Adam," came the doctor's request. "We know you're in there. And we'll come for you."

Adam was very quiet. He listened for the sound of the wind, the sound of the world. He listened for bullets or grenades. He counted all of their heartbeats in his head because he could hear them ticking like bombs ready to go off. Exit the fear. Exit the horror. Exit the quiet.

Adam raised his open palm, and in an instant his veins became electric, hot, burning the tips of his fingers. Each knuckle pulsed and gave way to a fiery reckoning. Beams of energy and flame showered down over the vultures, with their weapons and their metallic security. Again, he released it, the power draining him more and more.

"Enough!" he screamed, lowering his hand.

He didn't need to look down to see that human beings were burning. Their whimpers and cries floated toward the sky and died there.

"Adam. We w-wo-won't hurt her if you come quietly. I promise."

"Liar!"

"No more lies, son. I'm telling the truth."

Another voice shattered through. "Sooner or later that smoke's gonna fill your lungs. Real nasty. You won't be able to breathe and ask God to stop me from finishing her nice and good."

"Lamont, shut your trap. I won't have you ruining this. Now sh-shut-shut up!"

Lamont backed down as black spit crept out his mouth.

"Adam, come home," Krane pleaded, "where you belong."

"I don't belong wi...you," Adam struggled, the violent mist crawling into his bloodstream.

"Yes, you do. Come with me, and you will become what you were bo-b-born to be." With a nod, Krane ordered several men to sweep into the house. With his two-way radio, Lamont commanded a second group to swarm toward the back and break in.

Adam grabbed Emery's hand and raced across the upstairs hallway, where a man in a SWAT outfit waited. Around the corner, Adam saw three more bodies, hidden before by the darkness, sweeping into the rooms. He let go of Emery's hand and slid down the hardwood floor, beneath one of the attackers. With the heel of his hand, he struck him in the groin and brought him to his knees. In less than a second, Adam was standing over him, snapping his neck. But before finishing, a hand swallowed his shoulder. With one fluid motion, he clutched tightly to the hand and swung the almost weightless body into another enemy at the end of the hallway.

Emery went back to the bedroom and searched the bed and underneath the mattress, the corners of the room, and the closet for the gun Adam had brought out of Salvation. But she couldn't find it.

Adam continued to war. He held a uniformed soldier with a tight grip until the man stopped squirming, stopped breathing altogether. The thought of controlling weak flesh felt so enlivening, so enveloping. They were weak, easy. A nuisance, really, that he had to be rid of.

Grinding his teeth, he held on, not letting go. He could feel the heat transcend his bones, the pain in his ribs and all over seeming like nothing more than a bee sting when compared to the rage pumping into his blood. His fingernails burned into the man's neck, singeing flesh and throat, long after the man was gone. Adam finally released his victim. The floor absorbed a loud thud.

His eyes dropped briefly, and he listened for the feet of more soldiers coming to take him back to their cold prison. The footsteps rising from below began to mix with the footsteps on his level, confusing sounds he thought were certain. Was that Emery or another body trying to hurt her? More glass shattered. "Eme..." he tried. Was she all right?

A sound like hammers clamored in his eardrum. The doom edged closer. He shifted his weight toward the noise as black mist seemed to hover near him. As it moved closer, he realized it wasn't hovering at all. In fact, the mist was a series of bodies, and those bodies had weapons. Red lights sought him out in the fog and confusion.

With a scream, Adam let loose a wave of energy, a paralyzing force that knocked many back into walls, unconscious.

"I'll end you all!"

Darts hissed past him, so close to his face he could almost taste the poison dripping from the tips. One sting from the venom might knock him out. If he could stay strong enough for a little longer, then he could beat this swarm. He had to get to Emery quickly.

Before his brain could calculate another strike, Adam was falling, crashing down against the floor. Someone held him by the ankle. The smack of his bones against the hard surface sought to shatter his mind. But he couldn't let that happen. *Stay strong*, he thought, cursing at the thought that this might be the finisher.

Adam let his imagination rule the moment. In the dark quiet, his subconscious drifted. The grip on his ankle in seconds got weaker, and he knew the reason.

It was because of his thoughts. He created what he wanted to occur. What he thought in his mind was pain, unimaginable pain, and that pain was visiting his attacker now. She was no match, no matter how tough she seemed, how loud she grunted. Each new imagination came to life when he wished it. Adam pictured the agony beginning in the woman's ribs, where his own anguish now dwelled. From there, it leapt to her bones and fiercely spread, crawling throughout her weak, empty flesh, hollowing her, punching a hole right through. No, tearing her in half.

Before Adam's next breath, the pulse he'd felt seconds earlier deadened, and as he moved, the entirety of the woman's upper torso disconnected from the rest of her body and moved with Adam. He'd ripped her in half with a few thoughts. Shaking the dead flesh off, Adam opened his eyes. It still wasn't over.

His hearing was growing. He could hear Krane's words. "Come home, son. Do not f-f-fight it. Come back where you belong." He couldn't see him, but Adam knew that though Krane whispered those words from nearly fifty feet away, somehow they got misplaced in the pandemonium and the violence, and he could hear them. "No. Noooo!" Adam felt a burning in his chest, his hands. He controlled it. It wasn't the pathetic ball of fire he had toyed with in the shower. This was fiercer, deadlier. He flung himself back to hug the wall, and with a scream, released his fury upon the bodies climbing to take him away. Upon his next blink, he heard the gasps, the empty promises some made with their Creator to welcome them into paradise in spite of the lives they'd lived. The curdling of blood, the stopping of heartbeats.

He emptied his breath and filled his lungs again.

"Adam!" he heard Emery scream. She was terrified by what he'd done. Standing there, in the smoky hallway, their bodies ready to collapse, their hearts like lost ships in search of a harbor, a sea of horror set to overcome them.

Running to meet her, another jolt shocked his ribcage, and he could hear the whispers of the doctor inside him. "Don't fight it, Adam. I am stronger than you know." Adam didn't know how it was possible. But the whispers didn't stop, and the unfathomable vibrations didn't either.

Tilting his head, he lay on his back, hoping Emery would come to him. He needed her warmth, her hope, if any still remained.

With the edge of his fingernails, Adam dug into his side and created an open wound. Blood dripped out onto his hands and slipped into the floor. Deeper it went, the hole in his side growing wider. His fingers drifted, cold and slimy. His body nearly convulsed. Emery stared, bound.

"I have…to get…it out of me." It hurt so much he cried. Tears hot with hate bled down to his chin as the tips of his teeth crunched into dust. His entire hand was inside, up to the wrist. Another red puddle spilled out of him, washing over her hands now too.

"Adam, stop. Please stop," she begged.

"There, there it is," he said, his body jittering then shaking. He choked on what seemed like vomit, but there was no way to be sure. It was hot trying to come up. He looked into her eyes and pulled his hand out. In his palm was a piece of metal measuring just a centimeter in length with teeth on the edges and an unreadable symbol at the center.

Emery swore in shock when she saw it.

Adam prayed she wouldn't faint. He needed her strength, especially now. He shivered.

Emery bit her lip, and sweat drenched her cheeks. The smoke nearly choked them both.

"Adam…it isn't over." Krane's whisper haunted as more powerful shocks pulsated within him.

"Make it stop!"

"C'mon, Adam, they're outside. What do we do? What are we going to do? We can't stay." Her tears multiplied. "They'll take us back, and we'll never get out."

"He wanted us to get out," Adam said, almost choking again. "He wanted to test me. I get it…now. Make sure I still…had my abilities. Dam—"

"Save your strength, Adam," Emery said, limping with his hand swung over her shoulder. They walked down the stairs, over torched bodies and abandoned weapons. Emery stopped to get one.

The horrifying scene unfolded. The bodies so real and yet lifeless now. Some torn, others burnt black. Certain bones jutted out and were snapped. But the terrible carnage was necessary. This was war, and these deviant enforcers brought it.

"I'm going to be sick, Adam," Emery coughed. "I think I'm going to be sick." She vomited. "They're still out there," she said, wiping her mouth with her arm, the gun shaky in her grip as she noticed the wound on his side widening. "What are we gonna do?"

"Walk out the front door."

"Are you insane? They'll kill us."

"No they won't."

"If they bring us back, I might as well be dead," Emery spat.

"Adam!" Krane called, his puny voice reaching a height Adam had never before heard. "Adam!" A chainsaw was cutting through him, he swore. "It will only increase if you refuse me."

Adam counted the number of bodies on the lawn. Five. Krane, Lamont, and three others were left alive. They were armed. He heard them cock their weapons. Swallowing hard, he turned his imagination on. The weapons all aimed at Krane. No, not all. Just one. Blinking, Adam pictured the other three armed soldiers lifting their pistols to their own heads. Fearlessly, they pulled their triggers. From behind the door, Adam and Emery listened for the gunshots.

"What just happened?" Emery asked, wincing slightly, no doubt afraid the bullets had been aimed at her.

"I controlled them," he whispered.

Panic filled the two souls that remained. Adam heard Lamont's shock, waited for Krane's. It soon came. Cursing at one another, the two men drew back, exactly as Adam had decided.

"A diversion. That's right. Freak out. Only two left. This should be fun."

The door finally opened with a whine. Adam was now able to stand on his own, or dared to. His side was stained red, as were his hands, and a deep pain swelled beneath his skin.

"What's he doin', Doc?" Lamont asked, the dip swishing between his gums. He couldn't keep still. He was being pulled toward Krane. Meanwhile, the doctor walked backwards, and neither stopped until they were drawn together in the middle of the road, Lamont in back, Krane in front. Adam knew they were bewildered. He looked over at Emery while he controlled the scene. Lamont screamed.

"He's compelling us, Jeb. Using his powers to make us do what he wa-w-wants. You won't get far, Adam, I pro-promise."

The wind dragged through hair and jacket and fear. Cut down to the marrow. Snow littered their faces and the cars. The cold dropped from above and breathed over all of them.

"Was it like you remembered?" Krane asked. "Henry and I l-lef-left your home as it was when you stepped into your destiny. But this block was getting rather cr-c-crowded, don't you think?" A horrible cackle intensified the doctor's voice.

Adam exhaled, and as he did, he compelled Lamont to bring his weapon toward the doctor, simultaneously shifting Krane's body around. Now his enemies were face to face.

"You can feel it, c-can-can't you? The sharp stinging under your skin. I used it to help me find you. To take you back to your real home."

Adam ignored the doctor's threat. "Jeb hates your guts, Emanuel. Wonder if he wouldn't like to squeeze that trigger. It'd be quick and painless, isn't that what you always said?"

"Adam…" Emery began, stepping out of the shadow of the porch and into the icy, morning light.

Lamont swore in confusion and said, "Her face. It changed."

"You did what I could not," Krane said, almost defeated.

"You're not like us, Emanuel."

"She's qu-qu-quite beautiful, but will she be strong enough to s-s-survive it all? The more time I spent with her, the more I began to realize how unique you are, son."

"Don't call me that!"

"We've searched and studied and created. But you are a m-marv-marvel, Adam. You are pure."

"You used me. You promised me the world, but you took my life away from me! But I won't be your puppet anymore."

"You were never a puppet. You are so much more, to me. You were meant to f-f-fix this world. It is the future we all want. A per-p-p-perfect world."

"One for you and your sick species to rule," Adam seethed.

"If I am strong enough."

"None of you could ever be strong enough. I am the most powerful being on this miserable planet, you weak insect!"

"Then m-ma-make us like you. Fix us. Return. We will r-run-run the trials again. We will make humanity complete. Your blood can save us."

"Like it saved Frances? Your bodies will ruin. Mankind could never be what we are."

"But there will be more. You know this. We can change this world. We wish to rebuild it, Adam. It is such a flawed, p-p-pathetic excuse for a home. This race is tired. From the womb to the grave goes man. But we c-c-can purify it with fire and ashes."

"I am more than fire and ashes."

Krane shivered. "I know."

"All their blood will be on your conscience!"

"Our conscience, A-Ad-Adam. You are darkness. And you are the life we crave. This world will fear you as a god. The way it was always meant to be. I believe you were intended, b-b-born-born, to destroy. Born to create again. We will start fr-f-fresh, as a new race. Like you."

Adam laughed. "You will die, Doctor, before the end of all of your dreams." With the pistol digging into his forehead, Krane turned pale, his neck moving to face Adam and Emery. Lamont grabbed him suddenly by the throat and clenched his grip. "The world will turn, brother against brother, mother against daughter, son against father!"

"But the diseases and famines and wa-w-wars will not last. Even if you refuse us. We are strong as well, Adam. We can adapt, if we must. Can you smell it in the wind? Can you t-t-taste it on your tongue? The evidences of our new order. It is coming without mercy. Why don't you co-c-c-come back and finish what we have started together?"

"No!" Adam screamed. "I will not save you."

"Your faith in what we've accomplished doesn't matter. I do not much matter. This world will become with or without me. You ca-c-cannot stop it."

The snow melted on Adam's face. He had missed so much. The cold wrapped itself around him and wouldn't let go. Emery moved closer, held his hand, the blood from both now stained on their skin. Adam guided her toward the vintage Firebird parked on the lawn. They stepped over the body that had undoubtedly driven the car and searched for keys.

"How far do you think you can get?" Lamont said, his mouth soaking in poison. "I'll find you again, swear to God, I will. I'll tear your eyes out o' your skull, and do her just to make me feel nice."

Adam scanned the two men. Squinting, he compelled Lamont to draw the gun on himself. With the pistol pressing against the agent's fat neck, Adam made Lamont pull the trigger. A bullet chewed through the meat in his throat and shot out the other side. Blood splattered against Krane's cheeks and clothes, some soaking his lips.

Lamont held his throat, falling to the ground.

"Can *you* taste it, Doctor?" Adam said.

"I'll…kill him!" Lamont said, gurgling, struggling just to breathe.

"You were stupid to come against me. Open your eyes, Emanuel. Your kind is a hand on a ticking clock. You're dead, and you don't even know it. I should kill you right now."

Krane practiced a sardonic laugh. "But you are human. You a-ar-are one of us."

"We are not the same!" Adam shouted. With a twist of his wrist, he caused Krane's ankle to snap. The doctor dropped to the pavement, smacking his head, his glasses breaking.

Emery unlocked the car door and sank inside the passenger seat. She then tossed Adam the keys and shut the door, grasping the weapon ever tighter.

Adam stepped into the driver's seat, straining as he gunned the engine. For a second, he looked back at the frail lives sprawled out helplessly on the blacktop. The doctor and his dog really were weak. Not much of a scare at all as they lay there, crying to the winter sky. He watched them shiver and crawl until the image of the men got smaller, eventually disappearing as the Firebird abandoned the past he once knew and sped toward an unknown future.

CHAPTER THIRTY-NINE

REDD NEVER WENT TO SLEEP. MOST OF THE NIGHT, SHE listened to the words of Joel and Aimee next door. Her cell phone relentlessly vibrated in her pocket. She didn't dare shut it off; Saul Hoven would lay into her pretty hard if he knew. But she wasn't prepared for a verbal confrontation with him. Not yet.

The imaginary demon inside her skin edged closer to her heart. A harvester or a serpent with maggot fingers reaching for the hollow chamber. There was a Bible in one of the drawers. But no priest.

The gun lay in a spread-out, disassembled mess on the bed. She'd spent several hours taking her weapon apart and piecing it back together and then repeating the process. But this last time, she left it disorganized, disarrayed, disintegrated. She toyed with round after round, the bullets like tiny hearts in her hand. Cold, hard. Steel shells. They had grooves, rough indentations where life might exist with the powder and the dust. The sharp tip of her fingernails got lost somewhere there, between grooves and the empty metal.

She checked her phone. Eleven voicemails. She kept her jobs close to the chest, chose when and when not to adhere to the vulture's demands. But what if she changed their fates? What if she left? What if she ran and washed her hands of it?

It won't make a difference, her thoughts groaned. *If it's not you who carries it out, someone else will.* They would still die. That much was certain. They should've died months ago, but she had made excuses for keeping them alive. Still, the last thing Saul Hoven needed on his plate was a pair of nosy parents sticking their faces where they didn't belong. It was only a short matter of time before the local authorities got involved. How long would it take? A day, maybe two, before they were in body bags and disposed of? The Atlantic, the deserts of Nevada, or their remains dusted over the Grand Canyon. There were many creative ways to dispose of human life, and Hoven was the master architect at constructing dark deeds.

Redd flared her nostrils. It had to be this way. Staying up all night, hoping for something to change in her, wishing for things to be different, when she knew full well they couldn't be, was lunacy. It was insanity. She could leave, sure, but once the Phoenixes were removed, soon *she* would be. But if her death were inevitable, it would not come at the hands of desperate men with evil spells; it would be hers to render.

She quickly located all of the intricate pieces of her weapon and began fastening the bits together. She could do it blindfolded. Redd may have been born without supernatural powers, but she was not without instinct. Skills for survival. She, like Lamont, was a dog of war. Not bred but turned. Like a sickness or a red spot bleeding on a shred of white paper, her cruel instincts were at play now, twisting, turning, binding together the once torn pieces of her weapon.

When finished, she held it in her wavering grip and pointed it at a target. She thrust a magazine into the empty space beneath of the gun and tempted the trigger. The body hanging by a sharp thread in the bathroom had become a part of this motel room. Redd swallowed and closed the bathroom door.

She slowly grabbed her bag and avoided the mirrors, the creaks in the floorboards, the drag of her feet atop fraying carpet. It was all just static. An ambivalent grin toyed with her lips. A rehearsal for the big show. Joel and Aimee and Ky—no. These *new victims* would not suspect a thing. They had no names. They no longer had faces. They were only victims, already dead.

Placing the gun in her back pocket, she stepped out into the winter morning. It was not yet eight a.m. The noise of her victims preparing for the day, no doubt believing Salvation was their last hope, hit her ears first. They were misled. Like unwanted words in a sorrow poem, they'd be blotted out and abandoned. In a few moments, this crimson assassin would harvest every last breath.

Redd's knuckles crunched into a fist and, with a vacant stare, she knocked on their door.

CHAPTER FORTY

ADAM WOULDN'T STOP BLEEDING. WHEN WOULD THE HEALING take over? Couldn't he fix it? His hand dipped into his side every several minutes, almost like he was massaging the wound or waiting for something other than blood to spill out. Emery's mind still reeled from the battle she had survived.

"Are *you* okay?" he kept asking.

"All this time away from home. All this strangeness. I thought I'd be ready to handle this stuff."

Adam winced as she spoke. She wondered how he could still focus on the road and drive when his fingers were digging into his stomach like that. She imagined them as bloody splinters. Had he even heard a word?

"I'm still waiting for the alarm to go off in my head," she continued. "Then it'll stop. I'll wake up from this nightmare."

Adam clenched his teeth. "This is real, Emery. There is no waking up."

Did he have to sound so hopeless? Couldn't he allow her five minutes to wish for something, anything? Maybe warring and running and thrusting his fingers into his ribcage was a typical morning for him, but it wasn't for her. A hundred different words scattered her brain. Words like *crazy* and *freak* and *terrified*.

"You showed a lot of power back there," she said.

Adam didn't respond.

"If you healed me, why can't you heal yourself right now?"

"I'm weak. When we escaped the asylum, I wasn't strong enough to use all of my powers."

That explained the gun.

"It takes a while for my body to catch up. It seems my powers have a deeper hunger than I can handle. My mind can take it, but my body sometimes can't. I'm weak, Emery. I used a lot of it. Not sure when it's gonna come back."

"Are we talking hours or days?"

"It's always different."

"So you're saying you lose it sometimes?"

He nodded.

"Well, what are we gonna do?"

"I don't know. Drive until we run outta gas or figure something out. I can't really think right now."

Emery didn't like *I don't know*. It failed to give her any kind of security or confirmation that they'd be all right. "I want to go home. I want to have a screaming fight with my mom. I want to hug my dad. I want this to be over."

How long would she wait for comfort that wouldn't come? The false hope of safety or of returning home created a void at the center of her being. She ached and had no way of making it stop.

"You're strong, Emery. Trust me."

"Trust you? It's because of you we almost died back there!" She didn't realize she was yelling.

"I saved us, Emery. You're welcome."

"Yeah, thanks. Whatever."

"Would you have preferred me to leave you back there? You wanted me to leave you there to die like him?"

A moment came and went. It was coming back to her now. Adam's story. Creating another. But who? The last few hours, all she had been worried about was staying alive. She hadn't had time to logically process everything. To sift through it all. The gunfire, the smoke. Adam's power like lightning and fire. All distractions to what she had always believed at the core. There was someone else back at the asylum. Someone like Adam.

"What did you say?"

"Nothing. Forget it." He punched the pedal.

"Adam, don't do this. Tell me, please. You know the truth. I've trusted you all night. Trust me now. Is there someone else?"

His eyes darted from her to the road. She counted the seconds between her question and his answer.

"Salvation is just the beginning. It's one of many other perfect prisons just like it. Places where they can create and pervert and *take*!"

Her lips stuttered, but nothing she was thinking made it out of her mouth.

"Emery, I got you out before it was too late. They were experimenting on you, on us. Years I've spent locked away, but no more. No more being afraid of them. No more."

"How many, Adam?" she said slowly. "How many others are there?"

"I don't know. More. Ten, twenty, a hundred. Who's to say? It's only a matter of time before the final location goes public. It's where they will begin their new order. That's the endgame, Emery. Look, we're different. Don't you get it yet?"

"Yes, I get! I get that's what you believe."

"It's not just what I believe. It's the truth. I had to save you."

She scanned the horizon. The sun was almost full in the sky now. The trees were whispering, one to another, something she desperately wanted to hear. The hum of morning and back road streetlights all blended together.

Looking down at her wrists and her shirt, she saw the blood. Whether it was Adam's blood, or other men's blood, she wasn't sure anymore. But it was blood. How long could they keep running before someone found them again? If he could lose his powers so easily, how could he protect her?

The words *I had to save you* replayed in her head like a broken record. She knew it was true, but she wished it weren't. All her life, she'd been waiting for someone to save her, to fix her, to make her right. Her father couldn't; her mother couldn't. She believed Arson could, but he wasn't here now, and even he could die. Was there anything strong enough to take on the darkness in this world? Humans, freaks, aliens, whatever they were. Flesh and blood and weakness. They cried. They bled. They had fears.

"Ever since they started testing me, they've been creating. Little by little. They're making fighters who will do their bidding. Shipments of my DNA code put in food, baby milk, drugs. I let them do it. For years I let them change humanity. But it takes time. They're creating a new species without warning and in plain sight. It's the biggest adaptation this world has ever been subjected to, and it may or may not survive."

"Adam, tell me the truth. Who is back at that facility? Who did we leave behind?"

He said nothing, one of his hands dripping with new blood. She was starting to get used to it.

Emery thought back to that day at the hospital, when she had been abducted. She had no idea why anyone would want her. Until Adam created this theory that she was different like he was.

But beams of energy didn't shoot from her wrists or her eyes. She couldn't heal her own face, for heaven's sake. She was convinced that maybe Adam was wrong. From what she could tell, what she could feel, she was just an ordinary teenager.

As new images danced to life in her mind, she relived that hateful day, being ripped from the only world she'd ever known, torn from the boy she loved. If she had no power, why would they take her? The frustration climbed her brain. *Think, Emery, think.*

They took her because she knew him; that had to be the answer. She knew Arson, and *he* had powers. The faces of the ones who sought to burn her again came flashing back. She experienced their fear, their melted flesh, their tormenting screams all over again. He was like Adam. He could do things, things that would kill a normal person.

Adam was focused on the road. The cars passed them, and the wind seemed to forget them on these country trails. If the world were okay, this picture of color, forest, and distant cities would have been beautiful. But today, it was miserable.

"Where is he, Adam!" she finally said. "Where did they take him?"

He was slow responding. "Who?"

"Don't lie to me. Don't you dare lie to me! Arson Gable. Where is Arson?"

"Who is Arson?"

"I'm not special, okay! I'm not some witch or warlock or super-human freak! They wouldn't want me! I'm nothing."

"Don't believe that," Adam said, his voice weakening. "You are special, Emery. You are."

"They took me because I knew him. That makes sense. I knew what he could do. Crap, how could I have not figured this out before?" Her eyes flashed with sudden revelation. "They took him, Adam. They had to have taken him. There's no other way.

He would've come for me. He would've…they knew what he could do. He's like you."

"He's nothing like me!"

Emery finally had the truth. Adam knew where Arson was. Maybe he'd known all along. She wanted the truth, and now she had it. But the torment that followed, the fear of not knowing, was eating her alive.

"He's dead. He didn't make it. Is that what you wanted to hear? I told you, he's not like you. He's not like me."

"I don't believe you!"

Adam pulled off the road. "Look into my eyes, Emery. Do I look like I'm lying? I'm not sure how this messed-up little story ends, okay? All I know is that I'm not gonna let anything happen to you. You're all I care about." His crimson hand brushed her cheek, blood sticking dry to her hair.

"He can't be dead. He can't be."

"Believe what you want, but I swear it's the truth. He died weeks ago." Adam was almost lifeless as he said it, like he didn't care about Arson. He must not have known him like she did. "His mind couldn't take it. Our power begins in our blood, but it is controlled by our minds. Most human beings can only use a certain part of it, but not us. The gene Henry Parker discovered in me, it's the same in you. I'm sure of it. They want us for a reason. They have a purpose. When my body no longer responded ideally to their trials, they focused more on him. They wanted to use him to destroy the world."

"That's impossible. One person can't destroy the world."

"What about Hitler, Nero, Alexander? Great men who conquered this planet. What if they had possessed something more? Imagine if they could do what I could. Imagine if they had entire armies that could, with a whisper, lay waste to our cities, our homes? One battle might endanger a continent. These leaders reigned with their words and daggers, but imagine if they could breathe fire and control the seas."

"No. No one is that powerful."

"I am. You don't understand yet. Listen, you witnessed a glimpse of the kind of thing I'm talking about, and still you do not believe. I'm weak now, but my powers will return, and every time they do, my body adapts. I become stronger. While they had me in that cage, they found a way to control me. They feared my unpredictability. Humanity trembles before that which it does not understand."

Adam leaned back with a sigh. "But he wasn't strong enough. I didn't know you knew that boy, I swear. Listen very carefully to me now, Emery. Let it sink in. They used me. They used my mind and my blood. They've got machines and an infinite supply of money. They influenced me to create more like me. Like us. They're triggering events that mankind isn't ready for. All this," he said, pointing around him, "it's the past. It's all gone. Cities, hospitals, churches, homes. Gone. Very little will survive. Most will die."

"This is crazy. Why would they want to destroy themselves? They're human beings. Why would they destroy each other?"

"God favored Abel, and Cain killed him. Brother against brother. We're the new kids in town. More powerful than ordinary humans."

"We *are* human, Adam."

"A part of us, maybe. But we're not like them. In time, my DNA, my gene, would sift through the children of men. It would become stronger because it would begin a new race. My line might be kings, maybe even gods. Nothing this world has ever seen would be able to stop us." Adam tried to hide his obvious agony. "But they stole it. They think they're controlling the cards now. But they can't fully fathom what we are or the consequences of what they'll do. They've blindly begun creating more, Emery. Arson Gable was the first of their experiments. Actually, he was an accident. His mother was Frances Parker, the girl I tried to fix with my blood. Remember this, Emery. They can adapt too. And their hands have been busy…for a long time."

Emery's cheeks flushed red then went pale. What he was saying was a reality she didn't want to believe. But Adam didn't flinch. His eyes were locked on hers for every word. His mouth didn't stutter. His hands shook some, but he obviously believed everything he told her. And he was asking her to believe.

"It's strange how little can stay," he said softly. "This world has changed so much. Nothing remains the same for long. Decades I wasted. The time I missed. I never should've trusted them. Humanity is dark. They're liars and thieves and murderers."

"And you think we'll be any different. You said it yourself, a part of you is human. *I'm* human. These people, they're not all bad."

"It's people like them who took us. They can't be trusted. They lie. They manipulate. And now they're going to control it all. These fiends will wage war on this planet so they can stay at the top of the food chain."

"So we're gonna run? We're gonna let the world burn because a few a-holes say so?"

"Emery, I've lost so much already. My sister, my family, everything."

"And I haven't? Look, there won't be a place to run to if they get their way, Adam. If we turn away now, then everything will be lost. We have to go back and do something. We have to stop it!"

"No. This is the future they wanted. Let hell sort them out. We must keep moving. We watch the streets, the news. When it happens, we'll be ready."

"It'll be too late," Emery said, her breath fogging the chilled window. She studied his breathing, a slow chore. He was in immeasurable pain, but she was so concerned for the rest of the world. The ruins she knew might become familiar if evil men burned these woods and the cities like them. Tore families apart and fulfilled their twisted plots while those they created with power fell in line.

Was her heart actually beating? Arson was gone. If Adam was telling the truth, he was dead. But he was so strong. He had saved her once. He had saved her. As the frightened shakes overwhelmed her body, the fear of losing everything she held dear, she swore to herself that it wasn't real.

"Emery, do you feel that?"

"Feel what?"

Adam's head fell back on the seat rest, his eyes spinning until at last they shut. His mouth lay open and void. His hands, stained with blood, went limp. His face, his arms.

"Adam! Wake up! Adam!" It didn't matter how many times she screamed his name. He was lost in some other place. She checked his pulse and put her ear to his mouth. But he wasn't breathing.

CHAPTER FORTY-ONE

ARSON WONDERED IF HIS VEINS WERE ICE, IF THEY WERE frozen the way he knew some men's hearts were. The door behind him had almost stopped swinging completely before Arson recognized what lay in front of him. His eyes were lost in a daze or some kind of bitter fog. Somehow this place smelled like ash. What he stared at he wanted removed. But there was this longing deep inside him, an unknown wish for reality and this place to collide so he could understand it all, if such a thing were even possible. There was no removing these things— mysteries, prophecies, or the darkness between. And that scared him.

He moved toward the table. It just lay there, like a riddle, desperate to be solved. The spying walls crept closer.

There was a body on the table, one that wouldn't move. A leg dangled at the foot of the steel bed, while he imagined the other leg crunched and with the heel cradled with the corpse's genitals. Pale blue flesh reflected all the darkest lights of the room. A sheet covered the naked body. It was odd gazing at things that should have life but didn't. All the vigor and hope a human shell like this one must have once possessed was traded now for mysteries left undiscovered.

Another footstep brought him closer. It was a terrible thing knowing there was no going back. A terrible, haunting thing to learn the truth. Arson was certain—dead certain—that whatever rested in this room would not bring him peace. Perhaps it was the manner in which the walls hugged every corner the way the dark hugs the earth, or maybe it was the unfiltered cold cutting through his eyes, his ears, even his throat. And the fact that this never-world, this nightmare prison, allowed him such indecent luxuries was mind-bending. The sickness of fear ate away at him bit by bit. There were no words to describe it, no sentiment to embody it.

Strange how a four-wall reality could twist the heart of a boy, make him think dangerous thoughts, bring out the worst in him, or the worst that memories could offer. Was this just a memory, or was it real? He still didn't perceive it perfectly. He didn't know anymore. It felt real. He stepped closer. It smelled real. It was the way teenage flesh stunk after the assault his fiery rage unleashed on Mandy's beach. The horrible, black taste he couldn't remove for hours.

Upon his next blink, he saw a crimson line slide down the center of the body and stain the cover. Suddenly his eyes weren't fixed on the corpse's curly hair spread over the head of the steel bed or the melted fingertips this young girl no longer had. Only stubs with little knuckle and far too much blood. Just then, a second stream of red bled down, dripping onto the grey floor. Every drip sounded like gunshots, and these red bullets could tear right through him. Deep breath, and then he reached for the covering. Flung it across the room. As it spiraled in the air it carried dust and memory he fought to reject. But it came.

Faces. Blurred.

A frenzy of souls crowded around this table. How this girl panicked for her very life, or the life inside her.

Back to the moment, Arson dropped his gaze and saw it. The emptiness at the belly of this girl, whom birth made a victim. A haunting birth. Some unholy thing that ruined her. What was it?

Did he know, or did he just wish he didn't?

Arson swallowed hard. Thought that drop of saliva would stay stuck in his throat forever. How he wanted to claw his way out of this room before he saw any more. It was too much to handle. He didn't want it.

"Who are you?" he whispered, but something told him he already knew.

It wasn't the flaps of skin from her belly that seemed like they were clawed at or the thick, red-black goo that painted the canvas of her womb that terrified him most. It was the emptiness at the center of her, where life should've been. One. Left. Emptiness.

"It. Was. You," the dead girl whimpered demonically. Her voice chilled him. Arson jumped back. No—he wanted to, but he couldn't move. He was terrified. "It. Was. You," she slurred a second time. Only her lips. Those eyes of hers, now stained white, were piercing, mucus mirrors Arson dared not reflect.

"It was gonna…make me better. But you killed me. Stephen, you killed me. Arson."

The last word, his name, seemed to burn its way out from her mouth. Her lips were crusted and blue. A drop of red slipped down her mouth and singed the floor as it fell. Different than before.

"Mom?" he finally could say. What was it pumping through him? Guilt? Rage? Hate? Sorrow?

The head now moved. It nodded slowly, but still he dared not look into her eyes.

"Mur…der…er," his mother whispered.

Arson nearly tripped backward. The tangled mess at his feet was an umbilical cord. His. Blood wrapped, and leading into one of the corners.

More whispering. A lullaby, a prayer maybe. It was Grandma's voice.

"Grandma," Arson said, hushed. "It's you."

Her face was covered by the dark. All he could make out were her outdated apron, those slippers she used to wear to bed, and that red cord he now knew she possessed.

And her voice.

"I pray the Lord my soul to keep…" she sang, every other second a piece of her white hair creeping out of the shadows. She was rocking something to sleep. The more she rocked, the more Arson saw of her. The wrinkles, her ivory knuckles, and a soothing voice that kept repeating the word *murderer* in a soft, still voice.

"Be fearful, Arson…" the corpse on the table—his mother—broke in.

The thing in Grandma's arms no longer moved. It was hushed. Asleep, he imagined. Or worse, he feared.

An intruder tore through. How he got there didn't make sense. The figure simply appeared out of the strange black of the room and his presence began to form color and flesh and clothes. A hand reached for Grandma's throat. Stayed there, a comfortable grip capable of ending life. Grandma's spine smacked hard against the wall, enough to snap, he was sure. Then she let go of the life in her hands, dropping the child to the grey floor, dead, covered with dust and blood.

"Murder," Grandma hissed when she could breathe for a second. "Funny, isn't it?" she continued. "One moment," she struggled, "the world makes sense…you're safe, hmm." Was it laughter at the back of her weak throat, her lungs cradling an ounce of painful happiness, or was it fear too that manipulated her laughter? "And then…murder, panic…end."

"Mur…" his mother chanted.

"…der-er," Grandma concluded.

They repeated it over and over again.

"Mur-der-er, mur-der-er, mur-der-er…" An endless chorus. Arson remained terrified at the sight of the child he knew he had once been. It lay before him, confused. This dark painting was becoming clearer to Arson; he recognized the horrible strokes and the merciless brushes disguised for creativity. Such cruel instruments of torment.

Still Arson did not know who it was that harmed Grandma. Still he longed to know and end it. Arson ran toward the wall where they warred, but he passed through them, like they weren't there at all, or like he wasn't.

"I won't let it happen!" he screamed, fighting the reality of her death. "I can save you, Grandma. I can save you."

No, she indicated, before her eyes went black. The man walked away from his destruction but not before dipping his fingertips in the blood-stained floor. With the blood he wrote words on the wall.

"Be fearful of the thoughts of men. Be wary of the traps of the end."

Arson said the words back to himself several times and his heart sank at the weight of it.

"What is all this?" he panted. "What am I seeing? Who is that!"

The red letters dragged across the wall as the man's fingers tapped the same melody Grandma sang when she tried to rock the child to sleep.

"Who are you!"

"Be fearful of the thoughts of men, son," his mother slurred, her last words before she stopped moving. Arson rushed to her side.

"Please, God, please. Not now. Stay with me. Please stay." He swore, bashing his hands on the steel table. Unknowingly, the table singed when he hit it, melting slightly, forming the shape of his knuckles. It didn't seem to matter.

His mother, this beaten, ruined corpse, ceased all movement. He ran his fingers through her hair, stroked her cheek with his face and his tears. "I don't want it to end like this. I'm sorry. I swear I wish I were never born. I wish I could take it all back."

And then her eyes found him. She didn't move, didn't speak, but those haunting white eyes poured into his, and he could see new things.

A hospital hallway enveloped them. Salvation Hospital was disturbed by the screams of this young girl. He knew they were not the screams of a child wrecked by a firecracker but rather the screams of the mother he'd lost at birth. Her voice cracked the air as she reached for a hand in the chaos. "Isaac, promise to love him," he heard her say.

In the here and now, Arson grabbed the corpse head with both hands, unable to let it go. He was watching his own birth. He'd seen this chaos before in part but never this clearly. It was as if he were living it, breathing the same air the souls in that hallway breathed, fearing the same thing they feared.

"Isaac," she gasped. Arson watched her struggle and claw at Isaac's hand, hoping he could bring her some kind of solace.

And then he saw perfectly through her eyes. In that moment he was her—her mind, her soul, her everything. And he saw the man. Isaac. The one he knew as Dr. Carraway.

"There's so much blood," Arson cried, watching it all unfold. "No more. No more!" A fire boiled in the young girl's veins. Red dripped from her ribs. Her hands were hot with the unrelenting glow of fire. Ash stained her mouth and bled out her eyes as two souls stared on. Arson felt rage unlike anything he'd ever felt before. Hatred. And more than anything, a feeling of no control. A sensation of losing his grip completely to the madness. But there was no fire to deliver him. And there was no angel of death to remove him from this cathedral of torment. Only the past he could not change. He shut his eyes finally as the cry of a child pierced through.

"My voice. My cries. My fault."

He wanted to write a new history. He wanted to fix it. All of it. The heat boiling in his blood, the fear of losing everything: his mother, Grandma, Emery. His mind. He cried out. He screamed and screamed until his throat nearly collapsed. And through it all, the man he had never called Father continued to stain the wall red with words Arson began to understand. All this time he could see things he had never experienced, never dreamed, never lived. They were not his dreams, but the dreams were linked by blood. The realities must have blended together.

"I wanted to save you…to save all of you…"

His hands, once dried and lifeless, came alive in the quiet darkness. He, kneeling in dust and ashes, sensed the distant, abandoned fire swell once more.

He stared at the man writing on the wall. His father, Isaac Gable. A villain in this nightmare. Arson had a thirst to end his life.

CHAPTER FORTY-TWO

THE ALARM EXPLODED THROUGHOUT SALVATION ASYLUM.
Saul Hoven dropped the phone back onto the receiver; it droned for
the next several minutes while he fidgeted with the intercom switch.

"Krane! What is it? You've started a panic, for God's sake."

"Sir, the situation has changed. Everything's changed."

"Try again, Krane, and this time, let's not be vague. I haven't
got the patience for it."

"219," the speaker buzzed. "The arson…he did it. His p-po-
powers have fully returned to him. And greater."

Hoven pressed the button and screamed into the device.
"What do you mean, Manny!"

"Sir, he burned every monitor without ev-even waking up.
He's still in the coma, I believe. And then, in sec-sec-s-seconds,
two of my men were…"

"Were what! Quit playing games, Krane!"

"Set on fire, sir. He s-s-set them on fire."

Hoven massaged his temple, rubbing the sweat already beginning to blend in around the creases of age and fatigue. "It's finally
happening. All things come to him who waits," Hoven said with
a twisted grin. A cackle bellowed into the intercom speaker.

"What are we to do?" Krane asked.

In the background static, Hoven heard Lamont's troubled voice blend through. "Get outta here before he goes nuclear."

Panic erupted over the intercom, so loud Hoven pulled back to avoid shattering his eardrums. "What's happening now, Krane!"

"He's killed another member of my team, sir. The f-f-fire is spreading. The floor is burning along with the ceiling. It's every-ev-everywhere! We can't make it stop."

"I'll be down immediately. Sedate him. We must keep him controlled."

The intercom speaker clicked, and Hoven stepped away from his desk, grabbing his gun first out of the top drawer. He holstered the weapon and rushed out of the office, down the stairs, into chaos and violence.

Arson peeled back his eyelids.

Grey faces surrounded him as he took his first breath. Then his second. Feeling his heartbeat again was like being reborn. At first, the faces were frozen in place, immovable and uncertain. He looked at them, and they stared back. While his eyes were off in one direction, a nurse tried to stick him with a needle. At the slightest pinch in his neck, he flinched, snapping the needle in half. With one breath, he caused her suit to catch fire. A terrible yet soothing shriek distorted the air.

"Where is he?" Arson asked quietly. "Where is Isaac?"

Krane flinched at the mention of Isaac's name. A shudder fled from his lungs.

In seconds, the nurse who sought to sedate him was nothing but charred dust. Her remains melted into the floor. Arson's gaze located his next targets. His vision had returned. Each breath had measure and control. The horror he once feared in himself he would never again forsake. He embraced it. He wanted to.

As he leaned up from the steel table, Morpheus began to disintegrate. The vibrating motor clicked until it broke, producing a relentless hum that crawled inside Arson's head. He felt a blast release from his wrists, and in seconds, the fury engulfed the machine.

Stepping off the bed, the sheet keeping his body covered slid off his torso, nearly exposing him, except for the torn boxer shorts soaked with sweat. The floor tiles were already melting when his feet hit them. A singeing, hot sound seemed like it could echo. As he moved, the fire moved with him and grew stronger. The flames spread wildly and fast, climbing up the walls and scaling the ceilings like tortured spiders. Webs of fire decorated the dark corners and filled the space with a fierce glow. The heat was brutal and relentless.

"Where…is Isaac? Where is my father!" he yelled, searching the faces stitched with flesh and bone he could rip off in an instant. His eyes bled drops of red fire. Each pupil dilated, each blink rolling out waves of humid suffering. Wherever he looked turned to fire, and soon ashes. Water showered down over them. Their sweat; his carnage. Green lights flashed for a few seconds before dying.

"Tell me!" he ordered.

"I don't know," a terrified nurse replied. Arson walked toward her as she trembled. His hand reached to grab her face. He clutched her cheeks, her eyes, her mouth all within his palm. And he watched her disintegrate, veins blistering.

His neck suddenly jerked. The doctor had driven a knife into the side of his throat.

"Isn't this what you wanted, Doctor? Unbridled, furious power?"

The doctor shuddered, tripping backward. He was too paralyzed with fear to even crawl.

"You want my power, don't you?"

The doctor formed no reply.

"Speak!" As Arson roared, fire slithered out from his feet, the red-black serpents moving toward Krane rapidly. His shoes ignited first; then his feet began to swell. A haunting cry fought its way out of him.

The few who remained spied and were horrified.

"Where is Isaac Gable! Answer me, or I'll burn off every limb. I'll burn this whole world down."

Out of the dark came a scathing voice. One he had longed to hear all his life, until this very moment. "Son," the voice said.

A sigh exited Krane's dry lips, a murmur of gratitude. Like he'd been saved by Isaac's arrival. But when Arson moved his hand above his ribs, a small spark began to bloom inside the doctor's bowels. Something terrible spread throughout his weak frame. A fire that chewed his organs from the inside, crawling from vein to bone and flesh to flesh, consuming all that lay there. No sound left the doctor's mouth then. The heat held him. Still he picked and scratched at the infection, until he was consumed.

"So is it Stephen or Arson?" Isaac said.

Arson gave no reply but let new flames creep closer toward Isaac. "You left. You abandoned me."

"I loved you. I did not abandon you. I abandoned a monster. I abandoned the menace I thought you would become." Isaac coughed. "But look at you now. You're so much more than that, son."

"I am not your son! I'm your mistake."

"You're my second chance, Arson. Listen to me. I have made mistakes in my life. But I came back for you. I saw the light, and I had to get you out. I had to get you out of that nothing town. You would've died there, like they will."

"What?"

"You can't stop it. You can't. Your grandmother was a crutch, Arson. You have to believe me. Kay was nothing more than a waste of a human soul. She didn't love you."

"Liar!"

"You know I speak the truth. Kay Parker was your reason to believe you were normal. She was the lie, son. She was your connection to the human race. Like I said, a sick crutch."

"No!" Arson shouted. His eyes twitched, and suddenly Isaac grabbed his heart.

"You can burn me up, kill me. Hell, slice me into a thousand pieces if it makes you happy." He bit down hard, sweat dripping from his jaw. "I saved you for a purpose, son."

"You killed my grandmother! You took her away!"

"And you took my love away. Guess that makes us square." Isaac collapsed, tearing open his shirt. A deep color bloomed at the center of his chest. A fire, black and red and white. The colors stretched inside the loose skin. Arson knew what he was doing. He controlled every move. Tilting his head, he increased the flame's grip on Isaac's heart.

"If you kill me," Isaac gasped, coughing up blood, "you will never truly understand your role in all of this. Don't you see? You were made, son. You were an experiment. They tested your mother, tried to save her, but they couldn't. It is inevitable. They will control you. You cannot save this world."

"What are you talking about?"

"I came, I came back for you. To see what you were capable of. To see that I was wrong. I was trying to help you."

"You brought me here to die. You brought me here so they could stick me with needles and manipulate me. You lied to me! And you let them take Emery!"

"It was all done to protect you."

Arson grunted. "I don't need your protection!"

"Your mind does. You were safer here, with me. I was watching over you, really. Your mind could be harnessed and protected.

Out there, you're prey. Out there, someone else would've found you. You would've died with the rest of the weak, pathetic links of humanity. Believe me."

"Maybe I am already dead." A thousand images flashed inside Arson's mind. His memories of Grandma. A life without a father, without hope. A life blinded by guilt and torn by a merciless world in desperate need of salvation.

"I am lost, just like you," Isaac pleaded. "I too am alone."

The sound of a gunshot silenced everything. As the fire trailed above them and showers sprayed their faces, Arson's vision blurred slightly. A second shot came at him. But where was the shooter? A third bit right through his neck. A fourth punctured his ribcage. Several more tore into his limbs. Arson dropped to his knees. The bullets came at him from nowhere.

"You are mine," came a voice. "I control you. This is my Sanctuary. I call the shots. I say who dies!"

It was Saul Hoven. Fearless. Brave. And stupid. From behind him, he fired one last shot, aimed at the back of Arson's head, as Isaac screamed.

Jittery and uncertain, Hoven dropped the clip from the gun and reloaded. Cocked it again, ready for Arson to move.

"That's not enough to stop me," Arson said, not bothering to even turn around. He dropped to his knees, stared down at the bullet holes and the blood seeping out from each wound. Water and fire danced around him. It was quiet, enveloping heat. Darkness pushed his eyelids together.

He channeled every ounce of power from his body. Deep breaths flooded his lungs. Arson blinked, his eyes shifting color every time. Changing shape. Every move was on purpose. Every time the flames exploded from his shell like a merciless tornado, he controlled it. His head swung from side to side, all in a matter of seconds, and he saw the work of his hands.

It was so easy to war. To hate. To destroy. The flames stretched around him and the two other men left behind by the apathy of others. Left here to die with him.

He watched each flicker transform into fire. He studied the architecture of smoke as it built and built upon itself, rising into the vents, where more could be created. The fire spread. Arson looked around at the machines that were no more. The wires and monitors he had destroyed. His mind soaked it all in.

He listened for the sound of Hoven's anxious heartbeat. What a weak, pitiful man. It was like there was no time. No clock. No record to keep track of. Nothing but this moment. He stared at Isaac too, straight through him. What a ghost. Even if he were telling the truth, about any of it, could Arson ever truly trust him? Would it matter after tonight?

As more water hit his face, he was back in this hospital. Seventeen years ago. Experiencing it from the fixed stare of Frances Parker. He watched his mother freak out and then scream as fire consumed her from within.

"Be fearful of the thoughts of men," Arson said. "Be wary of the traps of the end. I see it now. I see destruction. I see the end." Was that all there was left?

He reached down into the grit of the filthy floor and picked up a handful of the black dust.

"Arson…" Isaac whimpered. Something told him what came next would be terrible. "Arson, wait."

"Ashes to ashes," Arson exhaled deeply. And suddenly, a new fire engulfed him. Needles shot out from his skin. A wave of heat thick enough to melt flesh ruptured from the center of his being. The tiles at his feet shattered. All that was near was first brought into the air by the violent, furious wind pushed out from his body. There it levitated, weightless before him, and the fire fed upon it like a starving beast. Arson lay huddled, his spine and flesh smoking.

Isaac's corpse blended into the floor where his soul would perhaps rot. Behind him Saul Hoven still suffered. A stiff life he never would've believed could end like this. Scream after scream. His face bubbled and oozed last, his eyes intact to watch the fire devour his humanity the way he had once devoured others.

And then…a stillness. It was always quiet after the flames went away. Nothing but smoke enveloped the room now. Arson shuddered as the bullets fell out of him and disintegrated on the dirt. There was no floor left. The asylum was destroyed. In the back of his mind, he could hear them. The victims. The patients. The dead. There was no peace whispering in the trees.

Arson tried to breathe, but what came were stuttering gasps for air and shaking. The smoke filled his lungs, and he felt safe, protected by it. It knew him.

"Arson?" he heard. "Arson?" A second time it pierced the silence. It was a voice he never thought he'd hear again.

"Emery?" Tears swelled in his eyes, burning on his face the way he knew they would. Some dropped to the dirt floor with a hiss. "Emery!" Suddenly he found that if he said her name, something would move inside him. It was like fresh, living water. He wanted to drown in it.

Her footsteps came closer. Where had she come from? How had she gotten here? He didn't care. He just needed her close. He needed her love; the love he wished would envelop him now. It started, but as he swallowed, as the sound came even closer, his spirit begged that this peace she brought might stay.

Then he saw her. Out of the smoke. She was here, finally here with him. He could see her, unchanged by time. A rock band t-shirt tight on her chest. Ripped jeans clinging to her small waist. Converse sneakers he surmised had to be uncomfortable. Shoelaces slinging back and forth as she ran to him. He even smelled her hair.

She had no mask.

Arson didn't say a word. Instead he reached for her and kissed her. Again and again, like he'd never done it or like he'd never be able to after this moment. Like he was alive because of her. He could feel her presence. So strong. Their lips stayed connected as he breathed her in. He never wanted to let her go. Arson stared at her for a long moment. He gently touched her face. He was desperate to hold her in his arms forever. "You're safe now. So beautiful. I'll never let you go again. I swear. I love you, Emery. I love you."

He poured his love into her with another kiss. Felt his hands heat up. But Emery didn't speak. They'd gone months without a single word to one another and she had nothing to say?

"Say something. Please, Emery, I need to hear your voice."

"You need to wake up, Arson. Wake up and change it, before it's too late."

A bullet split the air. It ripped a hole through her chest and sank into his. They both began to bleed. A hungry laugh disturbed them then and Arson turned to the shooter.

The shooter spoke. "Ah-ah-ah, boy."

It was then he realized that it was Lamont.

"You're still a prisoner, Arson. You're never gettin' out. She's gonna die, you know it. They're all gonna die!" With wide eyes, Lamont haunted him, and when Arson turned back to Emery, she began to fade in his hands like black sand. She didn't burn. She didn't stir. She simply faded. Her face, her hands, everything was...

Gone.

Arson shut his eyes and returned to that dark room where he saw his mother dead on a steel bed that was now her coffin. The torment chamber where Grandma rocked him to death. The cell where he watched her suffer at the hands of Isaac Gable, his horrible nightmare.

Arson nearly choked with fury and fear. The agony wouldn't stop. Had everything been a dream? His violent escape from the asylum? All of it? A dream trapped inside this nightmare? He had woken up, hadn't he?

"Let me out!"

He bashed the walls. Then, moving to the center of the room, Arson spread out his hands and waited, smoke and fire shooting out of him. The walls blackened and dropped backward into nothingness. New rooms formed around him. He burned another wall down and ran into the next chamber. The echo of mad voices calling him from that room clamored like nails hammering down into flesh and blood.

Arson ran and ran. As he moved, everything behind him burned. The fire wouldn't stop, and he didn't want it to. If this was his hell, he would make it home. Everything would burn; nothing could escape his relentless rage. Arson incinerated the classrooms filled with ridicule. He laid waste to every tormentor and broken memory. But there were no tears. He felt no sorrow. No remorse.

How dead inside had he become?

He searched for that small life he had talked to before. The one who had led him to that room. The one he called Danny. Perhaps his friend—that small, frail boy—could lead him away from this evil prison. Arson gritted his teeth and circled the places he'd already been. The ones consumed with fire. He prayed that in his recklessness he had not ended that boy's life, or spirit, or whatever kind of unnatural entity he was. Arson needed a way out. Desperation clawed at him.

"Where are you? Help me!"

And then he stopped. There, at the center of the black hallway, was a figure, walking through the fire and the smoke. A small boy, the one he recognized from his nightmares past.

"Don't look so surprised. It's not like you're not the only one with powers."

"Where have you been?"

"Running. Like you. I'm tired, and I'm wounded. But it has to stop. They have to pay for what they've done. Revenge is the only currency this world accepts. And it seems like you're finally getting it. I'm gonna help you. But just so we're clear, it's going to take more than vengeance to get you out."

"Who are you, really?" Arson asked.

The boy looked around at the flames, the hallway filled with red and black. "Love what you've done with the place."

"Who are you!" He knew now that this boy wasn't Danny. This boy wasn't afraid to step out of the shadow or approach him. There was something different in him.

"My name is Adam," the boy said. "I'm here to get you out. Forget what you see me as. It's not the real me, but it's a projection of what you needed to see. I call it sliding. When it happens, I have to use what's familiar in a person's mind. I used an image you already had in here."

Sliding? Arson didn't understand.

"Your mind's comfortable with your memory of Danny. He's not a threat to you. So you accept me as real."

"Are you real?"

"Yes. Very real," Adam replied. "I just needed you to believe I was real. How long have you been stuck in here?"

"I don't know. Feels like forever."

"I can imagine. Arson, your physical body's in a coma. I thought you died. I was wrong. They're keeping you alive. Your mind isn't ready to give up the ghost yet."

"What?"

"There's still some poison in your blood, though. If I'm right, it's the spider venom. I read the code in one of the other rooms. It's in your blood strong. It's gonna take some work to wake you up and get you out of here."

"Spider venom? That can take away my powers?"

"I think so. It can't take away your powers forever, but for a little while. Might kill a normal person. For people like us, it wounds us. But, like an idiot, you tried to use your powers before your blood filtered it out. And, voilà, do not pass go."

"How did you know my name?" Arson said, perplexed still.

"I'm in your mind. You can pick up knowledge about your host when you slide into their head."

"Whoa. So how exactly did you get into my mind?"

Adam stopped in his footsteps, turned around, and smacked Arson in the chest. "Do you wanna stay in here forever? We could sit around asking questions, or we could look for a way out."

"Fine," Arson surrendered. "I just need to know one thing. Do you know where Emery is? Have you seen her or heard anything about her? I need to know if she's okay. I need to know where she is. She was taken when I was taken. Do you understand?" Arson waited for something to change in the young boy's eyes. He hoped. "Emery Phoenix. She's seventeen, has…scars on her face. Have you seen her? Is she still alive?"

Adam waited a moment. "I haven't seen her. She could be alive, could be dead. I don't know."

A hopelessness drifted through Arson. Everything he had wished for collapsed. The fire began to spread out of control. Wild, fiery vipers took shape and slithered across the floor.

"Hey, get a grip," Adam ordered. "The whole reason you're in here is because you slipped. You let your mind go. You got careless. Stay focused!"

Arson wanted to see her one more time, to hold her, kiss her. In the outside world. Would she forever be a picture lost in his memory? This maze was torturous—a living, breathing curse of an existence. It was time to escape it.

Maybe Adam had answers he needed. Maybe he could help him. Maybe he could even save the world.

"You still wanna save the world, huh?" Adam asked. "Kids. Always wanna be the hero."

"You heard my thoughts?" Arson replied.

"We're in your mind. I can sense everything you do or think."

"Creepy."

"Look, Arson, I've wasted my life riding on the sick dreams of others. The world you so desperately wanted to save is ruined. It's filled with backward devils. Good souls don't exist anymore. Mankind is an outdated, forsaken creature. And yet you wanna be the brave hero?"

Arson didn't move. He honestly didn't know what he wanted anymore. He had wanted to save Emery. He had wanted to save Grandma, the ones he loved. But since he'd gotten lost in here, nothing was certain. Everything became a blur.

The world had put him here. The world had toyed with him all his life. For so long he had looked on people with hope. But those people had abandoned him.

Adam stood still, watching Arson war with his emotions. Hate. Love. Forgiveness. Rage. What Adam had said was true, and that was the worst part. What could redemption do now? What could anyone do to save such a lost cause?

Only fire could make it right; only fire could end the world and purify it again.

Adam read Arson's expression, the fury trapped behind his eyes. "It's too late, Arson. You know it's too late. Why save the world?"

"Why save the world?" Arson repeated, his eyes igniting once more.

Adam grinned. "Let's rule it."

I HOPE YOU ENJOYED ASHES. COUNTLESS HOURS WERE SPENT producing it and promoting it. But there are still readers out there who haven't heard of my work. This is where you come in. The best way to gain new hardcore fans is with the help of existing fans. Please leave a review and help spread the word about *The Arson Saga*.

Be a part of the movement. Be a part of the story.

AND NOW, A PREVIEW FROM

ARISE

BOOK THREE IN THE ARSON SAGA

CHAPTER ONE

"THE END IS COMING, MY FRIENDS. AND IT WILL COME LIKE a thief, like an unforgiving storm. A day of reckoning when all that we know, everything that we love…and trust in…will be consumed. Are you ready for what dark and terrible things the future has in store?"

The sanctuary was hushed. A sea of captivated faces now sat mystified by Joel Phoenix's grim introduction. The members of his congregation stared up like children waiting in fearful anticipation for some sort of satisfying climax to the bleak story. Never before had one of his sermons been delivered in such a fatalistic and hopeless way. He'd no doubt lose a few parishioners come twelve o'clock.

In response to the painful silence, he cleared his throat. In truth, a new perspective dripped out of him, and the bottle that perspective belonged to was currently tucked inside the left pocket of his pinstripe suit. He liked keeping her close. The liquor gave him new eyes, somehow bridging a divine gap, as if with every drop his mind became a little more illuminated, capable of understanding the greater schemes of God. Then again, he was very much aware of the material of which men who walked the thin line of faith were made, and how such broken vessels so often needed a reason to remain on the path. Lately, he wasn't sure if he could.

Look at them. All the lost faces. Friends. No, not even close. Can you even stomach it? Look how they sit with their arms folded, scratching at itches on their necks, all of them anxious for another sip from your tainted chalice.

He'd kept his chalice so very clean over the years, but the rust was beginning to show clearly.

Joel glanced down from the platform and saw his wife. Aimee sat in the front row, her usual spot. Ever since he could remember, she'd been there, waiting and wide-eyed, whenever he delivered a sermon. During his forty minutes of preaching, he usually took pride in how she took notes and asked Emery to keep from scratching at her face. He liked that kind of devotion in a wife. And he needed Aimee's input, especially when it came to their daughter. Emery had become challenging since the accident, and rarely played the role of obedient child. Knowing full well that burn scars had left her once beautiful face mutilated and changed, Joel could more than sympathize with the attitude. Emery had reason to be bitter, but did she need to take out so much of that bitterness on a father just struggling to cope? No matter how many times he'd offered to play chess, she seldom acquiesced; his requests that she let go of that wretched mask were met with disdain and refusal; and Emery had gotten careless with her tongue as well, forcing out a curse or two whenever possible.

But maybe she was safer inside that other world of hers, inside the mask of whom she wanted to be instead of whom she had to be. He hated seeing her so broken. But what he hated more was how some of the eyes in the crowd were so disturbed that his daughter still wore a mask at all, given all the time that had passed.

Her determination bothered them, he believed, the misguided enjoyment she got from creeping out little kids, kids who'd grow up to be pretty. You are disturbed by it too, buddy; let's not forget. It only took another blink for him to realize that neither Aimee nor Emery was even listening.

Schemer! Where will you hide when they find you out?

He'd never gotten drunk before a sermon, and now that his vision started to split, he knew it had been arrogant and stupid to even risk it. But it was the only way to quell the shaking nerves for a few hours. Arriving early on Sunday morning permitted him some alone time. In his youth, he had spent that time seeking wisdom from above, but now he spent it seeking a new addiction. The lust was birthed long ago, and he'd kept the sick child asleep for years, but lately he'd grown weak to the infant cries.

"I know that this message isn't what many of you want to hear," Joel continued. "I mean, who really wants to hear about a God who may be pissed off at them? A God seeking vengeance? Who comes to church because they're looking for an unhappy ending?" Joel tilted his neck to the side, feeling the bones crunch underneath frail skin. He was tense. A sliver of sweat soaked into his tight collar; his suit jacket constricted him with every flexed joint, and all of it added to the tension. Stepping away from the podium, he droned on, "But I wouldn't be doing my job if I didn't give you the truth. God" —it was a challenge to keep his recent sarcastic notions of the divine to himself— "is up to something. He is coming to the end of his story, and from my point of view, the Boss seems to be fed up. With all of it. But one cannot study Scripture, or marvel at the wonders of heaven, without also asking if we are the problem."

Silence. So silent he could hear slight static from the microphone.

"Don't just sit there like you have no idea what I'm talking about. Mankind has played the villain, church. We murder. We steal. We whore ourselves to one another." His eyes roamed around for women in his congregation who had, on several occasions, offered to get to know him a little more personally, advances he'd regretfully refused. "Wicked little things our hands have done. But did we honestly think we'd get away with it? None of us can escape the schemes our deception has set into motion. Since the beginning, we have chosen to follow our way. To run from grace, to spit in the face of mercy."

Do you believe a word of it? Do you really believe there's anyone on the other side of those long-winded prayers? Like he'd still listen to the likes of you!

"But then, you might think, as I often have, that our Father deserves our spite, our bitterness. He made us this way. He took our love, our trust, our hope, didn't he? Come now, let's be honest. This is sanctuary. If we can't tell the truth here, where can we?" He swallowed hard, spread his tongue over parched lips. "Is this God the same abusive deadbeat we've seen in our fathers past? Is he a similar frail, broken child? Maybe he's lost his way in all of this."

Tone it back. You're starting to sound confused. And you're losing them.

"Take me, for example. I've served him most of my adult life, yet he hasn't made me rich or famous. Still, I am called to preach about his riches week after week. You've probably grown numb to words of hope." He could feel the weight of his eyes, heavy. The vile taste of regurgitated liquor had climbed his throat, and he almost choked. Close call.

"Is there still a God in the universe keeping this all in order? Has he kept his end of the deal? Has he given you the desires of your heart or protected your loved ones…from harm?" Joel glanced at Emery, and he knew she was uncomfortable. She hated being a topic in his sermons, but her tragedy fit his purpose, so he used her anyway. When his eyes left hers she folded her arms and got up, storming out of the sanctuary. He didn't even flinch.

"Still, we are to say that he is good, right?" Joel asked with a smirk, a piece of himself refusing to stake true confidence in his claim. "His eye is on the sparrow—isn't that what we just sang, friends? That he loves us? That he suffered and died for us? That he is to make us his bride? But I stand before you now to ask if she has been faithful, or has she just played the frivolous whore? Selfish, unbridled, covetous, cunning, depraved."

His words and accusations were sporadic and wandered. The liquor coursed through him with a vengeance. He exhaled and clumsily walked back toward the podium, his throne for the moment.

"I thought it'd get quiet in here. We're all a little uncomfortable with the truth. But this bride has some spots on her, doesn't she? Maybe she likes the beautiful lie instead. The pretty little lie. The one that tells her everything is going to be all right in spite of the darkness we see all around us. In spite of the horrible things we've experienced or the wicked things we've brought on others. What a bunch of horse shit."

Several members gasped. They couldn't believe he had uttered a curse during his sermon. What's gotten into him? he imagined them saying, pinning remarks to a number of elderly faces. Maybe the teens were rooting him on, happy that he'd pushed the envelope. It was also likely that a handful of middle-aged members were secretly chanting his praises, thankful that somebody finally noticed the elephant in the room. The harsh economy had left so many jobless, homeless even, feeling like rejects and failures.

A young boy seated next to his mother in the back came into focus just then. Joel blinked to make sure his eyes weren't playing tricks on him. They had to be visitors because he'd never seen them before. Joel glided down the center aisle and stopped when he reached them. The child couldn't keep still, his shakes coming and going in minute trembles. It was heartbreaking to see someone so young confined to a wheelchair; it looked like a prison for a human body. Hoses connected to the child's veins, and mechanisms that cradled feeble arms and kept a weak neck tight. Joel scanned the boy's lower half to find twisted, deformed legs.

The mother's lost stare pierced. He half expected her to storm out the door at any second, like his Emery had done. But she stayed, hand gripping her son's hand like the last breath. What a sad, depressing painting they created. He eyed the boy, swore he was looking into a soul, and then he turned again toward the mother. She was husbandless. The boy was fatherless. Yet both remained, stuck perhaps, and waiting for a new hope.

"Why do we do it?" he said in a hush. "Why do we hang on with such faith? Why do we believe? Why do we have hope?" He chewed his lip, tearing at loose skin. He tasted a bit of his own blood. "Why stay in a marriage where the candle is now just a faint, dim glow?" He toyed with his ring. "Why insist on living as if we have all the time in the world? Have we not read it already? Do we not know that the end will come?"

"We do," several shouted in agreement.

He was finding a bit of focus, and in a few moments, he would attempt to back up his sentiments with some Scripture.

"We speak it as truth, but we do not believe with our lives in this true reality. The reality that can admit that we are just barely alive, barely hanging on to what is left. We hope—" Joel paused and gently stroked the arm of the trembling child whose disease had stripped his ability to speak. "But we are stuck." He leaned over and touched the shoulder of the boy's mother. "Give this woman new hope," he whispered in a prayer. If you can.

"Hope. Should we have hope in a sick world? In a world spinning so out of control? By our own hands, yes, but also by the hands of the wicked?" Joel paced back toward the altar, where he was the most gifted of actors. "The final book of the Bible, known as John's Revelation, is pregnant with mysteries and horrors, and that is where our message lies this morning. Yes, at the finishing of all things, there will be redemption…for some. But before it, there will be pain, friends. There will be blood spilled in our Father's name. Death will roam the fields, the streets, the cities. Division will arise. Mothers will suffer and weep. Children will be deceived and corrupted. Fathers will abandon their sons… those who remain. Husbands and wives will betray one another."

Aimee crossed her legs and tucked a strand of hair behind her ear. She looked so pretty when she didn't try, even when she wasn't with him. But he felt, however faint a feeling it was, that a part of her still was.

"Take a look around you. We've seen these things with our own eyes." He waited, allowing his analysis to grip them. "Turn on the television. Every godforsaken news story tells of vile deeds we've dealt to one another. Evil running rampant. Evidence of darkness is all around us. Hopelessness. The peculiar mechanics of a manufactured world. But, dear fr—friends, do we have reason to believe?" He prayed no one caught him slurring his words.

"Yes," a voice echoed from his right.

Maybe you're safe for now.

"Always," another cheered from his left.

Definitely safe.

Joel flexed his jaw muscles. "You cheer and shout as if you have full knowledge of what that word means, friends. I hope we do. I hope that when all is said and done, our Maker's bride outgrows her filthy rags, and becomes more than the whore I see day after day."

Whose side are you on?

"Hallelujah!" members roared.

Joel licked his index finger and opened the worn-down Bible he'd received from a gifted professor upon completing seminary. Usually, he opened his sermons with a reading then carried out a monologue with clear-cut points. But the rulebook didn't exist today. He flipped all the way to the back of the Bible, stopping when he got to the final book. "'And I looked,'" he began, "'and behold a pale horse: and his name that sat on him was Death, and hell followed with him.'"

Another hush spread over the blank stares and worried mouths—the faces of the people he had been called to minister to. A path he'd chosen but one he was also led to, he had once believed. But where was this hope he boldly spoke of? Where was the stuff that made men legends in the records of heaven?

Where was he?

He continued, "'The second angel sounded, and something like a great mountain burning with fire was thrown into the sea; and a third of the sea became blood.' I still get chills when I read that part. Hear me. We can't live our lives in this world blindfolded any longer. Believe me, times are coming that will test the very fabric of our being, times that may break our faith." Joel wiped his forehead with a handkerchief and took a sip of water. Finally, true focus had come. "This message is truth. Hear it, understand it. Believe, if you can."

But the skeptic in him was still alive and ill.

"You are my family. All of you."

What a sick, pathetic father you've put on display. Your mentors would be horrified.

"If the horseman came storming through our church doors right now, would you be ready to embrace the end? I can promise you one thing: You are not strong enough for what will come. No man, no woman, no child is. The earth may shake. The seas may boil and run red. The skies may fall. But though this world passes, the human soul and this word..." Joel lifted up the threadbare book, "...cannot die. Take heed of what I say. The days of playing games with your soul are over."

Hypocrite!

"The days of flirting with the devil must cease."

Schemer!

"The secrets in our hearts will spill out one way or another."

And yours will run red first.

He carried on for the next half hour, ignoring the ridicule tormenting him from the inside. He spoke of prophecies and the end of civilizations, borrowing from ancient Hebrew texts like Isaiah and Daniel and Malachi, along with various passages in Revelation. His sheep were engaged, even if many were taken aback by his harsh approach. Some became frightened, he could tell. But he didn't care. This message was more for him than for the deaf and stupid. He didn't know it, though, when he prepared the sermon over the course of the last six days, during which time he snuck in liquor and lied to his wife. Of course, Joel didn't have the guts to come clean, not now, not about any of it. He couldn't dare break down and tell Aimee that he was getting drunk or that his lack of faith was pulling him apart at the seams.

Then everything blended. The last twenty years of his life. His pursuit of the ministry. A dying marriage. Raising a daughter who liked hiding behind a mask. So abundantly clear. He was here, now, dropped on this rock to live and breathe the gut-wrenching fear this sermon inflicted. But would there be salvation for the weakest among men?

Joel's throat was dry again. The clock at the back of the sanctuary ticked even louder, it seemed. Every time the hand moved, a tremor shook his chest. His nerves split him, crumbling the façade he'd kept on display with precision. Joel blinked, flaring his nostrils and loosening his tie.

"Friends, either it's true or it isn't." His eyes glazed over. He reached for the glass of water that sat on one of the podium shelves, but it spilled. The water soaked into the rug. Joel perceived it to be blood, spilling deeper into the fabric. Thick, red blood.

As he knelt down to dab the carpeted altar with his hand-kerchief, the bottle of whiskey that he'd kept close to his heart fell out.

'The day is coming; it will burn like a furnace. The arrogant and evildoer will be stubble, and the day that is coming will set them on fire.'

A startled curse exploded through the speakers when the bottle hit the platform with a soft thud. His words sent a chill over the sanctuary. They'd overlooked his creative use of profanity in the context of a compelling albeit meandering sermon, but this was too much. He was as still as a dead man on the altar, his mind replaying the last five seconds on repeat. Joel's hair had shifted out of place. He attempted to brush it back with jittery fingers, skin turning the palest of colors—white, bloodless. The members drilled him with stunned, critical eyes. He'd fallen, for good, hadn't he? He'd lost the path. How on earth had he been so careless as to expose his little sin to a crowd of people who desperately looked to him for answers?

Joel felt his spine click when he reached down to retrieve the bottle. "It's just a silly thing, really. Such a silly, little thing that can turn you, that can fill your heart with fear." Suddenly, the light that shined upon his stage showed a frightened and tortured actor, unsure of his next cue. Embarrassed, Joel slowly tucked the bottle back into his jacket pocket and tapped his chest. The raised brow of his assistant pastor, Carl, stuck out to him from the murky sea of faces. Unspoken tension was born within the space between their eyes. He would pay dearly for this.

"God forgive me," he said, waiting for his heart to beat.

Dawn.

Joel didn't like the eerie quiet that came over the shabby, unkempt motel room. He wasn't able to sleep either, which meant his mind ran in circles. His eyes longed for sleep, but his body refused to grant it. He just wanted that beating in his chest to subside.

Joel existed with the quiet. He came to know it intimately. So much could come to life when not even a whisper was there to be heard. But he wished the quiet dead still, wished it a hundred times. If only he'd never stumbled into that college bar, maybe the regret now subsisting off his failures would have found another soul to haunt. He often wondered if being the son of a closet alcoholic assured he would evolve into a suitable replica. But there was more to him than regret. Joel had to believe that, in spite of everything, a fracture of hope remained. Kyro, loud-mouthed street hustler that he was, had summed him up just hours earlier. The little punk had been right about him all along. "I spent years living off the faith and hope of others, letting my own run dry," he finally admitted.

The Bible felt strange in his grip, but he held it tight. This weathered thing had kept him alive; he knew that now. Ancient words and ideas and full lives stretched across thin pages; they possessed power to breathe new existence into cold veins. It was not without a sense of irony that he stumbled upon the passage of Revelation. He'd preached on it a few years earlier, during his last sermon, before impolitely being asked to leave the church, but never had the concepts hit him with such power.

A deep breath retreated from his lungs. Kyro's snoring had been dormant most of the night, but the sounds suddenly returned the second Joel closed the book. Aimee must've been in a deep sleep not to wake. He envied her ability to rest at a time when he thought his chest might literally erupt. Staring at her now, he thought only of the kiss they shared, and while the Scriptures had unquestionably empowered him with a sense of hope, their real job was to suppress the compulsion to revisit old desires. Among Kyro's few redeeming qualities, acting as third wheel on a rescue mission to bring Emery back didn't seem to make the cut. Things got a little weird when the penny street hustler wandered back hours ago to find Joel's hand sliding up Aimee's shirt. The slight lack of discretion notwithstanding, an inescapable splinter of guilt now circled the fear at the pit of his stomach. For whatever reason, attempting to round second base with his own wife was the stuff of psychological scandal.

Soon to be ex-wife.

Joel rubbed his lips, torn. "Maybe it's not the end yet," he whispered to himself. He blinked and swallowed, more awake than he'd ever been.

A peculiar anticipation lurked cautiously on the inside. Running his fingers through his hair, a greasy, unclean mess, Joel placed the Bible on the mattress beside Aimee's ankle. He'd been sitting in one spot for hours, waiting for the sun to rise. Would he find Emery or—upon entering this alleged experimental facility—would he discover that he was too late? Discover that his Emery had been mutilated even more, hurt and ruined beyond repair?

"God, if you are still there…if you care at all, about any of this, please help me find her. Let her be all right. Allow me to fix this. I want so badly to fix this." Joel wept into his tired hands and clenched his teeth. "I want things to be different. I tried." He scratched the creases in his forehead, felt the lines that reached from the edges of his nose to his lips. "I'm just a man. Please save my child. I want to see her face again."

Kyro mumbled in his sleep. He mentioned something about getting revenge on all those evil scumbags, and how they had stolen his grandfather's crucifix, how he'd never be right again. Joel empathized. The kid was lost too, just looking for his way.

Joel dried his face. Perhaps it really had all come to this. To one choice. One day. One life.

Aimee lay like a mysterious angel on her side. He saw her, really saw her, for the wonder she could be, the person whose light had been stolen by his secrets and lies. She wasn't perfect, but neither was he. His wedding band felt tighter the more he studied her body. Heavier. With his left hand, Joel stroked her cheek, and, eyes shut, Aimee's lips stretched into a smile.

Seconds later, Joel wandered into the bathroom, flipped on the light switch, and stared at his reflection for a long moment. In the mirror he saw a man who looked like him, maybe even was him once. He examined the figure's profile—eyes, mouth, hair, skin. So very similar, but they were not the same being, not anymore. The man in the mirror was dead. A corrupt, egotistical, self-righteous creature who had no faith to truly call his own.

He was the real Joel Phoenix, not this imposter. He would be the father Emery needed, the man Aimee had fallen for.

Joel removed his clothes but not before glancing one last time at his mirror image, to be absolutely certain he was right. And he was. The old figure was gone, and a new peace flooded his lungs. A sliver of light cut through the motel curtains about fifteen feet away, breaking into the darkness of this room from the outside. He could see it now, maybe for the first time. A beautiful, supernatural light.